COLD COMFORT

COLD COMFORT

QUENTIN BATES

Heartfelt thanks to all those good people who cheerfully had their patience stretched during the writing of this book. *Kærar þakkir, gott fólk.*

Copyright © 2011 by Quentin Bates

Published by
Soho Press, Inc.
853 Broadway
New York, NY 10003

Library of Congress Cataloging-in-Publication Data

Bates, Quentin.
Cold comfort / Quentin Bates.
p. cm.
HC ISBN 978-1-61695-054-5
PB ISBN 978-1-61695-203-7
eISBN 978-1-61695-055-2
1. Iceland—Fiction. I. Title.
PR6102.A7847C65 2012
823'.92—dc23
2011040903

Printed in the United States of America

10 9 8 7 6 5 4 3 2 1

COLD COMFORT

Prologue

FREEDOM TASTED GOOD. To Long Ómar Magnússon freedom tasted of hot dogs with ketchup and onions and washed down with a cold can of malt. He thrust out long legs beneath the café's plastic table and belched luxuriously. A woman with a brood of children at the next table turned her head and frowned, but he met her stare and she thought better of saying anything.

"Where are we going now, Ommi?" asked the tubby girl at his side.

"Town. Your place."

"We can't go there," she wailed. "Mum'll go mad if she sees you. She knows you're not out for another year."

"Good behaviour, Selma. Tell her I've been a good boy and now I need some fun."

He drained the can of malt and stood up, shaking his legs. "Come on. There's stuff to do."

Selma hauled herself to her feet and trotted towards the door with Ommi towering beside her. As she squealed in surprise, the woman with the brood of children again turned her head in irritation, in time to see a broad hand stretched down to cup a buttock, half under Selma's short skirt. The woman opened her mouth to speak, but before she had decided what to say, the pair had gone, with Selma's squeaks receding into the distance.

Thursday 11th

"LAUFEY!" GUNNA CALLED FOR the second time. "Laufey Oddbjörg Ragnarsdóttir! School!"

She brushed her teeth hurriedly and examined herself critically in the mirror. Time for a haircut, she thought. Good teeth, strong nose, thick eyebrows . . . Cupping a hand to lift a mouthful of water, she swirled and spat as Laufey appeared in the mirror behind her.

"Finished, sweetheart. All yours."

Laufey nodded blearily and said nothing.

Gunna switched on the radio and waited for the kettle to boil while Channel 2's morning talk show chattered in the background. Laufey shambled back to her room and shut the door behind her.

"If she's gone back to bed. . ." Gunna muttered.

The kettle steamed itself to a climax and clicked off as Gunna poured cereal into a bowl.

"Laufey!" she called again. The bedroom door opened and Laufey appeared, dressed and holding her school bag. "You'll have to be a bit smarter getting up if you're going to college in Keflavík next year."

"Reykjanesbær, Mum. You shouldn't call it Keflavík any more."

"Keflagrad they call it at the station, there's so many foreigners there now."

"Mum, that's a bit racist, isn't it?"

Gunna sighed. "Maybe, but it's too early in the morning to argue about it. D'you want some breakfast? There's cereal or *skyr*."

Suddenly the radio caught her attention and she turned the volume up quickly.

"A prisoner who absconded recently from Kvíabryggja open prison is still at large and is reported to have been seen in the Reykjavík area. Police have issued a description of Ómar Magnússon, thirty-six years old. He's one-ninety-nine in height, heavily built, with medium-length brown hair. He has heavily tattooed forearms and was last seen dressed in jeans and a dark jacket. People are warned not to approach him, but to report any sighting to the police on . . ."

Gunna spun the volume dial down to zero.

"Friend of yours, Mum?" Laufey asked slyly.

"Yup, most definitely one of mine right now. Actually, he's from here."

"A criminal from Hvalvík? Really?"

"He left Hvalvík before we moved here. Come on, I've got to go in ten minutes if you want a lift."

Laufey yawned. "It's all right. I'll walk."

"It's raining," Gunna warned.

"S'all right. I'm meeting Finnur and we'll walk together."

"Fair enough. I should be back at five, unless something crops up. I'll let you know."

"I might not go to college in Keflavík," Laufey said suddenly.

"What?" Gunna said, startled.

"I might go to Hafnarfjördur instead. Their psychology department is better. If you're driving every day now, you could give me a lift in the mornings, couldn't you?"

Gunna thought for a moment of how early they would need to leave every morning to take Laufey to Hafnarfjördur and still get herself to work on time.

"Psychology? I thought you wanted to do business studies?"

Laufey frowned. "Business studies is so 2007, just not cool any more."

"We'll see, sweetheart. We can talk it over tonight. See you later," Gunna said, sweeping up car keys and her mobile phone.

"YAH, DIDDI. REMEMBER this face, do you?"

A look of alarm spread rapidly across the young man's heavy features. "Hey, Ommi. Good to see you," he said, his voice hollow. "Didn't know you were out yet."

"I'm not. Not officially," Ommi leered, dropping a long arm heavily across Diddi's shoulders and sauntering with him along the deserted street.

"What? Did a runner? So it's you they're looking for, is it? Brilliant!"

"Yeah. Where d'you live now, Diddi?"

"Just round there. Not far."

"Yeah, Diddi, but where?"

Diddi quailed and blanched. "Just up the road."

Ommi used the hand draped across Diddi's shoulders to haul him round in a half-circle, slamming him face-first against a raw grey concrete wall, a fist planted squarely over his kidneys. Diddi wanted to yell for help, but knowing that nothing would be forthcoming in a neighbourhood where people avoided involving themselves in other folk's problems, he steeled himself to stay quiet.

"What's the matter, Ommi?" he warbled.

Ommi leaned close. "Diddi, you let us down. You owe."

"Wha-what's that, Ommi?"

"You know."

With one hand Ommi gripped a handful of greasy hair, swinging with the other to land a smack to the side of Diddi's head that raised a whimper and left his victim in a daze. Ommi loved the satisfying smack of fist on flesh, the rush of adrenalin, the flush of power. He'd missed this in prison.

"You know," he repeated. "You owe. Soon you'll have to pay up. All debts will be honoured in full. Understood?"

Diddi nodded. Blood was starting to seep from his right ear on to the shoulder of his denim jacket, and his head was buzzing. "Yeah, I get it, whatever."

"Hope so. You haven't seen me. Don't know where I am."

"I didn't do it, Ommi."

"That's what you say," Ommi hissed, delivering a punch to the kidneys that left Diddi unable to stand on his own feet.

The whole thing had taken no longer than a minute, and already Ommi was nowhere to be seen. Cross-eyed with pain, Diddi wondered if Long Ómar Magnússon had really appeared and beaten him up in the broad light of morning. The ringing in his ears and the taste of bile convinced him that it had been all too real, as he threw up messily across the pavement. Across the street, an overcoated gentleman in a peaked cap kept his eyes to the front and his chin high, making sure that he saw nothing.

THE ADDRESS WAS only a few hundred metres from the police station at Hverfisgata and Gunna decided to go on foot. She strode through the encroaching darkness of the windy afternoon with Helgi loping at her side. There was already a patrol car and an ambulance outside with lights flashing as they arrived at the stairwell of the block of modern flats and found a young officer fending off interested people claiming to live there.

"Crime scene. No admittance," he announced as they pushed through.

"Serious Crime Unit," Gunna growled, watching the young man take a step back.

"Straight up. Fourth floor. The lift's not working," he said.

Helgi eyed the stairs. "Four flights?"

The young man nodded.

"Oh well."

Helgi set off up the steps with Gunna taking them two at a

time behind him. As they reached the open door of the flat, he was breathing hard.

"This must be it?" he gasped, battling to keep the fight for air under control.

"You want to pack in smoking, Helgi," Gunna admonished, stepping past him.

Another young officer stood at the door, this time one who recognized Gunna and stood aside to let them in.

"It's not a pleasant sight," he said dourly as Gunna snapped on surgical gloves and handed a pair to Helgi. She bent to pull covers over her shoes and again handed a second pair to Helgi as he fiddled with the gloves.

In the corridor, a young woman in police uniform, her face pale as the apartment's ivory walls, stepped back from the kitchen door to let Gunna and Helgi through to where a paramedic hunched low with his back to them. Gunna went carefully around him and Helgi stayed in the doorway.

"Are you all right, sweetheart?" he muttered to the young policewoman, who merely nodded back, eyes fixed on the paramedic.

"Dead, I suppose?" Gunna asked, crouching next to the man in his green overalls as she surveyed the scene.

"Well there's not much reason for us to be here, if that's what you mean," he replied shortly.

The body of a woman lay on the chequered tiles, arms splayed in front and legs crossed awkwardly. A mass of fair hair spread around her and a pool of dark blood had seeped over the floor.

"Touched anything?" Gunna asked the paramedic.

"Checked for pulse, that's it. Nothing's been moved."

"Good man. Not a chance that she fell and banged her head, I suppose?"

"Not a hope," the paramedic volunteered cheerfully. "Blunt instrument, this one."

Gunna looked up at the faces in the doorway. "Helgi, would you get everyone out and bring the technical boys in here right away? This one definitely needs to be sealed up and gone over before we do any snooping ourselves. Do we have any identification?"

Helgi and the paramedic both stared back at her.

"You mean you don't recognize her?" the paramedic asked.

Gunna took in the woman's long, ample figure, dressed only in tracksuit bottoms and a white singlet. The taut skin emerging from the sleeveless top was tanned to the point she would have described as being crispy.

"Something about her rings a bell, but I couldn't say," she admitted finally.

"That's Svana Geirs, that is. Was," the paramedic said with a mournful shake of his head.

"Ah, in that case you'd better make sure we don't get any intrusion from the gentlemen of the press. And not a word, all right?"

"Of course."

The paramedic stood up and stretched. Gunna looked at the woman's face, half obscured by waves of hair. The skin at the corners of the wide-open green eyes looked stretched, parchment-like, in a way Gunna felt would have been more usual in someone past retirement age. The abundant blonde hair was coarse and thick, and she wondered if its natural colour had been seen in the last twenty years. She tried to estimate Svana Geirs' age and put it at around thirty-five.

"We'd better get ourselves out and leave the place to the technical team. Are you off?" she asked the yawning paramedic.

"As soon as the doc gets here to declare mortality," he replied, stepping back and carefully not touching walls or worktops. "So, is this your first celebrity?"

"Sort of. I had a city councillor once. Heart attack jogging on the beach at Nautholtsv'k. Stone dead by the time we got there. Shame about Svana, though," he sighed. "I used to have a poster of her on my wall when I was a student."

GUNNA AND HELGI left the technical team swarming over the flat and met on the first-floor landing to compare notes. As many uniformed officers as could be found had already been dispatched to scour the area for anything that could be a murder weapon, and to start the long process of knocking on doors.

"Tell me about Svana Geirs, then," she demanded. "The name's familiar, but that's it."

"Well we'll have to do a bit of digging. I suppose she was one of those people who are famous for being famous, if you know what I mean."

"You mean she didn't actually do anything?"

"She was on telly for a while with a fitness show on Channel 2. My first missus used to watch it, so that has to be five years ago at least, doing these daft exercises in front of the box. Never did her any good. The show was less about keeping fit than Svana's tits bouncing up and down in a tight top. That's about it. She sort of disappeared from view after that, but she still pops up in the gossip mags."

"All right. So who wants to knock off a failed TV presenter? There was some real force behind it, and that was a single blow as far as I could see," Gunna said. She would dearly have liked a cigarette, but a promise is a promise, and Laufey would know the second she walked in that Mum had been cheating.

"Time of death?" Helgi asked.

"Don't know. Miss Cruz will give us an accurate idea later. It's getting on for six now, so I reckon this afternoon sometime. She was still warm when we got here."

The police's only forensic pathologist was on long-term leave and the post had been covered by a series of replacements recruited from overseas. The latest was a woman from Spain with a double-barrelled surname who had replaced a tall Irishman and had instantly been christened Miss Cruz by her new colleagues.

"Who raised the alarm?" Gunna continued.

"The cleaner. Found the lift wasn't working, climbed the stairs and saw the front door was open."

"Open? So whoever did this was out pretty quick without waiting to cover their tracks," Gunna said. "Did you check the lift?"

"Jammed between the third and fourth floors. Been like that for a week, the maintenance man says."

"Top flat. Nobody comes up here without a reason. What about next door?"

"Nobody home. No sign of life." Helgi frowned and rolled his shoulders as if they ached. "Well, whoever lives there is going to get a bit of a shock when he comes home from work. How do you want to organize this, Gunna?"

For a moment she wondered why he was asking her. Being in charge of a new investigation unit was a change that would take some getting used to after the years running the police station in rural Hvalvík, where weeks could pass with nothing more serious than a stolen bicycle. The offer of promotion and the shift to the Reykjavík city force had come as a surprise, and working as part of a larger set-up was already taking some getting used to. Although she had lived there in the past and knew the city intimately, Gunna felt vaguely uncomfortable in Reykjavík. Much had changed during the years she had taken it easy in her coastal backwater. The city's pace of life had accelerated steadily for years until the crisis that saw the banks nationalized and the country plunged into a recession stopped progress dead in its tracks.

She had moved into the Serious Crime Unit's new office as the protests outside Parliament were becoming steadily angrier, watching her uniformed colleagues disconcerted at the public fury they were on the receiving end of at demonstrations every weekend, while many of them felt a secret sympathy with the protesters and their impotent rage.

Gunna had flatly refused to move house from Hvalvík, and the forty-minute drive was proving a challenge in the mornings, but the journey home had become an oasis of valuable thinking time.

"Gunna?" Helgi asked again.

"Æi, sorry. Thinking hard for a moment. If you try and figure out what the lady's movements were over the last couple of days, I'll tackle the next of kin."

"Fine by me. I'm still looking for Long Ommi as a priority as well, you know?"

"Fair enough. Eiríkur should be here in half an hour and you'd better fill him in on all this so he can collect everything that comes in from the knocking on doors. I'm sure the lad will have some kind of theory he read in a book that'll boil down to ordinary common sense. Pathology will tell us what they can, but I reckon we've seen it already. Blunt instrument to the head, single blow aimed to kill."

"Any ideas?" Helgi asked hopefully.

"I was about to ask you that," Gunna sighed. "On the surface, it looks straightforward enough. When someone's killed like this, it's either a junkie who doesn't know what he's doing, or it's money or anger. Svana Geirs must have pissed someone off, or else she'd ripped someone off."

"Jealousy?"

"Certainly a possibility. You'd better find out who she was shagging, in that case. I can't imagine she lived like a nun. It'd be handy to know what she did for a living. I doubt somehow that a flat like this comes cheap."

"I'll see what I can dig out by the morning. Be in early, will you?" Helgi asked.

"Nope. Bjössi in Keflavík asked me to stop by the hospital

there and look in on someone in the morning, a friend of your chum Long Ommi, as it happens."

"All right. Give him my regards, will you? Björssi, that is, not anyone who might be a friend of Long Ommi's."

Friday 12th

A NETWORK OF lines fanned out from the corners of the nurse's eyes. Working too hard, Gunna thought.

"This way, please," the nurse said quietly, her gaze flickering back and forth.

"How is he?"

"Not great. But he'll live."

"Can he speak?"

"Not easily."

She thrust open heavy double doors, strode along an echoing corridor and gently pushed aside a door that was already ajar. "Óskar? There's someone to see you."

The man lay back in bed, a wild tangle of black hair against the white pillow and fury in his eyes.

"Good morning, Óskar," Gunna said with as much warmth as she could muster at the sight of the man's lower jaw swathed in bandages. She tried not to imagine the splintered bones underneath, in addition to the split lip, puffed black eyes and the livid bruise colouring one cheekbone.

"Can I leave you to it?" the nurse asked. "We're short-staffed today."

"Of course. Thanks. I'll come and find you when I'm finished," Gunna said, looking sideways at the patient as if he were a naughty schoolboy.

The nurse nodded and padded silently away. Gunna sat at the bedside and opened her folder. She took her time to read the notes, while the bed's occupant looked at her stonily through his bruises.

"Right, then. Óskar Óskarsson, isn't it? Your mates call you Skari?" she asked without waiting for a reply. "You know who I am?"

"A cop," he mumbled with difficulty, his voice a hoarse baritone.

"Ah, so you can talk. That's good. Just so you know, I'm Gunnhildur Gísladóttir. Until a few weeks ago I was the station sergeant at Hvalvík, and now I'm with the Serious Crime Unit. Your file has stopped with us. So, now then. What can you tell me?"

Gunna scanned the notes as Óskar glared truculently at her. "Your legal address is Sundstræti 29, Hvalvík. Full name, Óskar Pétur Óskarsson, married to Erla Smáradóttir. Three children."

"Five."

"Five?"

"Erla got two already."

"From what I've been told, you turned up at Casualty in a right old state and declined to explain how you managed to get in this condition. So you'd better tell me what happened, and don't say you fell down the stairs."

"Pissed. Argument," Óskar muttered sourly.

"Argument? Who with?"

"Bloke."

"Who? Where?"

"Keflavík."

"Who was this person?"

"Dunno," Óskar replied slowly. "Big bloke. Polish."

"Ah, so what were you arguing about?"

"Can't remember. Pissed."

Gunna scanned the notes in her file. "It doesn't mention intoxication when you arrived at Casualty, only hypothermia."

"Pissed," Óskar replied firmly.

"No. You weren't pissed. What was this about? If we've got someone on the loose beating people up with this kind of savagery, then we need to find them as soon as possible. Skari, you're lucky to be alive. You could have been dead of exposure."

Óskar's eyes focused on the wall behind her, and Gunna recognized the determination in them. This would be a battle, and the whole story would probably never come out.

"Heard from Long Ommi recently, have you?" she asked, throwing out the question without expecting a reply as there was a tap at the door.

"Are you finished yet?" asked the nurse. "I can't leave you too long. He'll tire quickly."

"It's all right. I'm finished," Gunna said, looking at Oskar and noticing the sudden panic in his bruised face. "But I'll be back. If you've a minute, I could do with a word."

The nurse nodded. "I'll be at reception."

"I might as well come with you," Gunna said, rising to her feet and slotting her notes under one arm. "See you soon, Skari. Look after yourself."

The injured man looked balefully back but said nothing. He fumbled with his uninjured hand for the remote control and his eyes glazed as the TV blared into life.

By the reception desk, Gunna and the nurse sat on a sofa for waiting relatives behind a coffee table stacked with thumbed gossip magazines in a variety of languages.

"So, what can you tell me about this guy?"

The nurse shrugged. "His jaw's broken in a couple of places and I don't suppose he'll ever be able to eat or speak easily again. The other injuries are broken ribs, broken fingers on one hand, plus some cuts and bruises across his face and shoulders that'll heal quickly enough. He's been given a beating, as far as I can see, and a very heavy one. Somebody really wanted to hurt him."

Gunna scribbled quickly. "He was brought in yesterday?"

"About six."

"No ideas who may have done this?"

"Nothing at all."

"Right. I need your name for the notes."

"Sjöfn Stefánsdóttir."

"I don't think I've seen you before. Been here long?"

"Just a few months. We moved here from Akureyri."

"I see. Well, welcome to the wonderful Reykjanes Peninsula."

"Thanks. I'd have preferred to stay in the north, but my husband got a job down here, so here we are."

"I'm from the Westfjords, and I've never really got used to it here. It rains all the bloody time instead of snowing properly."

"Not looking forward to next winter."

"At least there's a whole summer ahead of us yet. But down here winter just means the rain's a bit colder than in summer. Anyway, I'll have to leave it there for now. I'll be back to ask our boy a few more questions."

Gunna extracted a card from a pocket in her folder. "I'd appreciate it if you could give me a call if anything changes."

"Been busy already?"

"Yup."

"Tell me, then," Gunna said, shrugging off her coat and wondering if she was overdressed. After years in uniform, deciding what to wear every morning wasn't easy. The suits she had bought were too dressy for anything but formal wear, and she was already falling back on the comfortable, shapeless things that she habitually wore at home, or simply going to work in uniform. She reflected that, being in charge, maybe she ought to be a little more careful about dressing than her colleagues. Helgi always wore the same corduroy trousers and plain jacket that looked as if they had been inherited from an elderly relative, while Eiríkur, the youngest detective, shame-lessly wore jeans to work.

"All right," Helgi said, scanning his notes. "Svana Geirs. Real name Svanhildur Mjsll Sigurgeirsdóttir, born in Höfn eighteenth of December 1976, making her thirty-three," he added, peering across at Gunna.

"You really were top of the class in maths at school, weren't you?"

"I was," Helgi replied, letting the sarcasm go over his head. "According to the technical team, we have a single wound to the head and secondary injuries where the victim hit the floor."

"Which we knew already."

"Yup. Undoubtedly the cause of death, as Miss Cruz will tell us later, along with every detail of the young woman's physi-ology. We have plenty of fingerprints and quite a few full palm prints, at least half a dozen sets," Helgi continued. "We'll find out soon enough if any of them match anyone we already know, but my feeling is that none of them will."

"Why's that?" Gunna demanded. "What's your reasoning?" she asked more softly.

"Just intuition, I suppose," Helgi replied. "I get the impres-sion that this wasn't premeditated, happened on the spur of the moment, and whoever did it simply ran for it. Hence the open door."

"You may well be right, Helgi. Do we have a time of death?"

"Miss Cruz says that Svana had probably been dead between three and six hours, and she may be able to narrow that down for us."

"So we can reckon she was knocked on the head between twelve and three."

"That's it."

"What background did you manage to unearth?"

"Ah, fascinating. Svana Geirs started out as a model, Miss

South Coast when she was a teenager, then was part of a pop group called the Cowgirls in the nineties, though they didn't do all that well. You know the ones, playing all over the country in bars and whatnot? Don't you remember Eurovision about twelve, fourteen years ago? She sang the Icelandic entry and came nineteenth or something. Nowhere near the top, did abysmally, like they always do. Then she tried her best with a solo career and a bit of acting but didn't get far. For five or six years she was on TV with the boob-bouncing fitness show. That ended three years ago. Since then, she doesn't seem to have done a lot, although she's part owner of a fitness club on Ármúli."

"Which one?"

"Fit Club."

"That's a new one on me. So where did you find all this out?"

"I asked my daughter," he admitted.

"Ah. Fine police work, Helgi."

He beamed back at her. "Wasn't it just? Parents are Sigurgeir Sigurjónsson and Margrét Thorvaldsdóttir, Tjarnarbraut 26, Höfn. Both living. They've been informed, probably on their way here already. Svana was married twice, and lots of squeezes, mostly sporty types, football players, plus a few businessmen. A popular lass, always in the papers, but never for having done much as far as I know. Just for looking good, I reckon."

"We'd better have some names."

"Will do." Helgi nodded. "Oh, that flat and the smart jeep outside weren't hers. Both are owned by a company called Rigel Investment."

"Aha. Now that's interesting. Eiríkur can look into that. Where is he, anyway?"

"Going to be late. He called in to say his wife's ill, so he has to hold the fort for an hour or so."

"Ah, the joys of parenthood."

"It's all right for you. That's all behind you now," Helgi

said grimly. Gunna knew that Helgi lived at a frenetic pace. With a son and a daughter in their late teens and a failed marriage behind him, he had embarked in middle age on a second marriage that had resulted in two small children in rapid succession. She wondered how he managed the sleepless nights and the aggravation of living with toddlers a second time around. He was always in a hurry, generally had something child-related on his mind, and a pair of child seats were strapped permanently in the back of his venerable Skoda.

"Too right," she said firmly. "I can just wait until the grandchildren start to show up."

"No sign of that, is there?" Helgi asked with alarm.

"I should bloody well hope my Gísli has more sense than that, for the moment at least. And Laufey's still at school. Although that doesn't seem to stop them a lot of the time," she added gloomily. "Anyway, when Eiríkur gets in, will you put him on to tracing the owner of Svana Geirs' flat and car? You said her parents are on the way?"

"Yup, flying here today or tomorrow morning."

"I suppose I'd better look after them. See if you can fix a time to meet them, would you?"

"All right," Helgi said, as Gunna pulled her coat back on. "Hey, where are you off to?"

"Not far. I'll be back in an hour."

JÓN FLIPPED THROUGH the pile of post and put the envelopes with windows at the bottom of the pile. Anything that looked like it might come from a lawyer or a bank received the same treatment, and this left him with a single postcard telling him that the jeep was overdue for a service.

As the jeep was no longer his, he dropped the card into the bin. After a moment's thought, he dropped the rest of the post, unopened, on top of it. It felt good, but he knew that later in the day he'd retrieve the envelopes and open them.

The house echoed. Half of the rooms were already empty, as Linda had taken some of the furniture and virtually the entire contents of the kitchen, apart from the white goods, which would doubtless be repossessed sooner or later.

Some days were good ones, when Jón could shrug it off and convince himself that he didn't care any more. This was a bad day, as he constantly ran through the trail of events that had tipped his little family over the brink into disintegrating. The smug face of the bank's personal financial adviser, with his ridiculous gelled-up haircut, was the focal point that he had trouble excluding from his mind.

CAFÉ ROMA WAS quiet. The pre-work customers had all gone to their desks and the mid-morning drinkers hadn't got as far as a break yet. Gunna watched with amusement as Skúli came back with a mug of coffee that he put in front of her and a tall glass with froth on the top for himself. They sat on stools at the long bar in the window with a view of the bank opposite where a very few customers hurried about their business as the wind whipped fat drops of rain almost horizontally along Snorrabraut.

"How's the new job?" Skúli asked shyly.

"Different. And yours?"

He grimaced. "Not great. Everyone's waiting for the chop. No idea who owns the paper now. The editor's gone, went to set up some kind of internet operation. Jumped before he was pushed, we all reckon."

"So things aren't great in the world of newspapers right now?"

"Things are, well, not easy? Got a story for me?"

"Possibly."

"Anything to do with Svana Geirs?"

"Why do you ask?"

"It's common knowledge that she's dead, but of course we can't say anything more than 'a woman was discovered dead in her apartment last night' until all the relatives have been informed. It's not something you can keep quiet for long, though. The obituaries are already written, just waiting for the word to go."

"Actually I don't have anything to tell you, Skúli. It's more the other way around."

Skúli looked expectant.

"I'm after background, any dodgy deals, unpleasant friends or acquaintances. Who Svana's friends were, any enemies she might have had. That sort of thing. But it needs to be a bit quick. The story's all yours, assuming I can swing it when the time comes. But I need information that I won't get from talking to her parents or business partners."

"There've been rumours about that fitness club she owned part of up in Ármúli going into administration. No idea if it's true."

"Do you know who else owns it?"

Skúli thought for a moment and sipped his coffee-coloured concoction delicately. "Agnar Arnalds. You know, the footballer? They were an item at one point and I know for a fact he's a shareholder in the club, or was. Apart from him, I couldn't say."

Gunna knocked back the rest of her coffee.

"You can get a free refill," Skúli said.

"Not this early. Otherwise I'll be peeing every five minutes for the rest of the day," Gunna replied and watched the tips of Skúli's ears glow. "And I really need to get back to work. You'll let me know if you come up with something other than the stuff everyone knows already?"

Skúli nodded. "I'll ask around."

"Good man. See you later, and thanks for the coffee," Gunna said and shoved the door open against the stiff wind that did its best to slam it shut again.

• • •

Eiríkur was downstairs by the door to the car park, in no great hurry to get back from a quick smoke break outside.

"They're here."

"Who's here?" Gunna asked, trotting up the stairs with Eiríkur two steps behind.

"Svana Geirs' family."

"Family? Already?"

"The whole crowd. Dad, Mum, little brother."

Gunna put her shoulder to the door to heave it aside as Eiríkur hurried to keep up.

"How are they?" she asked.

"Angry, distraught. I thought they were getting a flight, but it seems they drove."

"From Höfn? They must have been on the road five, six hours?" Gunna speculated, imagining the five-hundred-kilometre journey through the night along the south coast.

"The old man probably did it in four, I reckon, and I don't suppose he even stopped at Vík for a pee and a sandwich."

"Where are they now?"

"In the interview room. Not looking forward to this one," Eiríkur admitted.

Gunna picked up the file of notes from her desk and strode towards the interview room.

"Hey, you too, if you don't mind, Eiríkur," she called out as he sat at his desk. She could see a look of pain on his face and knew exactly how he felt. Dealing with shocked and grieving relatives was one of the things she would never get used to.

Three people were clustered around the table. A corpulent older man glowered, his face red. A small woman sat with pinched face and pursed lips, her coat still buttoned to the neck, while a younger man slouched with a deep frown on his face and his legs stretched out in front of him.

"Good morning," Gunna greeted them, trying for a blend

of formality that would mix sympathy and business. "My name's Gunnhildur Gísladóttir and I'm the officer in charge of this unit."

"G'day," the older man said in a voice so deep that it seemed to Gunna to emanate from somewhere near his boots, scraping the chair back as he rose to his feet and extending a meaty hand. "Sigurgeir Sigurjónsson. This is my wife Margrét and our son Högni."

Gunna extracted her hand from Sigurgeir's grip and sat down opposite the family group, back straight and eyes to the front, the thin folder on the desk in front of her. With all of the chairs in use, Eiríkur stood behind her.

"This is Eiríkur Thór Jónsson, one of my investigating officers who is also working on this case. First I'd like to offer you my deepest sympathy on your loss. I know this is an extremely hard time for you, but we have a great many questions, so we must ask you to bear with us while we—"

"Shit. Who the hell did this?" Högni had half risen from his seat. "You tell me and I'll go and fucking sort this out properly," he snarled, a fist no less impressive than his father's curled and ready for use.

"We don't have any suspects yet. The investigation is at a very early stage. It's vital that—"

"What the hell do you mean, you don't know?" Högni accused. "Quiet, boy," Sigurgeir growled. "The girl's doing her job. Sit down and shut your mouth, will you?"

Högni deflated back into his seat, lips moving but no sound emerging. Beads of perspiration had started to form on his forehead.

"Did you have much contact with Svana?" Gunna asked, determined to bring things back to a businesslike level.

"She called sometimes. Not often," Sigurgeir replied.

"Was there any indication that she was uneasy or that she felt she was being threatened?"

Sigurgeir shrugged and Margrét spoke for the first time, her voice as dry as dead leaves.

"Svanhildur Mjöll left home when she was seventeen and she's not been back more than half a dozen times since. We didn't see much of her," she whispered, and Gunna noticed the use of the unwieldy Christian names that Svana had abandoned along with her distant home town. "Högni saw more of his sister than we did."

"When did you last hear from her?"

"Christmas. She called from a hotel in Spain or somewhere," Sigurgeir said through a cough that shook him from head to toe.

"Högni?" Gunna asked, looking over at him.

"I saw her last week. Seemed all right."

"Was there anything unusual about her?"

"No," he said eventually, looking Gunna in the face. She guessed him to be in his mid-twenties, which would have made him a child of around ten when his big sister had left home.

"Was she her normal self? Did she appear concerned about anything?"

"She was all right."

"Do you know how long she had lived in the flat?"

Högni shrugged in exactly the same way as his father. "A while."

"A month? A year?"

"Since before Christmas sometime, I guess."

Gunna decided that this line was going nowhere. "We're doing what we can to track Svana's movements, but with no diary, mobile phone or anything like that, we don't have a lot to go on. It would be a great help if you could point out any particular friends she had."

Sigurgeir and Margrét looked blank.

"Svanhildur Mjöll never bothered to contact any of her childhood friends after she moved south," Margrét explained. "She cut home off completely. If we didn't live there, she'd have never set foot in the place again. She came home occasionally for Christmas or family funerals. That's it."

Margrét's face was composed, in contrast to those of her husband and son, both of which radiated anger and loss. Gunna guessed that the woman had long ago done her grieving for her lost child.

"Do you have any knowledge of her finances? We know she owned a stake in a fitness club, but are there any other businesses she was involved in?"

"She seemed to be doing well for herself," Sigurgeir said. "Bought a nice flat and everything."

Gunna wondered whether to mention that the flat and car were owned by a company, but decided against it. "Friends, acquaintances, business partners?"

"Don't know," Högni said, dropping his gaze.

"Svana had been married, hadn't she?"

"Twice," Margrét said through pursed lips. "The first one was a nice enough boy, but that only lasted five minutes. We never met the second one. That didn't last long either."

"We may need to interview both of them. Do you have their names?"

"The first was Sigmundur Björnsson. The second we only heard of as Bjarni; he's a sportsman, or so we were told."

"Bjarni Örn Árnason, the weightlifter," Högni broke in.

Behind her, Gunna could hear Eiríkur writing the names down. "When will you release the, er . . . When can we have her back, I mean?" Sigurgeir asked uncertainly. "Where is she now?"

"At the National Hospital. I can't say yet how long it will take to release Svanhildur to you," Gunna said apologetically. "I'll find out later today what the situation is and let you know. Where are you staying?"

"With my aunt in Kópavogur," Margrét said quietly. "Álfhólsvegur 202."

"Thank you for your co-operation," Gunna said, rising from her seat as the three on the other side of the table did the same. "We appreciate you coming to us so promptly. If you could give my colleague a contact number, he'll show you out. I'll be in touch as soon as I can with any information we can share, and I expect there will be a few more questions as well."

Sigurgeir nodded his head, shoulders rounded as if with a great weight, while Margrét held herself proudly upright and Högni carried himself like a clone of his father. Gunna left Eiríkur to lead them out to the car park behind the building and made her way back to her office, reflecting on how little the parents knew of their daughter's life once she had cut herself off from her own roots. But the young man was a different matter. The way he had dropped his eyes told her that Högni knew or suspected more than he was prepared to let on, at least in front of his parents.

IT WAS LATE in the day when Gunna dropped herself into what had once been her office chair and put her folder of notes on the empty desk. "Haddi!"

She was answered with silence and cursed quietly to herself until the sound of a distant flush confirmed that she was not alone in Hvalvík's police station. Haddi appeared with that morning's Dagurinn folded under one arm.

"You called, ma'am? Decided to come back, have you?"

"Indeed. Park yourself down and tell me everything you know. But not until we have lubrication," she instructed.

Haddi shuffled out, returned with two mugs, and made himself comfortable in the office's other chair. Gunna opened the window and longed for an illicit Prince from the dwindling pack in what had been her desk, while Haddi fussed with a pipe in defiance of both law and regulations.

"Now. What do you want to know?"

"Óskar Pétur Óskarsson. Tell me about him."

"Who?"

"The guy who had his jaw smashed up."

"Oh, Skari Bubba. Not much to tell, really. He was a bit of a bad lad as a youngster. Seems to have settled down since he took up with whatshername."

"Born in Keflavík fifteenth of April 1977," Gunna read from the notes in front of her. "Parents are Óskar Kjartansson and Fanney Ágústsdóttir, couple of older siblings. He has convictions for breaking and entering, vehicle theft, assault, drugs, drunk and disorderly, the list goes on. Nothing after 2001. Why's he called Skari Bubba?"

Haddi's pipe gurgled. "Well, the story goes that his dad, old Skari, isn't actually his dad at all. You know Bubbi, the feller who runs the pumps at Hafnarkaffi? Rumour has it that old Fanney had a bit of a fling one summer while the old man was away on the prawn fishing and next spring along came little Skari. Not that old Skari ever put two and two together. He's a decent chap, but not the sharpest chisel in the box."

"Fair enough, that's the man's ancestry sorted out. What else?"

"Skari left Hvalvík around the time you came here, I suppose. He went to Reykjavík for a bit and was in all kinds of trouble for a couple of years. Then I reckon he met this woman he's been living with and she must have straightened him out. Anyway, they've got some kids and about a year ago they turned up here. He's been working over in Keflavík in some warehouse and she waddles round the village with a pushchair full of children. You must have seen her; a tubby lass with lots of frizzy hair."

"They live in that little house near Jón Kidda's place?"

"That's the one. It was his granny's house. She must have left it to him when she popped off, and I suppose that's why they came to live here."

"All right. Now, what about Skari when he was a youngster, before his girlfriend straightened him out?"

Haddi sucked his teeth. "He was a right bloody tearaway. He and that damned Ommi caused all kinds of mayhem."

"Long Ommi?"

"Yup. Gulla the Post's eldest lad."

"Ah. The one who's escaped from Kvíabryggja nick?"

"And hasn't been seen since," Haddi said. "He was put away for murder ten years ago, beat up a chap outside a nightclub. Or so they say."

Gunna raised an eyebrow. "And what else do they say?"

Haddi coughed and cleared his throat noisily. "Well, according to the gossip, it wasn't Ommi at all, but he took the rap for it."

"We got the wrong man?"

"In a manner of speaking. Ommi confessed and everything, and from what I'm told, strictly on the quiet, you understand, he was made a generous offer to do the time in return for a decent payday and a good drink at the end of it all. It's not as if he wasn't used to being in and out of the nick as it was. Litla-Hraun must have been pretty much a second home for him, and being shifted up to Kvíabryggja's more like being at a holiday camp."

"Did Ommi and Skari fall out at some time?"

"Couldn't tell you, they both left here all those years ago, and when Skari came back he settled down like a good lad, or at least as good as he could manage."

"How far back do these two idiots go?"

"Right back to playschool. They grew up in the same street and knocked about together since they were learning to walk. A right pair of troublemakers; spent my first couple of years on the force knocking their heads together, not that it did much good."

"It sounds like I need to ask Skari a few more questions."

Haddi shrugged. "Rather you than me. I've seen enough of those bastards to last me a lifetime."

Gunna nodded absently as she thought. The atmosphere was different and it felt decidedly uncomfortable to be back in what had been her office for so long. The place felt unfamiliar, even though she had only transferred to Reykjavík a few weeks before and still went past the Hvalvík police station every day.

"You know I'm not gone yet, don't you, Haddi?"

"What's that?"

"You ought to know I'm only seconded to this new unit on what Ívar Laxdal calls a permanent temporary basis, whatever that means."

Haddi wheezed with what Gunna recognized as laughter. "I suppose it means that as long as you're a good girl you keep the job, and if you screw up they can send you back to us with a boot up your arse?"

"Probably, and it means that Keflavík is still paying my huge salary. Thought maybe they'd bump you up to sergeant. I did recommend it, you know," she added.

This time Haddi looked surprised. "That's good of you, but I'm too old and past it, you know. Maybe young Snorri'll get it instead." He grinned slyly.

"I'm afraid not, Haddi. We're just going to live with the recruitment freeze for a good while to come and there won't be a lot of promotion if it means going up a grade in salary. It seems my inspector's grade has yet to be approved, so I'm still on a sergeant's salary."

Saturday 13th

GUNNA STOOD OUTSIDE the Co-op. Eventually the elderly woman she was waiting for appeared, the shop's first customer of the day, buttoned up in a thick herringbone coat of a kind that had become unfashionable forty years before but which was hard-wearing enough to have lasted. Fanney's hair was covered with a scarf that whipped up around her shoulders in the stiff breeze as she stepped outside.

"Need a lift?" Gunna asked, nodding at the bags the woman held in each hand.

"I don't need a lift, but if you're offering I'll accept one," Fanney answered, looking about to see who was watching.

She sat silent and stiffly upright, as if a ride in a car was a rare treat to be savoured.

"I suppose you want to come inside now?" she asked with resignation as Gunna pulled up outside the modest house one row up from the harbour.

Gunna sat patiently at the kitchen table while Fanney made coffee and set about emptying her shopping bags. The kitchen of the little house reminded her of a museum, so little had changed in the last thirty years, from the antiquated fridge to the old metal kettle on the stove.

"What was Skari like when he was a lad?" Gunna asked softly.

Fanney pulled the scarf from her head and clattered cups on to the table.

"Nothing but trouble, that boy, from the moment he was born," she snapped. "I don't know what he's been up to now but he'll be off work for a good few months, I reckon. I don't know how his Erla puts up with him."

She poured for both of them and leaned back to reach for a milk carton.

"He's not a bad boy, you understand," she went on. "Not bad at all. But he's easily led, follows the others all the time, always has done. Wants to fit in with the crowd. If it wasn't for Gulla's boy, you know, the one in prison, he'd have been fine. But no, my Oskar just had to do everything Omar told him to do. I thought when he took up with Erla he was letting himself in for too much, what with her having a couple of children already and being older than him, but I was wrong there and they seem happy enough." She sighed again and paused for breath.

"Have you been over to Keflavík to see him?"

"No," Fanney said bitterly. "Erla's been to see him, but she hasn't thought to ask me along to see my own son yet."

"Well. I have to go over there tomorrow, so I'll drop you off at the hospital if you like."

Gunna watched Fanney stifle an internal battle between pride and anger.

"I wouldn't want to put you out," the older woman said icily.

"As I said, I have to go over there anyway, so it's no trouble at all."

"Thank you."

"I'll pick you up at ten."

Fanney reached for the coffee jug and filled the cups.

"Now, what can you tell me about Omar Magnússon?" Gunna asked. This time Fanney's face stiffened.

"That evil boy. Trouble follows him like a ghost with no house to haunt," she said with a shiver. "He and my Skari were the best of friends as kids and that arsehole of a boy did nothing but thieve, lie and fight. Led my lad a merry dance, he did, what with all the trouble he caused. He set fire to the old fishmeal plant for a bet, and that cost a dozen men their jobs. Then he stole cars and all sorts as soon as he could get behind the wheel, and talk about picking locks and thieving from peoples houses. The things I could tell you. . ." Fanney's voice faded away.

"Please do," Gunna invited.

"You don't think it's him as had anything to do with my Skari getting hurt like that?"

"I've no idea," Gunna admitted. "I'm simply trying to put together some picture of these boys. I came to live here about the time they both left Hvalvík, so I don't have the local knowledge and the background to go with it."

"You've been here so long now that people forget you're not from round here." Fanney sniffed, and Gunna almost felt a flush of pride at what was an unintentional compliment. "Omar and my lad knocked about as boys do and I suppose they were more troublesome than most. There was never anything bad about Oskar, just high spirits. But that Omar's a bad lot. They met up in Reykjavík, and his father and I never did find out what it was they got up to there."

"Oskar didn't tell you?"

"And we didn't ask. If he didn't want to say, that was his business." She sniffed again. "But I've no doubt that Omar was up to no good. He always was a wicked bastard, even when he was little."

"AH, DECIDED TO join us, have you, chief?" Helgi asked, glasses on the end of his nose and the phone slung precariously between shoulder and ear.

"Thought I might drop in," Gunna answered. "Been helping you out, as it happens. Now, where's Eiríkur? It's time we put our heads together."

"Here, chief," Eiríkur said cheerfully, standing up behind his partition. "Right then, gather round, gentlemen."

Helgi stayed where he was and Eiríkur brought over a stool to sit next to him while Gunna took off her anorak and opened her briefcase.

"Right. What's happening with Svana Geirs so far? Eiríkur?"

"I'm going through all the info the door-to-door enquiries came up with. It was a busy afternoon and the flat's close to the petrol station and the 11-11 shop up the road, so there was plenty of traffic and we have loads of sightings of suspicious-looking persons. Trouble is we have no idea at all if we're looking for a man, a woman, young, old or what, so we can't discount any yet."

"Plenty, then?"

"Too many. Dozens of descriptions, and I'll bet that most of them were just going to and from the bakery."

"Any CCTV?" Gunna asked.

"Not directly. There's a camera outside the lawyers' chambers round the corner in a blind alley. Been through it and there's nothing to be seen on it at all. The petrol station and 11-11 both have footage that I'm going through now."

"Prints from the flat?"

"A good few, they're still being worked on. Technical are a bit pushed at the moment."

Gunna drummed the table with her fingernails.

"You might have to push them a bit harder if they don't get on with it," she said, and Eiríkur looked dubious.

"I don't like to. I know they're doing what they can, and they're short-staffed."

"Aren't we all? Any news of the real chief?"

Örlygur Sveinsson, their superior officer and the man nominally in charge of the unit, while well known to them by reputation, had yet to make an appearance after having been signed off on long-term sick leave.

"Lying on the sofa being waited on hand and foot while watching Police Academy 12," Helgi cackled. They were all aware that enforced TV would be little short of torture for a man denied access to the golf course.

"Fair enough, it's all down to us, as usual. I have the guy who fitted the burglar alarm in Svana Geirs' flat coming over this morning to unlock a few things for me, and we need to start interviewing friends and acquaintances. Do we have a list to start with?"

Helgi laid a sheet of paper on the table, closely packed with names, addresses, phone numbers and indications of what each person's relationship to the deceased had been.

"We'll divvy that up between ourselves," Gunna decided. "Now, Long Ommi. Any sightings of our errant convict, Helgi?"

"Excuse me, chief, do you still need me?" Eiríkur asked.

"Not on this, but you might as well listen in, just in case Helgi decides to go on holiday and you have to take over. Go on, Helgi."

"Not a bloody thing," Helgi said morosely. "But a prize-winning idiot called Kristbjörn Hrafnsson, otherwise known as Daft Diddi, was admitted to casualty at the National Hospital on Thursday morning with a fat lip, various bruises, cuts and scrapes. What with Óskar Óskarsson in hospital in Keflavík, that pretty much gives us two definite sightings. The bastard might as well have just written 'Ommi was here' on the pavement and have done with it."

"All right. I've been fortunate enough never to have encountered this particular ray of sunshine, although I've met his mother. Now I've also spoken to both Skari and Skari's mum. The old lady loathes Ommi with a passion and Skari says nothing. So where does that leave us?"

Helgi lifted his hands up, palms in the air. "If he wants to keep his mouth shut, that's his prerogative. But with that sort of injury, there has to be a damned good reason . . ."

"Which is what we need to winkle out of someone," Gunna finished for him. "Right, guys. I have an appointment at Svana Geirs' flat in ten minutes, so I'll see you two in the canteen at lunchtime."

THE WOMAN HE had lived with for fifteen years looked blank-eyed at him from the doorway of her parents' house. Jón wanted desperately to sweep her into his arms and take her with him, not that he had anywhere much to go. Their own house had become a shell of the home they had both worked hard to make it. Practically everything that could be sold had gone. Even the living-room carpet had been exchanged for a couple of tanks of diesel.

"Have her back by eight, can you?" Linda said in the most neutral voice she could manage, although to Jón it sounded edged with barbed wire. He just nodded as his daughter skipped down the steps and put her hand in his. Didn't the bloody woman understand that every hard word was like a smack in the face?

Linda watched with folded arms as Jón carefully strapped Ragna Gústa into the front seat and the little girl waved happily to her mother, who found suddenly that while she could wave back, finding a smile was more of a problem.

"Where are we going, Daddy? To our house?"

"I don't know yet, darling. I thought maybe we'd go to Grandma's place for a change. How does that sound?"

"Good," she replied after thinking carefully for a moment.

Jón spun the wheel to take the van out on to the main road, and the tools in the back rattled.

"I like this."

"What's that, love?"

"I like being in your work van. It's funner than your big car."

"Not funner. More fun. . ."

"You know what I mean. This car's bigger and it smells

different." The only car now, Jón thought but didn't say out loud. He didn't know how to explain to her that the jeep had gone more than a month ago.

THE EXISTENCE OF a canteen was something Gunna was becoming accustomed to. In her years on the city force before leaving Reykjavík for the quiet of a post at the fishing village Hvalvík, the canteen had been a fixture where practically every officer met every other one.

She loaded two lamb cutlets on to her plate, added a single potato, some salad, decided to forgo gravy and carried lunch to where Eiríkur was sipping coffee over his empty plate.

"That's what comes of being late," she said, cutting into the cold potato and discarding it.

"There's no phone in Svana Geirs' flat, is there, chief?" Eiríkur asked. "No, don't think so."

"That's what's missing. No phone. Somebody like Svana Geirs must have had an iPhone or a BlackBerry. There's no way round it—everyone has a mobile these days. Even my dad has one and he's the world's most old-fashioned man."

Eiríkur rarely mentioned his parents, but Gunna knew that his father was a clergyman and that Eiríkur had several considerably older siblings. She sometimes wondered how easily Eiríkur's parents accepted his not being married to the girl-friend with whom he had a small child.

"It's a thought," she said, more to encourage him to continue than to say anything.

"She must have relied on a mobile. Even if people have a landline these days, it's normally just for the internet connection. You just can't function now without a mobile. So where's Svana's phone?"

"Do you have a number?"

"No. But I'm starting on some of her friends this afternoon and I'll see what I can get out of them. It stands to reason. If

we could get hold of it, it would give us a load of information
on her movements that day."

"Go for it. Let me know what you come up with."

"GOD! AND RIGHT next door!"

Svana Geirs' neighbour was alone at home and seemed
pleased to have company when Gunna and Eiríkur called on her.
She was a tiny, doll-like woman, casually and fashionably dressed.

"I mean . . . Svana. It's . . ." She floundered for the right
words and eventually gave up, letting a despairing fluttering of
hands speak for her.

"It must have been a shock for you," Gunna said.

"God! Of course! I know this is Reykjavík 101 and you
should expect it to be . . . er, like . . ."

"Rowdy sometimes?" Gunna finished for her.

"Yeah. Rowdy, lively. That's it. But, God," she said with
emphasis, dropping on to a plush sofa while Gunna and Eiríkur
stood. Gunna thought better of the sofa and lowered herself on
to one of the chairs arranged around a long dining-room table.
The room was spotless. Gunna gazed around her with a practised eye and saw nothing cheap, from the minimalist pictures
on the walls to the weighty crystal ornaments and the huge
screen that filled one wall. She placed her notes in front of her
and opened the folder.

"All right. You're Arna Arnarsdóttir?"

"That's me," she simpered.

"My colleague Eiríkur Thór . . ." Gunna looked over at him,
enveloped in the sofa's grip. "My colleague spoke to you yesterday, and according to your statement you recognized some of
the people seen leaving and entering Svana's flat. Is that right?"

"Yeah, God. I saw one of them on TV last night as well,"
she said in excitement.

"Who was that?"

"On the news!"

"RÚV or Channel 2?"

Arna's excited smile stopped in its tracks. "Er, I don't know. They're the same, aren't they?"

"Not quite," Gunna said. "Were you aware of the same people coming and going regularly? Or were there people you only saw once?"

"Well, both really."

"So, have you any idea who some of these people are?"

Arna almost bounced with eagerness and reached down to the floor beside the sofa for a stack of glossy magazines that she put on the table in front of her.

"I went through all these . . ."

"And you found some faces you recognized?"

"Yeah!" She opened the first one and flipped through it, peering at the pages. "Him."

Gunna moved over to the table and looked down at the magazine to where Arna pointed with a lacquered nail at a flashed photograph of a man in a dark suit getting out of a sleek car.

"But I don't know who he is," Arna said.

"Jónas Valur Hjaltason, it says there," Gunna pointed out, and looked over at Eiríkur again.

"Businessman," Eiríkur elaborated. "Fingers in all sorts of pies."

"Fair enough. Arna, it might be easiest if you could go through these and mark the people you recognize."

The idea seemed to confuse her for a moment. "What, and you'll come back later and get them, you mean?"

"No, I meant you could go through them now," Gunna said patiently. "That way we can ask you any questions while you do it."

Arna seemed to be thinking through the idea. "OK. Do you have a pen?"

"Eiríkur? Would you?"

Eiríkur stood up and took charge.

"Could I ask you to put the magazines over here where we can both look?" he asked sweetly, patting the dining table.

Gunna gratefully left Eiríkur to it, accepting that his patient manner would be far more effective than the irritable brusqueness she was having difficulty suppressing. Every few moments there was a giggle from the table as Eiríkur's and Arna's heads became steadily closer over the pile of magazines.

"Arna? Do you live here alone?" Gunna asked suddenly when there was a lull.

"No, of course not. My husband lives here as well."

"And he's at work at the moment, I suppose?"

"Yeah. Why?"

"Nothing special. I was just wondering if he might have noticed anything. When do you expect him home?"

Gunna could see that the pink tip of Arna's tongue was protruding from a corner of her mouth as she concentrated on the magazine pages in front of her.

"Him?" Eiríkur prompted.

"Yeah. I've seen him. What? Tolli's back tomorrow night. He's in London this week," she added proudly.

ON THE WAY down the stairs to the street, Gunna welcomed the reappearance of the city sounds that had been ruthlessly excluded from Arna Arnarsdóttir's hermetically sealed apartment on the top floor.

"So, Eiríkur, what kind of a haul do we have?"

"Half a dozen of the country's finest to try and talk to discreetly. Two shady businessmen, Jónas Valur Hjaltason and Bjartmar Arnarson, plus Bjarki Steinsson, a high-flying accountant, and a brand new MP," he said, counting them as he looked at his notes. "She said there were a couple of younger men who visited as well, but doesn't know who they are."

"Which MP?"

"Hallur Hallbjörnsson. Been a naughty boy, I reckon. Didn't think the Social Democrats went in for that sort of thing."

Gunna watched the street doors to the block hiss open automatically as they approached.

"Did you get any joy with that?" she asked suddenly, pointing to the security camera fitted above the door.

"No. The caretaker says it's been broken for weeks, so no security footage."

"Shame. Now, we'd best divvy these jokers up between us and see what we can get out of them. Do you want the MP or shall I?"

Gunna sensed Skúli's awkwardness from the set of his jaw and the thin line his mouth made. She waved to him and his face relaxed as he saw her.

"Sorry I'm a bit late. Traffic," he apologized.

"No problem. I don't have long, though."

Gunna sipped her coffee and glanced towards the counter, where a bored young man was waiting with a blank expression for something to do. Around them the shopping centre in Hafnarfjördur bustled with people buying their last-minute groceries under soothing artificial light.

"Already done your shopping?" Skúli asked.

"Nope. Left it to the boyfriend. D'you want a coffee?"

"Yeah. Why not?"

"Go on. Get me a refill while you're there."

He returned with mugs and a dry sandwich on a plate.

"Lunch?" Gunna enquired.

"Yup. Not much time to eat today."

"Now then," she said in a businesslike tone that made Skúli swallow and pay attention. "I'm sure we've been doing much the same sort of research on all this stuff, you and I. So tell me what you've found out and I'll fill in the gaps I'm allowed to."

"Svana Geirs was a talented dancer, did OK as a model, not very successful pop singer, even less successful actress, shameless self-publicist. Married twice, both times briefly. No kids. Numerous operations—"

"Operations?"

"Yeah, cosmetic. Thighs, tits more than once, I'm told, face lift, nose job, teeth fixed, liposuction. The works, more or less."

"OK, understood."

"She owns a third share of this health club, which has traded on her image from when she had a fitness show on TV. But from what I can figure out, the club has been struggling these last few months. Fewer customers since the bank crash last year, now that people don't have so much cash to spend, and they haven't been able to raise finance."

Gunna smiled inwardly, recalling how only a few months ago Skúli had been a shy young man surprised at everything around him in the real world after all his years of study.

"There's been a rumour flying around that Svana was linked with somebody prominent," Skúli continued.

"Linked businesswise, or romantically?"

"Either or both. The rumour is that she had been sleeping with someone prominent, but no names. Someone prominent and married, that is. But what's the state of things now as far as the police are concerned?"

"So the mystery deepens. We'll confirm officially first thing in the morning that the victim is Svana Geirs. The family have been notified, so it's all yours."

"Can I have that now?"

Gunna thought for a moment. "The confirmation will be at eight tomorrow. But I reckon you'd be safe enough if it goes on the Dagurinn website after midnight. That won't upset anyone and you'll still be ahead of everyone else."

"Brilliant," Skúli grinned.

"Right. I'm going home," Gunna announced, fumbling in her coat pocket for car keys. She looked down at their empty mugs, squinting at the remnants of sandwich on Skúli's plate. "You ought to eat your crusts if you want to grow up big and strong. I'll get these," she added, striding towards the slack-jawed young man staring into space behind the counter.

Sunday 14th

"Where d'you get the number from?"

"From the brother, strange character," Helgi replied. "I had to push him a bit, but he came up with it. It's as if he wants us to find out what happened to his sister, but he doesn't want to do anything that might actually help."

"He is odd," Gunna agreed. "You'd be odd if you'd grown up where he did. A country lad like yourself should know what these out-of-the way places are like."

"That's rich from someone who grew up in Vestureyri," Helgi shot back.

"So, what have you found out since last night?"

Helgi looked pleased with himself. "There are actually two numbers registered to Svana Geirs, neither of which has been used for months. Plus there's the number I managed to get out of Högni."

"And?"

"It's a contract phone, all paid up to date, and it's registered to Fit Club. I asked for a warrant to track the phone, and according to the phone company it's still switched on. It's in the vicinity of the flat and hasn't been far. At least, the connection has been through the same mast the whole time. And no, there's no answer."

"That's quick work. Well done. So what do you reckon?"

"No idea," Helgi said after a moment's silence. "It could still be in the flat, but the place has been searched thoroughly. Or else it's somewhere close by. Picked up by the killer and dumped in a bin, something like that?"

"Or been put somewhere we're never likely to find it, more like," Gunna said grimly.

"I don't know. I'd have thought that someone who wanted to get rid of it would have switched it off first, or just taken the SIM card out and destroyed that, rather than leaving the phone lying about switched on."

"Unless it's some kind of false trail?" Gunna wondered.

Fit Club was less than its website had indicated, but managed to be everything Gunna found uncomfortable. Sandwiched between a residential area of 1960s blocks and the business district of Ármúli, the short street of which Fit Club was the main feature was full of cars parked badly across the club's glass frontage. Gunna peered in and saw that a few of the running machines were in use. Rather than the bright young things that Fit Club's advertising indicated, these were being pounded by middle-aged women and a few men, all on a mission to get into something slightly smaller.

"Agnar Arnalds about?" Gunna asked the waif-like blonde at the front desk.

"Er, like, who are you?" the girl demanded in return, and Gunna wondered if she really was thinner than the sad yucca plant in a pot next to the desk, of if she simply looked that way.

"Police." Gunna flashed her wallet quickly in front of the girl.

"Sorry. We get a lot of older ladies asking for him," the girl apologized. She pressed a button on an intercom system that blared an error tone back at her. "It's not working. Wait a moment, I'll check. He's not always here this early on a Sunday."

"Older?" Gunna mouthed to herself as the girl disappeared through a door behind her desk, and she took the opportunity to look over into the reception desk. There was little to be seen other than a battered phone. An open notebook showed scribbled numbers, and packets of chewing gum and cigarettes were stacked out of sight of prying eyes.

"Good morning. You're not here to join us, are you?"

The man had appeared silently behind her as the girl returned to her desk.

"No, far from it," Gunna said. "Agnar?"

"That's me."

A beefy hand was extended, with a discreet hint of smile that indicated its wearer knew why she was there.

"Gunnhildur Gísladóttir, Serious Crime Unit. It's about Svana Geirs, but I reckon you'd guessed that already."

"Thought so. Come with me."

Agnar Arnalds stood over two metres tall, waves of brown hair falling to his shoulders, and Gunna looked appreciatively at the expanse of the man's muscular back as he took the stairs three at a time. Fit Club's office provided a remarkable contrast to the hardwood floor and floor-to-ceiling mirror walls downstairs. The decor in here was cheap chipboard, and Gunna guessed that it had been years since the place had seen a paintbrush. Agnar waved her to a seat, but sat himself on his own desk, feet on a chair. Gunna decided to stay standing rather than have the man towering over her.

"I'm here about Svana," she repeated. Agnar's face became melancholy as if a switch had been turned inside him. His shoulders dropped and the smile disappeared.

"Poor Svana," he sighed. "She was a wonderful person. So full of life."

"Right now I'm working on building up a picture of her movements over her last few days—who she spoke to, who she met, places she went to, that sort of thing. When did you last see her?"

"The day she died. She was here, took an early class in the morning for her foldies—"

"Foldies?" Gunna asked.

"Fat oldies. Sorry, I mean older ladies. When was she . . . killed?" Agnar gulped out the last word.

"In the afternoon. What time did she leave here?"

Agnar thought for a moment with his chin in one hand, a pose that Gunna was sure he must have practised frequently.

"She normally had three classes here between eight and eleven. But that day she had just one and someone else took the other classes. I remember she showered here and left. I think she had a meeting somewhere," he said carefully. "No, I don't know who with," he added as soon as he saw Gunna about to ask.

"All right. What's the nature of her involvement with this business?"

"How do you mean?"

"Svana was one of the three owners, or so I understand?"

"You've been doing your homework, haven't you?" Agnar asked with a winning smile.

"That's the nature of the job," Gunna replied coldly.

"There are . . . were," he corrected himself, "three partners in the company that owns this place. Me, Svana and an investment company."

"Which is?"

Agnar twisted uncomfortably. "KópInvest has a lot of shareholders. Svana owned thirty per cent, the same as me. KópInvest holds the rest. That's it."

Gunna consulted her folder of notes. "Svana's mobile phone, number ending 868. It's registered to Fit Club?"

Agnar nodded.

"Any idea where that phone is?"

Agnar looked blank and Gunna knew immediately that he had been taken by surprise.

"She always had it. Used it all the time," he said slowly. "Wasn't it with her?"

"No sign of it."

"Can't understand that. She was lost without it. She'd put it on silent when she had a class, but apart from then, it was pretty much stuck to her ear all the time."

"Did she have another phone?"

"Not any more. She changed numbers a few months ago after some deadbeat started making crank calls to her. Svana swore she was being stalked."

"Did she go to the police?"

"God, no," he said, rummaging in a drawer. "Here's her old one. It's a Fit Club phone as well."

"I'll take that if I may," Gunna said firmly as Agnar unwillingly placed the phone in her palm. "Did she report these crank calls? Any idea what sort of calls they were? Silence? Heavy breathing? That's the normal sort of thing."

"She didn't say, just that some creep was pestering her."

"All right. I could do with a list of friends and acquaintances. I take it she had a busy social life?"

"Just a bit."

"Any particular close friends?"

"Loads of them. Jenna Hrannars, Ásd's Ósk Gunnars, Hulda Gróa Waage. You must have read about them?" Agnar looked satisfied, as if there could be no greater accomplishment than having talked-about friends.

"Can't say I have," Gunna replied drily. "Any new acquaintances? Anything unusual?"

"Last week she had a screaming argument right outside here. That was a surprise," Agnar said, rubbing his square chin. "She told me afterwards that the bloke she was yelling at was her brother and that they'd sorted it all out afterwards. Svana wanted him to become a personal trainer."

"And what did you think of that idea?"

"Not a lot," he said flatly. "I spoke to him and I thought he was an idiot. Well overweight, so he'd need to lose a lot."

"How about Svana's lovers?" Gunna asked.

The look of satisfaction vanished from Agnar's handsome features and was replaced with a scowl. "A few. They came and went."

"Frequently? Occasionally? Who's in the picture? You?"

"That's ancient history," Agnar said with a sour look that appeared incongruous on his open features. "We were good friends and business partners. We worked well together, but we didn't share every personal detail."

"That's as far as it went?" Gunna asked, inwardly pleased to have found a chink in the man's self-satisfied armour.

"We were an item for a while about five years ago, after she divorced Bjarni Örn. That's all in the past. Nothing since."

"Fair enough. Do you know who was she seeing recently?"

"No. She didn't say and I didn't ask. But there was one she kept quiet, like she wanted to stay discreet about him. Maybe he's married, I don't know."

"Did she make a habit of that?"

"What? Screwing married men? It happens," he replied with a shrug. "Is it important?"

"Murders are generally about either money or jealousy. If anything comes to mind, I'd appreciate it if you'd let me know. How's business?" she asked abruptly.

Agnar scowled again. "It's OK. Could be worse. At least we're still in business, which is more than can be said for a lot of places. But I don't know how we're going to manage now. Svana was this place's main attraction, you know."

GUNNA SAW THE moment the door opened that Hallur Hallbjörnsson was sweating. His face was flushed, in sharp contrast to the urbane persona she had seen him present so skilfully on television.

His office was in the eaves of one of the old corrugated-iron houses a stone's throw from Parliament and the incongruously modern city hall bordering Reykjavík's shallow, duck-filled lake. Gunna knew that the city hall behind its modern columns was where Hallur had been a rising star in municipal politics before standing for Parliament. She was surprised to see just how small a junior MP's office was, a book-lined cubbyhole crammed into the roof space that had probably been a servant's bedroom a century before, and guessed that this represented a temporary drop in status compared to the echoing spaces of his previous workplace.

Hallur waved Gunna to a seat in the only spare chair in the room, and placed himself behind the desk in the corner, as if he knew the angled light coming in through the skylight would accentuate his chiselled features.

"Thanks for finding time—" Gunna began, but Hallur waved her words away.

"I'm often here on a Sunday morning when it's quiet. How can I help you?" he asked with a show of suavity.

"I expect you probably have an idea already. I'm working on the investigation into the death of Svanhildur Mjöll Sigurgeirsdóttir. You were acquainted with her?" Gunna said, going straight to the point.

"I, er, yes. I had an acquaintance with her," Hallur mumbled, and Gunna looked at him enquiringly. He raised his chin to speak clearly and met her gaze. "I did know her and I am deeply saddened by her unfortunate death."

Soundbite talk, Gunna thought, wondering if or when the mask would be allowed to slip.

"I'm trying to track her movements leading up to her death. When did you see her last?"

"On the fourth. Ten days ago," he replied promptly.

"You're sure?"

Hallur nodded. "I checked my diary when I knew you were on the way. I had an idea what you'd want to ask me about."

"And how did she strike you then?"

"As usual," Hallur said with a shrug. "Lively, happy, excited at the possibility of being back on TV."

"I take it she wasn't going to be hosting any heavyweight political debates?"

"That's an unkind comment, officer. She had an offer from a production company to front a fashion show of some kind."

"D'you know the name of the company?" Gunna asked, jotting down notes.

"I'm sorry. We didn't tend to discuss business."

"What did you discuss, if you don't mind my asking?"

A rivulet of perspiration made its way from the parting in Hallur's groomed dark hair and came to rest in the stubble on his jaw. "All sorts. But I wouldn't say we were close friends."

"What sort of friends were you? Lovers?" Gunna asked. A jolt of discomfort passed through Hallur's shoulders.

"We were. . . good friends," he admitted finally.

"It seems an unusual friendship," Gunna said drily. "A well-known politician with a high-profile wife and some strong opinions, and a rather shallow woman. From what I've been able to make out, you couldn't have had a great deal in common."

"Sport, mostly. I trained at Fit Club once or twice a week when I was a city councillor. It was as good a reason as any for getting out of the building for an hour when the office politics were making me lose the will to live."

Getting somewhere at last, Gunna thought.

"So you met Svana at Fit Club?"

"That's right. We'd bump into each other once or twice a week and chat over a coffee."

"And you continued to 'bump into each other' and 'chat' even when you'd stopped training at her club?"

Hallur nodded. "Svana had a very wide circle of acquaintances. A very disparate group of people."

"All men?" Gunna observed.

He nodded again. "I don't believe she had many close female friends. You understand?"

It was Gunna's turn to nod. "You still haven't told me the nature of your relationship, other than that you chatted occasionally over a latte. I have to tell you that you have been identified as a regular visitor to Svana's apartment."

Gunna could see that Hallur's composure was gradually failing.

"This isn't on record," she continued, "and you're not sworn to tell the truth, although I wouldn't expect anything else of someone in your position."

"This goes no further?"

"Unless it leads to material evidence that requires further investigation."

Hallur's shoulders dropped. "We were occasional lovers. I knew there were others and it didn't bother her that I'm married. It was just physical . . . We'd meet up every couple of weeks and . . . y'know . . ." His voice tailed off as if he were a schoolboy caught with a pocketful of contraband.

"Always at her apartment?"

"Pretty much. We had a weekend once, in Copenhagen. But it wasn't comfortable. There are so many Icelanders there that I was terrified of being spotted. This is confidential, isn't it? It would destroy my marriage if this got out."

Gunna bit back a caustic reply. "It's between ourselves, as I said, unless this leads to material evidence that we need to pursue further. However, you mentioned that there were others?"

"Yes. Of course. I couldn't expect her not to see other men. Svana was . . . how shall I put it? She liked to experiment."

"We have people already identified as being Svana's acquaintances in the same way that you were. But if you could provide names, it would help. As I said, we are making every effort to track down a killer, but it doesn't help when much of the victim's life was either right in the public gaze or else hidden completely."

Hallur's head bobbed in agreement and his trademark boyish smile began to reappear. "I know that Svana had several friendships. But I don't have any names and I never asked."

"In that case, I'll leave you alone. For the moment, at least," Gunna said, rising from the chair. Hallur was on his feet instantly and stepped around the desk with his hand held out.

"I'd like to thank you for being discreet," he breathed with a flash of the television smile.

"Anyway, thank you for your time. I'll be in touch if we need to speak to you again."

"Of course, please call if you need anything."

He stood holding Gunna's hand in his for longer than a usual handshake would warrant. "You know, officer. Would you be free for lunch sometime? I'd like to know more about the way the police work, from the inside, so to speak. Law and order is an issue that I have a deep interest in."

Gunna extricated her fingers from Hallur's soft but insistent grip. "Thank you. But that would hardly be appropriate as long as you're a potential material witness, I'm afraid."

"Maybe when the case is closed, then?"

"Possibly. Thanks for your time."

Gunna clattered down the narrow wooden staircase from Hallur's office. Outside, she breathed a sigh of relief.

"The cheeky randy bastard," she muttered to herself, striding past Hotel Borg and toying with the thought of going inside to use the bathroom and wash the hand that Hallur had shaken.

THE AIR TASTED slightly stale and the flat no longer felt as if anyone lived there. The kitchen floor where Svana Geirs had twitched as she died in a widening pool of her own blood was scrubbed clean, as if the flat's occupant had simply moved out. Gunna went from the kitchen to the living room, frowning as she wondered what she was actually looking for. The place was tidy and Svana Geirs' belongings were all still where they belonged. Eiríkur and the technical team had taken only a few items that they felt needed to be fingerprinted or checked at the laboratory.

In the blue and pink bedroom the huge down quilt had been carefully folded into a square and placed on a corner of the mattress, while the sheets and duvet cover had been taken away to be checked. She slid back the door of the wardrobe that filled an entire wall and ran a hand over the expensive fabrics of the dresses and coats on hangers, wondering how many of these had ever actually been worn.

She went through the hangers one by one, checking the pockets of all the jackets and coats for anything that might have been left, but finding nothing. At the far end, behind a couple of colourful summer dresses that she doubted would see much use in a short Icelandic summer, and some revealing nightdresses, she found herself looking at two hangers that had been carefully pushed out of sight.

"Good grief," she muttered, lifting up a hanger that held a skimpy French maid's outfit consisting of more lace than mate-rial. Behind it was a bizarre version of a nurse's outfit that she realized with distaste was made of some kind of plastic.

She debated with herself whether these ought to be taken for testing as well, but decided that if anything were to be found, the bedclothes or the contents of the washing basket would probably be likelier sources.

She hung the items back in their places respectfully, pain-fully aware that their owner had only been dead a few days. She wondered who had been the beneficiary of Svana Geirs' magnificent figure in these bizarre, titillating outfits. She looked at the vast array of shoes at the wardrobe's floor level, shook her head and shut the double doors.

The place was unnervingly silent. Any traffic noise was shut out entirely by the triple-glazed windows, excluding any sense of the outside world. The flat resembled a cocoon cut off from reality. She sat at the head of the bed and felt herself sink in the dense mattress, resisting the temptation to bounce on it. The two drawers of the bedside table on one side were empty, but the side nearer the window revealed the TV remote, sprays and jars of creams and a party box of condoms in a variety of colours and, as far as Gunna could make out, flavours—she decided that banana probably didn't refer to size. The lower drawer contained handcuffs, a small vibrator that emitted a rattlesnake buzz at the flick of a switch, and packets of pills from paracetamol to heavy-duty prescription painkillers. But no phone or little black book were to be seen. In fact, Gunna reflected, as she paced to the window to look out at the quiet street four floors below, nowhere was there a scrap of paper, a magazine or a book.

Suddenly all her senses sharpened in a single flash of alarm as a groan, muffled but unmistakable, came from the corridor. She turned slowly and listened for it to be repeated, stepping as gently as she could towards the bedroom door. She was wondering if she had definitely closed the flat's door when the groan came again, longer this time and ending on a higher note that was almost a squeal.

In the passage she stood and listened. She could hear someone's breath coming in short bursts, and this time she swept towards the kitchen, certain that the sound was coming from there. In the kitchen doorway, she scanned the room. The breaths panted and morphed into a low moan that rose and suddenly stopped, cut off as if by the flick of a switch. The flat was silent again.

Gunna stood in the middle of the kitchen floor and turned in a slow circle, looking in every direction. She smiled to herself, reached into her jacket pocket, took out her phone and thumbed the green button twice.

"Helgi? In the office, are you? You have Svana's phone number? I'd like you to call it right now from your desk phone, OK? And stay on the line."

The silence in the kitchen was broken only by the faintest hum from the fridge. Gunna was uncomfortably conscious of her own breathing, and even of the rustle of her still unfamiliar non-uniform trousers. When it began, she thought at first that the innocuous buzz was from the fridge itself, a low but insistent pulse. As she squatted down on her haunches, aware that the sound was coming from near the floor, the groan echoed through the kitchen a second time, tinny against the room's hard surfaces. She listened, eyes half closed, and the second groan began, rising to a squeal of what Gunna could now make out was supposed to be ecstasy.

She cast about as the voice began to pant. She lay flat on the floor and peered under the fridge and then under the dish-washer, where a mobile phone sat in the only patch of dust she had seen in the whole flat, flashing and vibrating to itself as the voice rose from a moan to burst into a climax.

"Ah. There you are," Gunna said as a grin spread across her face, reaching with a wooden spoon under the machine to retrieve the phone. It was still vibrating and howling in pleasure as she sat up with it in her hand in triumph. Suddenly it stopped flashing and the screen went dark as the phone switched itself off.

"Damn, battery must be flat," she muttered, fumbling for her own phone. "Helgi? What happened there?" she asked, Svana's lifeless mobile in her hand.

"I let it ring and ring and then it went dead," Helgi said. "What was all that shouting?"

"That was Svana's ringtone, and she was faking it. I'll be back in a minute."

• • •

Ragna Gústa had been named after two old ladies. Linda had wanted to christen the little girl with her mother's name, and Jón realized that his own mother would consider it a lifelong slight if the child didn't carry her name as well. Now he thought it vaguely amusing that his daughter would go through life carrying in close company the names of Ragnhildur and Ágústa, two elderly ladies who couldn't stand each other.

Jón could see the serious expression she had inherited from her maternal grandmother on his daughter's face as Ragna Gústa painstakingly nibbled the nuggets of chocolate from her ice cream before devouring it.

"Daddy?"

He wondered if the bloody man had the faintest idea what turmoil had been wreaked on the lives of ordinary hard-working people. He had fought for months to keep everything together, but finally he'd had to admit to himself that he couldn't keep the pretence up any longer. The jeep had been the first thing to go. Linda hadn't minded, as she hadn't liked it anyway. What had been painful was having to pay more than a million in cash on top just for the privilege of being rid of the loans secured on it.

"Daddy? What's that?"

If only he'd had the sense to take out a loan in krónur instead of letting himself be persuaded to borrow in yen and Swiss francs, then he wouldn't have been hit by the spiralling exchange rate that had doubled his repayments. The boy who bought the Land Cruiser was only a youngster, but a youngster with a berth on a trawler and a pocketful of cash. Jón reckoned he'd actually got the lad to agree to a good deal, once he'd seen the young man's eyes lingering over the massive tyres.

It hadn't been painless, but at least he was shot of the mush-rooming repayments that had been crippling him.

"Yeah, sweetheart? What's up?"

"Daddy, are we going to see Grandma today?"

"No, sweetheart, not today. Shall we go to the pictures instead?"

ALBERT STOOD FOR a moment in thought, Svana Geirs' phone in his hand. "Quite a new model, this one is," he said, as if to himself. "Now, over here . . ."

Gunna watched as he dived into a box and rummaged, emerging with a black box bound round with a lead.

"This one might do it. We'll see," he muttered, plugging the charger into the wall and then into Svana's lifeless phone. "We'll give it a minute to build up some juice and then we can give it a try. So, how are you getting on with being out of uniform?" he asked with a lopsided smile.

"To tell you the truth, Albert, it's bloody weird," Gunna replied as he tapped a computer's keyboard to bring it to life. "I feel like an old frump most of the time, all dressed up and nowhere to go."

She eyed Albert, who was now watching the screen of the laptop perched on a pile of phone books on the workbench in front of him. One of the force's forensics officers, a fascination with anything to do with communications and computers, as the amassed collection of chargers, battery packs, spare parts and other paraphernalia stacked under the workbench demonstrated. Gunna was certain he was absorbed in establishing a link between Svana's phone and the laptop and was no longer hearing a word she said.

"So some mornings I wonder whether to go for the leather miniskirt and the slashed tights, or just put on the little black cocktail dress," she continued.

"Ah! Got it," Albert said in triumph. "The phone's charging and I can open a link to download the call log data, but I'll need a code to get into it."

He ran a hand over the top of his bald head and tapped at the keyboard with the other. The computer beeped back and

Albert's mouth turned into the downward bow of a petulant frown. He rapidly tried another combination, with the same result, and reached for the desk phone, cradling the receiver on his shoulder as he jabbed at the keypad, hardly taking his eyes off the laptop screen.

Gunna felt entirely excluded from Albert's world as he grunted into the phone still jammed between a shoulder and the side of his head.

"Hey, mate. Yeah. Got a D700i. Yup," he mumbled as Gunna tried to make sense of the one-sided conversation. "Two of them, yeah. No, can't see it. It's the new one with the expanded memory. Got an unlock?"

He grunted monosyllabic responses into the phone and tapped at the keyboard, which refused to accept the code with an imperious alert tone.

"No, didn't do it."

He tapped again, and this time there was no answering beep from the laptop.

"Gotcha. Yup, thanks," Albert grunted into the phone. "We're in," he announced, looking up at Gunna as if returning to the real world and flourishing an outstretched palm to show the data marching across the screen.

Gunna shifted her stool closer to the high workbench and peered at the laptop.

"I had complete faith in you, Albert. OK, what do we have?"

"Everything. There's a trace of every piece of data that has ever gone through this phone. What are you looking for?"

"Calls to and from, especially over the last ten days or so. SMS messages, stored numbers."

"No problem. D'you want me to email it all to you?"

"Can do. How long will that take?" Gunna asked dubiously. "Not sure. Where's your office?"

"At the end."

"In that case, I reckon I can get it to your computer quicker than you can get there."

"In that case, I won't hurry." Gunna smiled. "I'll need the phone as well. Evidence."

Albert nodded. "It's a nice one. Quite a new model that came in at the end of last year. It's had a lot of use, I reckon. The keypad's quite worn and you can see it's been in someone's pocket a lot from the way the lacquer's gone off the corners. Where did it come from?"

"Murder victim."

"Svana Geirs?"

"That's the one."

"You'd better take the charger with you as well and charge the battery right up," Albert said, squinting at the screen and scribbling on a scrap of paper. "I've reset the security code to 4321, just in case," he added.

"Thanks, Albert. Much appreciated," Gunna said, unplugging Svana Geirs' phone and weighing it in her hand. "I'll leave you to it, then."

Albert was already deep in his laptop as she swung open the door, and she was startled when he called out with the door closing behind her. She poked her head back in the room.

"Yes?"

"The leather mini, I reckon," Albert grinned.

GUNNA REGRETTED THE decision to print out the document that was waiting on her PC when she reached her desk after hurrying from Albert's workshop downstairs. Pages spewed unrelentingly from the printer, crammed with lines of numbers, times and dates.

Scanning the list of logged calls, she saw that at the top was a withheld number from that morning and guessed that this was Helgi's call that had helped her locate the phone under the dishwasher. Below it were a dozen more calls from withheld numbers over the past few days, as well as from mobile and landline numbers that Gunna marked with a highlighter.

The last call that had been answered was on the same day that Svana Geirs had been found with the side of her head crushed on the kitchen floor, the call timed at 13.53 and lasting less than three minutes.

"So she was still alive at five to two," Gunna mused.

"Say something, chief?" Helgi enquired.

"Albert got all the data out of Svana Geirs' phone. The last call that was answered was at 13.53 on the day she died, so she was alive then. Narrows things down a bit, I suppose. Her cleaner turned up just before five, by which time Svana had already been dead for a while."

"We showed up just after five, and Miss Cruz said that Svana could have been murdered between midday and three, so that fits. But 13.53 is only an indicator if we assume that Svana answered her own phone."

"Don't make things complicated yet," Gunna admonished. "Although you're right. We have to take into account that someone else could have answered it."

"Where did you find it?"

"Under the dishwasher. Got you to call the number and listened out until it rang. Remind me to let you hear her tasteful ringtone properly sometime." Gunna riffled through the top sheets of the printout. "That's it. That's the last activity on the phone, except for a load of missed calls from mostly withheld numbers."

"So how about she had the phone in her hand when she was actually attacked?" Helgi said slowly. "Surely if the attacker wanted to get rid of it, he'd have taken it with him and dropped it off a bridge. I reckon we can be sure that Svana didn't deliberately put her own phone under the dishwasher. What d'you think?"

"It sounds more likely. You'd have thought an attacker would have taken it and disposed of it rather than stash it under the dishwasher," Gunna agreed, staring at the heaped printout. "Where's Eiríkur? I need some help going through all this stuff."

"He's off today."

"OK. You know, Helgi, I have a strong feeling that you're absolutely right. Svana gets a bang on the head, hits the ground like a sack of potatoes and anything in her hand's going to go flying. Which means that there's a real possibility that she was taking this call when she was attacked—which could give us a very precise time of death."

"What's next, then?" Helgi asked dubiously.

Gunna felt her stomach growl. "It's all boring detective work, starting with going through the names and numbers in Svana's call log. Are you still looking for Long Ommi?"

Helgi rolled his eyes and Gunna saw his shoulders droop. "God, yes. The bastard's about somewhere, but I'm damned if I can find out where he's holed himself up. Normally there's someone who's only too ready to pipe up and it takes about two days to track these deadbeats down, but I don't know what Ommi's doing right this time."

"I'd better leave you to it. Can you put Eiríkur on to this tomorrow?"

Helgi's eyes narrowed. "You're not here tomorrow?"

"Yeah, afternoon shift. See you at lunchtime," Gunna said, pulling on her anorak.

"Hæ! Anybody live here?" Gunna called out, kicking off her shoes in the back kitchen of Sigrún's house among all the boots scattered in front of the wire-mesh cage that occupied the corner. She swung open the kitchen door to be greeted by steam and the aroma of fish soup from the pot on the stove. Baleful eyes glared from the cage.

Sigrún looked up and gently closed the laptop on the kitchen table in front of her. "All right? Good day?"

"Not bad, apart from a smarmy git trying to smooch his way into my knickers."

"But you say it like it's a bad thing?" Sigrún grinned.

"Hallur Hallbjörnsson."

"The handsome-and-knows-it MP?"

"Yup."

"Yuck. You can lock people up for trying it on with a police officer, can't you?"

"If only."

Gunna fumbled in her pocket for the packet that wasn't there any more while lifting a mug from the tree on the worktop behind her without having to look. She placed it in front of her and Sigrún poured.

"Is Laufey here?"

"I sent her to the Co-op with Jens."

"Ah, peace and quiet for five minutes."

"Not for long." Sigrún looked preoccupied and frowned.

"What's up?" Gunna asked, recognizing the signs. "Jörundur behaving himself?"

"Well . . ." Sigrún began.

Gunna sipped her scalding coffee and waited.

"I don't know what you think. . . and I really hope it's not going to be a problem for you, what with Laufey and everything. But Jörundur and I have been, well, you know, talking about everything. And he's been offered a job."

"That's great," Gunna said warmly. Sigrún's surly bear of a husband had been one of the first victims of Iceland's financial turmoil, as the construction business had ground to a halt even before the banks had admitted that their coffers were empty. "But it means moving, right?"

Sigrún nodded. "Norway."

"Norway? Good grief."

Gunna wondered, as so many times before, how she would ever have managed to juggle work and family without Sigrún down the street to feed the children when police business called. With Gísli now away at sea much of the time and Laufey turning into an independent young woman in her next to last year of secondary school, Sigrún's help was less frequently needed, but still invaluable.

"He's been unemployed for the best part of a year, and things don't look like getting any better. It seems that one of the guys he used to work with up at the Kárahnjúkar dam got a job there on some tunnel-building project and they need people with experience, so he called Jörundur up and told him to apply. Jörundur's good at what he does, you know. They told him to come over as soon as he can and the job's his."

Sigrún looked suddenly tearful before taking a deep breath.

"We've been over it again and again, but he's set on it," she continued. "I've told him often enough that if we're careful we can live on what I bring in. There wouldn't be any holidays in the sun, but I can live with that."

"But not Jörundur?"

"Ach. You know what blokes are like, and my Jörundur's not what you'd call a new man. As far as he's concerned, a man provides, and if he can't, he's a waste of space. I suggested he could go back to college for a year and retrain, but that was the stupidest thing he'd ever heard."

"So when are you leaving?" Gunna asked softly.

"Next month, probably."

"You'll be fine," she forced herself to say. "Something new."

"We thought about him commuting. You know, a week at home and two weeks over there, something like that," Sigrún continued as if Gunna hadn't spoken. "But that'd never work out. You know what Jörundur's like. A couple of beers with the boys and he'd be off on one again."

"I understand. What about your job? What happens there?"

"That's no problem. The council's so desperate to cut the wage bill that they couldn't wait to tell me I could have a year's unpaid leave whenever I want."

"So it's there if you want to come back to it?"

"That's it. But it's not as if work's going to disappear. People keep on having children, so the demand for nursery school teachers isn't going to go away."

"More, if anything. There seem to be more and more pregnant women than ever around these days. You'd have thought the recession would put people off having kids, but it seems it's the opposite."

"Got to find something to cheer yourself up when times are hard," Sigrún grinned, a smile returning to her round face at last. "There's nothing like do-it-yourself entertainment. Are you eating? There's enough fish for everyone."

Suddenly the back door opened and swung in with a bang as the wind caught it.

"Mum! Guess what?" Laufey yelled from behind the gurgling toddler as she steered the pushchair through the door.

"Hæ, sweetheart. What should I guess?"

"Didn't Sigrún tell you? She's moving to Norway and she said we could look after Krummi."

Gunna sighed.

"All right, young lady," she said, trying to sound stern. "But you'll have to look after him. And I still think Krummi's a ridiculous name for a rabbit."

JÓN LAY IN the dark, unable to sleep. The sofa wasn't as comfortable as it had looked, but it was better than sleeping in the workshop. That afternoon he'd toyed with the idea of splashing petrol over the house and putting a match to it before handing the keys over to the bank's representative, a silver-haired man in a long overcoat who had seemed genuinely sorry to be doing his job.

The sofa belonged to Jón's younger half-brother Samúel, a secondary school teacher in his twenties who lived alone during the week but at weekends shared the flat with a boyfriend, another teacher who arrived joyfully every Friday evening from his weekday job in a flyblown town a couple of hours east of Reykjavík.

Jón and Sammi were too far apart in age to have spent much of their youth together. Sammi was the late and accidental result of their mother's second marriage, and had been pampered in ways that had made Jón furious with envy over the toys and treats he had never enjoyed. Sammi had made it plain enough that the sofa was Jón's during the week, but when the boyfriend turned up on a Friday evening, the two of them preferred to have some privacy. The trouble was, Jón didn't have anywhere else to go.

He tried to blot out the murmurs of conversation and the muffled laughter coming through the thin wall of the flat's only bedroom, and concentrated instead on the faces of people he held grudges against. First was that bastard at the bank, the one who had encouraged him to borrow so much. It wasn't even as if the personal financial adviser was someone with experience; just a lad with a stupid haircut and a pink shirt who had done a week's personal banking course.

Second was the bastard who owned all those flats. It had been a big job and just what a small company keen to make a name with the quality of its workmanship needed. It had meant working evenings and weekends, as well as calling in a few favours and bringing in some mates from the trade as sub-subcontractors. But it had been worth it, and Jón had proudly handed over a completed set of kitchens and bathrooms a week ahead of schedule in time for the flats' buyers to move in before winter.

Unfortunately Ingi Lárusson's company had gone into receivership a few weeks later. No money was available and Jón could only become one of a great many creditors. When he finally spoke to Ingi, he understood that the developer had defaulted and they were all in the same boat. Everyone down the line had been out of pocket, with Jón's mates who had done some of the work also cursing him.

A couple of hours on Sammi's computer told him who the real bastard was, and he couldn't find it in his heart to blame Ingi Lár when Bjartmar Arnarson's development company had failed to honour its debts.

He tried to go to sleep, but whispers and muffled giggling continued to seep through the wall. Eventually he wrapped the pillow around his head to blot it out.

"NINETY-SIX."

Diddi took a number and waited. He used to enjoy going to the bank when he was a boy, depositing half of his week's money every payday and watching the total add up to a tidy sum. These days a visit to the bank was a different affair, the savings book long since emptied, and this was a shame, as Diddi still liked the place. The lights were bright and friendly, the ladies behind the counters smiled and there was always unobtrusive music that didn't hurt his head like the music his neighbours played.

"Ninety-seven."

Diddi looked at his ticket again, even though he knew his number was ninety-nine. Three of the cashiers' desks were open, so that meant only a few minutes to wait. He perched awkwardly on an uncomfortable plastic chair, sweating in his thick parka, knowing that what he was about to do was wrong. He badly wanted the toilet, but that would mean missing his turn and having to get another number and queue all over again.

"Ninety-eight."

A hard-faced lady in a fur coat stepped quickly past him and a blast of wet air disturbed the bank's controlled atmosphere before being suddenly cut off as the door eased itself shut again. Diddi gulped.

"Ninety-nine."

He looked up and saw that the youngest of the three

cashiers was waiting for him, a woman with thick brown hair and a toothy smile. Diddi quailed and stood up, stared at the desk in front of him and looked up to focus on the girl's teeth. He knew she was saying something, but he didn't hear it for the roaring in his head.

He fumbled with his parka and hauled down the zip to put in a hand and pull out the carpet knife that he had been careful to keep inside, terrified that he would cut his fingers.

"One hundred."

The cashier at the next desk had seen nothing, but the one facing him was staring in disbelief. Diddi looked straight at her and in a moment of clarity took in the heavy mask of make-up on her face that wrinkled as her mouth opened.

"Quiet," Diddi ordered. "Please. Give me money. N-n-now," he instructed, trying to sound as if he meant it, and then remembering what he had been told.

"Don't make a noise and don't make any alarms go off," he ordered, mind on autopilot. He stuffed the crumpled carrier bag that had been in his pocket through the gap. "Put it in there," he instructed. "If you don't mind," he added as an afterthought without having a clear idea why.

The girl recovered her composure and quickly busied herself behind the desk. Diddi realized he had forgotten to tell her to keep her hands where he could see them, and felt suddenly that things were going wrong, telling himself that he shouldn't panic. The woman at the next desk was staring at him in amazement, and the man in the green jacket she was serving had realized that her attention wasn't on him any more, but on the young man in a parka with the pudding-basin haircut and bewilderment in his eyes.

"What's happening?" the man ventured, and Diddi raised the knife, trying to look threatening.

"Please, don't say anything, and keep calm," the woman at the desk murmured as the carrier bag appeared in front of

Diddi, stuffed with notes. He picked it up with his left hand and backed away from the counter, keeping the two cashiers and the man in front of him.

"One hundred and one."

The third cashier still had not noticed what had taken only a matter of seconds, but squawked as she looked up and saw Diddi standing in front of them uncertainly, knife held out.

"Look here, young feller," the man with the green jacket was saying in the same authoritative tone that Diddi had hated hearing at school. "Look, give me the knife and everything will be all right. You understand?"

Diddi backed away as the man advanced, the stern look on his face clashing with his false smile. He proffered a hand for Diddi to put the knife into, when suddenly Diddi remembered what he had been told.

"No, f-f-fuck off! Leave me alone!" he yelled, slashing wildly and turning to run. He registered the door swinging to behind him and the shock of cold air hitting his face outside as a shrill alarm began to ring somewhere in the distance. He raced round the corner and along the street before remembering his instructions. He cut down a footpath and emerged in a street of quiet houses where a battered red car waited.

Panting uncontrollably, he collapsed into the passenger seat. The car was moving before he had even closed the door.

"OK?" asked the denim-clad, thin-faced driver as they stopped politely at the intersection to join the main road towards town. He smiled at Diddi cowering in the seat as they heard the first sirens coming the other way, a police squad car followed closely by an ambulance, and took the car as close as he could to the curb to allow the emergency vehicles a clear path down the middle of the road.

Diddi started to breathe more normally as they approached the main road, and he closed his eyes, trying to overcome the panic he could feel inside and to stop himself sobbing. He still clutched both the bag and the knife.

The mid-morning traffic was fairly sparse, and as the car pulled up at a set of traffic lights ready to turn into another quiet residential area, the driver looked over at him.

"Knife," he said.

"What?"

"Knife," he repeated, winding down his window.

Diddi silently handed it over. As the car moved off and around the corner, the thin-faced man sent the carpet knife spinning away into the thick hedge of someone's front garden.

S ɪ ɢ ʀ ú ɴ   ʀ ᴀ ɪ s ᴇ ᴅ   ᴀ questioning eyebrow as the newsreader finished the announcement.

"Robbing a bank? Do people really do that?" she asked. "I knew that kiosks and shops get held up sometimes, but not banks, surely?"

"It happens, though not often," Gunna said thoughtfully, rummaging through the pockets of her fleece for her phone. "I'm just going to call Helgi . . ."

Sigrún stood up and refilled the percolator jug absently while Gunna listened to the phone ring.

"Hi, Helgi, busy?"

"No more than usual, chief. Plenty to do and not enough time to do it."

"You want to take a morning off now and again. Does you good," she replied. "Here, I just heard the news. Who's the bank robber?"

"Ah. Actually, I was wondering if I should give you a call, and then I thought better of it."

"Why? Me being off duty has never stopped you before."

"No, that's Eiríkur, not me."

"Sorry. But OK, is there anything to this?"

She heard Helgi chuckle.

"The world's stupidest bank robber, it seems. Daft Diddi walked into a branch of Kaupthing with a knife in one hand and got away with about a million in cash."

"A million? That's not much of a payday, is it?"

"Wouldn't even get you a decent second-hand car these days."

"And where's Diddi?"

"No idea. The uniform boys are doing the rounds and we're keeping out of it for the moment. The silly bastard only walked into the branch where he has his own account and the girl behind the counter knew exactly who he was. No attempt to hide his face, nothing, but he managed to disappear, so I doubt he was doing this alone. Poor lad, now he's going to get into some real hot water."

"He'll get a suspended sentence, I suppose, when he shows up."

"No chance. There was a chap there who tried to be a have-a-go hero and got in the way of Diddi's knife. Slashed the tendons in one arm, so Diddi's going to be facing GBH."

Sigrún put mugs and a plate of biscuits on the table, while Gunna shook her head in despair.

"Unbelievable how stupid these people can be, isn't it? Let me know what happens, will you? We ought to have a word with Diddi when he's finally brought in and see if we can get him to admit that it was Ommi who beat him up."

"Way ahead of you, chief. I've already warned the uniform boys that Diddi may have been keeping some bad company. I'll let you know if anything exciting happens."

"Fair enough. See you this afternoon," Gunna said, ending the call.

"What was that?" Sigrún asked.

"Ah, the usual stupid, immoral people we have to deal with. A disabled lad walked into a bank with a knife, demanded money and got away with about a million in cash. But he slashed someone's arm while he was at it, so it'll probably be an additional case for us once the boys in uniform have brought him in."

"Don't you ever get tired of these people?"

"And how. But a morning off helps, and chocolate biscuits don't do any harm. What's happening with Norway?"

"Jörundur's there now for a week, on a strict promise to behave and not touch a drop. If it works out, he'll go back and I'll go with him for a couple of days. The job sounds good. A year's contract, decent earnings plus subsidized accommodation."

Gunna absently dipped a biscuit a little too long in her coffee and it unexpectedly disintegrated.

"Damn," she said mildly. "I mean, it's going to be quiet without you two here. Laufey's going to miss babysitting Jens and having a second mum to go to when I'm at work."

Gunna made her way up the stairwell of a pastel-coloured concrete block of flats. The building was indistinguishable from the rest of the row that formed the final border of an out-of-the-way housing estate at the far end of Breidholt. This was where some of the city's cheapest housing could be found, in cramped apartments that had once been smart and in demand as the first rung on the property ladder. More recently they had started to be seen almost as ghettos, where those down on their luck lived alongside the city's more recent immigrants, as the spicy aromas in the stairwell bore witness to.

Gunna sensed the sharp smells of garlic and ginger, mingled with the more subtle tinges of spices she did not have names for, as she peered at a door that was bruised and had clearly been repaired more than once. A broken pushchair containing a black plastic sack of rubbish occupied the corner of the landing.

A thickset teenager wearing a black T-shirt and with a baseball cap sideways on his head answered the door with a frown across his face. "Yeah?"

"I'm looking for Justyna," Gunna said.

"Who wants her?" he demanded truculently.

"Police. Where is she?"

The boy shrugged his shoulders and jerked a thumb towards the flat's passage before turning on his heel without a word. Gunna knocked on the first door and opened it gingerly. A bright light inside shone above a heavy sewing machine festooned with orange fabric and a pale-faced woman hunched over it as the machine hummed. A pencil secured an untidy bun of greying fair hair and she held a pair of oversized scissors crosswise in her mouth.

"Justyna?"

The woman looked up and nodded, finished the seam she was stitching and stood up to pick her way through the folds of fabric to the door, which she shut behind her with relief.

"Kitchen," she said firmly, before yelling, "Nonni! Where are you?"

There was no reply from further along the corridor, but an insistent beat that pervaded the whole flat was enough to tell them both that the teenager was there.

"Your son?" Gunna asked, wondering if the boy had shown up in any of the reports passing across her desk.

"Yes. His father is not here any more, so now we two are here only," she said stiffly.

"How long have you been here?" Gunna asked.

"Fifteen years," Justyna replied, lighting a cigarette and leaning against the kitchen units. Gunna opened her notes and looked over at the tired woman staring back at her. "I'm investigating the death of Svana Geirs. I understand that you cleaned her flat?"

Justyna nodded.

"And when was the last time you cleaned it?"

"Every week. So a week before she died."

"Always on the same day?"

"Yeah. Always same day, but not same time. Sometimes morning, sometimes later. Never cleaning if she have people there." Justyna ground out the stub of her cigarette into a saucer and fiddled with the packet in her other hand.

"Is this a private arrangement of some kind?"

"Is agency. They arrange, fix times. Most times I cleaned her flat when nobody there. Two, three times she was home when I clean. Not more."

"Which agency?"

"Reindeer Hygiene. They clean many houses, flats, offices. But I guess business not so good now."

"Do you do much work for them?"

"Before, every day. Even Sunday. Now, two, three days every week."

"And you do other work as well?" Gunna asked.

"Work, work, always work," Justyna replied bitterly with a frown that deepened the web of lines around each eye. "Teenager is expensive and no maintenance any more. Two, three days cleaning houses. One day, maybe two, cleaning hotel."

"And what are you sewing?"

"Extra work. Not black," Justyna added hurriedly. "Tents. Repair before summer comes. Tent company rents them to tourists."

"All right, I'm not concerned with whether or not you're working on the black. I'm interested in Svana Geirs. Did you ever speak to her?"

"Only the first time I go there. She show me around."

"OK. So, tell me about Svana's place. Was it clean normally?"

Justyna looked thoughtful. "I see lot of people's houses. Svana's place . . ." She shrugged. "OK. Same as most. If people are too lazy to clean themselves . . . it's not hard."

She shrugged again and looked around the flat's tiny but spotless kitchen. "This place should be cleaner. Not easy with teenagers."

"Tell me about it," Gunna agreed with heartfelt conviction. "I have two. Now, about Svana's flat. I'm interested in anything unusual that you might have seen."

"Nothing special. I see lots of strange things in people's houses. Svana, she have lots of friends. Or maybe same friend come a lot. I always change the bedclothes and take to wash. Always very dirty, drink, food, other stuff," Justyna said with a curl of her lip. "Bedroom toys as well, she sometimes leave them on the bed. I put them away."

"So you cleaned everything."

"Ceiling to floor. Every week."

"Wiping everything down?"

"Everything."

"Always the same way?"

"Always the same. Start with kitchen, then bathroom. Then big room, bedroom and hall last. Polish everything. Vacuum everything."

"And was this regular, the things you saw? The bedclothes, the toys and things like that?"

"I think so. A lot of drink, lots of bottles. No food, only takeaway. Pizza and things. But whisky, vodka, gin, wine always, always bottles to throw away. Always lots for bathroom, empty packets."

Gunna raised an eyebrow and Justyna curled thumb and forefinger into a circle that she slid sharply down the index finger of the other hand to indicate a condom.

"Also make-up, lots of make-up, hair dye, stuff to look younger. All rubbish. Sleep good, eat good, you look younger."

"How about the keys? Do you have a key?" Gunna asked.

"Key at agency. We collect keys for all the houses each day. Sign for them, give back when we finish."

"And the alarm code?"

"Is new code every week. Also get from agency."

"And the day you found Svana, did you have a code?"

"Yes, I go with code and key, but everything open."

"So you wouldn't be able to get into a house on a day when you weren't cleaning?"

"No. Only if the code is not changed. But still no key."

"Understood," Gunna said, reflecting what an opportunity such an arrangement provided for scams of all kinds to be set up. "It's a very security-conscious operation."

"Of course. Rich people in smart houses don't trust for-eigners in their homes," Justyna said with a mischievous smile that lifted the fatigue from her face. "Too many criminals come from other countries."

GUNNA BROUGHT THE car to a halt in a puddle that widened visibly as the rain pelted down from a belt of black sky chased by a distant blue promise of sunshine to come. She waited, toying with the idea of going for a hot dog at Bæjarins Bezta, until the sight of Skúli running through the rain towards her put the idea out of her mind.

"Not going to drip everywhere, are you?" she asked as Skúli sat in the passenger seat trying not to shake excess water from his head. "Can't help it. I'm soaked."

"You could have waited a couple of minutes. But it's all right, this is a rental car," Gunna told him as the rain stopped beating on the roof and sunlight began to glimmer again on the puddles.

"You rent cars?" Skúli asked.

She hauled the Golf out into the stream of traffic and kept pace behind a lorry as it trundled towards the harbour. "When there aren't enough in the pool, they rent a few for us to use."

"A fine use of taxpayers' cash," Skúli observed, and lapsed into silence as Gunna drove the short distance to pull up out-side Kaffivagninn. They sat in the café as a second wave of rain hammered on the iron roof over their heads.

"What's happening at Dagurinn, then?" Gunna asked when Skúli had made short work of a sandwich. He shrugged.

"No idea. I'm on compulsory unpaid holiday. Got to keep the wage bill down, or so they say."

"Oh, right. I thought you were still at work."

"I am. I'm doing some freelance stuff for Reykjavík Voice. And Dagurinn doesn't mind?"

"Dagurinn can go to hell," Skúli said with a sudden flash of anger. A new side to him, Gunna thought. "It wouldn't be a surprise if there's no job to go back to when my two months off are up, so what the hell?"

"And this other one you're working on, what's that?"

"It's a freesheet with daily news on the web, half in English, half in Icelandic. It's not bad, but the money's lousy."

Gunna nodded and wondered at the change that had come over Skúli since the previous summer, when he had been finding his feet in his first real job since leaving university. Iceland's financial crash had taken him by surprise, and Gunna had followed his growing disillusionment.

"But at least Reykjavík Voice is more or less independent and we're not just plugging Rich Golli's business interests and political chums, which is more or less what Dagurinn is there for," Skúli grumbled.

"Will you go back to Dagurinn if you can?" Gunna asked.

"I'll have to. Jobs aren't easy to find, and even though it's shit, if there is a job once my mandatory unpaid holiday is over, I'll still have to stick with it. Unless Rich Golli's closed it down by then."

"Ach, you'll be all right," Gunna tried to reassure him. "Things'll pick up soon enough."

"Yeah. That's the Icelandic way, isn't it? 'It'll work out' is what everyone always says. But I don't know . . ."

"When the force finally decides to employ a press spokesman, I'll put in a word for you," Gunna said with a thin smile.

"Would you?" Skúli asked, the serious tone of his reply taking her by surprise.

"Of course. I don't know if they'd even look at it, what with the state of the finances. There's nothing spare anywhere. I'm even bringing in light bulbs and toilet paper myself now and again."

"For Christ's sake," Skúli muttered. "You realize the amount of money the taxpayer will eventually have to fork out for the Icesave thing would be enough to run the Greater Reykjavík police force for more than a hundred years?"

"No, I didn't," Gunna admitted. "I'm afraid that with those sorts of figures it just becomes telephone numbers, completely unreal. Anyway, do you have anything you can tell me?"

"About Svana Geirs?"

"Anything from a new angle would be useful."

Skúli sipped his coffee and grimaced.

"Strong."

"Good grief. What do you expect in a dockers' café? And people wonder why the descendants of the Vikings have become a bunch of weaklings," Gunna observed seriously. "Now, Svana?"

"Prostitution," Skúli said quietly, wiping his mouth and looking around him.

"You're joking."

"Nope. From what I can gather, and absolutely nobody wants to be quoted or interviewed on this, you understand, Svana Geirs had turned herself into a top-class hooker."

"Bloody hell. That explains a few things," Gunna said as Skúli put down his mug, fumbled in his coat pocket for a notebook and flipped through it.

"Here we are," he said, reading with his finger on the page. "'A skilled and enthusiastic purveyor of some highly specialized services who really enjoyed her work' is what one bloke I spoke to said with a huge grin on his face, so I got the impression he was speaking from personal experience."

"And who's this guy?"

"Can't say. He said it was a while ago, though, a good few years."

"Fair enough. What I could really do with knowing is if she worked alone, or if there's someone fronting for her. This is something that's becoming a real problem these days."

"Since the law was changed, it's certainly been driven even further underground," Skúli agreed.

"Didn't you interview some Eastern European woman last year about this?"

"Yup. Could have been a fantastic front page, but it was the same week that the banks went belly-up and I suppose there was bigger news and my story got buried near the back."

"All right. Tell me what you can, then. D'you want a refill?"

"Yes please."

"Get one for me at the same time, will you? I'm going to nip to the loo."

Gunna returned to find Skúli sitting in front of two mugs and reading through his notes.

"That's better. Now, where were we?"

"Svana Geirs," Skúli replied, and sipped. "As far as I can see, there wasn't anyone fronting for her business, if that's what you can call it. The whisper is that there's a little club who quietly shared her services. I don't know how many there are, but she didn't do what you might call freelance work, and I gather she was well paid enough by her group of 'friends' not to need to."

"Hell, so this was an organized operation, then?"

"Absolutely. Very small and discreet, the most exclusive club in town."

"And some exclusive members, I suppose?"

"Very much so. Not men who would welcome publicity."

Giving in to temptation, Gunna put a lump of hard sugar between her teeth and filtered a mouthful of coffee through it.

"Don't stare, Skúli," she admonished.

"Sorry. I thought it was only old men who did that."

"YOU'RE SURE?" THE National Commissioner's deputy asked.

For a second Gunna looked at Ívar Laxdal's knitted brows and wondered how this thickset barrel of a man managed to wear a hat as ridiculous as a beret and still radiate authority.

"I'm sure enough. Sure enough to warrant leaning hard on some of these people."

"What sort of people?"

Gunna ticked them off on her fingers. "The regulars are two businessmen, one accountant and one MP."

"Which party?" Ívar Laxdal demanded.

"Social Democrat."

He snorted. "Wishy-washy liberal types. But they're part of the government right now and therefore able to kick us where it hurts. And they'll close ranks to protect their own," he rumbled. "These politicians worry about their own skins first and the rest of us afterwards."

"It's probably best I didn't hear you say that," Gunna said quietly to remind him that politics and policing should stay separate.

"No coppers on that list?"

"Not as far as I know."

"That's something to be grateful for. But I suppose even a chief superintendent wouldn't be taking home enough to get him into that sort of club," he said, almost as if to himself. Gunna reflected that she hadn't given him names and he hadn't asked for them.

In the park behind the Hverfisgata police station they stood next to her son Gísli's treasured elderly Range Rover. Gunna frequently reminded herself that one day she would have to buy a car of her own, reliable enough to commute in, and stop borrowing Gísli's car while he was at sea. Gunna had deliberately waylaid Ívar Laxdal outside to preclude any chance of being overheard. He stood in thought, one hand clasped in the other, then spun round and glared at Gunna as if she had dropped a hand grenade into his lap.

"If this is mishandled, it could be a disaster. I'm warning you, Gunnhildur."

"Warning me of what, precisely?" she asked with a shiver of trepidation and anger.

"I'm warning you that if this isn't dealt with sensitively, it could blight a lot of people's careers. Yours included," he added.

"By 'dealt with sensitively,' just what are you trying to tell me? Not to look too hard in any particular direction?"

"Hell, no," Ívar Laxdal thundered. "It's a bloody disgrace. And don't be so damned suspicious. I mean you're going to have to keep this very discreet and be sure of your ground. You know what this country's like. Just a whisper out of place and everyone knows. Shit always sticks and I don't want to see it sticking to anyone without good reason. Understand? You included."

"Thanks. That's what I thought you meant. Just wanted to be sure."

Ívar Laxdal deflated slightly and Gunna felt there was a ghost of a smile about him for once. Maybe the man could thaw out occasionally, and she wondered idly what kind of life he led out of uniform.

"In that case, you'd better get on with it. All right?"

"Understood. Er . . ."

"What? Anything else?"

"The usual," Gunna sighed. "Manpower. There's only three of us in the department. My superior officer is on long-term sick leave. We're all working flat out as it is."

"Who's your chief inspector?"

"Örlygur Sveinsson."

"That old woman . . ." Ívar Laxdal grumbled, smacking one fist into the other hand as he thought. "Leave it with me. Report to me on this. I'll square things with Örlygur if he comes back."

Gunna noted the "if" rather than "when" and wondered whether there might be something that she should be aware of.

"Anything else?" he barked.

"Well, yes. I'm still a sergeant. I expected to be made up a grade with this post."

"Still? Damn. Leave it with me and I'll see what I can swing, but we're going through tough times, you know, Gunnhildur. Tough times," he repeated, marching across the car park towards his own car, which looked suspiciously like this year's model.

FOR ONCE THERE was no wind, and a pall of black smoke hung in the still air. Gunna parked along the street and fought her way through a crowd gathered a respectful distance from the ambulances and fire engines that hid the house, set well back from the road in a well-heeled suburb.

A pale-faced young police officer was slowly unrolling Police—Do Not Cross tape and stringing it between the skinny trees in the front garden.

"You can't go in there," he barked as Gunna lifted the tape to step under it.

"Serious Crime Unit," Gunna barked back, aware once again that being out of uniform was going to take some getting used to.

"In the garage at the side," the young man advised her. "It's not pretty," he added, shaking his head.

"Thanks. Didn't think it would be, somehow. Who's here so far?"

"Fire, ambulance."

"I can see that. Who's the senior officer?"

"That's me, I suppose, until Pétur Júlíusson gets here from

the station," he said ruefully. "We're a bit short on manpower these days."

Gunna nodded and crunched her way along a gravel path between scrubby lawns by the side of the house. A trampoline that looked as if it had spent all winter outside occupied the middle of one of the lawns in front of a thick hedge at the garden's boundary.

No view, so no witnesses, I'll bet, Gunna thought as she reached the double garage, one door closed, the other half open, the white paint on it blistered into bubbles and the ground in front of it scorched black. A paramedic and a fireman she recognized were standing by the garage's open side door.

"Evening, Röggi," Gunna offered. "I heard the F2 call on the way home. What do we have?"

"Hæ, Gunna. It's a bloody mess," the fireman replied grimly. "Garage went up in a right old fireball. Can't have lasted more than a minute, but the heat must have been phenomenal."

"Casualties?"

"One, in the ambulance. Not a happy lady, shock and smoke inhalation. Could have been a lot worse."

"What happened, d'you reckon?"

Röggi spread his hands. "No idea. Absolutely no idea."

"A massive fireball like that, could it have been an accident?"

"I'd say not. There's nothing sensible you can keep in an ordinary garage that will produce that kind of thing."

"Chemicals?"

"Could be. Or just petrol, a lot of petrol."

Gunna nodded and thought. "I take it we can reckon this wasn't an accident, unless it's proved otherwise?"

"Sounds reasonable," Röggi admitted. "There'll be an investigation, and with a casualty involved, they won't give up until they know what caused it, especially in a posh place like this."

"Whose house is this?"

"Bjartmar Arnarson. You know, the businessman. I reckon that's his missus they're taking off to hospital."

"Sounds interesting." Gunna frowned, the name instantly setting off alarm bells in her head.

"You have a suspicious mind, Gunna."

"It's in the job description. What are you up to now?"

"We'll stand one of the appliances down and send it off home. I'll be here with the other one until the site's secure and nothing else is likely to go off pop."

"Good. I'd better marshal my forces, then," Gunna decided, knowing that there would be no access to the scene itself for some time.

She made her way back to her car, looking carefully at the faces lined up on the other side of the road and noticing lenses already trained on the house. She wondered if the press had been quick off the mark, or if these were more likely neighbours with cameras. When she had been a young police officer, anyone with a long lens would be a press photographer and she would have recognized most of them. But these days enthusiastic amateurs could have newer and more expensive kit than the professionals.

Gunna sat in the driving seat and clicked her Tetra set on. "Zero-two-sixty, Ninety-five-fifty. You there, Helgi?"

She waited for a reply, knowing that Helgi was one of the few CID officers who made a habit of using his communicator. After a minute she gave up, picked her phone up from the seat and dialled Helgi's number.

"Ah, so you are there," she said accusingly as he answered.

"Sorry. Been busy this afternoon. Anything serious?"

"Just a bit—and don't reckon on getting home for a good while yet. House fire, looks mighty like arson to me, one casualty and a burnt-out garage."

"Shit. And we had a babysitter lined up this evening as well."

"Sorry. Can't be helped. This one really stinks," Gunna said, trying to sound apologetic. "And here's the fun bit of it: Bjartmar Arnarson's house. One of Svana Geirs' little band. Looks like his missus is the casualty."

"Whoo-hoo. That does sound like a load of fun."

Gunna spelled out the address to him. "I need you over here, but first I want you to find out where Bjartmar is."

"Yeah. Sure. D'you need Eiríkur as well?"

Gunna thought, looking up and acknowledging with a wave the burly form of Sigmar from the technical department wading through the crowd at the roadside, bags slung over each shoulder.

"No, we'll let the lad off the hook if he's already gone, but he's going to have a tough day of it tomorrow. Got to go, Technical's here."

She ended the call, quickly located another number and waited patiently while it rang.

"Hæ, Sigrún. Yeah, it's me. Is it OK if Laufey comes to you after school?"

"Not a problem. Busy, are you?"

Gunna wondered what to say.

"Something serious has come up and we have to get on with it right away," she replied eventually. "I expect you'll see something about it on the news tonight. The TV crews are here already."

"All right. Tell me later, but will you send Laufey a text and let her know?"

"Yup, will do. Thanks, Sigrún," Gunna said gratefully, ending the call. She rapidly thumbed buttons on her phone to send Laufey a message as she walked quickly from her car back to the house, and by the time she was by the garage's side door, Sigmar and the serious young woman with him were both wearing the all-in-one white coveralls that she could hardly imagine Sigmar without.

"It's going to be a long job, this one," he announced morosely as if accusing Gunna of playing a practical joke on him.

BJARTMAR ARNARSON TOOK the news impassively. Gunna wondered if this was determination or indifference. Discreetly taken aside at passport control and led to an interview room, he constantly rolled an iPhone that chimed and throbbed at intervals between his fingers.

"What happened, then?" he asked finally, having brushed aside sympathy from Gunna and the two airport police officers in the room.

"We still don't know," Gunna admitted. "This only happened a couple of hours ago. Your wife has been injured in a fire at your home and we believe it wasn't accidental."

Bjartmar shrugged. "Who would want to harm Unnur?"

"I'm hoping you might be able to shed some light on that."

"Are you insinuating something?" he asked silkily. "If you are . . ."

"I'm asking, not insinuating," Gunna tried not to snap back.

"Can one of you get me some water?" he demanded suddenly. "It's hot in here and it's been a long flight."

One of the airport officers left the room, shutting the door silently behind him.

"What I need to know initially is if there has been anything unusual that your wife may have noticed recently. Any odd activity, if someone may have been following her, if she's been involved in a dispute of any kind, anything of that nature?"

Bjartmar's mouth opened and he was about to answer when his iPhone buzzed just as another ringtone could be heard, a basic chime like an old-fashioned desk telephone. He looked at the iPhone with annoyance and put it down, at the same time pulling a bulky old-fashioned mobile phone from his jacket pocket.

"Yeah?" he grunted into it before his voice softened. "No, just a hold-up with baggage. I need to speak to some people before I clear immigration. No, it's not a problem. I'll be right with you. Ciao."

The airport officer who had gone for water reappeared with a small bottle and placed it on the table within reach of Bjartmar, who glared truculently at Gunna.

"Look, how long is this going to take?"

"Not long," Gunna replied. She had taken an instant and deep dislike to Bjartmar and his indifferent attitude. The man showed no shred of interest in his wife's state of health and was again fiddling with his iPhone. She tried to glare at him, but Bjartmar appeared not to notice. "If you don't mind . . ." she ventured in an acid tone.

Bjartmar looked up and stared back. "Sorry. Business."

"Anyone who might bear a grudge against your wife?"

Bjartmar shrugged. "Undoubtedly. You don't become wealthy without making enemies."

"All right. Anyone in particular?"

"Almost anyone who worked for her. Everyone was sacked sooner or later. There were always a few outstanding court cases for wrongful dismissal in the works."

"What's her business?"

"It's very smart, so I'm not surprised you haven't heard of it. It's a restaurant called ForEver."

Gunna took the jibe in her stride.

"As it happens, I've been there," she said smoothly. "Who runs the place? I take it your wife doesn't spend her time waiting on tables?"

Bjartmar stifled a yawn. "Don't know. Last I knew there was a manager, but she may well have walked out since last week. The chef's the guy who keeps everything going and the only one Unnur doesn't want to upset too often."

"When did you last see Unnur?" Gunna asked.

"The week before last. When I left to go to the States."

"Was there anything about her then that struck you as unusual? Anything odd?"

Bjartmar's teeth smiled but his eyes remained expressionless. "You mean apart from the carton of yoghurt that she slung at me? No, don't think so. I heard it hit the door as I shut it behind me and I suppose she left it for the Thai girl to clean up."

"You mean you and your wife aren't on good terms?"

"My wife and I haven't been on any kind of terms for the last few months. We have been leading pretty much separate lives, except when we meet, and then that's generally to argue about something or for her to demand more cash to prop her restaurant up a little longer. Apart from that, everything's been just wonderful," he said with the first traces of bitterness in his voice. "Look, officer, I don't know if you're married or what. But it has run its course. We've been together for almost ten years and it's got to the point where we just don't like each other any more. It happens."

"It does," Gunna agreed in a neutral voice, making quick notes on the pad in front of her.

"And are you?" Bjartmar drawled.

"What?"

"Married? Shacked up?"

"Not any more," Gunna replied after a pause.

Bjartmar leaned back and picked up his iPhone again.

"Like I said, it happens," he said in triumph. "Walk out, did you? Or did he? Or maybe she?" he leered.

"He died," Gunna said sharply. "Now, if you don't mind, can we continue?"

HRAFN KRISTJÁNSSON SAID nothing as he drove into town with a silent and fearful Diddi at his side. There was plenty he wanted to say, but he refrained from commenting,

certain that he would be unable to contain his fury at the
people who had led his son astray.

Diddi stared out of the window at the street lights flashing
past and knew deep inside that from now on nothing would be
the same again. The people he had thought were his friends
had let him down disastrously. He had both feared and admired
people like Long Ómar Magnússon, men who went their own
way and did what they liked without bothering too much
about tiresome rules and regulations.

Ommi had just taken the bag of money and grinned at him.
There had been no pat on the back, no "Well done, Diddi,"
nothing to say he had lived up to expectations. Diddi had just
sat in the corner as Ommi and the man who had driven the car
split the cash between them and ignored him, not even
noticing as he left and went home to find his father sitting
there waiting for him, his face like thunder.

Even at a few minutes to midnight, the place was busy when
Hrafn pulled up outside the police station on Hverfisgata and
turned to his son as he switched off the engine.

"Come on then," was all he could find to say, and Diddi
stepped out of the car into the cold evening air.

The old man took his son's arm as they went up the steps
and into the building, where he opened the door and made
sure the boy went inside first.

The desk officer looked up and smiled.

"Haven't seen you for a while, mate," he began, until he saw
the morose figures father and son made.

He picked up the phone and dialled.

"Sævaldur? Yes, Sigvaldi on the front desk. You might want
to come down here. The lad you've been looking for all day has
just walked in the door."

Tuesday 16th

Gunna typed Bjartmar Arnarson's name into the police computer network, waited for results to show up and drummed her fingers on the desktop when nothing appeared other than the man's date of birth and records of a few speeding and parking tickets.

Frustrated, she went to an internet search engine instead and typed in the same name. A second later a list appeared and she set about reading the reports from newspapers, websites and gossip magazines. In ten minutes she had learned that Bjartmar Arnarson had made himself into one of Reykjavík's lowest-profile millionaires with a fortune amassed from property speculation. It appeared that he had no expensive hobbies apart from a penchant for cars that did not extend to anything flashy, had only occasionally spent time fishing for salmon on exclusive riverbanks, and made a habit of travelling economy on scheduled airlines.

"Helgi?" Gunna called out, turning around in her chair.

"Yup?"

"Bjartmar. What do you know?"

"Probably about as much as you do."

"Not much, then?"

"Nope."

"Any joy with Omar Magnússon?"

"That bastard," Helgi grumbled. "As far as I can make out, he's been busy settling scores. There have been a few sightings,

including an off-duty officer who says he saw him in a kiosk in
Selfoss last weekend and a woman who's certain she saw him
in one of the petrol station snack bars in Borgarnes on the day
he did a runner."

"But nothing you can use to track him down?"

"Ah, you may well ask. I want a word with Daft Diddi as
soon as Svaldur's finished with him."

Gunna frowned at the mention of the recently promoted
Sævaldur Bogason, an efficient but abrasive character she had
always had difficulty getting on with. "He's dealing with this
ridiculous bank job yesterday, is he?"

"Yup. Pretty much done and dusted. Diddi admits he did it.
All three cashiers and the bloke whose hand he sliced have
identified him. But we don't have the knife he used, we don't
have the million or so in cash and we don't know how he disappeared after leaving the bank."

"So, Sævaldur has it all tied up, apart from the bits he
doesn't?" she asked wryly.

Helgi shrugged. "That's more or less it. But Diddi turned up
in Casualty the other day babbling that it wasn't Ommi who
beat him up. Which is what tells me that it was. So I have an
idea that if Diddi doesn't know where Iceland's latest Jesse
James is hiding, that's probably where the cash disappeared to."

"Seems logical," Gunna agreed.

"The woman who saw him in Borgarnes the day he absconded
said he was with a young woman, and the description matches
our Ommi's girlfriend, Selma. Better still, I searched around and
found that Selma's mother's car, which is a flashy 5-series BMW,
was caught by the speed camera at Fiskilækur going north and
again that afternoon in the Hvalfjördur tunnel going back to
Reykjavík. So Selma's mum gets two speeding fines in one day
and the timing fits perfectly."

"So Selma needs to answer a few questions?"

"Doesn't she just?"

"And when are you going to ask them?"

"As soon as I can find the bloody girl. She's been off work for months, supposedly sick, and she's not at home with her mum, who says she has no idea where her daughter is."

Gunna stood up and looked out of the window of the two-person office that now contained three desks.

"Going out for a minute, Helgi. If Johnny Depp shows up, just ask him to get undressed and wait for me, would you?"

THE ECONOMIC CRIME Unit's offices were larger than Serious Crime's, as well as being in a building around the corner on Raudarárstigur instead of in the old Hverfisgata police station. The Economic Crime officers all looked young and fresh, although the young man who took Gunna aside had bags under his eyes. She extended a hand.

"Gunnhildur. Serious Crime."

"Ah. We all know who you are. I'm Björgvin."

"Busy?" she asked.

"And how. If there were another dozen of us, we'd still have more than enough to keep them at work."

"All right. I'll keep it quick. Bjartmar Arnarson. Can you tell me anything about him?"

Björgvin filled a plastic cup from the water cooler and sipped. "What do you need to know?"

"I need to know who might want to try to kill his wife, and why."

"That fire in the Setberg?"

"That's the one. Apart from a few parking tickets, the man has a squeaky-clean record."

Björgvin grimaced. "He's as sharp as a knife, I'll give him that. He's been up to his eyeballs in all kinds of dirty tricks but has always kept himself at enough of a distance to avoid too much investigation, let alone any kind of a case to be built against him."

"All right. Background?"

"Unusually for the crimes we investigate here, he's not a lawyer or a banker. He was a wheeler-dealer of some kind for a few years and the drug squad took an occasional interest in him, but nothing concrete. He owned part of a place called Blacklights at the end of the nineties."

"I remember it well," Gunna said grimly.

"Bjartmar was doing all right for himself, but things really took off when his dad died. Our boy inherited a boat in the Westmann Islands with a few hundred tonnes of cod quota. He promptly sold the lot and became straight virtually overnight. You remember when the banks were privatized?"

"Around 2000?"

"That's it. Suddenly everything changed. They started lending stupid amounts to homeowners. Bjartmar saw what was happening and put all his fish money into property, bought up land and houses all over the city. Within a year, property prices had gone through the roof. He bought and sold dozens of properties and made an absolute killing. That's when he became respectable."

"And started wearing a suit?"

"That's it. Got himself a trophy wife at the same time and started making even more money when he set up a property agency. You must know it, Landex? They advertise all the time, or used to. Business must have taken a hit recently, but I'm sure he has a good bit salted away somewhere. We know he has significant deposits overseas, as Landex had been expanding into Mediterranean property as well. The Spanish operation is called Sandex. Right on the beach." Björgvin squeezed the empty cup until it crackled and dropped it into a bin by the water cooler.

"So how respectable is Bjartmar? Is he all legal these days?"

"It's hard to tell. I doubt it. But he's not involved with any of the banks or the financial institutions in a serious way and he's nowhere near the top of our list of priorities. He can be confident that Economic Crime won't be knocking on his door for a few years yet, unless it's linked to laundering cash or avoiding currency controls, in which case we'd jump on him. But he's too smart for that."

"Well, thanks for your time," Gunna said with a smile. "That certainly helps me out on the man's background."

"You're welcome. D'you think he might have had any involvement in this fire? He wasn't always a criminal with a briefcase, and there are stories about extracting cash with menaces from years ago. But of course, nobody's ever been prepared to point the finger."

"At the moment I have no idea, but it wouldn't surprise me."

Björgvin nodded. "I'd appreciate it if you'd keep me informed. Bjartmar is pretty ruthless. He's cut out business partners in the past and left them high and dry. It's amazing when you think about it that he's not a financial genius, just a dope-dealer who got lucky," he said with a thin smile. "Unlike the real financial whizzes, who are mostly bankrupt now."

HELGI HAD THE radio tuned to a classical station. As a young man he'd preferred prog rock, but as his hair gradually fell out, he felt the call of the old-fashioned music that his father liked to listen to in the cowshed, claiming that it helped the milk yield. Helgi had even toyed with the idea of getting his old accordion out, but the look on Halla's face on the rare occasions he had mentioned it had been enough to make him think again. Although they got on well, the difference in their ages was a source of occasional discomfort for him.

When Halla's forty, I'll be past fifty, he mused, sitting in the dark and watching the house where Eygló Grímsdóttir, mother of Long Omar Magnússon's girlfriend Selma, lived with her cherished BMW on display in the drive. The area was one of the better parts of the city's suburbs, a quiet few rows of newish houses flanked on both sides by empty developments that were likely to stay empty now that the property market had come to a crashing halt. Halla had even taken Helgi to view one of these brand-new terraced houses and they liked both the area and the price. But with as much chance of selling their flat in a faded 1970s block as of a winning lottery ticket, there was little choice but to stay put.

Helgi reflected that if Eygló were to decide to go for a drive, his Skoda would struggle to keep up. The clock in the dashboard had stopped months ago, so he tapped the keypad of his mobile phone to light the screen and saw that the time was later than he'd thought.

Ten minutes more, then I'm going home, he decided, peering through the dark at the lights of the long living-room window. He had always been a patient man, something he had learned in his teens waiting on the moors with a shotgun cradled in his arms for migrating geese to pass within range.

He could see people moving in the living room and guessed that there were at least three present: Eygló, Selma and a third person, a man, he guessed, judging by the silhouettes. He turned down the radio and eased the window open, listening to the night and the music coming from the house. The germ of an idea came to him and he picked up his communicator from the passenger seat.

"Control, zero-two-sixty. Is there a patrol car at a loose end anywhere near Vesturmóar?"

"Zero-two-sixty, zero-one-fifty-one. Just coming up to Hamraborg. Need us for something exciting, do you?"

"Just a quick look at something. Meet me in the bus stop at the top of Vesturmóar. I'm in a green Skoda."

"We all know what your old rattletrap looks like, Helgi. See you in a minute."

The squad car pulled up behind him and Helgi got out to talk to the officers sitting in it, a burly youngish man and a young woman new to the force. He quickly explained what he wanted them to do and set off on foot down the slope towards the row of houses that backed on to Vesturmóar, cursing the mud at the side of the road where the new streets still had no proper pavements. When he felt he had a good view of the back of Eygló Grímsdóttir's house, he clicked his communicator.

"Zero-one-fifty-one, zero-two-sixty. In position."

"OK," came the laconic reply.

Helgi peered through the clear night air and watched. He could see the lights of Eygló's kitchen window and guessed where the back door was.

"Zero-two-sixty, zero-one-fifty-one. Silla's knocking on the front door now."

"Got you."

"Door's opening."

As the words crackled into his earpiece, the back door swung open and a figure stepped out of the house and into the night.

"Zero-one-fifty-one, zero-two-sixty, that's great. Stick around for ten minutes just in case, then you can wrap up."

Helgi jogged along the road, keeping the dark figure in sight as it flitted from the glare of one street light to the next. Suddenly it disappeared, and Helgi set off down the slope, trying not to let his footfalls crunch too much on the rubble underfoot. He caught a glimpse of the bulky figure turning a corner ahead of him and realized that he would hardly be able to keep up without making more noise and risking alerting the man to his presence, when the sound of a door clicking shut stopped him in his tracks. He concentrated on the direc- tion the sound came from and pointed himself towards it, emerging into the next street of empty houses made up of terraces of six. Every one was dark and empty, the first street of a new development.

Feeling uncomfortably conspicuous, he walked along the street as if he had a perfect right to and was simply taking a short cut. At the far end of the second set of six blank-eyed houses, a narrow ribbon of light glimmered faintly past one edge of a badly fitted garage door.

So, Ommi. That's where you're keeping yourself, he congratulated himself. I think you might be getting a visit in the morning.

JÓN STUMBLED AND leaned against the wall. His head was swimming. He had always been a thirsty man, but his love of a good drink was something he had easily suppressed during the years when he had worked hard and had a happy home life.

That had all changed now, and he felt his thirst clawing at him more often, whispering to him that a drink would help and that the day would pass more easily with a sharpener. With no more contract work to be had, he found himself relying on word-of-mouth jobs paid in cash to keep himself in funds. Friends of friends kept his phone number pinned to a board somewhere, just in case the dishwasher developed a leak or something went wrong with the heating.

He was enjoying it in some ways. For years he had meticulously kept records and rarely did black work other than for friends. Now, with the taxman and the child support people all chasing him, he had found a pleasurable release in ignoring them all. In any case, with no home to go to any more, it would take a while before their letters started reaching him again.

Slumped against a shop front, Jón lifted the half-bottle from his pocket and spun the cap, which flew off and tinkled as it hit the pavement. He cursed briefly and decided that as the bottle now didn't have a cap, he'd just have to drink it all.

"All right, are you?"

He turned to see a pair of police officers in uniform looking down at him.

"Yeah. I'm doing OK."

"On your way home, are you, mate?" the youngish police-woman asked kindly, handing him the bottle cap while her older, larger, male colleague surveyed a party of revellers clattering along on the other side of the street.

Jón nodded. "Yeah. I'm going to get my head down now," he slurred. "Far to go, is it?"

"S'just up there."

He waved a hand vaguely uphill and tried manfully to get to his feet.

The male police officer frowned down at him, still keeping an eye on the other side of the street.

"Where do you live?" the policewoman asked, squatting on her haunches to talk to him.

"Dunno," Jón admitted. "It's up there, big green house in Sölvagata. Top floor. It's my little brother's place. He's a poof," he added, and then wondered why he'd said it.

"All right, mate. Look, if you can stand up and walk as far as the next corner without falling over, I haven't seen any-thing. All right?" the policewoman said in the same friendly tone, extending a hand to help him up.

Tears came unbidden to Jón's eyes and coursed silently down the red stubble on his cheeks as he pulled hard on the woman's hand and found himself upright.

"G'bless you, darling," he muttered, weaving from one side of the pavement to the other as he made his way uphill.

"Job done," the policeman said appreciatively to his col-league. "And no paperwork."

Wednesday 17th

HELGI'S DELIGHT COULDN'T be concealed.

"And what are you so damn cheerful about this morning?" Gunna demanded.

"Found where Long Ommi's hiding away."

"Really? Well done. The sooner we can get the bastard back to the nick, the better for all of us. Spill the beans, then. How did you find him?"

Helgi beamed. "Easy. I got a patrol to knock on Eygló's front door, asking if anyone had noticed a joyrider in a stolen car belting around the area. The back door opened as soon as the patrol rang the doorbell, and all I had to do was follow him."

Gunna nodded appreciatively. "Nice work. So where is he?"

"You know that new district in Gardabær, just above the Smárinn sports hall? All those new houses?"

"Yup. I drive past it every day."

"He's in one of those. The whole place is empty, not a single one's been sold yet and it's like a ghost town. The place he's camped out in is Hátúnsbraut 21 and I think he's using the garage to live in as it doesn't have any windows, so nobody looks in and no light gets out—or it wouldn't if the garage door hadn't been put in crooked."

"What's that?" Eiríkur asked, dropping his briefcase on to his chair and shrugging himself out of his coat.

"Our man has tracked down Long Ommi. Now we'd better go and collect him," Gunna replied.

Helgi frowned. "I'd like to track him for a day or two, find out what he's up to. He's a right evil bastard and I'm positive he's up to no good."

"You think so?" Gunna asked sharply. "I reckon we get the uniform boys to pick him up and ship him over to a month in solitary at Litla-Hraun once we've asked him a few questions. Job done."

"I don't know," Helgi murmured. "It doesn't make sense, to my mind. He had less than a year of a long stretch to go, in a low-security nick where life isn't hard. So why abscond? Why now? All right, he's set a national record for being on the run, which is an achievement in itself. But I'm sure setting a record wasn't what he set out to do."

Gunna watched as her computer started up, wondering how many of the emails in her inbox could safely be deleted unread.

"Ommi's from Hvalvík, Gunna. Didn't you ever cross paths with him?" Helgi asked.

"He'd left Hvalvík before I went to live there. I know who his mother is, though. Nice enough lady, very strict, I always thought. Religious as well, sings in the church choir."

"I really think we ought to watch Ommi for a day or two. I'm certain it was him who gave Skari a beating in Keflavík, and Daft Diddi, and the word is that there have been more broken noses than usual around. But I'm sure he didn't abscond from Kvíabryggja just to settle old scores that could have kept for a few more months."

Gunna thought quickly. The unit had more than enough to do with the murder of Svana Geirs and now the suspected arson at Bjartmar Arnarson's house.

"We don't have the time or manpower to keep tabs on Ommi, but Eiríkur, can you keep a watch and log who goes in and out of there tonight, and we'll pick him up in the morning. Until then, please get on to finding out about Bjartmar's dirty deals when you have an hour. A list of business interests and property would be handy, and his tax records."

• • •

HALLUR HALLBJÖRNSSON'S SMILE of welcome was sicklier than it had been when they last met, and Gunna's expression was grimmer. This time a dowdy and flustered researcher showed her to the rooftop office, which seemed smaller as Hallur glowered behind the desk in the corner. Today the sun was out and slanted in through the window to bring out a touch of bronze in the hair that swept unfashionably down to his earlobes.

Wasted on a bloke, Gunna thought, reminding herself that her own unruly thatch was overdue its usual workmanlike trim.

"Good morning," she offered, sitting down opposite him without waiting to be asked.

"More questions, Sergeant?"

"I'm afraid so. This isn't a bad moment?"

"Not at all. Always ready to help the police," Hallur said, and Gunna saw him gulp as he spoke.

She nodded and looked sternly over the cluttered desk. "I don't feel you've been entirely open about your relationship with Svanhildur Mjöll Sigurgeirsdóttir. We spoke a few days ago and you gave me the impression that you had conducted an occasional liaison with her, but now I understand that there was rather more to this. I'd be interested if you'd elaborate."

Gunna could sense fear as Hallur coughed and looked from one corner of the room to other as if seeking inspiration. He's cornered and terrified, Gunna thought. Be gentle. Don't overdo it.

"I, er, I'd like you to know that this could be deeply embarrassing, you know . . . Very unpleasant for a lot of people. My wife . . . and the Prime Minister . . ."

There was real anguish in his voice. Gunna looked impassively at the wild eyes frowning back at her and let him continue.

"It would be a shock to her if this were made public. A huge shock," he concluded, nodding in emphasis.

"Unfortunately that's beyond my remit. My concern is to identify who was responsible for this woman's violent death. You'd best be open about it and tell me what you know."

Hallur fidgeted. "What do you know already?"

"Let's just pretend that I don't know anything and you start from the beginning."

"I think I ought to have my lawyer present," he blurted out.

Gunna shrugged. "Up to you. That's if you want me to suspect you were involved with her death, in which case we'd be best off doing this as a formal recorded interview at Hverfisgata and not an informal chat in your office."

Hallur deflated visibly and his whole body sagged in his chair.

"Did you, for instance, support Svana financially in any way?"

"What? Good grief, no."

"Not at all?"

"I paid for a meal sometimes," he said with a flash of his smooth public persona breaking through. "I'm old-fashioned like that, don't believe in going Dutch. Of course I paid for everything that time we met in Copenhagen, but apart from that, certainly not."

"And your financial records will bear this out?" Gunna asked quietly.

"You want to go through my bank statements?"

"It's possible. So this is the sum total of your involvement with Svana Geirs, is it? An occasional meal, one dirty weekend away, the odd screw? No cash changed hands?"

Hallur blanched and he shook his head, jumping as his desk phone rang. He snatched up the receiver as if it were a saviour and yelped into it, nodding as he spoke.

"Yes, yes, of course. That shouldn't be a problem. But could you ask him to call me in an hour? I'm in a meeting right now and it's not entirely convenient. Thanks."

He dropped the receiver reluctantly. "Sorry. I'm supposed to be on the way to meet a group of Japanese investors."

"You know Bjarki Steinsson," Gunna said, framing the question as a direct statement.

"Er, I, yes. Of course. What do you want me to say? We belong to the same clubs, he's a member of the party and attends meetings regularly."

"I want you to tell me the truth and all of it, just as you would in court," Gunna said grimly. She was certain that Hallur was close to telling her everything as long as she could maintain pressure on him. "And how about Jónas Valur Hjaltason? Another friend?"

Blood drained from Hallur's face, leaving him gaping at her. "How much do you know?" he gulped finally.

"Tell me about the syndicate," Gunna said quietly, ignoring his question.

"It was Jónas Valur who started it all off."

"Go on."

"Yeah. He'd known Svana for a long time. The idea came up when we were at Jónas Valur's salmon lodge, I don't know, three years ago, a whole bunch of us. Jónas Valur's son Sindri was there as well, and he was boasting that he'd slept with Svana. He was pretty drunk, and all of a sudden he spat out that Svana would do it for cash for the right people. We had a laugh and a joke about it and that was that."

Gunna stared at him as he sat bolt upright in his chair, looking blankly at a point on the wall behind her, hands playing nervously in his lap.

"So the next night we had a few bottles of Jameson's on the table and it was Jónas Valur who suggested that we could form a syndicate and take turns, y'know, once a week or something.

We all thought it was a brilliant joke, but Jónas Valur was completely serious. It took a while before we realized that. He just called her up there and then and put it to her, and she agreed right away. Don't know if she was serious or not at the time, but he's a proper salesman, the old bastard, a real charmer. A few days later he took her out to dinner and convinced her. Mind you, Svana was always short of cash, and I suppose she saw it as some sort of security."

Hallur sighed. "What now? What else do you want to know?" he asked in the same blank monotone as before.

"I want to know how long this arrangement has been going on."

"Since about this time two years ago."

"And how often did you have a meeting with Svana?"

Hallur hesitated. "It varied. Sometimes it would be a couple of times in the same week. Other times not for a week or two. I don't think any of us kept a log or anything like that," he said with distaste. "We're all friends and trust each other."

"When and where did this take place?"

"At Svana's flat. Sometimes we'd meet at Fit Club and go on from there. Normally I'd just go straight to her flat in the afternoon after a workout, we'd spend an hour or two together and then I'd go back to work. I don't know about the others. I guess Jónas Valur had evenings, as he doesn't have the same family ties as the rest of us."

"And was Svana paid in cash, or what?"

"Direct to her bank account."

"From your family account?" Gunna asked with disbelief.

"Well, no. I have a separate account that my wife doesn't, er . . . doesn't know about. I do some journalism and public speaking, that sort of thing, which is paid into that account."

"So your freelance activities funded your part-time mistress, so to speak?"

He nodded silently.

"I'd prefer it if you don't mention this conversation to the others. Of course I can't prevent you from getting in touch with them, but you ought to be aware that we will be interviewing them as well, and if your stories all tie up too neatly, then there might be something to get suspicious about. So, not a word, please."

"No, no, of course not," Hallur said blankly.

"I'll be in touch with you again in a few days."

It was as if he had snapped out of a reverie as his eyes lifted despairingly. "Is it possible to keep this quiet?" he asked quickly. "I have a lot more at stake than the others—wife, family, career."

Gunna wanted to reply that he should have considered that before, but kept the comment to herself. "It's very difficult to say. Strictly speaking, an offence has been committed. It's largely down to the prosecutor's office to decide whether or not to press a charge. But at present, I'm looking for Svana's killer."

"None of this is on record, is it, Sergeant?"

"No, but if there's reason to investigate further, then it might have to be done at Hverfisgata, which would mean a formal interview."

"I could deny everything."

"I think, under the circumstances, that would be far from wise," Gunna said quietly. "But certainly for the moment, if you keep this conversation to yourself, I'll do the same."

She rose to leave and picked up her unopened folder. Hallur levered himself from his seat behind the desk and made his way around it, extending a hand. "Thank you. It's much appreciated. Of course my offer still holds good."

"Offer?" Gunna said blankly.

"Dinner sometime?"

The familiar boyish smile spread across Hallur's face, and Gunna could see why old ladies voted for him in droves.

"I'll be in touch," she said coldly, letting go of his hand and stepping outside.

She took the stairs two at a time and waved to the researcher half hidden behind her computer monitor before taking a breath of fresh, damp air on the steps outside the old building. She looked up and could see Hallur's tiny office window propped open up in the eaves.

"The cheeky bastard. Dinner? My arse," she muttered to herself, wondering just why Hallur had avoided mentioning Bjartmar Arnarson's membership of what she had started to think of as the Svana Syndicate.

"WHY ARE WE in this place?" Eiríkur asked, craning his neck to take in his surroundings.

"We're here because Helgi and I like it," Gunna replied. "It's also quiet, and if anyone we know pops in, we'll see them straight away."

Gunna had taken a window table at Kænan, the harbour café in Hafnarfjördur, with a view of trucks rumbling steadily along the road outside to and from the dock gate a hundred metres away. With the lunchtime rush over, there was still food on the menu but the place was quiet enough for them to talk.

The remnants of lunch, Gunna's fried fish, Helgi's lamb stew and Eiríkur's burger, had all been taken away. The sallow waitress had hardly even bothered to look at them, but Gunna could tell the woman had sensed that they were police officers. She tried to catch her eye as if to reassure her that she didn't interest them in the least, but the waitress stared steadfastly over the trolley in front of her.

"Coffee, boys?" Gunna asked brightly.

Helgi grunted what she knew from the tone to be a yes and gazed out of the window at a forklift truck making precarious progress with a pallet of scrap metal on its forks, waiting to see whether the driver would notice if anything fell off.

"Mocha, please," Eiríkur said, and Gunna chuckled grimly as she went to the counter and poured into three mugs. Helgi took his appreciatively, while Eiríkur looked at his with surprise.

"Sorry," Gunna apologized. "There's only two kinds of coffee here—black or white."

"Come on then, what's it all about?" Helgi asked. "Either going out for lunch is some bizarre team-building exercise, or you've a good reason for taking us somewhere quiet."

Half an hour earlier the tables had been packed with men in overalls and heavy boots. But as the magic hour of one o'clock approached, Kænan had emptied, the queue at the counter had vanished and the tables were deserted. A knot of smokers gathered outside for a few minutes before the boiler suits and boots disappeared to the workshops and factories around the harbour. Only a group of retired men sat at a table in the far corner of the long room, looking wistfully at the small boats at the quayside over the road and idly flipping through the day's newspapers as they wished there was still work for them.

"The long and the short of it is that we have something that's more than a little sensitive on our plates right now," Gunna explained. "And you're right. I wanted to get away from flapping ears for an hour or so."

"Svana Geirs?"

"Got it in one. I had a chat with Ívar Laxdal. I don't reckon Örlygur's coming back from sick leave, and we're reporting direct to Laxdal himself on this."

Helgi guffawed. "I can just imagine Örlygur nursing his bad back at home, hoping it won't get better. I'll bet he's scared shitless he might have to return to work."

"Well, Örlygur's bad back aside, we don't have a senior officer in charge of this department and we probably won't for a while."

"Are you going to put in for it, Gunna?" Eiríkur asked, taking her by surprise with such a direct question.

"No comment's all I can say. Let's just say it's doubtful," she said finally.

"A bar to a star's a bit of a jump," Helgi observed, referring to the one bar of a sergeant and the star a chief inspector would carry on each shoulder.

"Well put, Helgi. Now, Svana Geirs. The word from Ívar Laxdal is that this has to be under wraps, which is why we're here and not in the canteen at Hverfisgata. No publicity, no leaks, no charging in without some very good reasons. Other stuff has to go on the back burner for a few days."

"All right. Is it just us, or do we get any help?" Helgi asked doubtfully.

"It's down to us for the moment. We still have uniforms knocking on doors around Svana's flat and searching bins and whatnot for a possible murder weapon, but we have to concentrate on her private life. We've been over this already, but to make sure we all have the basics, Svana Geirs was the shared squeeze of a group of prominent men who between them contributed to keeping her in a pretty comfortable lifestyle," Gunna explained.

"Names?" Helgi asked.

"There's Bjartmar Arnarson to begin with, which throws a whole new light on a few things."

"And Svana's flat and car are owned by one of his companies," Eiríkur chipped in.

"By the way, did you know that Bjartmar and Long Ommi have a bit of history as well?" Helgi added thoughtfully.

Gunna raised an eyebrow.

"That's right," Helgi continued. "Before Bjartmar became respectable, Ommi was some kind of freelance muscle for him."

"So maybe we can ask Ommi, when we catch up with him. Which might not be for a while if we have to devote every waking moment to Svana Geirs. Anyway, these are the others," Gunna said grimly. "Our big hitters are Jónas Valur

Hjaltason, chairman of Kleifar, shareholder in shipping and transport businesses, as well as running his own export operation. He's a grandfather and older than the others, in his mid-fifties, separated, lives alone. Then there's Bjarki Steinsson, who runs an accountancy firm. Bjarki sold a whole raft of holdings in one of the banks weeks before the crash and made a packet out of it. Björgvin at Financial says that everything he owned has been transferred to a company in his wife's name. It's already part of a wider investigation, so we have to be extra careful not to muddy the water there."

Gunna paused.

"Any more?" Eiríkur asked.

"Plus Hallur Hallbjörnsson, and as far as we know, that's all. Right. We'd better divvy these magnificent specimens up between us and see what we come up with. Start with any records we already hold, I'll check with Financial, and we go on from there."

"So who wants what?" Helgi asked.

"We might be best taking some of them in pairs, I reckon," Gunna decided. "Eiríkur, can you chase up the phone records and suchlike? I can continue to be brutal with Hallur as I've already had two goes at the slimy bastard and he's not as squeaky clean as he wants me to think. Helgi can come with me to see Bjartmar, Bjarki and old Jónas. Agreed?"

"Agreed," Helgi said, rattling his mug on the table. "You know you get a free refill here, don't you?"

KLEIFAR'S OFFICES OCCUPIED half the ground floor of a squat old building with little to indicate that it housed a successful export company with a subsidiary in Portugal. It was a stone's throw from what Gunna still thought of as the old Morgunbladid building overlooking the open space of Ingólfstorg with its skateboard rink that fizzed with life during the long summer days. But on a chill winter's afternoon the square and the empty restaurants surrounding it exuded a forlorn air, with only a handful of hiking-booted tourists to be seen, going from one shop window to another huddled into their thick parkas, tutting over the prices of Icelandic woollen sweaters.

Kleifar's outer office was pleasantly warm, and a secretary with an air of discipline about her looked up as Gunna entered with Helgi behind her.

"Can I help you?" she asked, head back and eyes heavy-lidded. She took off a pair of black-rimmed glasses and let them fall to hang on a chain around her neck.

"We're here to speak to Jónas Valur Hjaltason. Is he in?" Gunna said, trying to sound friendly in the face of this clearly unfriendly woman.

"I'm afraid Jónas Valur has a busy schedule and is occupied in a meeting all afternoon. Could I ask who you are?"

"Police," Gunna replied. "His name has been mentioned in connection with an investigation and we need to go over a few points with him."

"Can I ask what it concerns?" the woman asked in a razor voice. "I handle all of Jónas Valur's appointments."

Gunna was aware that Helgi was showing a great deal of interest in the antique maps hung on the walls of the office, standing with hands behind his back and bending forward to peer at the faded gothic lettering of some place names.

"I'm afraid that I can't tell you. But I assure you it's a serious matter and it's important that we speak to him."

"And I'm afraid he's not available."

"His car's outside," Gunna pointed out, reasoning that the Mercedes with the personalized number had to be his. "So I assume he's here."

The woman's face remained a mask. "Jónas Valur sees people by appointment only."

"People like Svana Geirs?" Gunna asked in the sweetest voice she could manage.

The woman's eyes bulged for a fraction of a second.

"Wait," she ordered, and disappeared through a door behind her. Helgi stood behind Gunna, lifted himself on tiptoe and leaned forward to whisper in her ear.

"You're going to get in trouble again," he half sang, stepping back and exhibiting an innocent smile by the time she had turned round to frown at him. She burst into a grin just as an animated but muffled conversation could be heard through the panelling of the wall.

"I'll say it was you," she decided.

"And I'll say you told me to," Helgi responded, smothering his crooked smile as the secretary slipped in through the door, as if she had wheels instead of feet.

"Jónas Valur will see you shortly, if you'd like to wait."

Gunna could almost imagine icicles cracking and falling from her voice. The woman indicated an uncomfortable-looking sofa against the far wall, the cracked leather of its ancient covering not designed to encourage waiting.

"We'll stand, thanks. I'm sure he won't be long."

IN CONTRAST TO Jónas Valur Hjaltason's smooth confidence, Bjarki Steinsson blinked like a small animal caught in the beam of a headlight. He hardly looked like a high-flying accountant, dressed in faded jeans and a polo shirt embroidered with a discreet logo that quietly proclaimed the name of the company he worked for and ostensibly owned a substantial share of.

"You're here about Svana?" he asked before Helgi even had the opportunity to open his mouth, and Gunna guessed that Jónas Valur had passed on a warning, probably before they had even left Kleifar for the five-minute drive to where Bjarki

Steinsson's company occupied a floor of one of the Shadow District's newer office blocks.

Gunna clicked the door shut behind them. While this stopped any sound escaping from the man's office, she noticed that a pair of eyes at every desk was keeping tabs on the two strangers talking to the boss. This time Helgi would ask the questions while Gunna watched and listened.

"We are investigating the murder of Svanhildur Mjöll Sigurgeirsdóttir," Helgi confirmed portentously.

"So it was definitely murder?" Bjarki asked, eyes wide, brimming with a sadness he could not conceal.

"Without a doubt."

"She didn't just, er, fall or something?"

"Absolutely not. Can you tell me where you were on Thursday afternoon last week?"

Bjarki Steinsson sat down heavily while Helgi kept him fixed in the headlight beam. "I couldn't tell you offhand. Here, probably. I can ask my secretary to check the diary if you like."

"I'll ask myself. Of course I'll need to have confirmation of where you were at that time. Now," Helgi said, sitting down without being invited to do so, "your relationship with Svana Geirs. Tell me about it."

Gunna stood by the door and listened, hands behind her back, concentrating on watching Bjarki Steinsson's face as he responded to Helgi's questions. As far as she could make out, the man was genuinely distressed, with beads of sweat forming on his forehead.

"What do you need to know?" he asked quickly.

Helgi sat back as if he had the whole day and the evening stretching ahead of him. "Let's just say I need to know everything?"

Bjarki Steinsson slumped as if deflated. "All right. Svana and I had a relationship that went back two, three years. Something like that. I don't recall precisely. We used to meet occasionally."

"How often?"

"Sometimes we wouldn't meet for a month. Sometimes we might see each other several times in a week."

"And what did you do?"

"What did we do?" he asked blankly. "How do you mean?"

Helgi sighed. "Surely I don't have to spell it out for you? Did you go out? Hold hands? Screw?"

The sudden coarseness jolted Bjarki Steinsson and his eyes bulged.

"Our relationship was a physical one," he said finally, as if overcoming a painful barrier. "Look, how far is this going to go? I have a wife . . ."

"This is just an informal talk, nothing more," Helgi assured him, and paused. "For the moment, that is."

"Which means what?"

"It means that if I have reason to believe you're concealing something that has a bearing on Svanhildur Mjöll's death, then we'd need to make this more formal."

"I see," he replied and was silent.

Gunna rocked imperceptibly on her heels, watching the man in distress behind his vast granite desk, and at the same time watching his staff in the open-plan office outside at their chipboard workstations, trying not to stare too obtrusively.

"I, er," he began, and coughed. "I take it you've spoken to the others already and you know about the, er, arrangement?"

"Let's pretend I don't, shall we?" Helgi said softly.

Bjarki Steinsson looked down at the floor under his desk and Gunna imagined him as a small boy caught with a pocketful of purloined sweets.

"A group of us. We, er, shared Svana's time. She acted as an escort to us all in turn, by prior arrangement. In return for a financial consideration," he said bleakly.

"Ah. There is a word for this, and I presume you're aware the law is also quite clear on this kind of activity?"

He nodded without raising his head. "Yes. I know. Look, officer. Nobody was hurt or harmed or did anything they were unwilling to do or was in any way coerced or forced. Everything in this arrangement was entirely consensual and amicable."

"I can see that. But Svanhildur Mjöll was selling her company, which included sexual services. An offence has been committed by each of the participants. As I said, there is a less pleasant word for this kind of arrangement."

A tiny spark of anger could be seen deep behind Bjarki Steinsson's eyes.

"Officer, have you any clue what a loveless marriage is like?" he asked bitterly. "My wife . . . My wife and I have had nothing to say to each other for years. We live in the same house. A divorce would be a disaster financially, and for her it would be deeply uncomfortable in social terms. The circles she moves in . . ." He sighed. "Listen. We know and trust each other to that extent. I earn a considerable amount. My wife has a comfortable position based on that income. We each respect that the other has a private life. Understand?"

"An open marriage, sort of thing?"

"If you want to put it like that."

"And have you made a habit of procuring services of this kind?"

"If you're going to be offensive, I'd prefer it if this interview was recorded so that I have grounds for complaint," the accountant snapped.

"I'd prefer it if you would just answer the bloody question," Helgi replied with a new harsh note in his voice.

"Not . . . not recently."

"During your relationship with Svanhildur Mjöll?"

"No, of course not."

"Why 'of course not'?"

"That was the agreement. No other partners, spouses excluded."

"Do you think the others kept to this agreement?"

Bjarki Steinsson shook his head. "I don't know. It's not something we discussed. Possibly not."

Helgi seemed satisfied with the answer and Gunna saw an air of defeat in the man's reply.

"Now," Helgi said. "When did you last see Svanhildur Mjöll?"

"On Thursday," he whispered. "In the morning."

DIDDI SAT CRUMPLED between his lawyer, a young woman with a plump, friendly face, and a social worker huddled in a denim jacket.

"All right, Diddi? How are you?" Gunna asked, taking a seat opposite him.

"I'm OK," Diddi replied, a dazed expression on his round face.

"You're aware that everything is recorded in here and anything you say could be used in evidence in court?"

"I'd like to make it plain," the plump young woman began, "I'd like to state, that my client has a history of mental illness."

"Actually, I know Diddi of old." Gunna smiled. "Isn't that right, Diddi?"

"Yeah, Gunna."

"So, for the record, you're Kristbjörn Hrafnsson, you're thirty-four years old and you're on invalidity benefit. Is that right?"

"Yeah."

"Now, Diddi. Would you like to tell me about what happened to your face?"

The lawyer frowned but said nothing.

"I fell over," Diddi said finally.

"If you say so. But how did you manage to fall over on both sides of your face at the same time?"

"Is this relevant?" the lawyer asked.

"If it wasn't relevant, I wouldn't be asking," Gunna answered, glaring at her. "All right, Diddi. Your dad brought you into the station on Monday night. The branch of Kaupthing in Grafarvogur was robbed by a man with a knife that morning. Now, Diddi, it was you, wasn't it?"

"Yeah."

"That's fine. I just wanted you to confirm it, because there's no doubt that it was you. You understand that?"

"Yeah," Diddi answered. He appeared to be close to tears.

"What I really want to know is where you went after the robbery. How did you get back to town? You don't drive and I'm sure you didn't catch a bus, did you?"

Diddi sitting in silence, staring at the floor, reminded Gunna immediately of Bjarki Steinsson looking guiltily at the floor of his own office that afternoon.

"Come on, Diddi. You have to tell me, like you said you would. The truth, remember?"

"Promised I wouldn't."

"Who did you promise you wouldn't tell? Was it Long Ommi?"

"No!' Diddi squeaked. "No. I haven't seen Ommi. It wasn't Ommi!"

"Diddi, we've known each other for a long time. You remember how long? You remember when I hauled you out of the bus station that time those boys set fire to your coat? Remember that?"

Diddi nodded.

"And you remember when all that money was stolen from the kiosk on Sólgata? That wasn't you, was it? But those guys said it was and I didn't believe them. Remember that?"

Diddi nodded again, while the lawyer knitted her plucked eyebrows and pretended to understand what was happening. The social worker glanced at his watch.

"Now, Diddi, my friend," Gunna said softly. "Don't you think it's about time you told me the truth?"

This time his features crumpled and tears flowed down his cheeks as he howled as if in pain, turning to the social worker with an imploring look on his face. Gunna sat impassively and looked over at Diddi as the volume of his howls increased.

"Can we stop? Please?" the social worker demanded. "He's distressed enough as it is."

Gunna nodded without taking her eyes off Diddi, who stared right back through his wails of anguish.

"Interview suspended," she said sharply, and immediately the volume from Diddi went down a notch. "Eiríkur, would you get Diddi some water."

"Can I have a word, outside?" the young lawyer asked.

The top of the lawyer's head came roughly up to Gunna's shoulder.

"What are you doing in there?" she demanded with a pugnacious curl of her lower lip.

"I don't know about what you might think, but what I have here is a pretty watertight case, what with witnesses, CCTV and all that. No weapon or cash, but we don't even need that. Why? What's your problem?"

"You'll never get a conviction, never."

"Really? You'd better tell my colleague Sævaldur that."

"Come on. Look at the man. There's a history of mental health problems going back years. We'll plead diminished responsibility and he'll be off. So why are you pushing him so hard?"

Gunna looked down into the young woman's earnest face and wondered if she had graduated yesterday or the day before.

"Look, Valbjörg," she said, and a look of surprise shot into the woman's eyes as she realized Gunna had remembered her name. "I know Diddi of old and he's had an absolutely miserable time since the day he was born. D'you really think I want to see him banged up in Litla-Hraun? Even with a GBH charge he'll probably get a suspended sentence at worst, and that's fine with me."

"Yes, but my client—"

"Is definitely guilty. No question, and unfortunately he hurt someone rather badly. But where did the cash go? Where's the weapon? How did he make a getaway? Who organized this? Diddi can only just about manage to decide what to have for breakfast, so there's someone who forced him into this and that's who I'd love to see in a cell, preferably for ever."

"I see," the lawyer agreed, grudgingly.

DIDDI WAS CALMER, but sniffed as he sat in a corner of the interview room. "He's very distressed," the social worker announced. "I should call a doctor, really. He needs medication."

"If you think that's appropriate," Gunna said dubiously, sitting next to Diddi, hunched in his grubby parka. "Diddi," she said softly, "listen to me. I've asked your dad to sit with us. Is that all right with you?"

He nodded in reply.

"Will you be happier with him here as well?"

Diddi nodded again, slowly this time.

"Is there anything you want to tell me before he gets here?"

He shook his head and Gunna patted his shoulder. 'Don't worry, Diddi. Don't try and make anything up. Keep to what really happened and you'll be all right."

"Am I going to prison?" he asked in a small voice.

"I don't know, Diddi. That's not for me to decide, but you did something wrong when you cut that man's hand."

"I didn't mean to. He got in the way, shouting at me like that."

He looked up mournfully at the social worker. "I'm not going to prison, am I, Axel?"

"Not if I can help it," the man replied.

"All right, Diddi," Gunna said in the kindliest voice she

could manage. "Your dad will be here in just a minute, so shall we start again?"

"All right."

"I'm going to be completely straight with you. I'm not really interested in you robbing the bank, and if that man who tried to talk to you hadn't been hurt, I'd do my best to make as little of this as I could. Understand?"

Diddi nodded wretchedly.

"But I suppose you panicked and he was hurt. There's nothing we can do to change that, and you'll be charged. What I'm really interested in knowing is why. Why did you suddenly need a million krónur? In fact, I don't believe you needed a million krónur. I think somebody else wanted the money and made you do it. And I think that somebody is the same somebody who gave you a black eye. Am I right?" Gunna asked gently, her voice soft as Diddi looked up at her, his face a picture of misery.

"Yes," he whispered.

"Long Ommi?"

Diddi twisted his fingers and nodded again.

"Yes," he said finally. "Ommi told me to do it. He said I owed him money and he wanted it."

"Did you owe him money?"

"I don't know!" Diddi wailed.

"And he drove you away?"

"His friend. In a red car."

"Do you know Ommi's friend's name?"

"No. He's ugly."

"Now, I want you to take your time and tell me just what happened after Ommi's friend drove you away from the bank. Can you do that?"

"WHAT DID YOU get out of Daft Diddi?" Helgi asked, turning on to Kringlumýrarbraut and pulling down the sunshade in the front of the hired car to shield him from the full glare of the low springtime sun, shining directly into his eyes from beneath a cover of thick white cloud in the west.

"Hell," he swore, as the sunshade dropped down in front of his eyes and Gunna leaned over to lift it back. "The bloody thing's broken again," he apologized.

"What a surprise. What were you saying?"

"Diddi. Any progress?"

"Yeah, he came clean eventually. Long Ommi gave him a light smacking to start with and then demanded a million in cash. Diddi asked where from and Ommi or his mate told him how to go about it, gave him the knife and so forth."

"Where are we going now?"

"Bjartmar Arnarson, one more time."

"Oh, be still my beating heart. Another hour with a soulless bean-counter. It'd be fantastic if we could get the knife with Ommi's prints on it, wouldn't it? You want Ommi brought in?"

"Oh, yes. As soon as poss. We'll sling the book at the bastard."

"All arranged for early tomorrow. These guys sleep late, shouldn't be a problem to give him a surprise wake-up call."

"Sounds good. Come off past the petrol station. Bjartmar's office is at the top there."

Helgi parked between a sleek Mercedes and a Land Cruiser on tyres that wouldn't have looked out of place on a truck.

"After you, chief," he said gallantly as Gunna pushed open the door.

Bjartmar looked up from the table in the corner where three people were talking over empty cups. He smiled, stood up and came over, hand extended.

"Gunnhildur, isn't it? Come in," he said with a friendliness that took her off guard. He led the way to a conference room with a view overlooking the busy main road outside. "Take a seat, please. Coffee?"

"No thanks. But I expect Helgi wouldn't say no," she told

him as she settled herself in a leather chair so soft it felt like sinking into warm mud.

"No news on the fire, I suppose?" he asked, a pained expression appearing across the strong features that were more relaxed and, she had to admit to herself, more handsome than those of the jet-lagged, unshaven man she had interviewed at Keflavík airport only two days ago. Bjartmar's hair had been cut and his shirt was pressed and smart, open at the neck to show a fine gold chain. His attention was entirely on Gunna, and Helgi sat ignored, wondering if coffee was going to appear after all.

"No breakthroughs, I'm afraid. The technical division is working through a pile of forensic evidence that might help, or it might not. The fire was definitely petrol, though."

"Both our cars are, were, diesel. There was a small petrol can in there for the lawnmower, though it could have been empty for all I know. But that would never have been enough for a blaze like that, surely?"

"How's your wife?" Gunna asked bluntly, and Bjartmar's eyes lifted.

"No idea," he said with a shrug. "We don't communicate a lot."

"Svanhildur Mjöll Sigurgeirsdóttir," Helgi broke in. "She was found dead in her apartment a week ago and we have good reason to believe that you had a relationship of some kind with her. Would you explain?"

Bjartmar's smile froze for a second, then thawed as he looked over at Helgi before focusing his attention back on Gunna. "I've known Svana for years, since she was in the Cowgirls. That's going back ten, twelve years. Why are you asking me this?"

Helgi planted his elbows on the polished wood of the table and Bjartmar winced at the sight of his greasy anorak. "We understand there was a syndicate, a group of prominent men who shared her favours, and that you're a member of this group. Is that correct?"

"It is," he said with only a flicker of rapidly stifled irritation.

"When we spoke before, you mentioned that your marriage had been rocky for some time," Gunna said quietly. "You didn't attempt to hide it and you certainly gave the impression that you and Unnur were likely to part company shortly. I'm given to understand that you have another relationship now?"

"This is personal," Bjartmar said stiffly.

"It certainly could be," Helgi said gruffly. "It could be very personal if whoever killed Svana Geirs also tried to kill your wife."

Bjartmar's jaw hung slack for a second. "Do you really think . . . ?"

"We don't know. But it's an angle we have to consider and there are a few things we need to ask you about," Gunna said.

"God. Hell, yes, anything. Ask away if it helps."

"First, the syndicate. We have a pretty clear idea of how this operated, and the legal department are now deciding whether or not to proceed with prosecutions."

"Prosecutions? Why?"

"Because it appears that offences have been committed in purchasing sexual services."

"It was a consensual private arrangement between adults."

"Were you a member of the syndicate from the start?"

"We all were. There have never been any new members. Actually, I'd more or less dropped out and hadn't seen Svana for a while."

"Why?"

Bjartmar's eyes sparkled, although his face remained set. "I met a new lady and we're getting on just fine."

"And you even bought her a business?" Gunna asked.

"Look, where did you hear that from?" he demanded angrily. "That's a private matter. As it happens, I already owned a controlling share in the place and bought out my partner. Then I asked . . . my new partner to manage it, and she has, very competently."

"Is that partner as in business partner, or partner as in girl-friend?" Helgi asked.

"Both."

"And your wife? Is she still a business partner as well?"

"I suppose so."

"And how is her restaurant doing now that she's not available?"

"Better, thanks. The chef's running things for the moment and it's going a lot more smoothly without Unnur in charge. I might keep him on."

Gunna wondered how Bjartmar felt about his wife's injuries, or if he was more concerned about the damage to the house.

"Where were you when Svana Geirs was killed?" she asked.

"Abroad," he answered without hesitation. "I returned from the States the day of the fire, as you know. Before that I'd been away for almost two weeks, Belgium, Germany, Spain and then Chicago. All verifiable if you want to see tickets and reservations."

"You know, I'd been wondering about you, and then I remembered. You used to run Blacklights, didn't you?"

Bjartmar frowned and his jaw pushed forward, as if he were unprepared to have his past dug over. "That was one of my earlier ventures, yes."

"I thought so. At the time, we were always as sure as we could be that there was a lot more to that place than met the eye, but never anything that could be pinned down," she recalled as Bjartmar's eyes narrowed. "So what happened to the place? Did you sell up?"

"Someone else took over that business. We still own the building. In fact, The Fish Lover is exactly where Blacklights used to be."

"And this is a better business than the nightclub?"

"Not as profitable as a nightclub, but without the head-aches. There's a better class of customer, and we never have to throw anyone out these days."

"I see," Gunna said. "How about your old friend Long Ommi? Heard from him recently?"

"What?" Bjartmar asked, as if Gunna had dropped a fire-cracker on the table in front of him. "Ommi? Why would I have heard from him?"

"That's what I'm asking you. Ommi and you go way back, I'm told, until he was put away."

"Listen, I don't know where your information comes from, but I haven't seen or heard of him for years," Bjartmar snarled, and Gunna was pleased to see that the suave businessman had vanished.

"Just how many years?"

"Eight, nine. I don't know. A long time."

"I'll refresh your memory, in that case. Ómar Magnússon was jailed in 2001 for murder and got a fifteen-year sentence. He would have been up for parole next year, and as he's been a good lad inside, he'd have been out within a year. But for some reason that nobody has been able to fathom, he did a runner from his comfortable open-prison billet at Kvíabryggja last month and is still at liberty."

Bjartmar sat with his fists clenched so the knuckles whit-ened. Gunna noticed suddenly that they were not the soft hands of an office worker, but shovel-like and better suited to a farmhand than a businessman. For a second she recalled the old story about the size of a man's hands being relative to other parts of his anatomy—or was that feet?—but dismissed the thought irritably. She leaned forward and looked Bjartmar in the eyes.

"What I'm wondering is whether Ommi is going round set-tling scores on his own account, or whether he's clearing up for someone else, carrying out a contract, so to speak. And if he's doing business for himself, who's next, and why? Has he been in touch?"

Bjartmar's face was the colour of parchment and the veins stood out on his neck as his jaw jutted ahead of him.

"I'm not prepared to discuss this any further," he said hoarsely.

"Now that's a shame, because I have a distinct feeling that you know a good deal more than you're obviously prepared to let on," Gunna said gently. "I have a feeling that you and Ommi have probably been in touch since he's been out, and I don't doubt that he'll spill the beans in return for some kind of a deal when we catch up with him, which will be soon enough."

"Iceland's a small country and you can't stay hidden for long," Helgi added.

Bjartmar stood up suddenly and his chair shot back on its wheels to hit the wall behind, where it rolled over and crashed on to one side.

"I'm not prepared to continue this," he rasped. "You two had better leave. Now, right now."

Gunna stayed sitting down for a moment and took a long look at Bjartmar flexing his fists, shoulders tensed, before she got slowly to her feet without taking her eyes off him.

"Well, thanks for your time. Very interesting in many ways. I'm sure we'll speak again soon."

"You can call my secretary, and I'll have my lawyer here. I have nothing more to say."

Bjartmar swept from the room and left them to find their own way out through the office space where staff tried not to look up, reminding Gunna precisely of Bjarki Steinsson's staff staring fixedly at their computer terminals.

She looked back as Helgi pulled the door open to see Bjartmar gesticulating with his phone to one ear, the fury apparent on his face rendered silent by the soundproof glass wall of his office.

"Coming, are you?" Helgi asked. "I thought you two were getting on so well when you had to go and spoil it."

"I DON'T KNOW about you, but I'd dearly love to haul all of them in and chuck them in cells overnight before we give them a proper roasting."

"You think so?" Helgi asked, listening to the gearbox rattle with a pained expression on his otherwise mild face.

"Yup. The whole lot of them in the cells. What a bunch of shitbags! Are most men like that? Have you ever paid for it, Helgi?"

"Not as such," he said distantly, stopping at a junction and peering left and right.

"What does 'not as such' mean?"

"I met my first wife at a country hop at Húnaver, talked her out of her knickers that night and almost twenty years later I'm still paying for it," he said grimly.

"Æi, you're a cynical bastard, Helgi Svavarsson," Gunna grinned. "What do you make of Bjartmar?"

"Wouldn't buy a second-hand car off him."

"Did he do it?"

"His alibi's pretty perfect. Involved? More than likely."

"And the others?" Gunna probed.

"I don't reckon I'd put much past Jónas Valur. Who knows? He'll be a very tough nut to crack and he's certainly covered his tracks. As for Bjarki Steinsson, I felt almost sorry for the man. He was clearly besotted with Svana, so I can't see him being responsible for her death."

"Even though he saw her that day?"

"Even so," Helgi said firmly. "The man was shattered. You saw his face when we walked in. How about Hallur?"

"The same. He has an alibi as well, he was speaking in Parliament at two that afternoon. But somehow I have less faith in the innocence of the ones who do have alibis than I do in Bjarki Steinsson, who doesn't. Ah well. Back to the office, please, my good man, and we'll see what our young sleuth has dug up."

Thursday 18th

HELGI FELT HIS nerves jangling. He knew that while having slept badly would catch up on him later in the day, later could wait. Two patrol cars were parked in the street and one in the street above. Six officers from the Special Unit in black overalls waited by their van for the word to go, breath steaming in the cold clear morning with the sun just rising.

The sergeant in charge of the squad, a solidly built man called Steingrímur, rubbed his gloved hands together, relishing the moment. "How many numbskulls are in there?" he asked.

"Should be three. Ómar Magnússon, did a runner from Kvíabryggja last month. Then there's Addi the Pill, small-time dealer, nasty bit of work. Don't give him any second chances, just cuff him quick. Then there's Ommi's girlfriend Selma, who's the only one I don't really expect to come at us with a baseball bat. That's it unless we've miscounted somewhere along the line."

"Good. Whenever you're ready."

"Let's go, then. Big key or quiet key?"

"Let's keep the noise down, shall we?" Steingrímur decided and murmured instructions to his team. Two of them slipped along the row of houses to watch the back. Steingrímur looked over at Helgi. "Ready with the car, are you?"

Helgi nodded and retreated, taking his place in one of the squad cars. He started the engine and listened to it mutter into life as Steingrímur spoke into his communicator to warn the pair at the back of the house.

"Go on, boys," he said crisply. "Make a mess of it."

The brand-new front door splintered quietly as the hydraulic key levered the lock apart in fascinating slow motion. Helgi eased the patrol car forward up the drive until its bumper was an inch from the garage door. The sound of booted feet piling into the narrow hallway greeted him as he stepped from the car and joined the burly, black-clad queue.

The house wasn't big. Two of the officers quickly checked the kitchen, glanced into the bathroom and thundered up the stairs as two others made for the front room. Helgi quickly opened the back door to let in the two behind the house.

"Come on. Garage," he ordered.

The wiry young man in front made to put his shoulder to the door in the hallway leading to the garage, but Helgi stopped him and pointed to the handle. The young man opened it and stepped into the dark opening, backing away with a yell of pain and both hands clutched over his eyes.

"Fucking spray!" he howled.

So now you know how it feels, Helgi thought, and shouted to the others.

"Steingrímur! In here, quick!"

The heavy figure, wearing a full-visor face mask, appeared at his side.

"In there. The bastard's just peppered your mate," Helgi gasped.

Steingrímur shouldered his way into the opening, drawing his baton, and Helgi heard the ominous click as it snapped open. The spray hissed a second time behind the door, followed by a crack and a howl of agony. Helgi didn't wait and followed close behind, wondering as he did so how he could retreat with three more men behind him.

Inside the door he fumbled for a light switch and clicked it on. A skinny man wearing only ragged underwear and with a curtain of greasy hair loose around his thin shoulders was sitting on the concrete floor nursing one arm and whimpering. A can of spray rolled across the floor towards one of the mattresses along the wall, where a young woman held one hand blearily over her eyes and with the other lifted the hem of a sleeping bag higher over herself as she blinked in the bright light. At the far side, a lanky figure hammered ineffectually on the garage door.

"It's all right, Ommi. You needn't bother. Quietly, now."

"Bastard," he snarled back.

"You are arrested on suspicion of absconding from prison. You are not required to say anything, but anything you do say should be correct and truthful. You have the right to a lawyer at every stage of proceedings," Steingrímur intoned in a flat voice as he clicked shut handcuffs on Ómar's wrists.

The second man was hauled to his feet, still whimpering in pain and clutching one hand in the other.

"You'd better call an ambulance for this chap," Helgi decided.

Steingrímur stooped to pick up the pepper spray can and carefully placed it in an evidence bag.

"Police issue. That counts as assaulting a police officer, doesn't it, Helgi?" he asked smoothly.

"I certainly think so. You'd better send your lad to hospital with him and get his eyes washed out."

Helgi looked around the bare garage, lit by the glare of a trio of naked bulbs in the ceiling.

"Selma, isn't it?" he asked as the girl let the sleeping bag slip down. "What of it?"

"Put them away, will you, love? We've all of us seen tits before, especially small ones like those. But I think you and I need to have a little chat."

"Are you arresting me?" she asked petulantly.

"Not yet, but you might get lucky and find yourself in a cell," Helgi replied. "It's bound to be a bit more comfortable than this dump."

A PLEASURE TO see Bjössi again, Gunna thought. Even though the man acted like a world-class chauvinist, something that had landed him in trouble more than once, experience told her that there was a conscientious and painstaking detective underneath. Since her move to the new squad in Reykjavík, she had seen little of her colleagues at the tiny station in Hvalvík or the main police station in Keflavík to which it belonged. If she hadn't been so busy, she would have missed them.

Gunna and Bjössi talked over the case on the way to the hospital, where they sat themselves at Skari's bedside. The patient glared at them with undisguised loathing.

"What's this? Two of you?" He slurred through his broken jaw. "What's going on?"

"Just the usual, Skari. Time for you to tell us what really happened," Bjössi said lightly.

"Coincidence, you could call it," Gunna added. "Long Ommi does a runner and not long afterwards you get a beating. I'd say that's too much of a coincidence."

Skari glared back at them. "Don't know what you're talking about."

"Ah, but you do, Skari, you do," Bjössi said. "You know perfectly well what we're after. The fictional big Polish bloke who gave you a bit of a hiding hasn't been found, and he won't be, because he doesn't exist. We reckon Ommi did all this. But why?"

"Get lost. Find that Polish bastard," Skari said in a flat voice.

"No, Skari. I'm sure there wasn't a Polish bloke," Bjössi said. "We've been through CCTV from every angle we can get hold of and there's nobody anywhere who looks like your description of this chap. But there is a glimpse of Long Ommi."

"Haven't seen Ommi. Not since you put him away."

"Why did Ommi come all the way out to Keflavík to give you a good hiding? There has to be a reason. And what's more interesting is why you're so determined not to identify him. Come on, Skari, what's the story?"

"We have all the evidence we need to place Ommi a few hundred metres from where you were in Keflavík that day. No doubt about it," Gunna said. "In a little place like this, it would be odd if you two didn't run into each other. So why would Ommi want to come and see his old friend Skari? Could it be because he believes you tipped us off to where he was a few years ago?"

"Don't be stupid." Skari grimaced as fingers of pain shot through his jaw and up into the side of his head. "Ommi'd never. . ."

"Ommi'd never what, Skari?" Björssi probed.

"Ommi wouldn't—I never knew where he was hiding . . . wherever it was that you caught him," he said slowly.

Björssi stood up and walked over to the window to look outside. Although he pretended to be bored and uninterested, Gunna knew that he was listening to every word. "So where was he hiding?"

"I don't know!"

"All right. Let's backtrack." Gunna said firmly as Skari glared back at her. "You and Ommi. What were you up to ten years ago?"

"Shit. I can't remember. Having a good time. Getting pissed."

"Come on, Skari. You know better than that," Björssi admonished, without looking round. "You and Ommi were dealing on behalf of someone. When Ommi was put away after killing that lad, you got a bit frightened and decided crime wasn't for you any more. Something like that?"

"Don't talk shit."

"Don't tell me your Erla was the one who made you see sense."

"Yeah. That's it."

"Ah, isn't that sweet? Ain't love grand?" Bjössi sneered.

"Bjartmar Arnarson," Gunna said suddenly, watching the patient's face for a reaction that she was inwardly delighted to see. "Does the name mean anything to you, Skari?"

"Who?"

"Ah, now I know you're bullshitting me. You know perfectly well who Bjartmar Arnarson is. You and Skari were both working for him in some capacity or other at the end of the nineties. Remember Blacklights?"

"Yeah . . ." Skari answered slowly. "You mean the guy who owned the place?"

"That's him. Now we're getting somewhere."

"I was on the door. So?" Skari said, eyes wide with confusion.

"So was Ommi. Bjartmar was there as well. So was the lad who had his brains scrambled when your mate Ommi gave him a beating in the car park out the back. Did you maybe have something to do with it as well? Is that what happened?"

"I was out the front. Didn't see anything," Skari said quickly. "The coppers took a statement off me then."

"I know," Gunna said. "I've read your statement and all the other statements. I'm wondering how it all ties up so neatly and why Ommi admitted it quite so quickly and quietly. Not like him, you'll have to agree."

"Dunno. You'll have to ask him," Skari replied, retreating into his taciturn persona.

"I will," Gunna said. "Don't you worry."

"You'll have to catch him first."

"Ah, but I'll be having a long talk with Ommi this afternoon, and there's plenty I'll be asking him about, including Blacklights."

"You've caught him?" Skari yelped, almost sitting up in spite of the pain in his broken ribs.

But Gunna was already on her feet and Bjössi looked at Skari with a grin, tapping the side of his nose.

Outside the hospital Bjössi tapped a filterless Camel from its packet and lit up with relief. He proffered the packet, but Gunna shook her head. She unwrapped a stick of chewing gum and popped it in her cheek.

"Given up, have you? What's that about? Is this Steini's influence?" Bjössi asked.

"Hell, no," Gunna groaned. "This is Laufey Oddbjörg's doing."

"How so?" he asked, exhaling a plume of harsh smoke.

"My daughter," Gunna said with a shake of her head. "One morning she says, 'Mum, when are you going to stop smoking?'"

"'Don't know, hadn't thought about it,' I said. "All right," says Laufey. "'Maybe I'll start if you don't give up.' So I had to stop and think for a minute."

"Got a mind of her own, hasn't she?" Bjössi observed. "I wonder where she gets that from? How old is she now?"

"Fifteen going on twenty, I reckon. Bright as you like, but hard work."

"Like mother, like daughter," Bjössi decided. "Give her my kindest regards, won't you? Is she going to college?"

"So she says. Psychology's what she has her sights set on at the moment, but it could be something else by next week. A few months ago she wanted to be a vet, but that seems to have dropped off the radar at the moment. How about yours?"

"Same as ever. The lad just wants to take cars apart all day long. That's all he's interested in, it seems, apart from girls, obviously."

"Goes without saying if he's your son, Bjössi. Now, I'd appreciate it if you'd keep an eye on Skari. I'll be back to have more words with him once we've given Ommi the third degree. Can I haul you in on that?"

"Pleasure, as always," Björssi said. "What was the case you were asking him about? What was it Long Ommi did?"

"Don't you remember? Damn, I was on sick leave just then," Gunna said, and the old feeling of loss came hurtling back.

"Of course. It was just after Raggi died, wasn't it? Hard to believe it was that long ago."

"Almost ten years," Gunna said bleakly, and shook herself.

"It was a fight, wasn't it? A young man got a hell of a beating and died of his injuries without regaining consciousness. There were only a few scared witnesses, who wouldn't say much. Ommi fessed up, nice as pie, if I remember correctly. It was one of old Thorfinnur's last cases before he retired."

"Rumour has it that it wasn't Ommi, though."

Björssi looked suddenly surprised. "Really? I just remember the petty crime rate went down quite sharply as soon as he was out of circulation."

"By all accounts, Ommi was too co-operative: hands up and 'it's a fair cop' sort of thing. I've been hearing whispers that he took the rap for someone else in return for being well looked after," Gunna said grimly. "And I'd love to know who he's been standing in for."

"WANT THE GOOD news, chief?" Helgi grinned with unaccustomed joy.

"Örlygur Sveinsson's decided to come and give us a hand for a couple of days?" Gunna hazarded.

"Not that good."

"Go on, don't keep a lady in suspense."

"It's the prints from Svana's flat. Positively identified, the cleaner's prints in the hallway."

"Which we knew we would."

"There's Svana's brother's prints, and Tinna Sigvalds, the police officer who was first on the scene." Helgi read from the printout in front of him, holding it at arm's length so as to be able to see without having to fumble for his glasses.

"Again, we knew Tinna's prints would be on the door at least. So what's your bombshell, Sherlock?"

"We have Hallur Hallbjörnsson all over the bathroom and the bedroom. Bjarki Steinsson's prints in the kitchen, bathroom and bedroom, and the big fat man's prints practically everywhere."

"You mean Jónas Valur Hjaltason?"

"That's the guy."

"And the other miscreant?"

"Bjartmar Arnarson is conspicuous by his absence. But there's a joker in the pack as well."

"Which is?"

"Long Ommi."

"What?"

"No doubt about it. Ómar Magnússon's prints were beyond question on the door of the fridge, the kitchen door, one of the worktops and the kitchen light switch."

Gunna sat back and thought for a moment with knitted brows. "In the kitchen where Svana was killed. It puts a new angle on things, doesn't it?"

"Doesn't it just?" Helgi agreed. "According to the technical team, there are some blood spots on one of the kitchen cupboard doors, which ties in with what Miss Cruz came up with."

"Which is what?"

"Three blows to the head, which looks very much like a single blow with something heavy to the back of the head, a blow to the forehead as she hit the counter on the way down and another one when she landed on the floor. She's done the autopsy and those are the only injuries."

Gunna nodded. "Sounds plausible enough. We're just missing

the heavy object for the moment. What else did Miss Cruz have to say? I'll read it all later, but give me the gist of it, will you?"

"Svana was pretty fit, as you'd expect. Loads of plastic surgery, though, some liposuction and some false bits added on, notably tits, hips, cheeks and lips. She had all her own teeth, no other significant injuries apart from some minor bruising to one forearm that's certainly a day or two older, marks on wrists that are consistent with handcuffs or a binding of some kind, but also several days old. Oh, and she'd had it off in the last few hours of her life."

"DNA?"

"Working on it. Also traces from the sheets and clothing."

"So Svana had been very friendly with someone that day. A quickie that morning, or maybe whoever she was friendly with knocked her on the head afterwards?" Gunna suggested.

Helgi shook his head. "Bjarki Steinsson admitted he was with her that morning."

"Another talk with Bjarki is called for, I think. Where's Ommi now?"

"Not going back to Kvíabryggja, at any rate. They made a bit of space and he'll be in solitary at Litla-Hraun tomorrow, but he's in the cells here right now."

"That's handy. He has a lot of answers to come up with," Gunna said grimly. "But as he's not going anywhere, I'd like to let the bastard stew while we have a chat with Selma first."

It wasn't a long drive to downtown Reykjavík, and Gunna reflected that she could have been quicker walking, with the added benefit of burning off a few calories. She parked near the lake and admired the reflection of the City Hall in the water, perfectly still for once, as she strode towards the old town house where Hallur Hallbjörnsson had his office.

As she turned a corner, a familiar figure leaped down the

steps three at a time and hurried towards the car park, fumbling for keys in one pocket while hugging an armful of folders. Gunna quickened her pace and reached Hallur's parked Mercedes just as he was stacking files and folders on the back seat.

"Morning. Need a hand?"

"Good morning," he shot back breezily, smiling as he looked up. "Ah, Sergeant," he said, his smile fading away suddenly as he recognized her.

"Nice car. What year?"

"Seventy-two. An uncle of mine had it from new and looked after it. Never drove it during the winter, always kept it inside. So I've tried to do the same. First time I've had it out this year. Anything I can do for you, officer? I'm afraid I'm in a hurry."

"A word, if you have time," Gunna said in a tone that indicated that anything else would hardly do.

"I was just leaving. I have a meeting in a few minutes."

"It won't take long."

"My office? I'm going to be late, and this is important," Hallur said helplessly.

"We can sit in your car if that's not a problem for you," Gunna said, and half regretted the suggestion. She sank into the leather seat and Hallur sat behind the wheel, fiddling with his keys.

"Is this still about Svana?" he asked.

"Why? Is there something else you need to get off your chest?"

"Of course there isn't."

Hallur had spoken more irritably than he had intended.

"Sorry, Sergeant," he said with a sigh. "It's been, well, difficult these last few days."

"I'm sorry to hear that."

"Word gets around. Everyone there knows that you've been here to see me more than once." He indicated with a dismissive nod the red corrugated-iron building where his office nestled in the eaves. "The rumours are flying already. I've had to explain myself twice to the party chairman and it's being made pretty clear that my position could become untenable."

His eyes flickered from the dashboard to the building on the other side of the car park and back to Gunna, who once again had the uncomfortable feeling that she was being sized up. She tugged the zip of her coat up past the cleavage line, even though her blouse was already buttoned almost to the neck.

"Results from the forensic examination of Svana and her flat. Your fingerprints are all over the bedroom and the bathroom."

"I told you they might be, and don't forget, I gave samples of my fingerprints willingly."

"Duly noted," Gunna replied. "Svana had a sexual partner the day she died. You?"

"Shit!" Hallur looked shocked.

"Fair enough. I have to ask, you understand. But I need an answer," Gunna said with iron in her voice.

"I find it very uncomfortable, Sergeant, having my personal life dug into in this way by a woman. If you don't mind my saying so."

"I don't mind your saying so and I do appreciate your position. But these questions need answers." She tried not to smile, and bit back a suggestion that he could at least stop trying to unobtrusively check out her legs.

Hallur grunted non-committally.

"So when did you last see Svana?"

"Like I told you. On the fourth. That was my turn."

"I'm not saying I disbelieve you, but there is evidence to the contrary. If you have anything to tell me, I'd imagine a man in your position would be very well advised to come clean. There's DNA evidence that's being tested now."

"Shit! Am I a suspect?" he demanded suddenly. "Because unless I am, I think you should stop pressuring me like this."

"If I'm pressuring you, it's because I don't believe you're telling me everything that a man in your position would have a duty to," Gunna said gently, but with a firmer tone behind the softness.

Hallur jammed the car key into the ignition. "I'm sorry, officer. I have a meeting that I'm already late for. Can I drop you somewhere?"

"Right here will do. You still haven't answered the question I asked you."

"And I don't have time to now. Understand, Sergeant?" There was a new harshness in Hallur's voice.

"Perfectly. If you're not prepared to co-operate with a serious police investigation, then you don't leave me too many options."

"What are you going to do? Arrest me?"

Gunna opened the door and swung herself down to the ground, not sorry to be out of the car.

"Maybe not yet. But I'm already wondering what else a smart young MP might have to be so nervous about. See you soon," she said, slamming the door before he could reply. She set off towards the lake with a smile on her face, wondering idly why she should be pleased with herself when Hallur's car sped past.

JÓN LAY ON his back in a widening puddle as his phone began to play the theme tune from Star Wars. It was too far away to reach easily and he decided to let it ring. He patted the floor at his side for the wrench he knew was there and closed his hand around it, the other holding the isolation valve in place under the kitchen sink. With a few swift turns the valve was secured and he hauled himself stiffly to his feet.

There was no number under the missed call message on his phone's screen. Jón put it back on the kitchen table and rummaged in his toolbox to come up with a set of mixer taps, as good as new, left over from another job.

This time he whistled as he set about fitting them to the kitchen sink, first taking the old leaking taps off and dropping them in the bin that normally occupied the space where he had been lying in the puddle.

"Almost done?"

"Yeah. Not long. Done the hard part," he said without looking round at the thin, blank-faced young woman who lived in the flat strewn with the debris left by small children with not enough space to play. Not bad-looking, apart from that miserable expression on her face, he thought. How old? No more than twenty-three or twenty-four? And how many sprogs?

"D'you want a coffee?"

"Yeah, please."

He heard her take the jug from the percolator and fill it in the bathroom. Before long it was spluttering and hissing as the aroma of fresh coffee filled the room. Jón swung himself back under the sink with a tap spanner in one hand and gently tightened the nuts holding the new tap unit in place. As he emerged, he saw her sitting at the table with two mugs in front of her.

"Almost done," he told her, and she nodded as he delved into his toolbox for a tube of silicone.

"I'll just put a squirt of this around the back of your sink. If you get water into the worktop, it'll swell up and rot, and that's a hell of a job to replace," he said.

Jón stretched and flexed his shoulders after an hour hunched under the sink, just as his phone began to ring again.

"Yeah?"

"Jón?" a voice asked. "This is Hrannar Antonsson at the bank."

Jón instantly regretted answering the phone, as "private number calling" on the display generally meant trouble.

"Yeah, what do you want now?" he demanded, dreading the

reply and noticing for the first time that the woman sitting at the table had brushed some life into her limp hair and changed from the loose sweatshirt she had been wearing when he arrived into a blouse that hid nothing.

"We'd really like you to come in so we can review your status," the personal financial adviser gabbled. "Of course we realize that things aren't easy for any of us right now, but there are a few items that we need to regularize."

Regularize? Jón thought. Is that really a word?

"All right," he sighed. "When?"

"Well, no pressure, obviously, but this is getting urgent and we've been trying to reach you for a couple of days now . . ."

"So there is pressure, if you say it's getting urgent."

"Well, yes. Er, no. I don't want to pressure you, but we do need to achieve a settlement that's agreeable to everyone so that we can normalize your banking status and hopefully reinstate your privileges—"

"This afternoon?" Jón broke in. "I can be there in an hour or so."

"Er, yeah," Hrannar said, taken aback. "Could we make it tomorrow, maybe?"

"It's today or next week," Jón said, anger rising inside him as he imagined the young man sitting behind his desk at the bank. The woman stared at him with a vacant expression as she listened to the conversation.

"My diary's already full for today and I just don't have a slot for any more appointments," the personal financial adviser protested.

"Look, mate. I'm at work and I don't have time to mess about. Today, or next week."

"In that case it'll have to be Tuesday. How's about three twenty-five? OK for you?"

"No, it's not. What time do you open?"

"We're here at nine thirty."

"Nine thirty, then. I'm not going to pack up a day's work somewhere to come into town just to hear more bad news."

"If that's the way you feel, I can make you an appointment at nine fifty," Hrannar shot back, irritation plain in his voice.

"I have to say, I feel you could be more co-operative—"

"I'll be there when you open," Jón told him, and ended the call without waiting to hear more, tossing his phone into his open toolbox. "Bastards . . ."

"Finished?" the woman asked.

"Pretty much. I'll just give it all a wipe-down," Jón replied, turning on the new tap and watching the water gush into the sink. He snapped the water off and put the rest of his tools and unused parts back in the toolbox.

"Your coffee's on the table," she reminded him softly and with the first smile he had seen from her.

"Thanks," Jón said, sitting down and taking a mouthful. "Good coffee. Lived here long?"

"Almost a year. It's too small for us, but it was all I could afford."

"How many kids?" Jón asked.

"Three. All under five." She sighed. "How much do I owe you?"

"Call it fifteen thousand for cash. That's an hour's work and I'll only charge you five thousand for the taps as they were off another job. How does that sound?"

"That's great. But, er . . ." She looked down at the table and leaned forward, providing a clear view down her blouse. "The thing is, I don't have fifteen thousand right now. My maintenance hasn't come through and the kids needed shoes and I'm a bit short."

Bloody hell, another one. Poor cow, Jón thought, staring at her timid smile and deliberately looking into her face and not at the nipples on display. Hardly even a handful, not like Linda's.

She glanced down at his hands clasped around the mug.

"Maybe there's some other way we can settle this?" she said in a silky voice, looking him in the eyes and giving her shoulders a discreet shake that set off tiny tremors across her bosom.

Jón sighed. "Sorry, love. I'd rather have the cash. I'm a bit short as well right now."

"But I don't have fifteen thousand."

"I really don't want to take those taps off again."

"God! No! Don't do that! Five, and I'll blow you off?" she suggested with a weak smile.

"What's your name again?"

"Elín Harpa."

"Are you on your own?"

"Yeah. Guys don't hang around me for long," she said with resignation.

"Bloody hell. You shouldn't have to offer plumbers blow jobs, darling. Tell you what," Jón said firmly. "Make it five and I'll pop back next week for the other ten."

DROPS OF WATER glittered on the man's beard and spiky iron-grey crewcut hair. He concentrated as he tied a spoon to the end of his line, gave it a quick tug to check the knot and looked at Helgi with one eye closed in a quizzical half-wink.

"What brings you out here, then, Helgi? How's business at the old firm?" The retired chief inspector cast his line and listened to it spin off the reel with a satisfying hum. It hit the surface of the lake with scarcely a sound, but sent out a widening ring of ripples that died before they came close to the strip of black rock and sand that separated water and deep turf.

"Biting, are they?"

"There's a big feller in there. I've seen him before, but he's too smart to take a hook. You know I don't come up here to fish. I'm here to get out from under the old woman's feet for an hour or two. If she wants fish for dinner, I'll buy a couple of haddock fillets on the way home."

"You might get lucky one day." Helgi shivered. He wasn't prepared for the damp that the mist deposited on him, and wasn't dressed for outdoors.

"You remember Ómar Magnússon? Long Ommi?"

"How could anyone forget an evil bastard like that one? Why? Is he bothering you?"

"Don't watch the news, do you, Thorfinnur? He escaped from Kvíabryggja. We've got him back now, but there's something shady to all this that we haven't figured out."

Thorfinnur nodded sagely, his eyes on the line as he gently reeled it in.

"There's plenty going on," Helgi continued. "He's implicated with another murder, a couple of beatings and a bank job. Now the chief has the idea that Ommi was sitting out his stretch for someone else."

"He's been a busy boy. Go on."

"You were on the case. One of your last, wasn't it? I'm wondering if you recall anything that might cast light on all this?"

Thorfinnur Markússon watched his hook emerge, reeled it in and cast again before he replied, his eyes fixed on the point where the spoon had sliced into the water.

"It was all pretty straightforward, as I remember it, like most murders. Two drunks had an argument, took it outside and it went too far. All the witnesses corroborated each other's statements, more or less, so it was just a case of finding the bastard, which was something we had you to thank for, wasn't it, Helgi?"

"Yup, stumbled across him pretty much by accident."

"Makes no difference," Thorfinnur Markússon rumbled. "You got the bastard and brought him in. So why are you here? What is it you want to know?"

"One of the witnesses, Sindri Valsson. D'you remember him?"

"Vaguely. A young chap, wasn't he?"

"Same age as the deceased, more or less. Very well connected, and with a rich dad. But he had a record."

"For what?"

"Mostly assault, but nothing recent. There are a good few arrests on his sheet for fisticuffs of one kind or another. It seems the man has something of a short fuse."

"And you think we got it wrong and he might be the real killer?"

"I don't know," Helgi admitted. "The chief thinks so, although she hasn't said so outright."

"What's this chick like, then? Good grief, serving under a woman would have been unthinkable in my day."

"She's tough and she gets results," Helgi said. "There was a scandal a good few years ago when she arrested a city councillor for drunk driving. The bloke got a bit shirty so she cuffed him, had a look in his car and found a couple of wraps of coke."

"Oh, her!" Thorfinnur Markússon whooped. "I remember that! No end of a fuss. Normally that sort of thing could have been sorted out quietly, but she wouldn't have it. I can't remember the man's name, but that was the end of politics for him."

"That must have been a good fifteen years ago. Before I joined the force."

"It was impressive," Thorfinnur Markússon said. "She was as stubborn as a mule on that one, said that the man had been abusive and she wouldn't back down. Rumour has it he called her an ugly fat bitch and said he'd have her up in front of a tribunal if she didn't back off. So what's she like to work for? Is she an ugly fat bitch?"

"She's fine," Helgi said. "Very straight, no hide-and-seek office politics. Just likes to get things done."

The hook again appeared from the water, and this time Thorfinnur laid the rod down on the bank and lit a cigarette. The mist seemed to Helgi to be thickening, and the scrubby trees at the top of the slope on the far side of the lake had dissolved into the grey shroud that surrounded them and muffled their voices.

"How about . . . ?" Thorfinnur asked, miming an hourglass figure with his hands and grinning.

"She's a big girl. Plenty up front. I'd bet she's a bundle of fun in the sack."

"A word to the wise, Helgi. Keep work and play separate. Even if she has a shirtful of goodies that could keep you happy every night of the week, it's not worth it."

Helgi felt distinctly uncomfortable and shuffled his feet, while Thorfinnur Markússon grinned broadly, sensing his embarrassment. "Lay off it, will you? I wasn't born yesterday."

"Anyone'd think you had a crush on her, Helgi," he teased.

"Yeah, right. I'm on marriage number two as it is, so I definitely need shenanigans in that department like a hole in the head," he snorted. "About this Sindri Valsson. Anything you recall?"

The retired chief inspector blew out smoke from his nose and thought for a moment before shaking his head.

"Nothing that springs to mind. I remember him vaguely: young chap, and arrogant with it. Now that you come to mention it, everything tied up very neatly, open and shut. Long Ommi confessed as nice as pie after you brought him in. But this Sindri, well, I suppose we must have interviewed and taken statements from several dozen people altogether, and I can't say that he stood out particularly."

"How about the singer?"

"You mean the one who was in the band there that night? Who'd forget that! Tits like ripe peaches and legs up to here, gorgeous. It's just a shame the poor girl was so dim," Thorfinnur said, tapping one temple with a gloved finger. "Like they say, nice bodywork, shame about the electrics. But, here! Isn't she the one who was done in?"

Helgi nodded. "That's her all right."

"Any connection there?" Thorfinnur Markússon asked sharply.

"No idea. It's starting to look that way, but nothing you could pin down. Gunna'll get to the root of it. Look, I'd better be on my way. Good to see you again, Chief. I'll pop by again in a day or two and see if you've remembered anything more."

"You do that, Helgi. Good to see a face from the past now and again," the older man said gruffly, picking up his rod and casting once more. He reeled the hook in slowly this time, his mind elsewhere as he heard Helgi's car start up and drive away. Far out on the water, ripples formed around the line and he felt a tug.

"Yah! A shame the lad didn't see that," he crowed, reeling the line in until it went slack.

"Blast!"

He reeled in the rest of the line and laid the rod down before pulling a phone from his coat pocket. He dialled a number that wasn't in the phone's memory and waited for the voicemail announcement.

"Hæ, it's your old friend. Listen. Mention to your boy that questions are being asked, all right?"

Friday 19th

IT WAS LATE morning and it was Helgi's interview. He was relaxed behind the desk while Long Ommi sat slouched in a chair opposite him. Ommi's lawyer, a middle-aged man with thick glasses and a bored manner, sat uncomfortably next to his client leafing through a sheaf of documents. Gunna felt she had been right to wear uniform for a change, deciding that it lent an air of formality to the proceedings and contrasted with Helgi's habitually baggy brown clothes. She sat back behind Helgi and admired a tapestry hung on the wall. The interview room was much airier and lighter than anyone would have imagined, with comfortable chairs and walls hung with pictures dotted about.

Helgi turned to the computer on his side of the desk and inserted a blank disk.

"You know the procedure well enough, don't you, Ommi?"

"Yeah. Been here before once or twice."

Helgi pointed a finger upwards at a microphone hanging above the desk and the opaque dome of a surveillance camera in one corner. "You're aware that everything that happens in this room is recorded?"

"Yeah. I know."

Ommi settled himself deeper in the chair and thrust his legs out in front of him, crossed at the ankles. He folded his arms, displaying lurid tattoos peeking from the sleeves of his shirt.

"All right. We're ready to roll. Present are suspect Ómar

Magnússon and legal representative Karl Einar Bjarnason, police officers Helgi Svavarsson and Gunnhildur Gísladóttir," Helgi said formally for the benefit of the recording. "Agreed?"

The lawyer nodded without looking up from his papers.

"Right, Ommi, it's been a while. How have you been keeping?" Helgi asked in a friendly tone.

"Not bad, until I saw your ugly mug in front of me," Ommi responded.

"You absconded from Kvíabryggja prison on the eighteenth of last month and set a record for being on the run. How about telling me what you've been up to in the meantime?"

The lawyer rolled his eyes towards the ceiling and Ommi bridled. "I've been keeping to myself. Having some fun with Selma. Y'know."

"And the man in the garage with you? What's your relationship with him?"

"Dunno. He just turned up."

Helgi smiled. "As it happens, we had been watching you for a couple of days. Considering you spent the best part of a week in the man's company, you must have spoken to him once or twice."

"He's just a mate," Ommi retorted.

"Don't play the fool. Addi the Pill's up to his ears in Ecstasy, and don't try and tell me that you didn't know."

Ommi shrugged. "I thought there was something dodgy about him. I'd have called the police if I'd known."

"What were the two of you doing in Selfoss? Or was that just a little drive in the country?"

"Selfoss? Never been there."

"We have definite evidence that you were there last week with Addi. What were you up to?"

"Sorry, mate. You must have made a mistake."

"What made you want to run off from Kvíabryggja?" Helgi asked cheerfully. "A year to go of your stretch in a comfortable open prison. Breakfast in bed, conjugal visits, everything a man could ask for. Come on, Ommi. There has to be a good reason."

For the first time some anger showed in a flush that suffused Ommi's face. "Mind your own business."

"This is my business." Helgi leaned back in his chair and crossed his arms to mirror Ommi, who immediately uncrossed his arms and leaned forward.

"Look, I just wanted a break, man. Been in there for too long and I felt like a break. That's it."

"I don't believe you. Someone like you doesn't do that. You had less than a year to go, now you'll get a good bit more and you'll be back in Litla-Hraun instead of comfy old Kvíabryggja."

The lawyer coughed. "Er, I ought to point out that you should not be threatening my client."

"Threatening?" Helgi asked.

"Yes, you intimated that he would receive an extended sentence. Nothing has been proved."

Helgi shook his head.

"Keflavík. A week ago. What were you doing there?" Gunna broke in.

"Keflavík? Haven't been near it."

"If you can't account for your movements, we'll have to assume that you were there. There's witness evidence to support it."

Helgi glanced to one side at Gunna, his face one big question, and Ommi grimaced.

"D'you want me to check my fucking diary?" he sneered.

"Please do. I'd love to know how Óskar Óskarsson wound up in hospital with a broken jaw, missing a few teeth, and with four broken ribs, broken fingers, bruises everywhere. Care to elaborate?"

"Nothing to do with me, but I guess he had it coming." Ommi grinned.

"Explain, please, Ómar," Gunna said quietly.

"Well, Skari's always been a twat. He's always winding up the wrong people. Sooner or later someone gives him a good smacking. It's not the first time."

"And by coincidence, someone looking remarkably like you happened to be there that very day. There are broken bones here and GBH is a serious matter. You could be looking at a good few years on top of what you've already got left."

"Fucking hell, come on, man, call her off, will you?" Ommi appealed to his lawyer, who spoke with a voice as smooth as milk.

"I have to agree with my client. This appears to be an unrelated matter and therefore I would ask that you confine your enquiries to the case in hand."

"I assure you that this is very relevant to the case," Gunna replied. "But we can come back to it. Helgi, would you continue?"

Helgi sat back and knitted his fingers together over his paunch. "Tell me about Svanhildur Mjöll Sigurgeirsdóttir."

"Who?" Ommi asked. "No idea."

"Svana Geirs."

"Svana?"

"When did you last see or speak to her?"

Ommi frowned and glared at Helgi. "Years ago, man. Years ago. We had a bit of a thing going back in the nineties. Ancient history."

"All right. Tell me about your relationship with Svana."

Ommi whistled. "That's so long ago. Like I said, we got together for a while, had some fun."

"All right, where did you meet, and when was this?"

"In some club, I guess. When, hell, I don't know. Ninety-six, something like that. Before she started to get popular. Anyway, what's all this about Svana?" he demanded. "What d'you want to know for?"

"How long were you together?" Helgi asked blandly, ignoring Ommi's question.

"Hell, a few months . . . listen, this was years ago. We were kids."

Helgi nodded, as if this were a nugget of information he had been searching for. Gunna suppressed a smile of satisfaction and watched Karl Einar Bjarnason as carefully as she watched Ommi's reactions to Helgi's questions.

"So what was the nature of your relationship with Svanhildur Mjöll? Did you live together?"

"No, we never shacked up like that. She had a flat with Elma and the other girl from that band they were in. I was around there a while."

"Where were you living?"

"Where did I live in 1996? What's all this? Are you going to let them carry on with this crap?" Ommi demanded of his lawyer, who merely shrugged in reply.

Helgi picked up a sheet of paper from the desk and pretended to consult it.

"According to the National Registry, your legal residence until you went to prison was at Hraungata 19 in Hvalvík. I take it you weren't actually living there?"

"That's where my mum lives. I haven't even been near that dump for years."

"How long did your relationship with Svanhildur Mjöll last?"

"A few months."

"Why did it come to an end?"

"I don't know. I got tired of her."

"Not because you were abusive and violent? You have a record of violence against women."

"Don't drag that up again. That was years ago, and only the once."

Helgi gazed at Ommi and tried to gauge just how angry he was getting with the line of questioning he did not see the reason for. "Isn't it true that Svanhildur Mjöll threw you over after you hit her?"

"No! I dropped her. And I never smacked her, even if I wanted to."

"Why would you want to?" Gunna broke in.

Ommi shook his head. "She was just nuts. She'd drive you mad sometimes, wanting this and that, wanting to go here or there and always right now. Maybe she's slowed down by now. Felt sorry for that poor bastard she married, twisted him right round her little finger and dropped him the minute he wasn't going to be a rich footballer."

"You mean Sigmundur Björnsson?"

"Yeah. What happened to him? He just vanished the second Svana crossed her legs." Ommi looked up truculently into Helgi's eyes, as if challenging him. "Why all this stuff about Svana?"

"You were involved with Svana, and so was Óskar Óskarsson," Helgi guessed. "You guys were the best of friends, so what was going on there?"

"Æi. Me and Skari. We were best mates and we were always trying out each other's cast-offs. I had Svana first. Then Skari had a go at her for a while. We were mates. We shared these things like mates do."

"And Skari and you aren't the best of friends these days," Helgi said. "Why's that? Where were you on Thursday last week?"

"Can't remember."

"Try. We have CCTV evidence that puts you at the N1 petrol station in Keflavík shortly before Óskar Óskarsson was admitted to hospital."

"Yeah?"

"Yeah, Ommi. Now, what happened between you and Skari? You'd been best mates since you were in kindergarten. Grew up on the same street. Went to Reykjavík together when

Hvalvík wasn't big enough any more. You were both involved in all kinds of stuff, pinching cars, flogging dope, collecting debts for Benni Sól—"

"I never worked for Benni," Ommi interrupted.

"Ah, but you did. The man told us himself that you'd run errands for him."

The lawyer coughed discreetly at Ommi's side and Helgi's voice hardened. "You. Skari. What went wrong?"

"Shit, man. We just fell out. It happens."

"Over what? Svana?"

"Well, yeah. I suppose," Ommi admitted. "She was part of it, I reckon. Skari didn't have it in him any more, went soft."

"When did you last see her?" Helgi asked.

"Svana? Hell, I don't know. Didn't see a lot of her after she got famous on TV and married that weightlifting guy, got too smart to talk to her old friends any more."

"So when did you see her last?"

"Dunno. Before you lot banged me up."

"Sure?"

"Yeah. Course I'm sure," Ommi snarled.

"My client has been asked the same question a number of times now, officer," the lawyer pointed out, trying to stifle a yawn.

"In that case it would be useful for you to explain how come we were able to retrieve your fingerprints from Svanhildur Mjöll's flat. These prints weren't more than a week old when we lifted them."

Ommi's face set hard and the lawyer's eyebrows shot upwards.

"Ommi, we have Óskar Óskarsson in hospital in Keflavík to start with. Kristbjörn Hrafnsson, better known to you as Daft Diddi, was admitted to Casualty and when asked what happened told the officers who took him there that "it wasn't Long Ommi." So why did Diddi say that? And now Svana. Did you decide to settle a few scores, just for old times' sake, Ommi?"

"What's this with Svana?"

"If you've been holed up for a few days, maybe you're a bit behind with the news. Svana Geirs was found murdered in her flat. It's common enough knowledge, but maybe you haven't been watching the news in your little hideaway?"

"Svana's dead?" Ommi asked, eyes wide.

"Yup, and your prints are in her flat."

"I think I need to talk to this guy without you listening," Ommi said, ashen-faced, turning to the now wide-awake lawyer at his side.

In the canteen, Gunna found Eiríkur talking to one of the police legal team, a sharp-faced woman who was respected but not generally liked. As Gunna made for their table, the other woman stood up, nodded and left with a stack of papers in one hand.

"What did our legal eagle have to say?" Gunna asked.

"Questions over why Addi the Pill has a broken wrist. I told her that he resisted arrest and assaulted an officer in the process."

"And was she satisfied with that?"

"Oh, yes, especially when I told her to ask Helgi for details, as he was the officer in charge of the operation. I gather she rather likes Helgi."

"Poor Helgi. Right, what did you get out of Addi the Pill?"

Eiríkur grimaced. "Shit, what a thug. Have you seen his record? There's a bit of practically everything there." He sighed to himself. "A real head case, this guy is. I've no doubt he's the one who drove Diddi to the bank and drove him away afterwards. He fits Diddi's description perfectly, doesn't have an alibi. There's a red Ford that also fits the description parked a few streets away from the house in Gardabær, registered to a sixty-three-year old woman who reported it stolen from outside her house in Reykjanesbær ten days ago, and the keys were in

Addi's jacket pocket. Technical are going over it for prints and whatever else can be found."

"Good going, young man," Gunna said approvingly.

"He's having his wrist checked by the doctor again, says it hurts. When that's done, I'll have another session with him. How goes it with Ommi?"

"He's tying himself in knots, but won't admit a thing. I'm leaving Helgi to look after him while I go for a chat with Selma."

"She's in floods of tears, or so I'm told," Eiríkur said with satisfaction. "I take it that's not going to make you go soft on her, is it?"

Gunna stood up and cracked her knuckles. "You know, Eiríkur? You lot all see me as this evil old witch who's had every shred of sympathy surgically removed. Well let me tell you, under this rough exterior there's a heart of pure stone. Don't you worry about Selma. She'll be singing like a bird before you know it."

"You know her mother's downstairs?"

"What? Evil Eygló? Well, she'll have a long wait."

SELMA WAS NO more collected or calm than she had been when she and Ommi had been delivered to the police station at Hverfisgata to be searched and checked in, while Addi the Pill was having treatment for his injuries and roaring about police brutality to anyone who would listen.

She sat tearfully opposite Gunna, who spread her elbows on the table in front of her to provide even more of an imposing figure than normal. A middle-aged man in an ill-fitting grey suit had been appointed as Selma's lawyer and sat next to her, flipping unconcernedly through sheets of notes that Gunna guessed had little to do with Selma's case.

"Is my mum here?" Selma asked querulously.

"Yup," Gunna said.

"Can I see her?"

"No."

"Why not?"

"You are aware that everything that happens in here is recorded?" Gunna asked, ignoring the question.

"Yeah."

"Right, then. I've read your statements from yesterday when you spoke to my colleague. You helped Ómar to abscond from prison? Why did you do it, Selma?"

"I didn't know he was running away," Selma wailed. "Not until he said for me to drive out of that place, y'know, whatsit-called? You have to do what Ommi says. He's a sweet guy, but he can be really angry sometimes."

"Like when?"

"If someone doesn't agree with him, or doesn't respect him properly."

"Like this person?" Gunna held out a photograph of Diddi, and Selma studied it carefully.

"I don't know," she replied innocently. "Who's that?"

"Kristbjörn Hrafnsson, otherwise known as Daft Diddi. He's a nice enough lad, but has some mental problems and has lived in a hostel for years. Right, then. The truth, please, Selma. Have you seen this guy before?" Gunna demanded.

"Yeah."

"When? Where?"

"In town. Last week. With Ommi and Addi. The guy was downtown so Ommi offered him a lift and we went for a drive around."

"Who was driving? You?"

"Yeah."

"In your mother's car?"

"No! In Ommi's car that he bought the other week. The red one."

"He bought it? Who from?"

"I don't know. Some guy."

"Some guy who stole it," Gunna said.

"Oh."

"When Diddi was in the car, what did they talk about?"

"Money and stuff. I didn't listen much."

"And what was your impression of Diddi? How did he come across? Frightened?"

"Er, maybe. A bit," Selma said after a long moment's thought.

"Come on, Selma. Don't play games with me. I think Ommi and his mate threatened Diddi and forced him to go into a bank with a knife. In fact I know so, and unless I'm convinced otherwise, I won't have much of an option but to see you as an accessory."

"Please, officer," the lawyer at Selma's side said without looking up from his notes.

"What's an access . . . sery?" Selma asked.

"It means that you would be seen as having taken part in the alleged crime," the lawyer said in a dry voice.

"But I didn't! It was them!" Selma squawked.

"Ah. So now we're getting somewhere. You're saying that Ommi and Addi forced Diddi to commit a crime?"

"Yeah," Selma said sulkily.

"What did they tell him to do?"

"They said that he owed them money from sometime years ago before your lot put my Ommi in prison. Diddi said he didn't have it. Ommi said he could help him find it and all he had to do was go into the bank and get it. Look, I was just driving them around, OK?"

"Which one of them gave Diddi a lift on the day?"

"When?"

"Don't act stupid, Selma. Which one of them drove Diddi

to the bank, parked in the next street and drove him away afterwards?"

"I don't know. Not me."

"Selma, why did Ommi abscond from Kvíabryggja?"

"Ab-what?"

"Do a runner."

Selma's shoulders rose and fell in a shrug. "Dunno."

"There has to be a good reason for it. He had less than a year to go and then he would have been out on parole. Why jeopardize that? Something to do with this Addi? Did they have some business together?"

"Dunno," Selma said quietly, the sour looked fixed to her features.

"Come on, Selma. I know you're not as thick as you make out. Ommi's going away again for a good long time and if you're not careful, so will you. What was Addi there for? Why did Ommi do a bunk? Something to do with Addi's business, or was it something else?"

"Dunno," Selma repeated stonily. "Look, I want a cigarette. I've been here for hours."

"Sorry," Gunna said. "It's a government building, so it's a smokeless zone."

It was past six o'clock when Gunna, Eiríkur and Helgi gathered to compare notes. All of them were tired after spending a full day in the interview rooms with Ommi, Selma and the taciturn Addi the Pill when he was brought back, one wrist in plaster and prepared only to comment bitterly on his ill-treatment. Gunna felt her uniform shirt sticking to her back and longed for a shower.

"I'm leaving in . . ." She looked at her watch, "five minutes and not a second longer. What have we found out?"

Helgi yawned and his phone yodelled to him as he switched it on. "Daft Diddi's escapade was orchestrated by Ommi and

Addi. No doubt. Even if Ommi didn't have a good few years of his sentence ahead of him, we'd have grounds for keeping him. We have custody for Addi and it won't be a problem to keep him in. What about Selma?"

"We're letting her out tomorrow morning. Evil Eygló has been shouting about her daughter being banged up without good cause all day, so no harm in giving her a bit more to yell about."

"Did you get anything out of Selma?" Helgi asked, scrolling through a day's worth of accumulated text messages. "Shit. Halla wanted me home at four. Oh well. It's the doghouse for me tonight," he said, almost cheerfully.

"Selma knows a lot of it, certainly more than she's letting on. What I really want to know is the Ommi-Bjartmar-Svana triangle. How do these three tie up? What are the links? Who owes who a favour? Who did Ommi do time for, and in return for what? If there was some kind of a deal, why abscond? Is Ommi acting on his own initiative or what? Did he do a runner because of something happening outside? If so, what? Was it Bjartmar he was doing the time for?"

Eiríkur looked blank. "I've no idea, chief. Really no idea. It's like talking to a wall in there. I don't know how long Addi the Pill has been sampling his own merchandise, but the guy is completely spaced out."

Gunna shuffled through papers on her desk and screwed up tired eyes to look at the screen of her computer, scrolling through new emails and deleting as she went until only a few remained. She clicked Shut Down and stood up.

"All right, gents. We've done a long day's crimebusting and I've had enough. Time to go home."

THEY ALL THREE took gulps of fresh, cold air in the car park after a day inside. Helgi was fumbling for his keys as a patrol car entered the car park and drove straight to the admittance bay.

"Eight tomorrow, Helgi? I have a feeling that overtime isn't going to be a problem for the next week or two, or at least until we have Svana Geirs sorted out."

"Suits me," Helgi said. "My exhaust's on its last legs and a bit of overtime wouldn't do any harm."

Gunna squinted into the gloom and could make out Tinna Sigvaldsdóttir, the slightly built officer who had been first on the scene of Svana Geirs' murder, getting out of the driver's seat of the patrol car while her beefy male colleague emerged from the rear seat and a heavily built man in a leather jacket was unceremoniously hauled out with his hands cuffed behind him. Gunna caught a glimpse of a florid face, and even in the half-light and at a distance, she sensed that the man was drunk. The face was vaguely familiar and she wondered where from.

"Another pisshead, I expect," Eiríkur said without a second glance.

"Ach, you don't remember what it was like when we had real drunks in this country. Hard men who'd be on the piss for a week or more and travelled round in taxis with the clock ticking and a crate of vodka in the boot," Helgi said. "Now we just get these doped-up fuckwits instead."

"So that feller should get an award, should he, for keeping alive a grand old Icelandic tradition?" Gunna suggested.

"Bugger that, he should practically be in a museum," Helgi snorted. "I have to say I regret the passing of the traditional old-school Icelandic pisshead," he added sadly, while Eiríkur stared at him and Gunna burst out laughing.

"You sound like old Haddi when you say stuff like that. Sounds like you almost mean it."

"Well, given a choice of dealing with drunks or dopeheads, I know which I'd choose," Helgi said with finality, swinging his keys on his little finger. "Need a lift, Eiríkur?"

Eiríkur hesitated, seeing Helgi's Skoda lurking in a corner of the car park.

"Go on," Gunna urged him. "I had a ride in it once, and it's not that scary."

Saturday 20th

STEINI SNORED TUNEFULLY. It wasn't an all-out rumble, or even the occasional thunderous snort. It was more a musical tenor hum, Gunna reflected, lying awake. It felt odd, even uncomfortable, to have a man in her bed regularly after so long. In the little house with its thin walls they had done their best to be quiet, not knowing if Laufey in the next room was asleep, awake, or blissfully unaware of anything other than what Steini playfully referred to as the stream of "Beatle-music" coming through her headphones.

Glancing at the clock that she knew was ten minutes fast, she saw that it wouldn't be long before it would be buzzing angrily. Swinging her legs out of bed and shivering as her feet landed on the cold tiles of the floor, she wrapped herself in a threadbare dressing gown and made for the shower.

The penetrating coffee aroma brought Steini to the kitchen, wrapped in a towel and his eyes puffy with sleep.

"G'day." He smiled. "Been up long?"

"Long enough to have a shower and make coffee. Sleep well?" He hoisted himself on to a stool and reached for a mug.

"Working overalls today?" he asked, admiring Gunna's black uniform shirt.

"Yup, more interviews today and uniform makes things a bit more formal, impresses the rabble. And it's the easy choice."

"It looks good on you, you know. Same here. When I came out of the Coast Guard it took months to get used to wearing ordinary clothes again," Steini said, hopping off the stool to open the fridge in search of milk. As he did so, the towel came adrift and left him standing naked with a carton of milk in one hand.

"Speaking of which," Gunna said with an easy smile, "while I'm quite happy to have a naked man running around my kitchen, I have to get Laufey out of bed. So it might be an idea if you put some clothes on before you give the poor girl the fright of her life."

"Fair enough. Don't want to spoil the lass for when she gets a bloke of her own," he replied, retrieving the towel and retreating to the bedroom for clothes.

"Laufey! Laufey Oddbjörg Ragnarsdóttir!" Gunna yelled, tapping on the bedroom door. "Awake? I'm going in half an hour if you want a lift to basketball."

The response was a barely audible groan, but soon enough the sound of movement could be heard and Laufey eventually appeared. "Hi, sweetheart." Gunna smiled.

"What?" Laufey demanded waspishly.

"I said good morning."

"Oh. Yeah," the girl responded, disappearing into the bathroom and shutting the door behind her with more force than was strictly necessary.

"She all right?" Steini asked, reappearing in jeans, barefoot and buttoning a check shirt.

"I hope so," Gunna said with more than a little concern. 'It might just be, y'know, ladies' lurgy. I'll see what I can get out of her."

THERE WAS NO need to probe.

"Is he your boyfriend?" Laufey asked as they passed the Vogar turning on the main road, her voice abrupt after twenty minutes of silence.

"Yes, I suppose he is," Gunna replied, trying to keep her

own voice steady in spite of the nervousness within. "Is that a problem, sweetheart?"

"No," Laufey replied, nose in the air and looking pointedly out of the window at the jagged lava fields stretching out on the landward side of the new double-lane highway leading to Reykjavík. On the other side an angry grey ocean gnawed at the black rocks of the coast in the distance, reminding Gunna that her son Gísli was at sea in this weather.

"Don't you have a boyfriend?" Gunna finally asked gently once she had told herself, as so many times before, that Gísli was safe on a big ship and she had nothing to worry about.

"Maybe. But I don't sleep with him."

"Laufey, do you have something against Steini?"

"Mum! He's like, really old! Loads older than you!"

Gunna slowed to the legal speed and let a bright red car hurtle past in the outside lane, cursing briefly under her breath as it flung a sheet of water over the windscreen.

"He's not old. At least not old as in really old. He's only a couple of years older than I am."

"Twelve," Laufey said sourly. "That's really old."

"What?" Gunna demanded. "How do you know that?"

"Mum, I'm not stupid. I looked him up in the National Registry. It's not hard and there aren't that many people called Unnsteinn Gestsson. He's almost thirteen years older than you."

She sank back into accusing silence and glared out of the window while Gunna dropped a gear and peered into the thickening gloom that shrouded the sparse morning traffic. The entire world seemed to be damp and clammy with an unbroken succession of low grey clouds scudding in from the Atlantic. Ahead in the damp gloom she saw a flash of orange lights and gently braked.

"What now?" she muttered to herself.

"What?" Laufey demanded, looking up.

"Trouble ahead," Gunna said, clicking on the hazard lights as she slowed the car to a crawl and brought it on to the gravel at the side, behind two cars half across one lane.

"Laufey, would you pass me my coat from the back seat, please?" she asked, eyes on the cloud of steam rising from the little red car that she recognized as the one that had sped past a minute before, its bonnet crumpled into the side of a larger grey car. She shrugged herself into the thick parka, checked the mirror and opened the door to get out, passing her phone to Laufey as she did so.

"Sweetheart, I want you to call 112. Tell them who you are, who I am, and that there's a road traffic accident on Reykjanes-braut, eastbound, four kilometres past the Vogar turnoff. OK?"

"OK, Mum," Laufey replied, eyes wide as Gunna assumed a different, unfamiliar, businesslike persona.

"I'd best go and see if anyone's hurt. I'll be right back, OK?"

Gunna recognized one of the paramedics who arrived a few minutes later to casually ease a shocked young man from the wreck of the red car and a whiplashed elderly couple from their dented Volvo as the same young man who had attended Svana Geirs' flat.

"Hæ again, how are you?" he enquired with a cheery smile as the shaken old couple were taken away in one ambulance and the young man sat, grey-faced and wrapped in a blanket, on the step of the other one. "Not as bad as the last one, eh?"

"Could have been so much worse," Gunna agreed. "Silly bastard shouldn't have been driving that fast in this weather."

"Nope, hopefully these three will all be right as rain soon enough. Shame about their cars, though. You don't see so many of those old Volvos these days," he observed as a burly pair in orange all-weather overalls that made them look like cuddly toys winched the Volvo on to a truck while a uniformed officer from the Keflavík station watched.

"Hæ, Gunna. How goes it?" the officer greeted her with a smile.

"Snorri! Good to see you. It goes well enough, I suppose. Shame I have to stop and help you lot out on the way to work."

"You saw it happen, did you?"

"No. Just saw the red car go belting past and then saw them by the side of the road a minute later."

"Fair enough. I'll have to get a statement from you later."

Gusts of wind whipped rain across the road and into their faces.

"Right, that's us done," the paramedic announced. "We'll take matey here away and I'll leave the clearing-up to you guys," he said happily, and ushered the young man to a seat in the back of the ambulance, still wearing his grey blanket like a refuge.

"Thanks, mate," Snorri said to the paramedic and turned to Gunna. "When can I catch up with you, chief?"

"I'll drop in at your station tomorrow, if you like. Or you can stop by at home this evening. Up to you."

"OK. I'll see you tomorrow. I guess you need your peace and quiet of an evening these days," he said with a wink that bordered on a leer, waving as he got into his own car.

"The jungle drums are working overtime now," Gunna grumbled, getting back into the Range Rover where Laufey was busily texting.

"All right, sweetheart? You'd have been quicker on the bus today," she apologized.

"That's all right, Mum."

"Who are you texting?"

"Just letting them know I'm a bit late. Mum?"

"Yes, sweetheart?"

"Mum, why don't you see Snorri any more?"

"Because we're not working together now I'm back on the city force."

"Shame."

"Why's that?"

"Snorri's lush. He's loads lusher than Steini."

Gunna sighed.

"He'd be much better for you," Laufey continued slyly.

"Good grief, young lady," Gunna exploded. "It's enough that the whole bloody force seems to be clued up on my private life without you chipping in as well."

"But why not?"

Gunna shook her head in despair. "One, Snorri is a dozen years younger than I am. Two, he has a girlfriend. Three, I don't fancy him, even if he is lush. How's that?"

"I suppose . . ." Laufey conceded, lapsing into a silence that she did not break until the red-and-white checks of the aluminium factory appeared ahead.

"Mum?"

"Yes, sweetheart?"

"How do you get to be a paramedic?"

"I THOUGHT WE needed to have another chat, Selma," Gunna said cheerily.

Selma slouched in the chair and glared back truculently at Gunna, who had become certain that this young woman could be the key to unlocking a few mysteries.

"Had some breakfast, have you?" Gunna asked.

"I don't do breakfast. It's bad for you."

"All right, that's up to you. Now, can you account for your movements on the eighteenth of last month?"

"Duh. What day was that?"

"The day that you drove up to Rif and collected Ommi."

"Oh, that day," Selma said and lapsed back into silence.

"And?" Gunna prompted.

"I went up there to visit him, like I normally do, and . . ."

"And?"

"Well, he had a day pass so we could go out for a few hours. So we did."

Selma sat in thought for a moment and Gunna began to wonder if she had fallen asleep.

"Then he just said, 'I'm not going back inside. You're taking me south.' So that's what we did."

Gunna consulted a page of her notebook. "If you say so. Now, I've spoken to the prison authorities, and normally you visit on the second and fourth weekends of each month. So why was this visit in the middle of the week? You'd only been there a few days before, hadn't you?"

"Yeah, well, Ommi asked me to, didn't he?" Selma shifted uncomfortably in her chair, lifting herself from a slouch to sit up and perch forward, hands in front of her.

"I don't know. I'm asking you."

"Yeah. That's it. He asked me to come and see him. Said he'd got a day pass and we could go out for a few hours," she repeated.

"Do you normally do that?"

"Yeah."

"So where do you go?"

"Just for a drive, look around a bit."

"Do you have a job, Selma?"

"Not any more. I'm disabled. Nerves."

"Yet someone with your poor disposition can drive up to the far end of Snæfellsnes, pick up an absconding prisoner, drive him back to Reykjavík and then help him evade the police?"

"Yeah, well. It's Ommi, isn't it?"

"What does that mean?" Gunna enquired.

"Ommi's, well . . ." She shrugged, as if that were answer enough.

"I'm just wondering if it really was Ommi who asked you to drive up there and collect him."

Selma looked thunderstruck. "Course it was. Who else?"

"Plenty of people have an interest in him. Could be any one of them. I gather Ommi had some unfinished business to attend to. Tell me about it."

Selma yawned in spite of herself, puncturing the tough image she had been trying to project. "Y'know, Ommi came back with me, like he asked. I dropped him off near the bus station and he went to do his stuff. I don't know what."

"Tell me about Diddi."

"Who?"

"Don't play the fool, Selma. You know who Daft Diddi is. Why did Ommi want to see him?"

"Did he?"

"Ommi gave him a beating to start with. Why?"

"Æi, something about some job years ago. I don't know what."

"What sort of job?" Gunna asked with a new note of iron in her voice.

"Æi," Selma repeated and pouted. "It's Ommi's business. I don't know."

"You bloody well do. Ommi's already told us all sorts of interesting stuff that doesn't do you too many favours. Now you'd better start talking some sense for once if you don't want to wind up doing a stretch yourself for being an accessory," Gunna grated, eyebrows knitted into a single dark bar of determination across her forehead.

"Diddi used to deliver stuff for Ommi. That time you lot banged him up, Diddi'd been taking some stuff somewhere and hadn't come back with the cash. So Ommi wanted his money," Selma gabbled. "Diddi didn't have it 'cos he'd spent it ages ago, so Ommi told him to get it or else."

"So that's why Diddi tried to raid a bank?"

Selma nodded morosely.

"What 'stuff' are we talking about here?"

"Es and some coke," Selma replied. "A bit of everything."

"And where was this stuff coming from?"

"Dunno. That club, maybe?"

"Which club's that?"

"The one Ommi used to work at."

"Blacklights?"

"Yeah."

"Now we're getting somewhere," Gunna said. "D'you want anything, Selma? Coffee perhaps?"

Selma shook her head.

"The fight outside Blacklights. You were there that night. What do you remember?"

"That was years ago!" Selma protested.

"I know. But what did you see?"

"Nothing."

"Ah, but you did. You gave a statement at the time," Gunna said, lifting typewritten sheets from under her notebook. "According to your statement, the deceased, Steindór Hjálmarsson, threatened Ómar Magnússon during an argument at the bar. Then there was an altercation later during which Steindór received serious injuries. He died in hospital two days later."

Selma fidgeted in her seat and glared at Gunna with her face puckered in irritation. "I'm not saying anything."

"Half a dozen people gave statements, you included," Gunna continued as if Selma had not spoken. "Ómar confessed to having been in a fight with Steindór and to having hit him several times, both while he was on his feet and when he was on the ground."

"Yeah. And?"

"It all fits far too comfortably. Look, Selma, I've been a copper for a long time and I've split up any number of fights. If there are five witnesses, you get five different versions. Here we have half a dozen witness statements and they all dovetail just right. Steindór threatened Ommi. Later they meet up outside and there's a bit of fisticuffs that goes too far. Everyone agrees, Ommi is bang to rights and confesses as sweet as you like. I'd like to know what really happened. Who killed Steindór Hjálmarsson and why? Because I'm damn sure it wasn't Ommi."

"I can't tell you," Selma said finally in a small voice.

"Why's that?"

"I don't know who did it."

"But it wasn't Ommi?"

"No. He was with me."

"All right. Why?"

"He got paid for it."

"What, for doing the time for someone else?"

Selma nodded.

"Are you going to tell me who it was?"

"Don't know. I never asked. Ommi never told me. He just said we'd be all right after he came out."

"So what happened then? Why didn't he just finish his sentence quietly?"

"We were going to leave. Take the cash and go to Spain or somewhere. That was the plan, just disappear somewhere hot and not come back."

Tears had begun to roll down Selma's cheeks, taking with them smears of make-up that Gunna guessed had been there for days. She began to cry quietly, her words coming out in fits and starts between sobs.

"Ommi was really angry. He could be just totally crazy when he was angry. Said I should come up there and get him when he next had a day pass 'cos he had business to do in town. He said that he'd been double-crossed and the man he was doing time for didn't have the money to pay him for being there any more so he was going to sort things out himself," Selma said quickly, the words tumbling out. She took a deep breath that ended on a sob. "I was frightened. Really frightened. Ommi can be so scary when he's in a rage."

"I see," Gunna said as Selma's sobs receded and developed into hiccoughs. "And you don't know who this person is?"

"It's somebody rich. That's all I know."

"No ideas, no suspicions?"

Selma shook her head. "No. If I knew, I'd tell you. I never wanted to ask who Shorty was."

"Shorty?"

"Ommi always called him Shorty. He said Shorty would see us all right. And now Shorty won't."

"Yes? Can I help you?" asked a young woman who appeared around the side of the house with a disarming smile. "I was in the garden, didn't hear the bell the first time," she explained as a small boy hid behind her legs.

"You must be Hulda Björk?"

"Yes, that's me."

"My name's Gunnhildur Gísladóttir, I'm from the police, the Serious Crime Unit. I'd like to ask you a few questions about Steindór Hjálmarsson," she said, and the smile disappeared from the woman's face as if it had been turned off with a switch.

In the long garden Hulda Björk collected herself and they sat in the lee of the house's back wall in a patch of sunshine that had fought its way through a break in the thick cloud.

"That's a name I didn't expect to hear," she told Gunna.

"I'm sorry if I've reopened old wounds, but it's a serious case and I'm afraid I might have some uncomfortable questions."

Hulda Björk breathed deep and set her face firmly. "I'm OK now. Just ask."

"As you can imagine, it's Steindór's death that I'm interested in, and particularly the events leading up to it, but especially his, your, circumstances. How were you living at the time? Were you both working?"

"We rented a flat out in Mosfellsbær. We were both from

Dalvík and felt more comfortable up there out of town than down in the city. I was finishing my teaching degree and Steindór was an accountant with a job at an import-export company. It was fun, we were enjoying living in Reykjavík, but we both agreed that when we had children, we'd want to move back up north somewhere. Not Dalvík, but maybe Akureyri. Now I can't even visit Dalvík any more without it all coming back. Every house and every street remind me of him."

"But you're settled here now?"

"Yes. I met someone. Never expected to. He's been great and now we have Gunnar as well," she said, her proud gaze following the small boy as he rode unsteadily around the garden on a bicycle with stabilizers. "I never thought I'd get over it when Steindór . . . died so suddenly."

"I'm interested especially in the days and weeks leading up to his death. How was he? Was there anything odd you noticed about his behaviour?"

Hulda Björk spread her hands, palms upwards. "It's hard to say. We were both so busy then and not seeing as much of each other as we would have liked. Steindór was a workaholic. He'd work hours of overtime and he'd always been like that—a little obsessive. If there was something that interested him, he'd absorb himself in it. It was a bit annoying sometimes and I dreaded the thought of him discovering golf."

"But no unusual behaviour?"

"It's so hard to think back. He was a bit preoccupied. I don't think he enjoyed the job he was doing, but it was quite well paid and we needed the money after all those years of being poor students."

"The night he was attacked. Were you there?"

"No," Hulda Björk said abruptly. "It was some kind of outing with his uni friends. I wouldn't have gone anyway. It was a boy thing."

"Had either of you ever had any kind of acquaintance with Ómar Magnússon?"

"You mean the bastard who . . .?" Hulda Björk's eyes flashed with a sudden fury. "Of course not," she spat. "Neither of us had ever laid eyes on that scumbag. I saw him in court, sitting there with a smirk on his face. If I could meet him now, I'd . . ."

Her face was set in a hard mask.

"So there was no reason that you could think of for the assault on Steindór, other than, as Ómar alleged, that they had been arguing?"

"Nothing. I'm certain their paths never crossed. I suppose it's possible they could have had an argument. Steindór didn't drink often, but he enjoyed it when he did and could be quite boisterous. Whatever, that's no reason for beating him so badly that he died, surely?"

"No. But these people live by different rules," Gunna said sadly. "Can you tell me more about Steindór's colleagues and his work?"

Hulda Björk shook her head. "Not really. He hadn't worked there for more than a couple of months and didn't like it much, but the money was good. I don't think he got on well with the office manager. I met her once, a very cold woman, I thought."

"So what was he doing there?"

"Bookkeeping and invoicing, as far as I remember. He used to tell me and it went right over my head. Sometimes he had to talk to people in Taiwan or Nigeria, places they exported to."

"Exports?"

"Fish, mostly. Stockfish to west Africa, herring to the Ukraine, all sorts. That's what he was working with for the most part. But there was some property as well, buying and selling commercial buildings, I think. Workshops and shops, that sort of thing."

"Do you remember what the company was called, or if it still exists?"

"Kleifaberg Trading, at least the part that Steindór worked for. They used to have offices in the city centre, off Tryggvagata, I think."

"And there's nothing else that springs to mind? Nothing about Steindór's behaviour that you recall as being anything different?"

Hulda Björk shrugged. "I've tried to remember everything, but there's so much that's too hazy. You try and recall these things but it's like they're just that little way out of reach. Know what I mean? Of course you don't," she added.

"Actually I do," Gunna said quietly. "I know precisely what you mean and I know how hard it is when someone is taken away in a flash."

Hulda Björk looked at her with a new recognition, half screwing up her eyes against the unaccustomed spring sunshine that shone in her face and highlighted the band of freckles across her nose. She stood up and cast about the garden for the small boy, who had gone quiet.

"He must be up to something if he's not making a noise," she said, forcing a smile. "I don't think there's anything more I can tell you."

Gunna laid a card on the slats of the garden table. "My number's there. I'd appreciate a call if there's anything you remember."

"Ah, there he is," Hulda Björk said. She pointed to her son at the far end of the garden, using a bamboo cane to push an offcut of wood across a puddle. "I'd better stop him before he gets too filthy."

She turned to Gunna awkwardly.

"I'm sorry. I don't think I've been a lot of help to you somehow," she apologized. "But there's a friend of Steindór's you might want to talk to. He was at college with us. I haven't seen him for a long time, but he works for a magazine now. Gunnlaugur Ólafsson, his name is."

THE BASTARD HAD a big enough house, Jón thought, staring at the sprawling building on the far side of the quiet street. He'd taken a detour to see the place yet again. He had done this more than once, stopping by the curb on the other side of the road to glare at the house with its double garage, set between lines of young birch trees that already were bushy enough to shield the place from prying eyes either side.

Jón's own house had been away down the hill in a decent, yet less exclusive neighbourhood. If things hadn't gone so terribly wrong, Ragna Gústa could have found herself mixing with children at school from this very street.

Jón knew that Bjartmar and his snobby wife had no children. The gossip around town was that they weren't getting on well lately, and that the man had set up some woman he'd brought to Iceland with a business in the city centre. Jón didn't make a habit of listening to gossip, but any mention of the bastard who had tipped his business over the edge was always going to make him prick up his ears.

He sighed, gritted his teeth and started the van's engine. A woman in the western end of town with two small children was waiting for him to again patch up the worn-out washing machine that she couldn't afford to replace.

"YOU KNOW SOMEONE called Gunnlaugur Ólafsson?" Gunna asked, phone to her ear as she marched across the street to her car.

"Er. Not sure," Skúli said slowly. "Know anything more about him?"

"Not a lot," Gunna replied, switching the phone to the other ear as she unlocked the car and got inside. "He'd be in his early thirties, works for a magazine."

"Sales or editorial?"

"No idea. Editorial, I guess."

"I'll ask around, see what I can find. Is that all right?"

"Skúli, that would be wonderful," Gunna said, realizing that she had been unnecessarily sharp with him.

"Cool. Leave it with me, then," Skúli said crisply, and closed the connection before Gunna could say anything more.

She started the car and listened to the engine hum into life. She let it roll gently down the street and stopped at the end, wondering whether to go left or right at the junction. A few years of frantic property speculation had left the sprawling peripheries of the city criss-crossed with streets that she had no recollection of, as well as confusing new junctions that appeared to lead nowhere, left unfinished as the estates they were supposed to reach were boarded up.

She opted to turn left, immediately regained her bearings and decided to continue through the quiet estate of houses set back from the speed-bump-studded road. This was a smart neighbourhood, not fashionable, but populated by younger, two-and three-car families who clearly took the look of their homes seriously.

Gunna's phone rang and she pulled over to the side of the road to answer it. "Skúli, that was quick."

"And easy as well. Someone knew the guy straight away. He shortens his name to Gulli Ólafs, that's what threw me."

"Understandable. But do you know where I can find him?"

"You're not going to give him a story before me, are you?" Gunna could hear the grin behind his voice.

"Of course not. Hey, are you back at Dagurinn?"

"Yeah, just covering a few shifts for someone else." Skúli's cheerful tone vanished. "Two days a week at the moment. Gulli Ólafs works for a business magazine called Verslun. It went bust last year and someone came along and bailed them out, so it's still running and he is one of only about half the staff they kept on. They used to be in smart offices on Borgartún, but now they're above a garage down at Grandi."

"Excellent. Thanks, Skúli."

"No problem. Just wondering, do you have anything to tell me?"

"Not right now. But progress is being made. I'll let you know when I can say anything. Keep your eyes open, though. This could be bigger than I thought. But not a word out of place. All right?"

"You know, Gunna? Anyone else saying that and I wouldn't believe them for a second."

"But you know you can trust your Auntie Gunnhildur, don't you?"

"If you say so," he said dubiously.

"OH YES. ARE we just the finest detectives around or what?" Eiríkur asked, rubbing his hands with pleasure.

"We are, Gunna and me. Don't know about you, young feller," Helgi grunted in reply.

"Don't mind him, Eiríkur. He's had a bad night," Gunna said. "Teething again, Helgi?"

"Yup." Helgi yawned.

"Put 'em to sleep, boys. Calpol works wonders. I'd have cheerfully strangled both of mine without it," Gunna said. "What have you found that's making you so happy, then?"

Eiríkur put a stack of printouts on his desk and patted them. "Witness statements from the Ómar Magnússon case. Dug them out from the archives, and guess what? There are a couple of very interesting witnesses who say they saw Ómar having an argument with Steindór Hjálmarsson the night he was murdered."

He paused for effect.

"Go on, get it over with," Helgi grumbled.

"There's a statement from the lead singer of the band, Svanhildur Mjöll Sigurgeirsdóttir, and also from one of the doormen, Óskar Óskarsson, currently in hospital in Keflavík."

"Weren't you on that case, Helgi?" Gunna asked.

"Not really. I was with the team that arrested Ommi, but it wasn't actually him we were looking for. If I recall correctly, we were searching Evil Eygló's summer house for stolen goods when Ommi came wandering out of the bedroom rubbing his eyes. I don't know which of us was more surprised."

"So Skari and Svana both gave witness statements saying that Ommi and Steindór had a ruck?" Gunna asked.

"Yup. That's it. There are plenty more and I thought I'd check through the rest of them, just to see if there might be a name that pops up anywhere, and there's one that made me think. Sindri Valsson, the man's name is. He was also interviewed at the time and claimed not to have been aware of anything. So I did a bit of a check and it seems he lives overseas now, Portugal."

"Any relation to . . .?"

"Spot on. Jónas Valur Hjaltason's son. It threw me to start with because he calls himself Valsson and not Jónasson. But he's still a director of a few of his dad's companies, including the one that owns property in Portugal and Spain, and he's also a director of one of Bjartmar Arnarson's companies, Rigel Investment."

"So how did you stumble on all this?"

"Well, I'd already been checking out the ownership of Rigel Investment and saw the name there as a director. It wasn't until I saw the witness statement in his name that it jogged my memory and I put two and two together. But guess what? He was here last week, left on Friday on a flight to London."

"How did you find that out so fast?"

"I had a look through the passenger list archive and it seems he's a regular traveller, four or five times a year normally."

VERSLUN OCCUPIED A cramped space with a row of desks along one wall decorated with posters from the magazine's more prosperous days. A sharp-faced young man with gelled hair looked up from the front desk.

"Yes?"

"Gunnlaugur Olafsson?"

He looked at her suspiciously.

"Gulli's in a meeting. Is it important?" he demanded sharply. "What's it about?"

Gunna felt her hackles rise. She dug in her pocket and flashed her police ID card at him.

"Yes, it is important, and no, I'm not going to discuss it with you. Where is he?"

The young man deflated and retreated, opening a glass door and holding a conversation in whispers, punctuated with quick looks over one shoulder.

"Gulli'll be right with you," he said, returning and sitting back at his desk, where he proceeded to ignore Gunna and concentrate on the computer in front of him. In the glass door behind him, Gunna noticed a reflection of the young man's screen and saw he was devoting his attention to his Facebook page. Finally the glass door opened and a tall man with a harassed manner came out, sweeping a lock of untidy hair away from his face and frowning.

"You're looking for me?" he asked doubtfully.

"Yup, Gunnhildur Gísladóttir. Serious Crime Unit. A quiet word would be useful."

"I recognize you," Gulli Olafs said, eyes narrowed. "There was a feature about you in a newspaper last year, wasn't there?"

"There was," Gunna said gravely. "I can see that my notoriety goes before me."

"What do you want to talk about?"

"Can we go somewhere quiet?"

Gulli Olafs held his hands up and looked around the cramped office with its desks and a few booths. "There's nowhere right now. The meeting room's in use and I don't know how long they'll be. Is it something particular you want to ask me about?"

"Yes. Steindór Hjálmarsson."

Startled, Gulli Olafs took a step back and then looked around him. "I think we'd better go outside," he said heavily, nodding his head almost imperceptibly at the young man at the front desk.

They walked the few hundred metres to Grandakaffi, one of the workmen's cafés. It looked to be thirty years behind the times in the increasingly smart dock area, but still saw a thriving trade for its traditionally down-to-earth food.

"Been here before?" Gulli Olafs asked as they went into the quiet café with the lunchtime rush over.

"Many times," Gunna assured him, taking coffee and a roll, and fumbling for coins.

"No, on me," Gulli Olafs said, handing over a note and asking for a receipt, which he folded carefully away.

They sat in the far corner of the glass-fronted extension and Gunna noticed that deep stress lines ran across Gulli Olafs forehead, making him look older than he was.

"Steindór Hjálmarsson. You knew him well, or so Hulda Björk tells me?"

"Yes. I was one of his closest friends, one of his few close friends. You've spoken to Hulda?"

"I have. Steindór's death is linked indirectly to an investigation that we have in progress at the moment, not something I can say too much about. But I'm trying to get a picture of what happened, and why."

"Omar Magnússon, I suppose?" Gulli Olafs asked with a sideways look.

"Well, yes. It's not hard to put two and two together."

"Not when you're dealing with gossip all day long it isn't. I knew he had escaped from prison and wondered why. His sentence must be almost up by now."

"Well, no. There's about a third of it left to go, but he would have been up for parole at the end of this year and would probably have been out if he'd kept quiet and behaved himself. He's not someone you ever had any dealings with?"

"God, no," he said with a shudder. "I saw him at the trial and I have to say that he was one of the most evil people I have ever set eyes on. He just radiated arrogance and . . . How should I put it? There was a ruthlessness about him that was quite unnerving. Absolutely no shred of remorse to be seen."

"That about sums up Long Ommi," Gunna agreed. "I'm particularly interested in Steindór in the weeks before his death. Was there anything about him that was odd, different, maybe?"

Gulli Ólafs stared out of the window across the wasteland between the café and the empty dock and to the shell of the unfinished opera house on the far side of the harbour.

"Steindór had graduated the year before and had fallen into a fairly decent job at that import-export company. He wasn't happy there. He was being given more work than he was able to do comfortably and he was also doing work for other companies within the group, which had a very wide portfolio of business. There was fish, there were cars, scrap metal, electrical goods, all sorts," he said finally, speaking slowly as if trying to recall every detail.

"Kleifar? Or Kleifaberg, maybe?"

"That's it. But they were getting into property as well. This was before the banks were privatized and property prices hadn't started to shoot up. If I'd known, I'd have bought a house then," he added ruefully. "But about a fortnight before the, um, incident, Steindór came to see me. I was in my first real job as well, as a reporter on a daily back then. Steindór said that he was sure there was something going on that he wasn't comfortable with. Kleifaberg and a couple of others were buying up property at an unprecedented rate, a lot of it owned by the city, at some surprisingly low prices. It was being practically given away. This was land that has housing estates and hypermarkets on it today."

"A bit of insider trading going on?"

"Exactly. Some highly placed people within the city council were allowing potentially very valuable properties to be sold quietly to their friends."

"So what did you do? What did Steindór want you to do?"

"He was giving me a fantastic story, but unfortunately it was a bit too dynamite. It reflected badly on his employers and several municipal authorities. He promised me more information and some documents to back him up."

"But then he was killed in a fight?"

"Precisely."

Gulli Ólafs stared out of the window, where a fat black fly buzzed in the corner. He sighed deeply. "I had nothing to go on. No evidence, no documents. I asked some uncomfortable questions but got only fudged answers in response. The guy who was my editor at the time didn't want me to pursue it and discouraged me from digging into it."

"So what did you do?"

"There wasn't anything I could do. There were no real avenues open to investigate. Look, I was the new boy in the office. I'd been told in no uncertain terms that if I were to continue digging into this, my career would finish before it had begun. Then I had a warning."

Gunna frowned. "What sort of warning?"

"I remember it like it was yesterday. I left the office late one evening and was surprised when I got to the car and found it wasn't locked, but just thought I must have forgotten. So I got in and was about to turn the key when there was a hand around my neck."

"What? Someone was in the back seat?"

"Yeah, and a rope. Whoever it was pulled a rope round my

throat and round the back of the seat until I was practically choking. He said, very clearly, "Back off. Leave it. You know what." That was it. A deep voice. That's all I can say. Didn't see anything."

"You didn't go to the police?"

"God, no. I was terrified. Went home, threw up, bolted the door and stayed in for a week. It's a long time ago now, but I still wake up in the night sometimes. That's the first time I've told anyone about this, ever."

"I see. It may be a stupid question, but do you have any idea who it might have been, or who was sending you a message?"

Gulli Ólafs shrugged. "I'm as sure as it's possible to be that it was something to do with Kleifaberg or the people who owned it, and still do."

"And that is . . . ?"

"He doesn't do quite so much these days, but I guess Jónas Valur has made his pile and prefers to spend most of his time on a golf course in Portugal, especially now that he's a highly respectable figure and a well-known party stalwart."

Jónas Valur Hjaltason glowered. The urbane businessman with the convincingly sincere smile Gunna had spoken to before was gone, replaced by a snarling man who radiated suspicion.

"Where's your son?" she asked without any kind of preamble, after she had brought him unwillingly to his front door.

"He's overseas. He doesn't live in Iceland these days."

"Where?"

"You'll have to ask him that yourself."

"You're aware that obstructing an investigation is an offence?" Gunna snapped.

"I'm not obstructing anything. I don't know his whereabouts." Jónas Valur stood defensively in the doorway of the expensive flat that Gunna could see glimpses of behind him.

"Come on. Don't try and spin me a line. The man's a co-director of several of your companies. Do you seriously expect me to believe that you don't know where to find him?"

"I have email addresses. But I don't have a physical address." Gunna's look told Jónas Valur that she knew he was lying blatantly. "What do you want to talk to him about? Maybe I could send him a message and ask him to contact you?" he suggested with the ghost of a smile.

"He was in Iceland last week. He flew to London on Friday. Why did he leave so suddenly?"

"Sindri was here to see his mother, who is seriously ill. I only saw him for an hour before he flew back to Europe. I had no foreknowledge that he was going to be here."

"So where is he now?"

Jónas Valur spread his palms in answer.

"When do you expect to see him again?"

"I have no idea. Sindri has his own business interests overseas and has steadily had less and less involvement with this company, to the point that he takes practically no active part in the running of Kleifar any more."

"What about Kleifaberg?"

"What?"

"You heard."

"Kleifaberg is a company we wound up years ago."

"Why?"

"I don't know what you know about these things, officer, but Kleifaberg had served its purpose. That particular line of business came to an end, so the company was wound up. It's as simple as that."

"What kind of business?"

"Haven't you done your homework?" Jónas Valur asked. "I'd have thought you'd know already."

"I've asked a few questions and not had many favourable reports of it. So I'd like to hear it from you."

The return of the urbane persona alarmed Gunna. It told her that Jónas Valur was no longer on the defensive.

"Kleifaberg was a property development operation on a fairly small scale. We bought land and either developed it ourselves or found suitable partners who were capable of taking on projects like that."

"And this was principally Sindri's business?"

"It was. He's a smart boy, my son," Jónas Valur said, unable to conceal his pride. "He saw the writing on the wall and listened to the analysts. He sold up his interests and shifted overseas to a more stable business environment. He was, I believe, the only one who was pragmatic enough to get out in good time. As it happens, he could have held on for another year or more. But . . ."

The spread palms finished the sentence.

"What I'd like to know, officer, is why you are taking an interest in a smallish company like Kleifaberg, which no longer exists, which always operated entirely legally, and the activities of which were mostly so long ago that they fall under various statutes of limitations."

"I think you know I can't tell you that. But I think you also know as well as I do that your son has some questions to answer."

"Mum, are you going to be long?" Laufey asked as Gunna tried to make out what she was saying over the rumble of wheels on tarmac. In spite of the crackle of the poor connection, she instinctively realized that something was not right.

"What's the matter, sweetheart?" she asked, eyes on the road, one finger to her ear to push the earpiece a little more firmly into place.

"I don't know. Sigrún's really unhappy about something. She's been crying and all sorts."

"Fifteen minutes. I'm on the way."

"Thanks, Mum."

Gunna put her foot down a little harder. At the turnoff, she coasted the Range Rover down the brand-new slip road to the roundabout underneath it that she was sure would become an impassable snow trap if the south-west were ever to see snow on the scale that she had grown up with in the west of Iceland, and accelerated as the road south opened up before her.

The black lava fields that from a distance appeared devoid of life were starting to sprout the first green lichens of spring, which was bursting out of its winter dormancy now that the temperature was rising. She checked carefully before swinging the heavy car across the road to overtake a slow-moving truck laden with tubs of fish on its way south, and quickly wound down the window to extend a hand and wave to the driver, one of Haddi's relatives, taking freshly landed fish to a processing plant in Grindav'k. The truck's lights flashed briefly in acknowledgement before it disappeared behind a bend in the road.

Gunna brought the car to a halt in a flurry of gravel outside Sigrún's house and pocketed phone and keys before jumping down and striding straight round to the back door.

"Hæ! Anyone live here?" she called out, opening the kitchen door and looking inside. A row of bulging bin liners greeted her.

"Sigrún? You in?" she shouted, slipping off her shoes and padding into the house.

A stifled sob told her where to look. In the bedroom, Sigrún sat on the end of the bed surrounded by piles of clothes.

"Hey, what's up?" Gunna asked.

"Sod him. I've had enough," Sigrún said through a voice choked with frustration. "Bloody men, nothing but trouble."

Gunna sat down next to her and surveyed the stacks of shirts, jeans, jackets and socks. "What's gone wrong?"

"Bloody Jörundur. He went to Norway with that bunch

from where he used to work. He's been there a week. Just a bloody, sodding, bastard week, that's all. I got a text this afternoon saying he's not coming home, he's staying in Norway and would I send his stuff."

"He's not on the piss again, is he?"

"If only that was all," Sigrún said despairingly. "The bastard. I called him half a dozen times but he's not answering his phone. So I gave up and called his sister, asked what the hell's happening, and she finally told me. Jörundur's been seeing a woman over in Keflavík, and she's gone to Norway with him. His sister finally admitted it. She's not that bright and it didn't take long to get the truth out of her."

"Æi, Rúna. I'm so sorry . . ." Gunna began.

"Don't be. I'm best rid of the bastard."

She sat clear-eyed on the edge of the bed and surveyed the contents of the wardrobes, feet extended in front of her and rocking back and forth.

"You know, I always knew this would happen, always. I always knew deep inside that he'd let me down sooner or later. Eventually I wouldn't be what he wanted any more and he'd be gone. Why didn't I admit it to myself? Have I been in denial all these years, or what?"

"What have you done with Jens?" Gunna asked, feeling foolish.

"I asked Laufey to go to the shop for me and she took him as well. Couldn't face going out right now, especially now that all the old bags down there will have heard the news," she said bitterly. "Unless they knew it before I did. Did you know, Gunna? Did you?" Sigrún asked, turning to face her.

"No, I didn't. I had my suspicions that things weren't right. But no, I didn't know about his other woman."

"Sure?" Sigrún asked. "I need to be certain at least one person wasn't in on it. Jörundur even told his sister, and that's as good as putting an announcement on the radio."

"I had no idea," Gunna assured her. "You know I've always had reservations about the man, but I never thought he'd do this."

"All right then," Sigrún allowed grudgingly, her shoulders sagging.

"So what are you going to do with all this lot?" Gunna asked, waving a hand at the stacks of clothes.

"I told his sister to come and collect it."

"Is she on the way, then?"

Sigrún stood up with a tough expression on her face that Gunna had not seen for years. "I don't know and I don't care. I'm going to bag it all up and she can collect it from either the front step or the dump."

When Laufey returned with Jens crying in his pushchair and shopping bags hung from both handles, she found them enthusiastically stuffing clothes into black bin liners as the heap on the floor diminished and the wardrobes looked increasingly bare.

"That's a lot of clothes," Laufey observed doubtfully, holding Jens's hand as he took faltering steps into the room. Sigrún swept him up in her arms.

"Your daddy's an unfaithful lying bastard, little man," she crooned to the little boy, who grinned and gurgled back. "And if he comes back, I'm going to cut his balls off with a blunt kitchen knife and then Auntie Gunna can lock him up in a smelly cellar on stale bread and water for ever and ever."

"HOW'S YOUR FRIEND?" Steini asked softly, looking up from the book in his hands.

"Ach, she's all right. Well, she's not, but she will be in a day or two."

Steini lifted his feet off the sofa and Gunna shrugged out of her coat and draped it over the back of one of the kitchen chairs. She hobbled over and dropped herself down next to him. He leaned over for a kiss, sandwiching the book uncomfortably between them.

"So what happened?" he asked.

"Sigrún's husband, Jörundur, has been out of work since the crash. Then he got an offer through some blokes he'd worked with before, some big construction job in Norway, a tunnel or something. So he went to Norway to check it out and hopefully do a couple of weeks' work. But what he didn't tell anybody was that there's a woman he's been having it off with on the sly since Christmas, and she went with him."

"Ah, the perils of middle age," Steini said with a rueful nod. "Pleased to be past all that."

"Get away with you. Anyway, he's decided to stay there with his new woman, and the first Sigrún knew of it was when he texted her asking her to send his stuff to Norway."

"That's a considerate, sensitive way to behave. Have a good day, apart from that?"

"Not bad. Lots I can't tell you. But it's been non-stop excitement since I left the house this morning. You'd never believe how many really unpleasant, bad people there are out there, even in a quiet little place like Iceland."

"Really?"

"Really. Keep your doors locked at night."

Steini leaned forward and tipped the last of a bottle of white wine into a glass, then passed the glass to Gunna. She took a sip and wrinkled her nose at the slightly acidic aroma.

"Where did this come from?"

"Don't ask." He grinned.

"Oh, right. I'm starving. Are you hungry?"

Steini stroked the moustache that made him look a decade older than he really was.

"If there's food on offer, I suppose I could be persuaded," he said with a slow smile.

Gunna hauled herself to her feet and started to unbutton her blouse.

"Good. There should be some garlic bread in the freezer that you can microwave, some pasta salad left over from yesterday, and a few lamb chops in the fridge. If you put them under the grill now, they'll be done by the time I'm out of the shower."

"Jón, I didn't expect to see you today," Ágústa said with eyebrows arched in surprise.

"Sorry, Mum. Thought I'd told you last week that I'd be over this weekend," Jón replied. Rain dripped from the brim of his cap and Ragna Gústa quickly let go of his hand and darted behind her grandmother to vanish into the house.

"You'd better come in, I suppose. Not for long, though. Didda Geirmunds is coming round later and we're going out," Ágústa pronounced without troubling to hide her annoyance at having her routine disturbed.

Jón sat himself down in the kitchen after force of habit had made him open the fridge to check the contents. Ágústa set a cup in front of him and nodded at the elegant steel flask on the table. Everything about his mother and the way she lived was elegant, Jón reflected. The house was spick and span, expensively furnished without a single piece of self-assembly flat-pack furniture to be seen.

"So what brings you out here today?" Ágústa asked sharply.

"I'm sure I'd told you. Ragna Gústa's with me today and I thought you'd like to see her. Linda's taking her somewhere next weekend, so it's not as if you'll see her again for a while."

"It's such a shame," Ágústa said with pursed lips. "Divorce is so common, but I thought it was something that didn't happen in our family."

It bloody well has now, Jón wanted to yell at his mother. Instead he shrugged his shoulders.

"It's happened and it's not something I'm going to discuss," he said. It's all right for you, he thought. Buried two husbands and they both left you a packet.

"I just want to have a look in the cellar for some bits and pieces," he added, leaving his half-full cup on the table and pushing back his chair.

"All right. But don't be long. Didda will be here for me in half an hour."

Jón felt happier in the cellar. It was cool and quiet, apart from the discreet humming of a deep freeze in the corner. The cellar had the same dimensions as the outside walls of the house, with a large main room that housed the heating system and racks of shelves full of biscuit tins and jars that Jón knew were empty. Ágústa had not made jam or baked a cake for years.

At the far side a door opened on to a smaller room, fitted out with a wooden bench and with tools hung on the walls, everything covered with a fine layer of dust. Jón looked under the bench for what he knew was there, and the sight of the familiar case gave him a warm feeling deep inside, recalling autumn days spent sitting wrapped in a thick coat watching the skies.

He admired the clean lines and dull shine of the shotguns. One was old, but as a practical man he could appreciate the beauty of a piece of precision craftsmanship made by hand and with love before the days of lathes and drills controlled by computers. He caressed the wooden stock, looking deep into the whorls and grain, wondering what kind of timber had produced such a pattern. The feel of the gun in his hands brought back uncomfortable memories, and he tried to shake them off as he picked up the other shotgun, with its dull metal and plain stock, that had been his own.

This was a newer weapon, less of a work of art and more of a tool with a workmanlike feel to it. Rummaging further beneath the bench, he came up with an old sports bag. Carefully wrapping his shotgun in sheets of clean cloth, he gently stowed it in the bag with a box of cartridges nestling against it, and then swung the closed bag on to one shoulder as he snapped off the light to plunge the cellar back into darkness.

"Chilly outside," Bjössi announced, slamming the door and settling into the passenger seat. "Going to see Skari Bubba, are we?"

The hired Polo rattled and Bjössi winced.

"What's the matter with you?" Gunna asked.

"You might want to get this thing serviced, you know. It sounds a bit rocky," Bjössi advised.

"Not my car, though, is it?"

Pulling up outside the hospital, Gunna felt her phone vibrate and fished it from her pocket to peer at the screen.

staying @sigruns tonite. OK?

Resolutely sticking to spelling and grammar, Gunna texted back to Laufey.

All right with me. I'll pop in on the way home. See you then. x, she wrote, before texting a shorter message to Steini: ?xG

As they walked into the building, with Bjössi leading the way, her phone chirped again.

9-ish?xS

She chuckled and thumbed back, OK xG

"Steini still sending you erotic texts?" Bjössi asked.

"Yup."

"Thought you were more cheerful than usual."

"Well that's what happens when you get it regularly," Gunna assured him.

"Couldn't tell you, that was so long ago," Bjössi said morosely.

"Get away with you, you randy old goat. You've always been like a rat up a drainpipe," Gunna shot back, stopping to look for the room where Óskar Óskarsson was not expecting them.

She pushed open the door and saw that there were visitors ahead of her. Óskar's mother sat there with pursed lips, and a florid woman with a mass of ginger hair spilled across the other chair.

"Morning," Gunna greeted them. "I could do with ten minutes of your time, if you don't mind," she added firmly to Skari, making it plain that she expected none of them to object.

"Of course. We'll leave you to talk to my Óskar," old Fanney said in her clear voice.

The other woman opened her mouth to protest, but Fanney stood up, buttoning her coat as she did so.

"We'll go and look round the shops for half an hour, Óskar," she said with decision. "Just while this lady wants to speak to you. Come on, Erla. We can start in Krónan."

Gunna recognized the younger woman as Skari's wife. She had seen her many times around Hvalvík, but never otherwise than surrounded by a brood of similarly red-haired children and behind a pushchair.

The two of them left the room, leaving Gunna and Bjössi to take their chairs.

"I've nothing to tell you," Óskar rasped.

"Your voice has improved, Skari," Gunna said, trying to be friendly.

"Yeah. Full of drugs, so it doesn't hurt so much."

"Skari, I'd like you to cast your mind back, if you'd be so good."

The patient glowered and looked uncomfortable. "What?"

"Ten years ago," Bjössi said. "What were you doing then?"

"I was in Reykjavík. Why?"

"That much we know. I'd like you to tell me about Black-lights. You remember the place?"

"Yeah," Óskar admitted warily. "Why?"

"Steindór Hjálmarsson. Does the name mean anything to you?"

"Should it?"

Gunna extracted a sheaf of documents from her briefcase, paperclipped together.

"This is a witness statement made by Óskar Óskarsson to the effect that you saw Ómar Magnússon and Steindór Hjálmarsson arguing heatedly in Blacklights at around two thirty in the morning. You and two of the other bouncers, whose statements I also have here, separated them."

"Might be," Óskar repeated with a shrug. "It was a rowdy place. There was rucks going on all the time."

"Ah, but this was a bit special," Gunna said. "Further along in your statement, you said that you escorted Steindór Hjálmarsson from the building and that Ómar Magnússon followed him out. So don't try and tell me you don't remember this, Skari. This is part of the testimony that put your mate Ommi away for fifteen years, isn't it?"

Óskar gulped and his eyes swivelled.

"So all this lot, all these black eyes, broken ribs and the rest of it, was this Long Ommi settling a score, or what?"

"Nah. Like I said, Polish bloke. A right big bastard he was."

"No, Skari," Bjössi broke in gently. "Long Ommi did this. You screwed him over, and when he got out, he decided to pay you back for the favour."

"No, no, no," Óskar said emphatically. "Leave me alone, will you? I'm straight now, clean record these days. So lay off."

"Let's look at it another way, shall we, Skari?" Gunna suggested quietly as the panic in Óskar's face began to magnify and his eyes started to bulge. "I get the feeling that you've been spinning us a good few tales. Let's suppose a little bird whispered to me that your statement is a pack of lies? What then?"

Gunna held up the statement again, one finger on the

scrawled signature at the bottom. Surprise registered on Bjössi's face and he sat back to listen.

"Yours, I believe?"

"Whadda you mean?" Óskar blustered.

"What I mean is, you gave a statement putting Ómar right next to Steindór Hjálmarsson when he was killed. Am I right?"

"Yeah. And what?"

"Long Ommi was your mate, your best mate. You grew up together. You don't help the coppers do the dirty on your mates. You could easily have said that you saw nothing and just kept out of it. Your statement and Svana's statement helped put Long Ommi away. Your best mate and Svana's former lover, one of many, you included, I understand. Right?"

"Well, yeah, me and Svana had a thing going for a while. But Ommi, I didn't . . ."

"Didn't what?"

"I didn't make a statement to get back at him or anything like that."

"So why, then?" Gunna asked sweetly. "Why squeal on your mate? It's not as if you had any special love for coppers, is it?"

"Hell, no," Óskar spat through his broken teeth.

"So why?"

"Nothing to say," Óskar said firmly.

Gunna sat back and looked at Bjössi, his face one big question mark.

"All right, let's try another theory, shall we? Correct me if I'm wrong, won't you?" Gunna continued. "Of course you don't dump on your mates. But maybe your mate wanted you to testify that he was following Steindór Hjálmarsson?"

Óskar's eyes overflowed with panic and he looked desperately past her at the door, as if willing anyone in the world to come into the room and interrupt. Gunna leaned forward and looked straight into the smashed face and the frantic eyes.

"So who really attacked Steindór Hjálmarsson, Skari? Who

has Ommi been covering for all these years? Who promised him a payday when he's done the time? Who's being protected? And why is Ommi out now, ahead of time and causing trouble all round? Why has he been settling scores? Why were you thrashed and why is Svana dead? Who else is on his list? Come on, Skari. We're on to you. Spill the beans, will you?"

"N-n-n-nothing to say," Óskar squawked, drops of spit flying in every direction as the words came out faster than his puffed lips could cope with them.

"You're telling me everything I need to know, Skari," Gunna continued in a gentle tone. "If you have nothing to say, that tells me you have plenty to hide, so I have every reason to dig a bit deeper."

"Shut up! Fuck off out of it and leave me alone," Óskar yelled furiously. "Nurse! Erla! Where are you?"

"Skari, just who are you scared of? You're in hospital. Ommi's not going to come and break your kneecaps in here, is he?"

"Get out! Nurse! Come here, quick!" Óskar roared, sweat rolling in rivulets from his thick black hair and down his forehead. He wiped his face with a sleeve and continued to bellow.

"Jeezus," scolded the nurse as she came in, punching a button on the wall. "I'm sorry, you'll have to leave. You've really upset him and he'll have to be sedated again now."

Gunna and Bjössi stepped back as a sandy-haired young doctor appeared and strapped an oxygen mask around Óskar's face, while the nurse patted his hand soothingly. Gunna could still see Óskar's wild eyes, even though he began to calm down as the doctor administered an injection.

"You'll have to leave now," he said seriously. "If you've caused any complications . . ."

"Just doing our job, Doctor," Gunna assured him. "See you again soon, Skari," she said over one shoulder as they left the room and the door banged shut behind them.

"Hell, Gunna. Were you trying to give the poor bastard a heart attack? Couldn't you see what he was like?" Bjössi demanded outside.

"You were listening, weren't you?"

"You're serious about that, are you? That Long Ommi's been doing time for someone else? You weren't just winding Skari up?"

Gunna looked at him and frowned. "Bjössi, dear and trusted comrade-in-arms. Of course I was deadly serious. You don't think I'd push him that far if there wasn't something behind it? The more I find out, the more convinced I am. I want to be sure who did kill that poor bloke. There must be a bloody good reason for it, and anyone who can afford to give Long Ommi a payday for doing a long stretch must have seriously deep pockets."

"It's a right pig's breakfast," Gunna announced.

Ívar Laxdal's brooding presence dominated the room. Eiríkur and Helgi sat in silence, ready to be called on.

"Go on," he said. "Just the outline, not too many details."

Gunna took a deep breath and picked up a marker pen. The others sat in silence while she drew a circle on the board and wrote a series of names around it.

"Steindór Hjálmarsson was killed ten years ago in a fight. Ómar Magnússon was convicted of the murder, which is all on record. Our information tells me that Ómar wasn't responsible for the killing. It seems to me that someone was concerned that Steindór was going to blow the whistle on some very dodgy dealing with several municipal authorities in property that subsequently became extremely valuable. I'm convinced that Ómar was doing time for someone else."

She drew arrows across the circle on the board to indicate the relationships.

"Now, Óskar Óskarsson and Svanhildur Mjöll Sigurgeirsdóttir

were both among the people who gave statements to the effect that Ómar had argued with Steindór on the night he died. Ómar absconds from prison a few months before he would have been up for parole. While he's on the loose, Óskar is badly beaten and Svana Geirs is murdered. Also Daft Diddi is beaten and then intimidated into committing a violent robbery. With me so far, everyone?"

The three men nodded.

"We have all sorts going on here. Svana Geirs had turned herself into some kind of high-class hooker with an exclusive clientele. We've spoken to all of her regular clients, as far as we know, and some of them have sticky fingers. Bjartmar Arnarson and Jónas Valur Hjaltason didn't seem too concerned that we knew what was going on. In fact, Bjartmar appears to have dropped out of the Svana club. The other two, Hallur Hallbjörnsson and Bjarki Steinsson, are extremely jumpy. Hallur for understandable political reasons, and Bjarki because his wife will rip his balls off when she finds out."

Gunna paused for breath. "Questions?"

"Get on with it," Ívar Laxdal growled.

"We also have the problem of Bjartmar's wife, still in hospital after what looks like an arson attack. Bjartmar himself has a very unsavoury past. He owned the club where the altercation between Steindór and Ómar took place. Ómar and Óskar were both working for Bjartmar, ostensibly as bouncers, but both were certainly involved in Bjartmar's other illegal business interests."

"Such as?" Ívar Laxdal asked.

"Dope. Blacklights was a clearing house for all kinds of narcotics, but Bjartmar was very careful never to get his own hands dirty. The man came into some money in the late nineties, and within a year he'd gone legit and was probably making more money legally than he had done illegally."

"How?"

"Property investments, for the most part. He bought houses and sold them as soon as the value rose by twenty per cent. Prices shot up between 2000 and 2007, so he made a fortune and put a lot of it into a similar business in Spain selling property to elderly people looking to retire somewhere warm. But he was still heavily into property and development here at the same time. One of his companies, Rigel Investment, owns the building just round the corner on Lindargata where Svana Geirs lived."

"It's convoluted, isn't it?" Ívar Laxdal observed with a rare shadow of a smile.

"It's a step up from speeding tickets," Gunna admitted. "Everything is linked somehow. Wherever you look, someone else had an interest as well."

Eiríkur put a hand up. "Er, chief. Actually there's more. While you were out this morning, I did a bit of digging and spoke to Björgvin over the road. Bjartmar was a director of Kleifaberg as well. Don't know if you were aware of that," he said, as if this was something that he should have found out long before.

Gunna circled the company on the whiteboard, which was now covered in arrows, and added another between Bjartmar and Kleifaberg. "Good grief, anything else?"

"Well, yes, there is," Eiríkur said nervously. "There were a few more shareholders in Kleifaberg, including Bjarki Steinsson and a woman called Helena Rós Pálsdóttir—Hallur Hallbjörnsson's wife."

"Ah, so the plot continues to thicken, Gunnhildur," Ívar Laxdal said approvingly. "But I need to see results for the murder of Svana Geirs. Do you have anyone in the frame?"

"As it is, I don't believe we are close to an arrest. We have Omar Magnússon in the picture, with evidence that puts him there during the week leading up to her death, but the same is true of half a dozen other people. Bjartmar has a rock-solid alibi, but that doesn't mean he didn't get someone else to carry it out on his behalf. We can place Jónas Valur, Bjarki Steinsson and Hallur in her flat during that same week, Bjarki on the same day, but we still have no evidence that any of them may have committed the crime."

"Motives?"

"Ah, Omar is the obvious one, as she had been a witness over the Steindór Hjálmarsson murder in 2000, and this is what I feel we need to crack more than anything. Who was paying Omar to do the time? What went wrong and why did Omar abscond? If we can find that out, then I'm certain everything else will fall into place. I'm sure Oskar knows, but he's terrified. I'm sure Jónas Valur knows, but he's saying nothing, possibly to protect his son."

"Next step?"

"Oskar. I've already pushed him harder than I should have, considering he's a sick man. But I reckon he's our way in."

JÓN ADMIRED THE clean lines of the shotgun, the deep patina that much polishing had given the stock and the gunmetal menace of the twin barrels. He and the old man had shot geese and ptarmigan every winter while his father had lived, first using the old man's shotgun that Jón had left under the bench at his mother's house. A year before he died, Jón's father had bought him a shotgun of his own, and the two of them doubled their haul of geese that winter, to the consternation of his mother, expected to pluck, clean and roast them.

With the old man gone, Jón had little heart for spending time on the hills and fields they had walked together, and the shotguns languished in the cellar, occasionally taken out to be cleaned, polished, oiled and put away.

Jón winced to himself as he put the barrels between the jaws of the vice and gently closed them. What he was about to do didn't feel right, but he picked up a hacksaw from the bench and laid the blade against the barrels, shutting his eyes as he pushed the saw forward for the first rasping cut.

GUNNA LISTENED TO the hired car's suspension complain every time it hit a bump in the road. Helgi himself seemed blissfully unaware of the bumps and Gunna decided that he must have become so used to the noise that if it were to disappear he would start to be worried about it.

"Run out of cars again, have we, Helgi?"

"Yeah. Sometimes. Here, I've been thinking," he said and lapsed back into silence.

"About what?"

"Long Ommi. Svana Geirs was murdered between twelve and three in the afternoon, right?"

"As far as we're aware. That fits in with the last call on her phone, and Miss Cruz said that body temperature indicated she'd been dead between six and three hours."

"All right. So if she was killed at two, give or take an hour or so each way, twelve-ish at the earliest, then it would have been a bit of a rush for Ommi to get to Keflavík to give Óskar Óskarsson a hiding, wouldn't it?"

"You're saying he couldn't have done both?" Gunna hazarded.

"That's it. Óskar turned up at Casualty at six that evening, by which time it was already a couple of hours since he'd been beaten. So what do you think? Is Óskar Ommi's alibi?"

Gunna gnawed a lip in discomfort. The idea had been at the back of her mind, but for some reason she had deliberately not thought it through.

'I don't know, Helgi. I really don't know. It strikes me that he could have done both if he'd been quick off the mark, but it doesn't look good, does it? It's an hour's drive, give or take ten minutes or so. Ommi could have bashed Svana's head, run for it and been in Keflavík an hour later to administer some punishment to Óskar. It could just fit."

"All right. So Ommi knew exactly where to find Óskar, did he? He didn't have to search around for him?"

"It's impossible to say until one or the other of them throws us a rope. We'd better have another go at Ommi tomorrow. Fancy a little drive in the country?"

The route to Óskar's room at the hospital was becoming familiar. Gunna pushed open the door to see an orderly stripping the bed.

"Where's Óskar? The man who was in this room?"

"I not know. Ask sister," the orderly replied with a heavy accent.

In the corridor, Gunna cornered a tired-looking nurse who could only say that her shift had just started and went off to find someone more senior. Finally Gunna recognized the nurse she had spoken to the first time she had been there to interview Óskar.

"I can guess who you're looking for, and he's gone," Sjöfn Stefánsdóttir said. "He discharged himself very much against doctor's orders and left about half an hour ago."

"Dammit, couldn't you have told us?" Gunna exploded. "Can't you keep people in here?"

"Actually, I left a message on your voicemail as soon as I knew what was happening," Sjöfn replied sharply. "And no, we can't keep people against their will unless they're sectioned. That's a major step and it's not something we can do lightly; even then it's almost exclusively done when there are mental health problems, not when someone is fed up with being harassed," she added.

"I'm sorry. Really, I shouldn't have gone off the deep end like that. Do you know where he's gone?"

"No idea. But he left with his wife half an hour ago, so I don't suppose they've got far yet."

"Helgi, will you get on to the local coppers and see if they can have a look for Skari and Erla's car? They may well be on the way out to Hvalvík," Gunna instructed, then turned back to Sjöfn. 'I'd like to speak to the doctor who treated Oskar when he was brought in. Is that possible?"

"I think he's here at the moment. Come with me and I'll see if he's in the common room."

They padded along corridors with Helgi behind them, muttering into his communicator. In the common room, Sjöfn gently tapped the shoulder of a tall man dozing in an armchair with his feet crossed at the ankles and resting on a low table covered with notes.

"Jónmundur,' she said, looking down at him as he adjusted his glasses. "This lady is from the police and would like a word with you about Oskar Oskarsson."

The doctor removed his feet from the table and put them on the floor, coughing as he did so.

"The guy who discharged himself?" he asked.

"That's him," Gunna said. "You treated him when he was admitted? What were his injuries?"

"Bruises to the face and upper body, certainly received during a fight of some kind. There was concussion, a broken clavicle, broken ribs and broken fingers, as well as a broken jaw and half a dozen teeth knocked out. Not something we see every day, quite a thorough beating."

"All right, he arrived here around six in the evening, right? What I'm keen to establish is how long after the event that was? I need to establish the time the beating took place."

"That's not easy to say. The bruises were well developed, and he was black and blue all over, though that doesn"t take long to happen. But he was suffering from borderline hypothermia. He was quite badly chilled and it seems he"d been unconscious or asleep outside for some time, quite possibly a couple of hours."

"Two, maybe?"

The doctor thought carefully.

"You understand I'm not a specialist in this," he warned. "He was quite well dressed, that is in terms of protection from cold, in a thick fleece, a shirt and a singlet. I doubt that his core temperature was near a danger level, but his extremities were badly chilled."

"Three hours, possibly?"

"I'd say so, perhaps even more as the weather wasn't particularly cold, but it depends if he was exposed or out of the wind."

Gunna tried to adjust her calculations and resorted to fingers. "So, Óskar appeared here that evening, after being badly beaten and lying unconscious for as long as four hours, would you say?"

"I'd say that would be probable. Why are you so interested in this?"

"Because I have a strong suspicion that the person responsible for Óskar's condition committed another crime the same day, and I'd like to know if he had time to do both, or if I should be looking for two people. By the way, how was he brought in?"

"Ah, in that case I see why the timing's so important. A serious crime?"

"Oh yes."

"All right. I won't ask. Óskar wasn't brought in. He walked in himself and practically collapsed by the door. You could ask him yourself, but he discharged himself this afternoon, very much against my advice. Though I doubt it'll be long before he's back to get some more painkillers."

"Don't you be so sure. Óskar's not one to have too much trouble getting hold of pills if he needs them."

"He's asleep," Erla said querulously, opening the door a crack.

"He should be in hospital," Gunna replied. "Open the door, Erla."

She swung it back warily, and Gunna could see her haggard face, eyes red with tears and lack of sleep.

"I suppose you'd better come in," she said resignedly. "He'd still be in hospital if you lot didn't keep hassling him," she accused.

The little house's front room was a mess of mismatched furniture and toys scattered across the floor, dominated by a vast TV screen on which characters in a soap opera mimed to each other with the sound turned off. Fanney sat upright on a hard chair and looked accusingly at Gunna.

"Can't you leave my boy alone?"

"I'll leave him alone when he tells me the truth," Gunna replied grimly. "Look, somewhere out there is the villain who did this to him, and it's not just your Óskar who's been on the receiving end of all this. I'd love to catch the bastard, but I can't if Óskar won't say anything and just sticks to this stupid story about some Pole we all know doesn't exist. So, who's going to start the ball rolling?"

She looked from one woman to the other, challenging them to speak out. Erla gazed down at the floor. Gunna saw that a dewdrop had formed on the tip of her nose and she sniffed as she wiped it away. Fanney sat rigidly, staring into the distance, hands crossed in her lap.

"I told you," Fanney said at last, her fury surging to the surface, then she lapsed back into silence while Erla sniffed. Gunna stood by the door and watched the pair of them, waiting for one of them to say something.

"It was that Ómar," Erla suddenly sobbed. "He came here looking for Skari, him and another man. I tried to call him and let him know, but his phone was dead. They must have found out where he works and gone there."

With the tension broken, Erla continued to sniffle, her shoulders hunched and convulsed with each new spasm of misery, while Fanney sat, still in her overcoat, her mouth set in a thin, hard line.

"Have you caught him?" she demanded abruptly.

"Oh, yes. Ómar is firmly back in Litla-Hraun."

"That's a blessing, I suppose," the old lady admitted. "Erla, my girl. The man's back in prison. Don't you think it's high time you two stopped being so stupid and told this lady what's been going on?"

Erla's shoulders heaved, but a series of nods could be made out among the tremors.

"Where is Óskar?" Gunna asked softly.

"Up-up-upstairs," Erla said finally, parting the mane of wild ringlets that spilled over her face. "He's asleep and you won't be able to wake him up. He's taken a few pills to help him sleep."

Instinct began to ring an alarm bell in Gunna's mind.

"Show me where he is," she said in a tone that brooked no argument. Fanney stood up while Erla sat looking stupidly ahead of her with an open mouth.

Gunna took the steep stairs two at a time and Fanney followed behind. There was only one room in the house's attic, and Óskar lay sweating profusely and muttering to himself in a king-sized bed surrounded by the detritus of a family living in not enough space.

"Skari, can you hear me?" Gunna demanded loudly, sitting herself at his side while Fanney stood in the doorway, her habitual angry expression replaced for the first time by something approaching true concern.

The duvet that Óskar had thrown off was drenched with sweat, and Gunna felt for the man's pulse, finding it racing.

"What's the address here?" she asked suddenly.

"Sjávarbraut 18," Fanney replied. "Why?"

Without taking her eyes off the man in the bed, Gunna clicked her communicator. "Control, ninety-five-fifty."

"Ninety-five-fifty, control," the instant laconic answer

came back. "I'm at Sjávarbraut 18 in Hvalvík. Can you get an ambulance to me? Possible overdose."

"Will do. Conscious?"

"Semi-conscious," Gunna replied.

"They're on their way. Can you find out what he's taken? I've opened the channel so the ambulance team can call you direct. OK?"

"Thanks. Out."

Fanney looked horror-struck in the doorway at the wreck of her son in the bed. Gunna glanced at her questioningly.

"Fanney, would you tell Erla to come up here? Right now?"

Fanney disappeared, and moments later the clumping of Erla's heavy footfalls could be heard on the wooden staircase.

"Is he all right?" she asked fearfully.

"He will be. Now, Erla, come over here," Gunna instructed, placing Óskar's hand carefully across his chest and patting the bed beside her. "I want you to sit here."

She stood up and steered Erla into position.

"Right, all I want you to do is hold his hand and talk to him. I don't care what you say, just keep talking. Tell him what the weather's like or something. Just so he hears your voice. All right?"

Erla nodded and immediately launched into a patter about how much rain there had been, while Gunna backed down the stairs.

Fanney was standing at the bottom, fear in her face. "Is my boy going to be all right?"

"He's going to be fine. But he should never have left hospital, and he's going back there. Where are the kids, Fanney?"

"They're at Jóna's house."

"Jóna?"

"My daughter. The one who lives next door to the old bakery."

"That's fine, then. Can they stay there for a while?"

Fanney nodded.

"Good. Right, I'm going back upstairs to make sure Erla's all right. What I want you to do is stay here by the front door, wait for the ambulance to turn up and then show them where to go. OK?"

The old lady nodded her agreement a second time, and Gunna climbed the stairs again to where Erla was rattling through a childhood story while Óskar's eyes rolled in his head. She held his hand with an unfaltering iron grip.

"Skari, my sweet. It's a lot easier that way. Then you don't have to do it twice like we used to," Erla rambled. "But if you can get the old car fixed, then it would be so much easier to get to the shops."

Gunna took in the tiny bedroom with its huge bed, the TV in one corner with DVD cases stacked on top of it, the clothes spilling out of a rickety wardrobe and the pile of unwashed clothes heaped by the door. She quickly swept a collection of pill bottles into a bag and hunted around for more. It was a relief when she heard the wail of the ambulance.

Jón Jóhannsson strode through the dusk and the drizzle. He had thought hard about how to do this, and knew that short and sweet would be best. His feet crunched on the gravel of the garden path and he saw with amusement the blackened door of the garage and the smart 4 x 4 parked in front of it.

He stood at the door and rang the bell, hearing it chime sonorously deep inside the house and taking a step back. The door opened and light flooded out. A barefoot Bjartmar Arnarson, dressed in a white shirt and suit trousers, glared back at him.

"Yes?"

"You don't know me . . ." Jón began.

"So I don't know you. What do you want?"

He's pissed, Jón thought, and stepped forward to put a foot inside the door as Bjartmar took in Jón's bulk and clear menace and retreated instinctively.

"It's because of you that I'm fucking bankrupt, you thieving bastard," Jón snarled, unable to stop himself even though he had vowed that he would say nothing.

"Look, get out of here, will you?" Bjartmar protested angrily. "I'll have the police here in two minutes."

"Two minutes is fine with me," Jón said calmly, drawing the shotgun from inside his coat and watching alarm dart across Bjartmar's face.

He pointed it downwards and pulled the trigger. The report was louder than he had expected and echoed in the lobby of the house. The lead pellets sprayed Bjartmar's bare feet and ricocheted off the tiled floor as he howled and collapsed back against the wall.

Screams like a girl, Jón thought, stepping forward. He grabbed a handful of Bjartmar's shirt and hauled him sideways so that he lay on his back. The floor was already slippery with blood and he remembered to be careful not to lose his footing. He levelled the shotgun and looked into Bjartmar's eyes a second time.

"Hell is packed with shitbags like you," he said quietly, and wondered why he had said it as he pulled the trigger and sent the load of pellets into Bjartmar's chest.

With the numb feeling of a job well done, he stowed the shotgun under his coat and stepped back into the garden. The man was clearly dead, his feet mangled by the first shot and his chest a mess of blood and torn flesh surrounded by ribbons of charred white shirt.

He took care to walk over the damp grass this time. As he crossed the street, he heard doors bang and saw lights appearing in the doorways of neighbouring houses. He walked up the slope, keeping to the gutter, where rainwater flowed steadily downhill, washing his shoes clean of blood. A few hundred metres ahead he ducked along a footpath between the houses that took him back downhill, emerging into another quiet street. A second footpath took him further down the slope to where the van was parked.

The engine grumbled into life and he drove slowly along the residential street to turn into the main road towards town, pulling over on the way to let two police cars with wailing sirens and flashing lights overtake and hurtle past.

Instead of going back to Sammi's flat, Jón stopped off at the workshop, where he lit the stove with some scraps of paper and threw on handfuls of sawdust and woodchips. When the fire was burning merrily, he took off his trainers and added them to it, wrinkling his nose at the smell of melting rubber. It was only then that the pent-up tension reached him and his hands began to shake uncontrollably. He drew his legs under him in the workshop's ragged armchair and hugged his arms around them, letting the heat of the stove bring some warmth back to his chilled bones.

GUNNA LAY BACK and wiggled her toes, her feet perched on the edge of the table. Her head was against Steini's chest, the two of them lying against each other on the sofa, and she could hear his heartbeat. She could tell by his breathing that he was almost asleep. The TV burbled beyond her feet; she had stopped paying attention to it as her eyelids began to droop. If she hadn't been so comfortable, she would have suggested turning it off and going to bed.

"It's been a long day," she said lazily.

"Nothing but excitement for the guardians of law and order," Steini agreed, opening one eye and shifting slightly to settle himself even deeper into the sofa.

"Sarcasm is a an offence you can be arrested for, you know."

"Ah, but you don't have any proof. No jury would convict me."

"That's what you think, mate."

"Early night, maybe, after all that excitement?"

"I'll take it into consideration."

Her phone began to buzz and flash on the table in front of them, and Gunna hauled herself upright.

"Æi, don't answer it," Steini mumbled, opening the other eye.

"It might be Laufey," Gunna said.

"Isn't she at Sigrún's?"

"Yeah. I'll just check," she said, and was surprised to see Eiríkur's number on the display. Before she could answer it, the buzzing stopped and the "missed call" message was displayed. Gunna lay back.

"Who was it?"

"Eiríkur. If it's important, he'll call back," she said just as the phone began to buzz again.

"Must be important," Steini said.

"Eiríkur. What's up?" Gunna asked crisply. "I'm off duty, and you should be as well—"

"It's Bjartmar, chief," Eiríkur interrupted. "Dead. He's been shot." Steini sat up, registering the expression on Gunna's face as she listened.

"Bloody hell. Where?"

"At his house. It seems he opened the front door and bang, bang."

"Where are you?"

"On the way there now."

"All right. I'll be there as soon as I can," she said, closing her phone and rummaging in the pile of clean laundry for fresh socks.

"Anything serious?" Steini asked.

"A villain we've been investigating with all sorts of nastiness in his past. It seems someone knocked on his front door and gave him both barrels."

She scooped up her phone and pulled on a thick fleece, stuffing the phone into one pocket and casting around for her shoes.

"I've no idea how long I'll be," she said, lacing up one shoe and reaching for the other. She stood up. "Damn and blast it. Firearms. It was always going to be a case of when and not if," she said furiously to herself.

By the door she picked up a thick green parka and turned to Steini. She took a couple of steps across the floor and planted a kiss on his forehead.

"I'll be back as soon as I can. Keep the bed warm for me, will you?"

Jón rang the bell and waited. Rain pelted down in the darkness and he huddled under the shelter outside the house in the western end of town. The concrete of the shelter was crumbling and the rusted iron rods that reinforced it were poking out. He could see there was a light on upstairs, otherwise he wouldn't have rung the bell. It was past midnight and he couldn't face going back to his brother's flat.

"Hello?"

The door opened a crack and the woman's face appeared in the narrow opening.

"Hi. I, er, I'm really sorry to be calling so late. You remember me? Jón the plumber?"

The door opened a little wider as she stared out at him.

"What do you want this late?" she asked suspiciously.

"Look, I'm really, really sorry. I'm in a bit of trouble and was wondering if I could come in for a minute?"

She stared back with her lips pursed, then closed the door. Jón heard a chain rattle and a second later it opened again.

This time he could see that she was wrapped in a dressing gown that had once been white, with shapeless slippers on her feet and a quizzical look on her narrow face.

Wordlessly she stood aside to let him in. Another door behind her squealed as it opened and an elderly man looked out at them, a grey-faced woman peering over his shoulder.

"Another new boyfriend, Elín?" the man asked salaciously, while the woman scowled behind him.

"Oh go back to sleep, you nosy old bastard," Elín Harpa snarled, slamming the front door and turning to climb the stairs behind Jón.

Jón stood in the middle of the kitchen and dripped water from his jacket.

"I'm really so sorry to barge in on you," he stammered. "It's late and I don't have anywhere to go. Lost my house and everything. Been sleeping at my brother's place, but he doesn't really want me there and I thought . . . maybe . . .?"

"You can sleep here if you want," Elín Harpa told him in a flat voice. She went towards the flat's tiny living room, where a TV screen was the only illumination. More than half of the room was taken up by a double bed. She sat on the edge of it and looked up at him calmly.

"Is that your bed? I didn't mean . . ." Jón faltered. "I meant, don't you have a spare room or a sofa or something?"

Elín Harpa shrugged. Jón saw that the lifeless shoulder-length brown hair had gone, replaced by a short crop that nestled over the tops of her ears, making her look younger and more fragile.

"There's only one other room and that's where the kids sleep. So it's here with me or on the floor. Up to you."

She prodded a remote control bound up with sticky tape several times until the TV screen went black, leaving the room in gloom, while Jón continued to drip on the kitchen floor.

Monday 22nd

MORNING WAS NOT far off when Gunna parked Gísli's Range Rover outside and quietly opened the front door to the silent house. The only sound to be heard was the muted ticking of the kitchen clock. Her hands and feet, chilled in the hours spent searching Bjartmar's garden under the glare of flood-lights, had thawed on the drive home, but the fatigue of the long day and the shock of seeing Bjartmar's mangled corpse, eyes wide open and staring into the distance, had left her drained.

She hung her coat and fleece on the back of a kitchen chair, stretched her arms high above her head and breathed in deeply. She closed her eyes and lifted her chin, squaring her shoulders and trying not to visualize the man's last terrified moments.

She had finally been ordered home, along with Eiríkur and Helgi. Nothing but faint footprints had been found in the grass, so, leaving the technical team engrossed in the scene of crime, she and Eiríkur had joined the group of uniformed offi-cers conducting house-to-house enquiries, trying to locate anyone who might have been aware of anything.

An elderly gentleman walking a small dog recalled seeing a man striding uphill from the crime scene, but could give no description beyond the fact that he was tall and dressed in dark clothing. The enquiries stretched into the neighbouring streets and revealed only that a shabby white van had been parked there for a while, but nobody recalled the number, or even when it had arrived or departed.

Gunna pulled off her T-shirt and unbuttoned her jeans, then stood in front of the open fridge to take a long pull at a carton of the orange juice that she always tried to remember to buy for Laufey.

She wriggled out of her jeans, sodden past the knees, and rolled them into a ball with the T-shirt. Feeling sweaty and dirty after hours in the drizzling rain, on an impulse she clicked off the main light, leaving only the light over the stove on, stripped off the rest of her clothes and stuffed everything into the washing machine. She squatted and poured powder into the drawer, set the machine to run, and padded to the shower, where the sulphurous hot water soothed the knotted muscles of her shoulders.

It was much later when she crawled into bed, draping one arm over Steini's sleeping form.

"Y'all right?" he enquired drowsily. "Tough job?"

"Yup. Exhausted."

She squeezed him gently and Steini snaked an arm behind him to rest a hand on her thigh as he began to snore musically again.

THE NEWLY PROMOTED chief inspector Sævaldur Bogason took charge of the briefing. Gunna yawned as he preened at the front of the room, and noticed with interest that Ívar Laxdal stood at the back.

"Right, people," Sævaldur said loudly, calling the room to order, even though everyone there was already sitting in silence and waiting for him to start. "The deceased, Bjartmar Arnarson, killed at twenty-one forty last night, two rounds from a shotgun at extremely close range. No witnesses. What do we have?"

Albert from the technical team stood up and cleared his

throat. "Like you said, Sævaldur. Two shots. The first probably downwards and into the victim's feet. This wasn't a fatal injury, but would have been completely debilitating. No way he could have escaped or resisted. The second shot to the chest was the fatal wound. Death would have been instantaneous."

"Where's Miss Cruz?" Sævaldur demanded. "Why isn't she here?"

"She's still at the crime scene," Albert apologized. "She'll be carrying out the autopsy this afternoon, but in broad terms I don't think it will tell us much more than we know already."

"OK. Is there anything else to go on?"

"The place is like a slaughterhouse," Albert continued. "Blood everywhere. The splash patterns tie in with what I've already described. There are a couple of footprints. The victim was barefoot, so we assume the tracks are the killer's; look like very ordinary training shoes. We're going through the data to try and get a match, but it's a long shot."

"Any dabs?"

"Not that we've found so far. We're still checking the house."

"Ballistics?"

"Working on it. But without a cartridge case, there's not a lot to go on."

Gunna could see that Sævaldur was enjoying his role at the front. He looked at the assembled faces and singled her out.

"Gunnhildur. You've been investigating this man already. Can you give us a rundown?"

Unlike Albert, Gunna decided to stay seated, and saw Sævaldur frown.

"He had a complex set of businesses that are, as far as we can see, all legal, based on the cash he made in property. Before that he was involved in narcotics, but didn't get his own fingers dirty and nothing was ever pinned on him. He ran a club called Blacklights that many of us will remember fondly, which is now a smart restaurant, but he still owns the building," Gunna explained, habit making her refer to Bjartmar in the present tense.

"What's your angle on him? Why have you been chasing this character?"

Gunna hesitated, remembering Ívar Laxdal's instructions to keep the investigation into the Svana Syndicate as low-key as possible.

"Bjartmar had a number of companies, including one called Rigel Investment. The ownership is complex, to say the least. But Rigel Investment owns the building that Svana Geirs lived in, also the car that she had the use of."

"D'you think there's a link?"

Gunna threw her hands up. "Undoubtedly. Bjartmar had upset a great many people over the years with all kinds of business deals that were, strictly speaking, legal, but far from honest. He didn't have many friends and seemed to have a talent for making enemies as well as money."

Sævaldur grunted in acknowledgement. "Motives?"

"This wasn't a robbery. Nothing appears to have been stolen and the killer didn't go further into the house than the lobby," Eiríkur ventured. "It was quick as well. The 112 call was made at twenty-one forty-one by one of the neighbours who had heard the shots. The first car was on the scene at within three minutes and the Special Unit was right behind them, by which time the killer was gone. He probably walked up the hill and away. None of the neighbours recalled any kind of traffic along the street until we got there."

"Motive, if this wasn't a robbery?" Sævaldur asked, throwing the question to the whole room.

"Revenge," Gunna said firmly. "Bjartmar's wife is still in hospital after what looks to have been an arson attack. I don't know if that was an attack that was intended for Bjartmar himself, but it seems possible. Bjartmar and his wife weren't on good terms and he resented propping up her business, while I understand that she was pretty much a trophy wife. He had another woman on the side, who runs a seafood bar called the Fish Lover a few doors from his wife's restaurant. Bjartmar seems to have taken a perverse delight in setting this woman up in a business in direct competition with his wife's."

"That sounds bloody mad," Helgi observed, speaking for the first time.

"It does," Gunna agreed. "But we have no shortage of people only too happy to do the man a bad turn."

Sævaldur looked at his watch. There was no need to, as there was a clock on the wall, but the gesture was theatrical.

"We'll adjourn until seventeen hundred. Albert, could you report then with Miss Cruz on developments, and Gunnhildur, will you draw up a file of the man's particular enemies and co-ordinate interviews?"

He clapped his hands to dismiss the group, clearly enjoying the moment, while Ívar Laxdal caught Gunna's eye: the barely perceptible lifting of one eyebrow indicated that he wanted a quiet word.

JÓN OPENED HIS eyes with difficulty and wondered where the strange low ceiling had come from. Then the previous night came flooding back and he shut his eyes and began to shake.

"You're awake, then?"

Elín Harpa sat on the edge of the bed and looked at him questioningly.

"You've had a bad time," she observed.

"Yeah," Jón grunted, his throat dry, struggling to sit up. "Look, I'm really sorry about yesterday. I was desperate and didn't know where to go."

"S'all right. There's plenty of desperate people about these days."

"I'm really grateful you let me stay here. I'll be out of your way now."

"S'all right," Elín Harpa repeated, shrugging off the long-since-white dressing gown and wriggling back under the duvet. "Stay if you want. You'll have to buy some food, though. There's none here and I don't get any money until tomorrow."

GUNNA DEEPLY FELT the need for a cigarette, something she was sure she had conquered over the last few weeks and months of withdrawal. Sævaldur's briefing had triggered a craving inside that she tried to cure with a brisk walk around the car park in Ívar Laxdal's company.

In spite of his shorter legs, Ívar Laxdal walked at a pace slightly faster than Gunna's and she matched it by keeping to the inside track.

"Bjartmar Arnarson. Is this linked to the case you were already investigating?" he asked bluntly.

"Probably, yes. I'd be amazed if there wasn't some kind of link, even if not directly. The number of people the bloody man had upset over the years, we're spoil for choice for suspects until Technical come up with something to work on or we can find a witness to give us a lead. The best we have so far is a tall man in dark clothes and a van parked two streets away. That's it. No fingerprints, no witnesses, bugger all, in fact."

Ívar Laxdal's pace picked up and Gunna wondered how soon she would find herself jogging to keep up.

"Actually, we have a problem there," she said.

"The Svana Geirs case? What's that?"

"Our star suspect has an alibi."

"Solid?"

"He was beating somebody up a hundred kilometres away. It's possible at a stretch, but I don't think it was him."

"Long Ommi, you mean?"

"That's him. Even he can't be in two places at once. If he

was handing out a beating that means he couldn't have been anywhere near Svana Geirs' flat when she was killed."

Ívar Laxdal nodded as he walked. "Bjartmar is the priority now. Was this a vendetta of some kind? A professional killing?"

"God, I hope not," Gunna said with feeling. "There are enough firearms floating around the country but they've never been used. But I suppose it was always going to be a matter of time before we were to see gun crime. If this was a contract killing, it could open the floodgates for all the scumbags who have weapons to start using them."

"My feeling precisely. This has to be sorted out quickly, very quickly. Svana Geirs being bumped off is one thing; that could be what the French call a crime passionnel. Temporary insanity, the Americans call the same thing. But this is something we can't afford to get wrong."

"Are we getting the killer profiled?"

Ívar Laxdal snorted. "We are. But that's just to keep them happy upstairs. It'll be legwork that sorts this one out, just you see."

"And Sævaldur's going to do that?"

Another snort. "Sævaldur's going through the motions. I want you on the Svana case, ostensibly. I want every possible angle examined that could have any bearing on Bjartmar. Everything, understand? You can have all the overtime you want, but I don't have any bodies for you. There's no spare manpower for an emergency these days, I'm afraid."

"WHY DID YOU cut all your hair off?" Jón asked.

"Felt like it. This is easier. Not so much to wash."

"It makes you look younger. It looks good."

"How young do you think it makes me look?" Elín Harpa asked with a secretive smile.

"I don't know," Jón said, taken by surprise. "Twenty-six, twenty-seven?"

"Close. Twenty-four. And you? You're quite old, aren't you?" she said blandly.

"Thirty-eight," Jón answered, subtracting three years from his age and wondering why.

Jón had bought pizzas. He and Elín Harpa perched on the edge of the bed, while two of the children sat on plastic chairs and the smallest lay happily in the crook of his mother's arm, sucking on a bottle.

The little boy and his younger sister chewed the spicy slices and guzzled cola greedily, apparently unconcerned by Jón's presence. They watched the television constantly, engrossed in cartoons in English, until only one slice of pizza remained and both decided that they wanted it.

"Stop it!" Elín Harpa commanded as the two of them began to squabble noisily. "Stop! Now! Or I'll change the channel," she threatened as they ignored her.

She stabbed at the taped-up remote control until the channel changed and the two children howled at the injustice.

"Turn it up, will you?" Jón said suddenly, and the children fell silent, turning to the television, where a row of police cars was parked in a suburban street that Jón recognized instantly.

"Mummy, what's—?" the little boy began.

"Shhhh!" Jón admonished. "Turn the sound up, will you?" The television image cut away to a grim newsreader.

"A man was found dead at his home in Hafnarfjördur late last night. A police statement is expected later today but the man's identity is not being released until relatives have been informed," he announced in sonorous tones. "In Akureyri yesterday . . ."

"You can change it again now. That's all I wanted to see."

"Someone you know?" Elín Harpa asked.

"Sort of," Jón said. "Someone I used to work for."

• • •

THIS TIME GUNNA tracked Hallur Hallbjörnsson down to his home, a smart house on the periphery of the Vogar district in a shady, tree-lined street only a few hundred metres from the busy traffic of Sudurlandsbraut but shielded from the constant whine of traffic by a thick hedge.

Hallur, Helena Rós, Margrét Anna and Krist'n Dröfn live here, a carved sign on the front door proclaimed, and music coming out of an open upstairs window indicated that someone had to be home. Gunna rang the bell, and then knocked as well for good measure. A dog yapped inside, and through a small window set in the door Gunna could see someone approaching.

"Yes?" The copper-haired woman at the door looked doubt-fully at Gunna.

"Good morning," Gunna greeted her. "My name's Gunnhildur Gísladóttir and I'm from the CID Serious Crime Unit. I take it you're Helena Rós? I'd like to speak to your husband."

"We're about to have lunch. We have guests," she replied with a blend of frustration and irritation in her piping voice.

"Who is it, Helena?" a familiar voice asked as its owner approached. When Hallur appeared behind his wife, his face fell. He recovered quickly.

"Ah, good morning, officer. I have to say, this isn't a conve-nient time," he said, doing his best to mask his discomfort.

"I realize that fully, but I assure you this isn't trivial," Gunna said.

"In that case you had better come in," he said resignedly. "Helena, would you look after our guests?" He looked help-lessly at Gunna and pursed his lips into a thin line in irritation. "Come with me, please. We'll go to my study."

The book-lined den in the basement was reminiscent of his parliamentary office, but considerably larger. Hallur sat at a small desk and gestured for Gunna to take a seat on the other side.

"Last night a man was shot at his home in the Setberg. You've heard about this?" Gunna said without preamble.

"I heard something on the radio this morning, but I had a late night last night and haven't listened too carefully to the news yet."

"The victim's identity hasn't been released yet. But I can tell you that it was Bjartmar Arnarson."

"What?" The colour vanished from Hallur's face. "Do you know who . . . I mean, who did this? Who'd want to kill Bjartmar?" he asked helplessly as Gunna scrutinized him for reactions.

"Someone who knew just what he was doing, apparently."

"How? I mean, how did it happen?"

"He was shot by the front door of his house, twice, at close range with a shotgun," Gunna said grimly. "This wasn't an accident. Half the force is working on this one case now. What I'm after is a motive that could lead me to the killer. But what interests me right now is that Bjartmar not only had no shortage of people with not much love for him; he also had a good few partners in his various businesses. I'm concerned that there might be a list here, and someone out to settle grudges."

If Hallur's face had not already been white, it would undoubtedly have gone paler.

"How far back does your acquaintance with Bjartmar go?" she continued.

"A few years."

"All right. Let's not play games. Your acquaintance with Bjartmar goes back to the years when you were a city councillor closely involved with the departments and committees overseeing land procurement and sales."

"I don't know how you—"

"It's all in the records. All you have to do is dig deep enough," Gunna said quietly, opening her briefcase and taking out some photocopied sheets. "It's all here, minutes of the procurement committees, reports, financial forecasts, et cetera. The city quietly sold off land in Grafarvogur and plots in and around the city centre without any kind of consultation or bidding process on a number of occasions. Every time, these plots were sold to companies that were run by Bjartmar Arnarson and Sindri Valsson. There's a word for this, you know."

"What?" Hallur asked dazedly.

"I'd say it's corruption, but that's not my concern right now. I'm more interested in knowing who else the bloke with the shotgun might want to settle up with. Where's Sindri now?"

"Er . . . Portugal, I think. That's where he normally is."

"How far did all this go? And for how long?" Gunna demanded.

"Look, I don't think I ought to be speaking to you about this without a lawyer. I don't want to be in a position of incriminating myself."

"Don't be stupid. I'm wondering how many people you lot upset over the years, you and Bjartmar and Sindri between you. Just how many people are there who might hold a grudge against you?"

Hallur sank down in his chair and looked blank.

"There are so many," he said morosely. "I sort of kept in the background and did what I could to push business their way. Jónas Valur, you know, is an influential man, and quite a few of us owe him favours. Bjartmar and Sindri did the business side of things until they went their separate ways."

"And when was this?" Gunna asked.

"A few years ago, I suppose. We were at one of the informal gatherings we have occasionally."

"Who's that? The Svana Syndicate?"

"Well, yes," Hallur admitted. "Bjartmar and Sindri were in the process of winding Kleifaberg up. Bjartmar had already set up Landex and Sandex, so he was doing all right. But Sindri took us all by surprise. He said he was getting out. Of course we all thought he was completely mad. The economy was booming at the time. But he said he'd consulted analysts and gave it two years. In the event, he was entirely right."

"You mean he predicted the crash, sold his assets and emigrated?"

"He still comes back here sometimes. But, yes, he saw some-thing the rest of us missed and put all his cash into property in Portugal. Hotels, golf courses, that sort of thing."

"And Bjartmar?"

"God, I'll never forget the two of them arguing that night. They're both pretty fiery and it practically came to blows. I'm sure Sindri would have hit Bjartmar if his father hadn't been there," he reminisced, staring over Gunna's head at the wall behind her. "Bjartmar hasn't done quite so well. His Spanish portfolio has been stable, as far as I know, but he's had prob-lems here. He stretched himself a long way and some of his companies are struggling. Rigel's just about getting by but Arcturus Holdings is well over its limits. Both of those compa-nies built property that back in 2007 would have sold as soon as it hit the market. But then everything was turned upside down. Rigel Investment built those luxury flats on Lindargata. Some of them sold and some are rented, but there are still too many empty. Arcturus built all those terraces in Gardabær, about a hundred houses altogether, and they're practically all empty."

"Bjartmar Arnarson was in financial difficulties?" Gunna asked, reminding herself that this was the district where Long Ommi had been hiding in a brand-new empty house.

Hallur nodded glumly. "I'd say he was in serious danger of losing control of Rigel, possibly in the near future. It's quite possible that he only held on to ownership because the bank had enough on its plate already and the last thing they wanted was to suddenly own a hundred empty houses all at the same time."

"Are there creditors over these houses, then?"

"God, yes. Some of the contractors went bankrupt. But Bjartmar was pretty smart in a lot of ways. He owned the company that handled the project under a different tax number, so that operation went bust without directly affecting Rigel, which actually owns the properties."

"Wheels within wheels? The usual dodges? Doing favours for your cronies?" Gunna said with disdain.

"Business." Hallur shrugged. "Just business. That's how it works."

"Steindór Hjálmarsson. Does that name mean anything to you?" Hallur looked blank. "Don't think so. Should it?"

"Not necessarily. Tell me what your movements were on the day Svana Geirs died."

"Are you still on that? God, I'd have thought you'd have caught the bastard by now," Hallur said.

"A little more co-operation and we might have," Gunna retorted.

"Is this anything to do with Bjartmar?" he asked warily. "Are these murders linked?"

"That's what I need to find out. Now, details. Tell me what happened that day, without leaving anything out this time."

Hallur groaned. "I left here around six thirty, as usual, and went to my parliamentary office. There I went through paperwork, answered emails, all that kind of crap, had a meeting with a couple of colleagues—"

"About what?"

"The oil refinery proposal in the Westfjords. Basically it's an environment-versus-employment question. So whatever stand we take on it, we're going to be wrong," he said bitterly. "Personally I'd like to see the effort going into aquaculture, but I'm only a junior MP and so nobody pays much attention."

"You can give me the names of these parliamentary colleagues?"

"Certainly. Eyrún Valgeirsdóttir, Pálmi Marteinsson, Fannar Jónsson. There were others, but those are the ones that spring to mind. They'll vouch for me."

"And then?"

"The meeting came to an end at around ten thirty and I went out."

"To meet Svana?"

"I went to Fit Club and was expecting to meet her. She wasn't there so I did an hour of running and weights, showered and went back to work. Simple as that. I was due to speak at two, as you know."

"You say you were expecting to see her? Had you arranged to meet?"

"Not specially. But she was normally there at that sort of time."

"You had something particular to discuss?"

"No." He shrugged. "I enjoyed her company. Svana was a fun person to be around. Even though she was shallow in many ways, she was a lively personality and an antidote to dry meetings that go on too long."

"It seems she had an appointment. Any idea who with? Another of the syndicate?"

There was a sour look on his face.

"I have no idea. I hoped to see her. She wasn't there," he said with rising impatience.

"You've no idea who she was expecting to meet?"

"Not the faintest, officer, and if you don't mind, we have guests for lunch."

"I'm sure they'll leave some for you. When did you last see Bjartmar?"

"Before his trip to the US," Hallur said with a sour expression on his handsome face.

"And the rest of the syndicate?"

"I've seen Bjarki once or twice in the last few weeks. His firm looks after the books for my wife's media business and we're old friends."

"He doesn't have an alibi."

"Bjarki? Good grief, he'd never hurt a fly, let alone a person. Svana was so fit and healthy, she could have made mincemeat of him."

"Bjartmar was abroad. You were in Parliament. Jónas Valur doesn't have much of an alibi and Bjarki doesn't have one at all. I'm not assuming that one of the syndicate killed Svana Geirs, but you have to admit that you all make a good starting point. You had a motive in that if she were to reveal the arrangement, your political career would be in trouble."

"You think so?" Hallur asked with a grim laugh. "If the truth were known about the goings-on between political bedrooms in this country, more than half of us would be out of office tomorrow."

"Did you meet any of Svana's other acquaintances?"

"What? Her friends? No. I don't think she had friends like normal people do. She just had people who were useful to her. I'd sometimes run into her with people at Fit Club, normally the sort of fashionable women she used to associate with, sometimes men, but not often. Once I saw her laughing and joking with a troll of a man at Fit Club, who turned out to be her brother. That was a bit strange, because Svana never seemed to have anything like a family, ever."

"How so?"

"She never mentioned family at all. I knew she was from out of town somewhere, but didn't know where. I know it sounds funny, but it didn't fit somehow."

"How so?" Gunna asked again.

"I don't know," Hallur answered. "She'd never had any relations like the rest of us do, never mentioned parents. Finding out there was a family behind her was a bit like discovering a shameful secret that she'd have preferred to keep quiet about."

GUNNA LEFT HALLUR'S smart house with his wife's farewell scowl vivid in her mind and drove back to Hverfisgata thinking over the conversation. She made a mental note to find Björgvin in the financial crime department and ask if he had any knowledge of Bjarki Steinsson's activities. As an accountant, Bjarki undoubtedly handled affairs for his friends' companies, and although she knew little would be divulged beyond generalities, she felt that the man's demeanour would tell her enough.

Some of what Hallur had said triggered a mental note she had made to herself a few days earlier that had become submerged beneath a tide of other matters. She hurried through the rain, grumbling to herself that rain shouldn't fall from a virtually clear sky. Instead of going to the detectives' office, she climbed an extra flight of stairs to the cells and could hear someone snoring sonorously inside one of them.

An elderly man padded uncertainly from the toilet back to a cell, followed by a woman prison officer. Hearing her approach, both of them turned.

"Hæ, Gunna, sweet thing," the grey-haired man croaked.

"Had a night on the tiles, did you, Maggi?"

"Æi, Gunna. You know how it is sometimes. A little drink doesn't go far these days," he said, and yawned.

"Come on, Maggi," the prison officer encouraged. "You can have a few more hours' sleep and that's your lot."

The old man tottered forward, one hand on the wall, and the prison officer locked his door behind him, watching through the peephole as he settled himself back on the mattress inside.

"Gunnhildur, isn't it?" she asked. "I thought I recognized you."

"That's right," Gunna said, surprised. "You're Kaya?"

"Saw you in the paper last year."

"Ah, so you must be one of the half-dozen people who actually read Dagurinn instead of using it to line the litter tray."

"Sort of." Kaya grinned. "We don't have any pets, so I suppose we have to read it. What can I do for you?"

"Chap brought in last week. Thickset, pissed. Tinna Sigvalds and Big Geiri brought him in but they're both off duty today, otherwise I'd have asked them. Who was he?"

Gunna followed Kaya to the office, where she scrolled through the log on the computer.

"Last Friday? He was brought in about six thirty?"

"That fits."

"What do you want to know?"

"Not much. Just who he was. The face looked familiar and I wanted to be sure."

Kaya scrolled through the notes. "Nothing special. His name's Elvar Marínósson, legal residence at Hólabraut 60, Djúpivogur, date of birth twentieth of March 1986."

Gunna nodded, writing the man's name and date of birth down on the last page of her notepad. "What was he brought in for?"

"Being an idiot, basically. Pissed, had an argument with a cashier in a shop on Pósthússtræti. He lit a cigarette in the shop, refused to put it out and they called the police. He slept it off, the shop decided not to press charges and so we let him out the next morning with a thick head and told him not to do it again."

"OK, thanks. That tells me what I needed to know."

"Any time," Kaya said with a saw-toothed smile.

Gunna clattered down the stairs to her own office and waited impatiently for her computer to start up.

When it had stopped whirring and had settled down to its usual irritating hum, she went to the traffic database and typed in Elvar Marínósson's name and date of birth. A second later the man's driving licence details appeared, confirming his full name, legal residence and date of birth, just as Kaya had said. But the picture alongside it, although not a recent one, showed a pale-faced, fair-haired man with deepset blue eyes, not the beefy red-faced man who had appropriated his identity.

"Ah, Högni Sigurgeirsson. What game are you playing at?" Gunna asked herself quietly.

"CAUGHT HIM YET?" Gunna asked as Helgi appeared with Eiríkur behind him.

"Caught who?" Eiríkur said with a dazed look in his eyes.

"I don't know. Anyone, plenty out there to choose from. What have you been up to, then?"

Helgi shook his head in despair. "Have you any idea? Any idea at all how many vans there are in this country that are either white or light grey? I've just spent an hour with the old feller who thinks he saw our mysterious white van down the hill from Bjartmar's house, showing him pictures of vans in all shapes and sizes, every model under the sun. Guess what? It's a white van. That's the nearest he can get. Oh, but there might have been some lettering on the side. Or there might not."

He dropped the folder of photographs and brochures on his desk and sat down.

"How far did the Special Unit go with their hot search?" Gunna said, standing up and going over to a much-annotated map of Reykjavík on the wall. "They don't mess about, those guys. If it was there when they did their search, they'd have logged it. If it wasn't, then it must have disappeared at the critical moment," she decided. "If it was ever there at all."

She traced the road in which Bjartmar's house stood with one finger, before skipping across the next road to the one beyond it.

"Bjartmar's house is in the furthest street but one in that

district," Eiríkur observed. "So if our man escaped on foot, he must have gone downhill, because there's only one street of these yuppie mansions, and then lava fields behind it."

"Until some bright spark like the late lamented Bjartmar feels a need to build on it," Gunna added.

"Yeah, chief. Look, though. Our friend does a runner. No point going uphill, there's nothing there and no way out. Downhill, back towards Hafnarfjördur. So even if the van was nothing to do with him, he would have gone down there anyway," Eiríkur continued.

"Yes, and look here," Gunna pointed out. "In case neither of you had noticed, there are only two ways out of that district. So if you can find some CCTV footage from a minute or two after the shooting that shows a white van, then we might be on to something."

"You should apply for promotion, Gunna. With brains like that, you're wasted on us," Helgi assured her, while Gunna took a moment to decide that the comment didn't warrant a sharp reply. "As it happens, my young colleague has already been busily searching out CCTV footage. But what have you been doing, chief?"

"I've been annoying our elected representatives once again."

"You've made something of a habit of that over the years, I hear," Helgi said.

"That's what those idiots are there for," Gunna retorted. "Remember Högni Sigurgeirsson?"

"Who?"

"Svana Geirs' little brother."

"Yeah, a leery bastard if I recall correctly."

"Hmm. A very insightful analysis, Helgi, and right on the money. He was here last week."

Helgi's brows knitted. "What for?"

"Pissed and making a nuisance of himself, or so Kaya upstairs says, but he passed himself off as someone else."

"You've been to see Kaya?" Eiríkur asked, awe in his voice. "Alone?"

"Yes. What of it?"

"Watch yourself, chief," Eiríkur said as Helgi laughed. "She's a right lezzie, that one is."

"Ach, get away with you."

"True, chief," Eiríkur said. "An out-and-out lady in comfy shoes."

"Private is private, boys. Leave that stuff outside work, will you?" Gunna admonished. "Eiríkur, you were with me when we interviewed Svana's parents. Can you find the phone numbers, please, especially the number for Högni."

Pink at the ear lobes after having been gently scolded, Eiríkur went to do as he was told and disappeared behind his partition.

"Don't encourage the boy, Helgi," Gunna murmured to him. "Gossip is one thing, but it's different when it's in here. I know Kaya lives with a woman, but she doesn't need her personal life raked over by everyone in the building."

"Sorry, chief."

"Will you get on to Steingrímur and find out how far his team extended their hot search around Bjartmar's house? All right?"

"Already on to it. What about you?"

Gunna sighed. "Sævaldur's holding another briefing at five. You know, I have a nasty feeling he's angling to take over Örlygur Sveinsson's duties, assuming Örlygur's back finally gets him retired. Now, that would be fun and games, wouldn't it?"

Helgi looked blank.

"But right now, I'm going to have a little drive in the country while you gentlemen get some real work done," she said cheerfully. "See you at Super-Sævaldur's briefing."

• • •

THE DOOR CLANGED behind them and the warder took his place next to it as Ommi lounged behind the table. Gunna eyed him curiously. She suspected that his tough veneer was thinner than before.

"You know who I am, Ommi, so let's go straight to it, shall we?"

"You know my mum, don't you?" Ommi asked. "How is the old bag these days? Haven't seen her for years."

"She's fine, as far as I know. It's not as if I see her very often."

"And how are the rest of the idiots in that dump?"

"You tell me, Ommi. You were there not long ago."

"Haven't been there for years," he said sharply. "You'd have to pay me to go near that hole."

Gunna looked him squarely in the eyes. "Ommi, let's leave out the crap, just for once. I know that you and another man, probably that deadbeat Addi the Pill, went out to Hvalvík looking for your old friend Óskar. I have enough witnesses and evidence to place you there on that day and I'm not interested in listening to you arguing about it. Understand?"

"Evidence, yeah. You can fix up a few witnesses easily enough to lie for you in court."

Gunna declined to rise to the bait. "It's your pension scheme I'm interested in, Ommi. Tell me what the arrangement was."

Looking him in the face, Gunna was silently pleased to see a moment's panic behind the façade before Ommi's sharp-cut features returned to their normal sneer.

"What the fuck are you talking about?"

"Who really killed Steindór Hjálmarsson? Ommi, I know it wasn't you, so who have you been doing the time for?"

"You're talking shit now."

"Am I? You've been inside for the best part of nine years and would have been out next year. In those nine years there have been some fantastic advances in forensic science. There's all kinds of evidence from the crime scene that's been carefully preserved that we can take a much better look at these days. A victim's clothes, that sort of thing. We don't throw anything away and you'd be amazed what we can come up with now."

"Don't be stupid. The guy got in my way, so I smacked him. That's what happened. He saw me outside afterwards and wanted another go, so I gave it to him."

"No, Ommi. You were inside the whole time. I have witnesses who state that you didn't leave the building."

"What witnesses?"

"Never you mind. They're there," Gunna said. "You know, it's very strange, this is. Normally it's the other way round: crims trying to tell me they didn't do things. Why are you so keen to be guilty, Ommi? Normally you'd have been screaming blue murder about police brutality, fabricated evidence and miscarriages of justice."

"Show me these witnesses."

"All in good time. This isn't a formal interview. You're not going anywhere and we've plenty of time to go through it all with you in every painful detail."

This time Ommi looked genuinely uncomfortable. "What have you been told?"

"All kinds of interesting stuff. You'd be surprised what clear memories people have, even after all these years."

"Was it Selma?"

"I can't tell you now, Ommi."

"Skari?"

"So you have seen Skari?" Gunna asked quickly.

"I didn't say that."

"But I've spoken to him, and very interesting it was. He's not the brightest, is he?"

This time Ommi glared sullenly, but Gunna could sense that there were a dozen questions eating away at him.

"I'm interested in what happened that night when Steindór Hjálmarsson was murdered, but you know what, Ommi? It's ancient history now, water under the bridge. It doesn't look good for us to be reopening a case after almost ten years, admitting that we got it wrong."

"So what the hell are you here for?" Ommi demanded, angrily enough for the warden standing by the door to stiffen and frown.

"It's all right," Gunna assured him and turned back to Ommi. "What I'm really here about is Svana Geirs. I can place you at the scene. Your dabs are right there in her kitchen, where she was killed."

"That's stupid," Ommi protested. "I'd never have hurt Svana."

"Come on, be serious. Skari testified against you and was beaten to within an inch of his life. Svana testified against you and gets killed. I can place you at both locations."

"But I didn't hurt Svana. I'd never hurt her."

"So why did you go and see her?"

Ommi glared back sullenly.

"A quick shag for old times' sake?" Gunna suggested.

"Fuck you, you old bitch," Ommi retorted furiously.

"I can hang this one on you, Ommi. Between ourselves, this'll mean another ten years inside, and with your past form, it won't be in some soft open nick like Kvíabryggja. Think about it," Gunna said quietly and turned to the warder. "Ómar would like to go back to his cell now," she told him.

GUNNA JUST MADE it in time for Sævaldur's briefing. Out of breath after trotting from the car park, she took a seat at the back.

In her precise, heavily accented English that Gunna knew practically every male officer found deeply exciting, the severe Miss Cruz drily described Bjartmar Arnarson's injuries. As Albert had predicted, there was little relevant information that hadn't been known at first glance.

"Caucasian male, good general health, one hundred and ninety-one centimetres in height, one hundred and fifteen kilos in weight. No illnesses, no evidence of drug use. The injuries were caused by a shotgun with small-gauge lead pellets that resulted in multiple lacerations of the feet, which were bare at the time the injury occurred," she intoned, using one finger to push her glasses back up the bridge of her nose.

"I would estimate that the perpetrator was standing no more than one metre from the victim and he would certainly have been splashed with blood from the victim's injuries."

She paused to draw a deep breath and push her glasses up a second time.

"The fatal injury was undoubtedly administered at very close range, within thirty centimetres of the victim's chest, with a second round delivered from the same weapon. Mortality was instantaneous," she said flatly, and sat down.

"Er, how long between the two shots, do you think?" Eiríkur ventured.

"Not more than a few seconds. Very soon after. With the first shot, the victim fell to the floor. He collapsed first on to his knees, which show evidence of the impact marks on the floor, and then on to one side. The floor was also badly damaged by the shot and there are slivers of glass from the surface of the ceramic tiles everywhere. It's possible that these may have hit the perpetrator as well, but there are slivers of glass in the victim's right buttock and side, indicating that he fell on to that side. He was lying flat on his back when the second shot was delivered, so he may have rolled that way by himself or he may have been moved by the perpetrator into a suitable position. The victim's chest was completely destroyed by the second shot, with extensive damage," she said.

Extensive damage—an interesting understatement, Gunna reflected, thinking quickly to cope with Miss Cruz's English.

"Do the footprints tell us anything?" Eiríkur asked, more confidently this time.

"Just that the perpetrator stepped towards the victim to fire the second round," Miss Cruz said. "There are three footprints. I believe he stepped forward, right foot first, then left, fired, then stepped left foot back and right foot out of the door. There's nothing remarkable about the prints, nothing special. Training shoes that are quite well worn, size forty-eight, I estimate, so we could be looking at a perpetrator around two metres tall."

Helgi and Gunna looked at each other, thinking back to the witness' recollection of seeing a tall man in dark clothes walking fast. "Thank you, Miss Cruz," Sævaldur said.

"What's the situation with the criminal profiler?" Gunna asked, knowing that this would elicit a sour response from Sævaldur.

"Coming from Denmark and should be arriving tomorrow," he said shortly. "Now, ideas? What are we looking for? To my mind this was a professional job."

Gunna shook her head and scowled to herself, which Sævaldur immediately picked up on.

"You don't agree, Gunnhildur? Reasons?" he asked.

"The weapon, mainly," she said firmly. "A shotgun's messy. Someone setting out to kill and wanting to keep it quick and simple would use a handgun, probably with a silencer, not a shotgun."

"Handguns are illegal. Have been for years," Sævaldur objected.

"Yeah. Anyone who wants to can get hold of one for the

right price," Gunna said. "If this guy was a professional, it would have been a handgun. This wasn't a professional job."

The rawboned figure of Steingrímur from the Special Unit nodded in agreement.

"I agree with Gunna," he said. "A shotgun's awkward. From the way the pellets spread out, even at such short range, I'd guess we're dealing with a sawn-off weapon here. It looks premeditated, but sawn-off says home-made to me."

"And there are shotguns everywhere," Gunna added. "Anyone who wants a shotgun can find one somewhere. Is there anyone here who doesn't know someone who shoots? See?" she said, as not a single hand went up. "This may well have been a perfectly legal, licensed weapon for all we know."

"All right, so what the hell are we looking for?" Sævaldur demanded. "I've no idea," Gunna replied. "I think what's certain here is that this isn't the usual Icelandic murder. This wasn't carried out by some doped-up bum who didn't have a clue what he was doing. Whoever did it knew exactly what he was doing, and we need to find out if it can be linked to the fire at the same house. What I have been able to ascertain is that all the locals who would normally be mad enough to do something like this are already behind bars, or have solid alibis."

"Either this was premeditated and carefully planned, or else whoever did it was very lucky," Steingrímur said absently, as if he were thinking out loud. "I mean, we were there within minutes. You don't get all that far in a couple of minutes on foot, unless he—assuming it's a he—lives nearby and just went home."

"Or unless he had a car parked nearby and was able to drive off without attracting attention?" Helgi suggested. "There's the white van that was parked a couple of streets away that might have disappeared about the time of the killing, except that nobody remembers seeing it coming or going."

"What do you want to do? Check every one of the hundreds of white vans in the south-west corner?" Sævaldur sneered.

"That's just what we've been doing," Helgi said.

Behind him, Ívar Laxdal nodded in tacit agreement.

THE ELDEST OF the three children was the last one to fall asleep. The little boy looked angelic as his head lolled to one side and Jón lifted him gently into the top bunk.

"I always struggle with that," Elín Harpa said.

They had spent the day together in the little flat, with the children engrossed first in the television and later in a game they made up for themselves in their room.

"I thought kids didn't do that any more," Jón said, pleasantly surprised.

"Do what?"

"Play by themselves. I thought it was all TV and video games these days."

"It is most of the time," Elín Harpa said. They drank cans of beer from the fridge and talked about themselves with difficulty in staccato sentences.

"How about you?" Elín Harpa asked finally. "What went wrong?"

Jón shrugged. "Same as so many people, I suppose. Debts, lost the house. Not enough work. Wife pissed off back to her mother's."

"So where have you been living?"

"At my brother's. It's only a one-bedroom flat and we don't get on. He's a spoiled little poof. And you?"

"Boyfriend walked out three months ago, said he'd had enough and wanted some fun again."

"That's shit," Jón said bluntly.

"Yeah. I thought so."

"Is he the father of all of your kids?" Jón asked, and his voice faltered. "I mean, I know it's personal and I shouldn't ask, really."

"I don't care. No, the eldest two are from boyfriend number one. We split up when the second one was born and I moved south to the refuge."

"He beat you up?"

"A bit. Enough to get into the refuge, and then I got this place. Boyfriend number two moved in with me and it was fun to start with, while that lasted."

"What went wrong, if you don't mind me asking?"

"He's only nineteen and couldn't handle the whole kids thing, especially the baby. So he just went."

"Do you see him?"

"Not since the day he left."

"God, doesn't he even want to see his baby?"

"I guess not."

Jón's mind wandered to Ragna Gústa and the thought brought tears to his eyes. They sat in silence as Jón drained his can and opened another.

"You can stay, if you want," Elín Harpa said suddenly. "You're quite a nice man."

"Thanks. I'd like to but I don't think it'll be for long."

"Why's that?"

Jón hesitated. Because I shot a man in cold blood yesterday and tomorrow I'm going to shoot another one, he wanted to say. And after that I'll be in prison for the rest of my life.

"Æi, there's just so much shit going on at the moment. I need to try and get my head straight," he said lamely.

"Up to you. The offer's there," Elín Harpa said simply. "You were kind to me the other day, and it's nice to return the favour."

"I couldn't do anything else," Jón said helplessly.

"Whatever. The kids will be awake early and I have to get them to playschool in the morning. So I'm going to bed," she said, pulling her shirt over her head. "You coming?"

• • •

LAUFEY WASHED THE pots while Steini loaded the dishwasher. Gunna sat herself back on the sofa and lifted her feet gratefully from the floor.

"What shall I do with the leftovers, Mum?" Laufey yelled from the kitchen.

"Put it all in the fridge, will you?"

The clattering from the kitchen came to a sudden end as the dishwasher hummed into life and Gunna heard the percolator start to hiss and spit to itself. She had never fully got to grips with the TV remote and its rows of buttons, sticking to the half-dozen that she needed, but finally she managed to find the evening news.

The chief constable looked tired as the picture cut to him from a view of the street where Bjartmar Arnarson had been shot the night before. The statement was short and sweet, naming Bjartmar as the victim of the shooting and stating very little other than that the police were following a number of positive leads towards apprehending the killer. Gunna knew vaguely that the chief constable normally enjoyed these encounters with banks of microphones, but this time he seemed less at ease. As he spoke in short, sharp sentences, she could make out the stocky figure of Ívar Laxdal behind him.

"Is that the case you're on, Mum?" Laufey asked, appearing from the kitchen with a cloth still in her hand.

"It's just one of many, sweetheart. But right now that one's at the top of the list."

"Are you going to catch him?"

"I expect so. When we find out who he is."

"What makes people kill other people?"

Gunna looked up at Laufey, who still had her attention on the screen. "Why do you ask?"

"I'm just interested. Psychology. There must be reasons for it."

"The theory is that there are a very small minority of people

who are capable of committing violent acts just like that,"
Gunna said, snapping her fingers. "Nobody really knows how
many of these people there are, maybe only one per cent of the
population, maybe less. The rest of us are fairly law-abiding.
But when these supposedly normal people commit a serious
crime, there are all sorts of reasons for it."

"Are they sick?"

"Sometimes they are. Often they are desperate, and normally there are narcotics or addiction problems somewhere
behind it all."

"So these people are mentally ill?"

"As long as you see addiction as an illness, then yes."

Laufey looked round at her mother. "Do you think addiction and stuff are an illness, or what?"

"It's very hard to say. In general terms, yes, it's a sickness. I've
learned in the years on this job that there are no easy answers.
Drugs are frequently a refuge from another problem that can be
so deeply hidden that even the sufferer isn't fully aware of it,
problems of self-esteem, confidence, inadequacy, all sorts. But
I've also learned that no two people are the same and every case
has to be looked at on its own terms, especially something complex like this one." Gunna gestured at the screen.

"You should have gone in for psychology, Mum," Laufey
said, heading back to the kitchen as Gunna's phone began to
ring.

"Maybe I will, sweetheart. Maybe I will," she said to herself
as she stabbed at the green button with a forefinger.
"Gunnhildur."

"Hæ. See Papa Smurf on TV, did you?" Helgi asked and
Gunna had to stifle a laugh.

"Any progress after I left?"

"We have a few vans we're checking out, all seen within
half an hour of the incident and not too far away. Two look
good, clear number plates, so shouldn't be any problems. One

didn't have a number plate at all, and on two only half the registration could be made out."

"So there's a good bit of cross-checking to do there?"

"Yeah. Eiríkur's deep in the vehicle registry right now and Sævaldur has a patrol car quietly checking out the addresses where the identified vans are registered. What time are you in tomorrow?"

"Early, I expect, hopefully before seven."

"This is a weird one, chief."

"You're telling me. Normally a murder in this country is a straightforward affair, but this is baffling. Has this profiler turned up yet?"

Helgi chuckled. "Not yet. Seems the man's flight was delayed and he won't be here until tomorrow afternoon."

"Ach. Won't make a difference, I don't think."

"Didn't get a chance to ask you earlier, how did you get on at Litla-Hraun this afternoon?"

"Ah, Ommi and I had a very useful chat," Gunna said with some satisfaction. "I think we'll be talking again in the next day or two. I'll see you in the morning."

"G'night, chief."

The phone had hardly been replaced when it rang a second time, and Gunna swore as she picked it up.

"Hæ, Skúli. How goes it?"

"Getting a bit desperate right now, Gunna. Can you tell me what's happening about Bjartmar Arnarson? I've been to the chief constable's press briefing and he more or less said nothing at all, except that the man's dead."

"In that case he was very honest with you," Gunna replied, flexing her toes as her feet rested on the edge of the coffee table. "Where are you, outside the station?"

"Yeah, and it's just about to start chucking it down again," he grumbled.

"I'm knocked off for the day now, back bright and early in the morning."

"Any chance you could throw a dog a bone here?"

"If I had a bone to throw you, I would."

"You mean you don't know anything?" he asked disbelievingly.

"That's about the shape of it. It's Sævaldur Bogason who's in charge, not me. I'm just a foot soldier on this one."

"But you must have something, surely? Is it linked to Svana Geirs, d'you know?"

This time Gunna felt uncomfortable with Skúli being so close to the mark. "Who knows? All I can say, and completely off the record, is that's one possibility we're exploring."

"No suspects? No leads?" Skúli asked plaintively.

"So far, nothing. No witnesses, no dabs, no ballistic evidence, nothing. So no bones to throw."

"Hell. This has to be the front page tomorrow, and we haven't anything to put on there. The whole story is two paragraphs and some waffle. Was it a professional killing, d'you think?"

"I'm sorry, Skúli, I can't speculate. But if you were to dig into Bjartmar's business affairs, you wouldn't go far wrong."

She heard the grin in his voice. "Thanks, Gunna."

"The companies are Rigel Investment, Arcturus Construction, Arcturus Management, Landex and Sandex Property. It's all public record stuff. All you have to do is join the dots and you should find something spooky."

"Thanks, Gunna. You're a star," Skúli said with evident delight, and rang off.

THE VAN WHINED and complained, but eventually started. Jón waited for it to settle down and stop belching smoke before he chivvied it into the morning traffic heading out of town. It rattled through Gardabær as he thought about Elín Harpa and the unreal day he had spent in her tiny flat, numbed and isolated from the world outside.

It was yet another relief to think that he wouldn't have to worry about the van's exhaust, ready to drop off into the road at the slightest bump. After today, he'd have other concerns.

He took a detour past his old house, and then wished he hadn't. A car was parked in the driveway and there was a light in the kitchen. Somebody was having breakfast in the kitchen he had built, probably the same somebody who had started making an effort to tidy up the garden that had been at the bottom of Jón's list of priorities.

He felt physically sick as he gunned the van down the street and back to the main road that took him towards Hafnarfjördur and the half-finished industrial area where the workshop stood. According to the plans, it should have been demolished already to make way for a new development, but construction had come to a halt a year before and the workshop had been given a reprieve.

Jón fired up the stove and the heat spread quickly, the bare walls drinking in the warmth and the metal of the stove ticking happily. From force of habit he cleared up, sweeping dust and debris from the floor straight out of the door to be caught by the breeze and whipped away.

At the workbench, he took his bag from an overhead locker and carefully unwrapped his shotgun. The barrels were blackened and he was shocked to see that there were blood spots on them as well. He carefully wiped the weapon down with a cloth and ejected the used cartridges. These he dropped into the stove that had already eaten up the trainers and overalls he had taken off after the shooting at Bjartmar's house.

Wondering why he was being so careful, he clicked on the kettle. He hadn't been able to face breakfast as Elín Harpa's children had wolfed down cereal, but there was time for a mug of coffee before he needed to get to his appointment.

"HIS NAME'S JÓN Jóhannsson," Eiríkur said, eyes on the screen as he clicked and scrolled.

The man's image appeared before him, a cheerful character who looked unused to having his photograph taken and had a serious expression on his face that didn't suit him.

"You're sure?" Gunna asked, leaning forward to see Eiríkur's screen better.

"Yup. We have CCTV footage of a white van registered to this guy taken within ten minutes of the shooting at the intersection below the Setberg district. We could only make out three numbers on the registration plate, but that combination only fits one pale-coloured van on the vehicle registry—Jón Jóhannsson's."

"So this certainly points to our man. If not, he's still going to have a lot of questions to answer," Gunna said grimly.

"He's a plumber, apparently."

"How do you know that?" Gunna asked.

"His ID number. Then looked him up in the phone book."

"Address?"

"Here," Eiríkur said, holding out a slip of paper. "He lives in Hafnarfjördur."

"Then we'd better get the Laxdal to call the Special Unit out to pay him a visit, hadn't we? I hope he hasn't gone to work."

Steingrímur and his two black-clad colleagues emerged from the van and got into position. Helgi took a deep breath and marched up the garden path beside Gunna, gulping as she hammered on the door.

"Coming," sang a cheerful voice an instant before the door opened and a smiling young woman appeared, hair in a turban made from a towel. "Yes?"

Gunna flashed her ID.

"I'm Gunnhildur Gísladóttir from the CID Serious Crime Unit. This is my colleague Helgi Svavarsson," she said grimly. "We're looking for Jón Jóhannsson."

Her heart was pounding and she hoped her nerves didn't show.

"Jón? There's no Jón here," the woman said with a laugh that died on her lips as she looked past Gunna and Helgi to see three black-clad men with their weapons trained on the house. "What's going on?" she quavered.

"Jón Jóhannsson has this place registered as his legal residence," Gunna said with relief as the tension subsided. "As you can see, we need to speak to him rather urgently."

"But there's nobody here with that name," the woman said plaintively. "There's just me and Smári, and he's gone to work."

"I think we'd best come in and look around," Gunna said firmly, stepping into the hallway.

Inside, she took in the stack of cardboard boxes in the living room and the piles of belongings that had obviously been moved recently. Helgi, Steingrímur and the other two officers moved swiftly through the house and checked every room before returning to the hall where Gunna stood with the woman, whose makeshift turban was gradually coming adrift to unleash locks of damp hair.

"It might be the guy who lived here before us," she ventured. "There's some post over there."

Helgi picked up the pile of envelopes and flipped through it. "Letters for Linda Örvarsdóttir and Jón Jóhannsson," he said. "We've not been here long," the woman said plaintively. "In that case, I owe you an apology," Gunna told her.

"Need us, do you?" Steingrímur asked, his semi-automatic weapon slung on his shoulder behind him.

"All done, thanks, guys," Gunna said. "Sorry about the false alarm, but hopefully we'll need you sooner rather than later."

"No problem. There's two teams ready to go when you find him," Steingrímur rumbled as he and his colleagues disappeared with an unnerving swiftness on silent feet.

Gunna turned back to the woman, who had given up on the towel and let her wet hair fall down her back.

"When did you move in here?"

"Only a few days ago. We're still unpacking."

"I can see that. Didn't you meet the previous owner when you bought the house, or is it rented or something?"

"It was a repossession. We bought it from the bank and were really lucky to get a good price on it. I think the previous owner left a couple of weeks ago."

Gunna nodded as she took this in.

"Fine. Sorry to have troubled you, in that case. We'll leave you in peace now, but you'd better let me have a contact at the bank that handled the sale."

WITH A HEAVY heart, Jón parked the van near the middle of Kópavogur. He set off towards the centre, taking a detour, partly to kill time and partly because it was something he didn't expect to be able to do again.

He walked right round the squat modern church, leaned on the parapet of the bridge over the main road and watched the traffic hurtle past, strolled past the shops on Hamraborg, looked in the windows of the bakery and toyed with the idea of a quiet coffee somewhere. He decided against it as he felt the bulk of the shotgun under his coat. Instead he crossed the street and pushed open the glass door of the bank seconds after it had been unlocked at nine thirty.

"I have an appointment with Hrannar Antonsson," he gruffly told a cashier, who choked back a yawn and tried to smile.

"I'm not sure he's in yet. If you take a seat, I'll ask where he is."

Jón grunted and lowered himself into a chair from which he could see the doors as well as the desk where the personal financial adviser normally sat in that stupid pink shirt.

It was warm in the bank and the sun beating down on the front window promised to superheat the lobby later in the day.

"He'll be here in ten minutes," a voice said, taking him by surprise. Jón looked round to see the yawning cashier standing next to his chair.

"Oh. That's OK. I'm probably a bit early anyway," he said apologetically.

"No problem. He'll be right with you," the youth said, disappearing into the distance.

A GENERAL ALERT for Jón Jóhannsson's white van was circulated immediately. Helgi set to work as soon as they returned from their anticlimax of a visit to the house in Hafnarfjördur to try and trace the man's whereabouts, starting with the National Registry, while Gunna tackled the bank.

"That's right, Jón Jóhannsson," she repeated, and reeled off his ID number for the second time without having to look at the slip of paper it was written on.

"One moment, please. I'll put you through to Data," a

disembodied voice said, and Gunna fumed while muzak echoed tinnily in her ear.

"Data. Hello?" a second voice asked.

Gunna introduced herself for the third time and continued before the man on the end of the line could put her on hold or send the call on to someone else. "I'm trying to trace one of your clients and need to get as much information as possible about this person. It's extremely urgent."

"I'll have to call you back. Security," the voice said dubiously.

Gunna snapped out her direct number, put the phone down and cursed, certain that it would take at least half an hour for the bank to return the call. To her surprise, it rang almost instantly.

"Gunnhildur?" the voice asked. "All right. This is Árni at the bank again, sorry about that. Procedures, I'm sure you understand. Now, who are you looking for information on? There's only so much I can tell you, I'm afraid."

"The man's name is Jón Jóhannsson," she repeated and again reeled off his ID number, listening to the rattling of a keyboard at the other end as she spoke.

"All right then. This isn't being recorded or anything, is it?" asked Árni with a nervous laugh.

"No, of course not. But it's urgent, so do you have an address, contact number or anything for him?"

"The only address we have is the one we know he doesn't live at any more, as that house was repossessed and has been sold, but he hasn't changed his legal residence, so that's where any post for him is still going."

Gunna wanted to grit her teeth. "Phone number, maybe?"

"Er, yes. There's a mobile number."

"Which is?"

"Look, I'm not sure I can release that sort of information. Data protection and all that, you know."

Gunna breathed deep. "Where's your office?"

"Excuse me?"

"I said, where's your office?"

"Well, I'm in Borgartún, but I don't see what—"

"You will if I show up in front of your desk in ten minutes' time. Look, this is not a trivial case in any way. What's the guy's phone number?"

Árni reeled off seven digits that Gunna scribbled down.

"Thank you. How long is it since there was any contact with him? I mean direct contact, not just you sending out a letter."

The man's keyboard rattled again.

"Last week. His personal financial adviser spoke to him last week and I can see from the notes that they have a meeting scheduled for today."

"When and where?"

"I presume it'll be Kópavogur, as that's the branch he uses, but I couldn't tell you when for sure. You'd have to speak to the personal financial adviser yourself."

Gunna drummed the desk with her fingers. "And do you have a name and a number for this person?"

"It's Hrannar Antonsson, and his direct line is the bank's usual number, but the last three digits are 967."

"Thanks very much, you've been a great help," Gunna said, putting the phone down. "Eventually."

She wondered whether to call Hrannar Antonsson's number or the mobile number for Jón Jóhannsson. A call to him could alert him to the hunt, but surely the man would know already that he was being searched for—assuming he had been responsible for Bjartmar's death. She quickly punched the seven digits of the mobile number and listened to it ring for a long time before a small voice spoke at the far end.

"Hello . . .?"

"Hello. Who am I speaking to, please?" Gunna enquired politely. "Elín Harpa.

Who's this?"

"This is Gunnhildur Gísladóttir at the CID Serious Crime Unit. I'm looking for Jón Jóhannsson."

"Police?"

"That's right."

"He's gone out and he forgot to take his phone," Elín Harpa said defensively. "Why? What's he done?"

"This number came up in connection with an investigation and I just need to make some checks," Gunna said carefully, wondering who this woman was. "Are you his wife?" she asked, hoping that this would elicit an explanation.

"No. He just stayed here a few nights."

"Elín, look, I don't want to alarm you, but this could be in connection with a serious incident and there's a possibility that you could be at risk. I'd very much like to talk to you, but face to face would be better. Can you tell me where you live? I can be there right away," Gunna said, trying to keep her voice calm.

But the connection closed and the dialling tone wailed in her ear.

"Damn and blast . . ."

"What's up, chief?" Helgi asked. "Just been speaking to our man's wife, a nice enough lady, understandably worried about him. Says it takes a while to wind him up, but when he's angry, he has a right temper on him."

"Anything that sheds light on all this?"

"The man's a plumber, had his own business but they lost a load of money when a big customer went tits up. In a nutshell, they lost the house, the jeep, all the rest of it, and the bank's still pursuing them for this and that, all bought on foreign currency loans, even though they don't have anything left."

"That bloke at the bank I spoke to didn't tell me any of this," Gunna said angrily.

"Well I don't suppose they want to tell the whole world what a bunch of grasping bastards they are," Helgi observed.

"Anyway, Jón and Linda went their separate ways around the time the house was repossessed. She took the kid and went back to her mother's, who lives in Hella, and she hasn't heard a lot from him since then. She reckons he's been staying with his half-brother, doesn't know where the man lives, but he's a schoolteacher called Samúel Ólafsson."

"Eiríkur!" Gunna called.

"Yes, chief?"

"One for you. Can you track down a schoolteacher called Samúel Ólafsson? No idea which school, but do your best. Looks like he's our boy's brother and that's where he's been living." Gunna turned back to Helgi. "But I'd like to know who this Elín Harpa is and why she answered his phone."

Helgi raised an eyebrow. "No idea . . ."

"Can you alert the Laxdal and Steingrímur and warn them that we may be looking at an encounter with our man in Kópavogur, either in or close to the bank on the corner of Hamraborg?"

She pulled the phone back across, punched in the number for Hrannar Antonsson and listened to it ring.

"Hello, Hrannar's phone," a cheerful female voice greeted her.

"Good morning, this is Gunnhildur Gísladóttir at the CID Serious Crime Unit," Gunna said for the tenth time that morning. "I'm trying to get in touch with Hrannar Antonsson and it's urgent."

HIS STOMACH RUMBLED as he sat with his coat wrapped around him and his hands deep in the pockets, pushed through the lining to give him a grip on the shotgun. He looked around repeatedly, watching the time tick past ten o'clock, wondering where the bloody boy had got to.

The tension that had been building up in him all morning had disappeared as if it had evaporated suddenly the moment he had pushed the door of the bank aside. He felt slightly light-headed, but fully in control, as if he were watching the scene from above. He imagined looking straight down on himself, sprawled in what passed for an easy chair while the bank's activity went on around him in a blur of people moving between offices and desks. He felt his feet begin to numb and wondered just how long the bloody man was going to take.

At last the familiar pink shirt appeared and came across to him, a hand extended.

"Good morning. I'm so sorry I'm late. There was an accident on Vesterlandsvegur and the traffic backed right up. Shall we?" Hrannar asked with a smile, gesturing towards an interview room.

Jón grasped the proffered hand, gripping it for slightly longer than was comfortable or necessary, and noticing a flash of discomfort in the boy's smile. He kept the coat closed around him as he followed Hrannar to the glass-sided interview room and took a seat opposite him.

"I can see you've had a really rough time of it these last few weeks," Hrannar said, tapping at the computer on the desk. "I'm just calling up all your details so we can review your status."

Jón grunted in response. There was nothing to say. He didn't need a youngster with a ridiculous haircut to tell him that he was broke and bankrupt. He looked at Hrannar, thinking to himself how stupid it would be to have that patch of hair in the middle of your head slicked up like that.

He looks like Tintin, he thought.

The numbness in his feet had spread to his fingers and he could barely feel them. He flexed his toes and fingers as much as he could, but still felt ill at ease, not uncomfortable, but not quite right. Suddenly he realized that he had not listened to a word of what Hrannar had been saying and the boy was staring at him with a concerned expression.

"Jón, are you all right?" he asked. "Would you like a glass of water?"

"Yeah," Jón grunted, tightening his grip on the shotgun and slipping off the safety catch. As Hrannar made to stand up, a young woman with a name badge on a chain around her neck knocked on the glass door and put her head around it.

"Hrannar, there's a personal call for you," she whispered, her voice rising on the final syllables. "Urgent, she says."

Hrannar sat back down and dragged the desk phone towards him with a frown.

"Thanks, Sigga," he said as the girl made to shut the door behind her. "Could you bring this gentleman a glass of water, please? He's not feeling well."

She nodded and departed, while Hrannar peered at Jón, who was sitting wrapped in his coat in spite of the office's stuffy warmth.

"I hope you don't mind, I have to take a call quickly," he said, and saw Jón nod imperceptibly. "Hello, Hrannar Antonsson speaking," he said smartly into the phone.

Jón's eyes began to move, boring into Hrannar as he sat flustered behind the desk. The world began to move in slow motion. The cashiers at their desks smiled and tapped at their keyboards as if their world had been turned down a notch.

"Of course," he heard Hrannar say. "It's very difficult for me to speak right now. It's really not a good moment."

Jón's eyes lifted to meet Hrannar's, which filled with fear and he almost dropped the phone.

"Yes, he's with me right now. W-w-would you like to speak to him?" he said into the mouthpiece, eyes wide as Jón let his coat fall open and he found himself staring into the two gaping barrels that looked as deep and wide as tunnels. He stared at the two circles, scarred and raw where the hacksaw had cut through the metal, ringing the black openings with silver hoops.

The girl with the name tag pushed open the door with one

hand and stood frozen for a moment as she took in the shotgun trained on Hrannar's chest. The glass of water dropped from her hand and shattered on the floor as she screeched and took to her heels. A second later the clatter of hurrying feet could be heard, but Jón sat still with Hrannar petrified in front of him.

"You took everything away from me," he said steadily. "I had a home, a business and a family. Everything I worked for all those years, taken away. It's all gone," he repeated.

"I-I-I'm so sorry," Hrannar stammered. "I couldn't do anything. There are rules—"

"Rules?" Jón roared. "What sort of rules say you have to snatch everything away from someone? Everything, not just the cash. There's the dignity, self-respect, all that stuff. There's nothing left, just more fucking debts. You're nothing but lying, thieving bloodsuckers, the lot of you."

Outside, a siren began to wail.

"The police will be here soon," Hrannar ventured.

"That's fine. I've all the time in the world now," Jón said with the merest hint of a smile, the first one for weeks.

GUNNA, EIRÍKUR AND Steingrímur's Special Unit looked over the bank's interior. A technician dusted for fingerprints in the glass-walled interview room, wrinkling his nose at the smell.

"And? What's happening?" Sævaldur Bogason demanded, bursting in through the front door.

"All over, mate," Steingrímur told him. "Nobody's hurt and our boy's cuffed and on his way to Hverfisgata right now in the back of a van."

"I came as soon as I heard," Sævaldur said lamely, clearly furious that their man had been located and arrested quickly and with a minimum of fuss. "So what the hell happened?"

Gunna picked up a chair that had been sent flying when the

bank staff had evacuated the building, stood it back on its legs and sat herself down on it.

"He was right there, pointing a shotgun at the poor bastard who had sold him a bunch of foreign currency loans. It seems that the lad was the focus of all that anger when he lost his house and his business," Steingrímur explained. "But I'm sure that'll all come out at the station. I have to say, I feel sorry for the poor bugger."

"Sorry for him or not, what's that fucking awful smell?" Sævaldur demanded.

'Ah, it seems the lad he was threatening crapped himself with fright, right there in his office chair. He was gibbering when they drove him off to hospital. I reckon he might be off work for a while now," Steingrímur said with satisfaction.

"And how did you find him so fast?"

"Gunna found him. You just have to look in the right places, I guess," Steingrímur said with a smile that was guaranteed to provoke Sævaldur to further impotent rage.

"Well done, people," he said through a forced smile. "Is he definitely the one we've been searching for over Bjartmar Arnarson?"

"I'd say so," Gunna said. "Looks like he was going to give the personal financial adviser the same treatment as he gave Bjartmar, but thought better of it at the last moment."

"Lucky bastard," Sævaldur frowned. "Who was the arresting officer?"

Helgi grinned. "Tinna Sigvalds."

"Her?"

"Yup. Tinna and Big Geiri were the first on the scene when the F1 went up. She walked in, asked him nicely to put the weapon down and come with her, and he did, easy as you like."

"Hell and damnation. A little girl like that," Sævaldur fumed, and Gunna felt her own anger boil up inside her.

"And what the hell's that supposed to mean?" she barked.

"Tinna did a fucking magnificent job that takes a bloody sight more guts than most of us have, and all you can do is whine that it was some slip of a girl who took the gun off him! The man's locked up and nobody's hurt. If that's not a result, then I don't know what is."

Sævaldur quailed at the virulence of Gunna's outburst.

"Yes, well . . ." he blustered.

"You should be bloody ashamed of yourself," Gunna continued. "The girl deserves a fucking medal."

"Of course she did a fine job, but we all played our part in it."

"We didn't all play our part in it. You spent your bastard time in fucking meetings making sure you got noticed by someone upstairs while the rest of us did the legwork," Gunna shouted.

Sævaldur paled. "We'll continue this conversation at Hverfisgata," he said finally as Gunna headed for the door with Eiríkur at her heels.

Eiríkur sat in silence while Gunna drove out of the city and towards the east. She was collected and hummed to herself, as if a gathering storm was the thing that brought her inner peace. Eiríkur wondered how long it would be before Sævaldur initiated a disciplinary procedure.

"You're very quiet, Eiríkur. What's eating you?"

"Well . . ."

"Well what?"

"I was just thinking how great it was that you should yell at Sævaldur like that," Eiríkur blurted out.

"Ah yes," Gunna sighed. "I'll probably get a rap over the knuckles for that." She smiled wanly. "But I'm a big girl and I can take it. It's not as if it hasn't happened before."

"Is Sævaldur after Örlygur's job?"

"Don't know, but I'd be amazed if he wasn't."

"Shit."

"Don't you want to work for the big man, then?" Gunna teased. "He gets results, as we're constantly being told."

"I know. But he's such a bastard."

The pass over the heath still looked to Eiríkur like a scene from another planet, with its bizarre rock formations, unexpected pastel colours, and gouts of steam issuing from the ground at the side of the black two-lane highway. The descent down to the inhabited lowlands was almost a relief and the sharp sulphur smell of the steaming highlands receded. Eiríkur saw fields starting to turn to green as the first signs of spring showed themselves, while the layers of snow on the mountain peaks inland displayed a stolid determination to ride out the coming summer. He looked out of the window in the other direction and saw the distant blue shimmer of the sea in the distance.

"You're a city lad, aren't you?" Gunna asked.

"Yup, Seltjarnarnes."

"So this countryside stuff's a bit alien to you?"

"I'm afraid so. My parents were both from the country and moved to Reykjavík when they were young, but they never dreamed about going back to a farm or anything like that."

"So you weren't brought up on haggis and boiled sheep heads?"

"God, no. Mum and Dad used to love that sort of stuff, but they never made us eat it."

"I'll tell you a secret, young man," Gunna said, taking her eyes off the road to look over at him. "I never liked it much either. But don't tell Helgi. He'd eat sharkmeat and boiled skate for breakfast if his Halla would let him."

"Not a word, chief," Eiríkur promised. "What's the score with Ommi now?"

"Not sure," Gunna said. "I was going to leave him to stew for a few more days, but I reckon he'll have had a day and a night to think and maybe make a few calls that won't be answered. So we'll give him another go now. It all depends on how unsure of his ground he is, I think. He was nervous yesterday, and by now I'm hoping he'll be closer to frantic."

Gunna showed their ID and drove in through the main gates to park in front of the prison. She stopped the engine and listened to it tick. "If anything sounds odd, just play along with me, all right?"

"Sure, chief."

"Good. Let's go. By the way, don't worry about Sævaldur. His past misdeeds are going to come back and haunt him one day, don't you fret."

THE DOOR CLANGED shut and the same warder took his place in front of it, staring over their heads. Eiríkur stood next to the warder and noticed immediately that Ommi looked haggard and irritable.

"Jæja, Ommi. How are you?" Gunna greeted him jovially. "Sleep all right?"

"Yeah. Like a baby," Ommi sneered. "Who's the kiddie?" He motioned towards Eiríkur with his chin.

"That's Detective Constable Eiríkur Thór Jónsson, a rising star of the police force. I thought the lad needed to have a good look at you for future reference."

"Yeah. Right. What're you back for, anyway? You were only here yesterday."

"Been thinking, Ommi?"

"Might have."

"Come on. You haven't slept a wink."

Ommi shuffled his feet under the table and rubbed his hands together as if trying to comfort himself. It wasn't cold in the interview room, but he shivered.

"I might look at doing a deal," he muttered, eyes on the table between them.

Gunna sat and looked at him sideways before leaning forward with a sly smile.

"Ommi, you don't have anything to bargain with," she said slowly and clearly, not loud enough for Eiríkur to hear without listening carefully, although she was certain he was doing just that. "I have everything I need to hang Svana's murder on you and put you away until you're an old man. How old are you now? Thirty-three? How does being in here until you're past fifty sound?"

Ommi's jaw stiffened and his eyes blazed, but the colour drained from his face.

"You've spent too many years in here already," Gunna continued, keeping her gaze on Ommi, waiting for him to lift his eyes. She wondered how far he could be pressured before his temper would burst its banks and have him back in solitary confinement. "If you don't want to still be here when your hair's falling out, you need to start telling me some secrets, Ommi. It's not as if the people you're protecting give a shit about you."

Ommi sat up straight-backed, and Gunna did the same, maintaining eye contact and waiting for him to blink.

"I know already how the story fits together. All I need you for is to fill in the gaps," she said.

"It's between you and me," he grated with an effort, blinking at last, and his chin jutted again towards Eiríkur and the warder. "Send them out."

"You know I can't do that," Gunna said gently.

"You and me," he snarled with lips drawn back to reveal discoloured teeth.

Gunna looked enquiringly at the warder, who shook his head. She sighed.

"Maybe we can go for a walk around the yard," she said finally, and turned to the warder. "Can we do that?"

A QUARTER OF an hour later, Gunna and Ommi walked their first circuit of the yard. Eiríkur and the warder followed

at a cautious distance as a biting wind from the north made
Gunna shiver in spite of the heavy coat she had borrowed.
Ommi appeared not to feel the chill through his hooded fleece.

"Tell me what happened that night at Blacklights. What
really happened," Gunna began.

"I don't know it all. There was this bloke Sindri had some
problem with. Sindri has a temper, just like his old man, and
when he saw this bloke there, he blew. They had an argument
and some people calmed them down, and that was that. Sindri
was fucking furious; he'd been snorting and drinking all day
and was really on a roll."

"So it wasn't you?"

"No. Didn't even see it."

"What do you think happened, then?"

"I reckon Sindri hauled this Steindór bloke out into the car
park, gave him a good kicking and didn't know when to stop."

"So where were you when all this was going on?"

"With Svana and the rest of the band. They'd just come off
stage."

"And Óskar?"

"I reckon he was out the back with Sindri. Why? What did
Skari say?"

"So what happened next?" Gunna asked, ignoring the question.

"Shit, all hell let loose. Bjartmar wound the sound up to the
max and turned down the lights so the place was jumping.
People everywhere, loads of noise. Bjartmar and Sindri came
and found me, told Svana to get herself on stage and crank it
up. Then, fuck me, but old Jónas turns up, Sindri's dad, face
like doom, and the three of them put the screws on."

"Made you an offer you couldn't refuse?"

"Sort of. Jónas said he had a very important assignment for
me and it was urgent, had to be done right away."

"Which was?"

"That was it, he didn't say. But he put me in the back of his Merc and off we went."

"Into the night?"

"Yeah. It was starting to get light by then and we went right out of town. I don't like going past Mosfellsbær, me. But we ended up at this summer house and he left me there with Selma to look after me, said he'd be back in the morning and that there was a good wedge of cash in it for me."

"This was Eygló Grímsdóttir's place in Skorradalur, right?"

"Yeah. Nice place. I think old Jónas had a thing going with Eygló at the time."

"You already knew Eygló by then?"

"Well, sort of. Selma and me, we'd been sort of, y'know, off and on, so I knew Eygló."

They turned at the corner of the field and came back at a leisurely pace, this time into the wind, which stung Gunna's cheeks. Ommi huddled deeper into his fleece.

"So, what happened?"

"Well, I was left there with little Selma to keep me company, and the next afternoon Jónas turned up again with Sindri in tow, and Eygló coming up behind in her BMW with Baddó."

"Bjartmar?"

"Yeah. Well Selma was kicked upstairs and the three of them put their cards on the table."

"Three of them?"

"Yeah. Eygló went off with Selma, I suppose."

"All right. Go on."

Ommi frowned.

"Jónas said they had a problem. A crime had been committed that they couldn't sweep under the carpet. He said they needed someone to take the rap for it and there would be a wage in it, plus a bonus at the end of the stretch. Would I be interested? Well I thought they probably wanted someone to do a year or a few months or something. So I said yeah, I could do some time for the right price."

"But it was more than a few months?"

"Hell, yeah," Ommi said. "I could see it was Sindri. He was as nervous as hell, fiddling with his keys, biting his nails, all sorts. Your lot would've chewed him up for breakfast," he said with a slim smile. "Anyway, it took me by surprise when they said it would be a murder charge, and I said hey, that's a bit heavier than what I'd had in mind."

Ommi kicked a stone and sent it skittering towards the fence. "But that Jónas, he's a sly bastard. He said I'd already said yes, so now we just needed to agree a price."

"And I take it you did?"

"Yup. Shit, yeah. Those three . . . Life wouldn't have been worth living if I'd turned them down."

"How much?"

"A couple of mill a year, plus a five mill bonus when I got out, and he swore blind it wouldn't be more than ten years, out in six or seven, tops."

"And you agreed to that?"

"Pushed him up to two and a half a year, plus eight, and we shook on it."

"A done deal? What then?"

"They went back to the city; said I should stay put and wait there quietly. They left a case of vodka and a couple of beers, told me to enjoy the TV until I got a visit. So me and Selma, we made ourselves comfy. A week later you lot came calling and I just put my hands up and that was that."

Gunna nodded to herself. Very little that Ommi had said had taken her by surprise, except that he had been so open after such a long silence. They turned again at the top of the yard and she saw that he was starting to feel the chill.

"Want to go back inside?"

"Not yet."

"So you got a decent nest egg put away somewhere for you as long as you kept quiet and did the time. What went wrong?"

Ommi grimaced. "I'll tell you what. I was starting to feel all right in there. Stopped smoking, worked out every day. Put an inch on my biceps. Feeling good. Then I began to hear whispers. Sindri moved abroad. OK, fair enough. Then I hear Bjartmar's in trouble. He'd got right out of the speed and clubbing business, and went respectable, stopped being there when I called. That's what went wrong. I couldn't have the cash going into an account with my name on it, so I wanted it in Selma's name. But Bjartmar said he'd invest it for me, get a good return and I'd have a big old whack waiting when I got out."

"And did he?"

"Yeah. Put it all into the stock exchange here and there, a load into shares in banks, and lost the fucking lot when the banks went tits up."

"That's when you decided to walk out?"

"Yeah. I couldn't get through to Bjartmar or Jónas. Couldn't find Skari's number, like he'd dropped off the surface of the earth. Selma asked a few questions for me, but her mum and Jónas had fallen out by then. I wasn't getting any answers, so I reckoned I'd go and ask questions myself. Thought if it came to it, I'd just talk to you lot and tell you everything."

Ommi looked directly at Gunna for the first time since they had started walking. "I thought they'd stitched me up."

"Looks like they had."

"Maybe. I couldn't get to Jónas or Bjartmar. Calls stopped at their secretaries, and their offices are like this place," he said bitterly, waving a hand at the high wire all around them as Gunna recalled the security cameras outside both Bjartmar and Jónas's offices.

"The fire at Bjartmar's home, was that you?"

"Addi did that. A bit of a warning."

"And Svana? Why did you go to her?"

"To get to Bjartmar. I'd heard she was still shagging him sometimes. So I turned up at the gym one morning and waited until she came out. When she got in the car, I jumped in the passenger side and we went back to her place for a bit of a private talk."

"When was this? Which day?"

"Morning. Don't know what day."

"But she couldn't help you?"

"She said that she knew Bjartmar was away and she'd talk to him when he came back."

"That was true enough," Gunna said. "Bjartmar really was abroad."

"Was it? I couldn't be sure. Svana was sweet, but she was never that bright."

"And Daft Diddi? That was you, wasn't it?"

"Yeah. Look, I'm not proud of that, understand? I was getting desperate, out of cash. Eygló helped out with a few shekels and found us that place to crash in, but she's short of cash herself after she put hers into property that won't sell."

At the bottom of the yard, Gunna felt her phone begin to vibrate in her pocket but ignored it. As they turned, she could see Eiríkur and the warder following them, huddled miserably deep into their coats.

"So Svana was fine when you left her?"

"Yeah. Right as rain. She'd had a lot done since I saw her last, new this, new that, looked like a million dollars. I swear it, I didn't touch her, honestly. But if you bring the bastard who did it in here, I'll make him wish he'd never been born."

Gunna wanted to believe him, and for once Ommi's voice had an earnest quality that was startlingly fresh.

"Fair enough. But Skari? What happened there?"

"Jesus. Found out why I couldn't get hold of him. The twat had gone and moved back to Crapsville with his fat girl,"

Ommi said with a shake of the head. "Me and Addi went out there to look for him, and when we did find him in Keflavík, it wasn't the way it should have been. He just went apeshit. Said he was straight now and wanted to keep it that way."

"So Jónas had squared all the witnesses? Skari and Svana?"

"Yeah, and the rest of them."

"Understood. What was the upshot with Óskar? How come he's in such a bad way?"

"He went fucking wild when I told him he'd had his payout from old Jónas for saying his piece in court that put me away, but I'd been left out in the cold. He laid right into me and I gave it all back, plus a bit more." Ommi sighed. "I'm a lot stronger than when I was put away. I shouldn't have done it, but fuck it. He wanted a ruck and he got a proper one."

"And this was in Keflavík?"

"Yeah. Near where he works. Shit, I've told you enough, and it's cold out here."

WITH OMMI TAKEN away and back in his cell, Gunna remembered to check her phone for missed calls. Instead of the one that she had expected, there were fifteen, and she was scrolling through the numbers quickly, wondering which one to return first, when the phone started to buzz in her hand.

"Gunnhildur," she barked.

"Hæ, Mum. When are you going to be home?" asked Laufey to Gunna's relief.

"Oh, am I glad to hear you," she said.

"Why's that?" Laufey asked with suspicion.

"Nothing, sweetheart." Gunna laughed. "I was just expecting a call I don't really want to take. That's all."

"All right, Mum. But when will you be back?"

"I don't know. What time is it now?"

"Two."

"Should be around six, seven-ish. Why, do you need me for something?"

"No, not really," Laufey said, and there was a pause that set Gunna's alarms ringing.

"What's up?"

"It's not me, Mum. It's all right. It's Sigrún. She was asking about you and why she hasn't seen you for a few days."

"I know, sweetheart. But you and Steini haven't seen much of me for a while either, have you? Things are just busy at work as usual, and these days when there's overtime on offer, I have to take it."

"I don't think Sigrún's well, Mum."

Gunna looked up to see Eiríkur gazing at her enquiringly.

"OK, sweetheart. I'll be back as early as I can and I'll make a point of going to see her this evening. D'you maybe want to ask her and Jens to come and eat with us tonight?"

She could hear Laufey's breathing.

"What are you doing?"

"I'm walking down the hill to Sigrún's place now. I'll tell her, OK?"

"You do that, sweetheart. See you this evening."

She ended the call and looked at the screen to see a text message in the inbox. She pressed the button to display it.

Come and find me at H-gata before 1700. IL, she read.

That's going to be my bollocking for losing my temper with Sævaldur, she thought, and scrolled through the numbers of the missed calls again. Ten were from withheld numbers, three from Laufey and two from numbers she didn't recognize.

"Eiríkur, sorry about that. Time to go."

"You know Ívar Laxdal called you a couple of times and couldn't get through. Someone must have told him we were out together and he called me to ask where we were."

"And you told him that we were enjoying a relaxing mud bath in the Blue Lagoon, I suppose?"

"Well, no. I told him we're at Litla-Hraun interviewing Ómar Magnússon," he said innocently, and then broke into a grin.

Gunna started the Range Rover and reversed out of the parking space before swinging round and heading for the main road.

"You know, Eiríkur, Ívar Laxdal is one of nature's anomalies. There's a lot to be admired in a man like that, but I don't believe he's overendowed in the humor department, at least not where work's concerned."

"Maybe, chief," Eiríkur agreed. "What did you get out of Long Ommi?"

"Everything I expected," Gunna said grimly. "Everything and more."

On the way back to Reykjavík they stopped at a petrol station, and Eiríkur went inside while Gunna pumped diesel. He returned with cans of malt, a couple of sandwiches and a grim look on his face just as Gunna swiped her card through the pump's reader.

"All right?"

Eiríkur simply held out a newspaper so that she could see the front page of that morning's Dagurinn.

"Shit," she swore. "Jump in and I'll move off the pumps."

She gunned the engine angrily and had the newspaper out of Eiríkur's hands before the car had come to a halt on the far side of the forecourt. Högni Sigurgeirsson's mournful face filled the front page in unflattering close-up.

"'Högni Sigurgeirsson, 26, is devastated by the loss of his elder sister, well-known TV personality and fitness coach Svana Geirs, who was cruelly murdered two weeks ago in her downtown apartment,'" Gunna read out.

"'Nothing has happened at all. There has been no progress by the police and they've hardly talked to us, let alone kept us up to date with what's been going on,' says a heartbroken Högni Sigurgeirsson, who has taken extended leave from work to stay at home and comfort his grieving mother," she continued. "The scheming bastard! It's not as if he's been even remotely helpful either. Who wrote this shit?" she demanded, looking at the double-page article for a byline and reaching for her phone.

She scrolled, punched the call button and listened to the phone ring until finally it clicked into life.

"Skúli? This is the law. Just seen your front page."

"Me too. Nothing to do with me," he said, and coughed. "So who wrote this crap?"

Skúli coughed again. "A freelance, I'd guess. I'll ask and give you a buzz back."

Gunna's anger receded as she understood that the story wasn't one of Skúli's.

"All right, don't worry too much about it, but I'd like to know where it came from. It looks like Högni is telling the press stuff that he isn't telling us, but still moaning because we haven't caught the bastard who bumped Svana off."

"Fair enough. I'll email you when I've heard anything," Skúli said, and rang off as he dissolved into yet more spluttering.

"And?" Eiríkur asked.

"Don't know. At least it wasn't my tame journalist who wrote that shit. But it's definitely time I had another talk with Högni."

Eiríkur disappeared upstairs, anxious to check his emails, while Gunna wondered where Ívar Laxdal might be found and whether or not he actually had an office of his own.

The man appeared to come and go at will, often turning up where his presence was not necessarily unwelcome, but was certainly uncomfortable.

"A result, Gunnhildur," he rumbled behind her, and she turned to see him striding towards her with his arms full of ring binders.

"On what?" she asked, baffled for the moment.

"The Bjartmar Arnarson killing, of course. The man's in custody and Sævaldur's team are interviewing him now. I'm going upstairs. Talk to me on the way," he suggested in a tone that made it an order. "How did you get on at Litla-Hraun? Helgi told me you were following up on the Ómar Magnússon business. Progress?"

"Absolutely," Gunna puffed, stretching to keep up with him on the stairs and wondering how he managed to shift himself so quickly without appearing to move any faster than anyone else.

"And?" he demanded, marching along the corridor and swinging into one of the lawyers' offices.

"Confirmed a lot of what I'd suspected, plus some new leads. Ómar didn't touch Steindór Hjálmarsson. He was being paid pretty handsomely to do the time for someone else."

"How much, as a matter of interest?"

"Thirty million."

"Not a lot, I'd have said."

"Ah, but ten years ago, thirty million was twice as much as it's worth now."

"I'll grant you that. But it's still ten years in a concrete box." Ívar Laxdal put the binders down on a desk in the corner and made for the door. "Coffee?" he asked, striding down the corridor towards the canteen with Gunna again hurrying behind him.

Hell. I'm thirty-seven years old. Why does this blasted man make me feel like I'm ten? she wondered uncomfortably as

Ívar Laxdal poured black liquid into two mugs in the deserted canteen.

"A good place at this time of day, Gunnhildur, because there's nobody about," he said, sitting at a table in the corner and motioning for her to join him. "Tomorrow, I want to see you at nine for a disciplinary reprimand."

His black eyes bored into hers from under his heavy brows.

"Is this because I was stupid enough to give Sævaldur a piece of my mind this morning?"

Ívar Laxdal nodded.

"I'm sorry," Gunna said heavily. "The bloody man winds me up so much, and after what he said about Tinna when she'd taken the gun off the nutcase in the bank, I'm afraid I just saw red for thirty seconds."

"I know. Sævaldur has some difficulties adjusting to the twenty-first century. I know he makes an effort, but that's not always enough. But I'd appreciate it if you would cut him a little slack. Completely between ourselves, he's an excellent officer who should never have left uniform."

"In that case, completely between ourselves, is he likely to be taking over Örlygur Sveinsson's duties?"

"In confidence, Gunnhildur, the likelihood is minimal. But what's your next step on the Svana Geirs case? Where are you now? I take it you've seen the papers?"

Gunna pursed her lips and frowned. "I have. I'm no closer to Svana's killer than I was a week ago. If anything, I'm further away, as Ómar Magnússon was a prime suspect and now he isn't."

"How so?"

"I know more or less precisely when Svana was murdered, but Ommi doesn't. I know, but he doesn't, that he has an alibi. Though that might not be much of an alibi unless the chap he was administering a pretty brutal beating to at just that time agrees to identify him as his assailant."

Ívar Laxdal supported his chin in one hand and Gunna could hear his stubby fingers rasping the bristles.

"So who's your suspect for the murder of Steindór Hjálmarsson?" he asked suddenly.

"Sindri Valsson, Jónas Valur Hjaltason's boy. He lives in Portugal now, as far as I'm aware. He and his father have some business interests there. What's the procedure on this? Can we ask the Portuguese police to sling him on to a flight to Iceland for us?"

"Ah, you'll be interested to hear that there are already enquiries being made in that direction. The financial and computer crime division have been watching the gentleman for a while now, so you'd better liaise with them and see if you can pool some resources. Who knows, you might get a trip to Portugal out of it," he said with a twinkle in his eye. "But, Svana Geirs. We need some progress there. The papers are on to this and we can do without the bad publicity, or that's the word from above that's filtering downwards."

"And you're filtering it down to me? Point taken. Give me a day or two and hopefully we'll see things start to move. But I'm practically at square one again on this."

Ívar Laxdal nodded slowly. "A few days, Gunnhildur. Report back to me when you have a lead, will you?" He stood up, collecting both empty mugs from the table. "I'll see you at nine, and give my regards to Unnsteinn, would you?" he added, and marched from the room.

Sigrún dissolved into tears a second time over the remains of the pork steaks that Steini had cooked slowly to tenderness with tomatoes, onions and a few herbs that he flatly refused to identify.

"I'm sorry," she sniffed.

Gunna and Steini glanced at each other helplessly while Laufey fed a laughing Jens with a portion of mashed-up food.

Sigrún looked at Jens, gurgling and smiling to himself in the high chair that he was almost too big for, and dabbed her eyes.

"He looks so much like his father," she said miserably. "The bastard."

"Have you heard anything from Jörundur?" Gunna asked as a grim look passed over Steini's face and he stood up to start collecting plates. Gunna motioned to Laufey to lend a hand, but she pretended not to notice.

"No. He's at this place near Trondheim. His sister told me today when she called to ask about clothes that he's working on a tunnel, and the slag he took with him's had no trouble walking into a job. Would you believe it, I don't even know the cow's name?"

"I thought she was going to collect his stuff?"

"So did I, and if she doesn't, she can pick it all up from the dump." Sigrún poured herself another glass of wine. "Jörundur wants the house sold," she blurted out. "But he can bloody well think again."

"Is it worth anything these days?" Gunna asked. "I haven't even had the heart to have a look at the property pages and see what this place might be worth now, but I guess it's not much. Yours is quite a big place, though, so it should be worth a bit, shouldn't it?"

"Yeah. But we're in Hvalvík, not Reykjavík. Jörundur always was crap with figures and he can't understand that anything we might get for the house is going to be less than what we owe on it. If we sell, neither of us gets anything and Jens and I would have nowhere to live. But he doesn't want to see that side of it."

It was painful to see the change that had taken place in Sigrún and the growing bitterness in her since Jörundur had left so suddenly. Gunna and Sigrún had known each other since Gunna had arrived in Hvalvík, with Laufey as a toddler and a school-age Gísli, to take over the village's policing from the retiring officer in charge. She had found that her personal history was already well known and the subject of intense debate.

She looked up and saw the reassuring image of Ragnar Sæmundsson, complete with his uniform cap at a slightly more than officially jaunty angle and a mischievous smile on his face, laughing down at her from the top shelf in the living room.

She shook herself from brooding and felt deeply sorry for Sigrún, having watched the burgeoning romance with Jörundur from its beginnings and Sigrún's longing for children of her own that had culminated in the difficult and overdue arrival of Jens Jörundsson almost three years ago. Gunna had known deep inside her that Jörundur would only last a few years before straying elsewhere. The hand that had unexpectedly cupped a buttock and been swiftly swept away one evening in Sigrún's darkened hallway had confirmed that for her, and she had watched helplessly as Sigrún lavished all her love and attention on Jens, while Jörundur increasingly occupied himself elsewhere.

"Y'know, Rúna, I don't know how I'd have managed without you that first year we lived in Hvalvík," Gunna said as Sigrún upended her wine glass. "You remember all the trouble with the school? A real nightmare that was. If you hadn't been there to look after Laufey, I'd never have got through it all."

"God, yes," Sigrún recalled. "It's never easy in a small place like this. When I came here it was the same non-stop speculation about who I was, where I came from, who I was related to, what my bra size was, why I'd decided to live here and not in Reykjavík any more, why I was single, if I'd always been single. It was endless, and nobody asks you anything straight out. Crazy."

"Isn't it just? It was the same in Vestureyri, but I didn't notice quite how nosy people can be until I came to live here. And it's all just gossip and whispers, nothing said out loud."

"You remember that rumour that we were, y'know, lady friends who were more than just good friends?" Sigrún crowed.

"Good grief. The blabbermouths have a lot to answer for sometimes," Gunna said.

"You're lucky with Steini," Sigrún said with the minutest trace of envy. "He even cooks. What a gem."

"Yup," Gunna agreed. "There's a lot to be said for a bloke who's old enough to be retired."

"Not talking about men again, are you?" Steini asked, reappearing and shaking his head in mock despair.

"We are indeed. Tell me, Steini, how do you know Ívar Laxdal? He sends you his regards, by the way."

Steini sat down, looked at the empty wine bottle and took a sip from Gunna's glass.

"Little chap, built like a barrel? He joined the Coast Guard the same year I did. He was as sharp as a knife, certainly smarter than the rest of us and undoubtedly destined for great things."

"So why did he end up as a copper?"

"He had a touch of colour blindness, nothing serious, but enough to put the lid on a career as a ship's officer, as far as I remember. So I guess he decided to go elsewhere. What's he doing in the police force?"

"He's my boss at the moment, at least until Örlygur comes back from sick leave. If Örlygur comes back from sick leave."

"Well say hello to him from me, will you? It must be twenty years since I saw him last. What's he like to work for?"

"Y'know, I really don't know yet. Like you said, he's as sharp as a knife. But every time I have to talk to him, I feel like a schoolgirl who hasn't done her homework properly. And tomorrow I have to see him for an official reprimand."

"What for?" Steini and Sigrún asked simultaneously.

"Ach. Nothing serious. Just speaking my mind out of turn."

"Well," Sigrún said. "That's something you've always had a talent for."

Wednesday 24th

GUNNA DIDN'T HAVE to find Ívar Laxdal. He was sitting at her desk when she arrived at seven.

"Good morning, Gunnhildur," he said seriously.

"Good morning. Steini sends his regards, by the way."

"Thank you. Now . . ."

"You need to give me a ticking-off."

"That's right. Just consider yourself reprimanded. This goes on your record and there's nothing I can do about that, but I don't think you'll need to worry too much about it."

"That's fair enough. I should have known better than to yell at Sævaldur in front of the others."

Ívar Laxdal nodded wisely.

"That's quite right. If you want to yell, do it in private," he said. "What's next on your agenda?"

"Depends. What did Sævaldur's team get out of whatsisname—Jón Jóhannsson—yesterday?"

"Very straightforward," Ívar Laxdal said with a shrug. "The man admitted everything, from shooting Bjartmar to threatening the bank teller. The technical team have been through his workshop like a dose of salts. They found the barrels of his shotgun that he'd sawn off, and even splinters that match the floor in Bjartmar's house."

"How so?" Gunna asked, intrigued.

"His first shot was at Bjartmar's feet and it also did a lot of damage to the floor, so there were fragments everywhere. It seems that Jón burned his shoes and overalls in a stove in his workshop, and there were splinters in them that were left in the ashes. Simple enough," Ívar Laxdal said with satisfaction.

"Motive?"

"Ah, this is where you come in, and where you and Sævaldur will have to be careful not to tread on each other's toes too much. Jón Jóhannsson will undoubtedly be undergoing a whole barrage of psychological tests and it's anybody's guess what they'll come up with. Certainly the man was under enormous pressure. He was up to his eyes in debt, had lost his house, and his wife had left, taking the child with her. In fact, she's upstairs now as well. But what's clear is that he was fixated on two people as the reason for all his misfortunes. One was the personal financial adviser who had become the face of the bank. The second was Bjartmar Arnarson."

"And why was that?"

"Because Jón Jóhannsson did a great deal of work as a subcontractor for a subsidiary company of Rigel Investment called Arcturus Development."

"The property development company."

"That's it. Arcturus built many of Rigel's properties and went bankrupt leaving virtually all of its contractors high and dry, and some of those went under as well. Jón Jóhannsson came out of it very badly. That was six months' work, and he reckons if it hadn't gone sour on him, he'd probably still be in the black."

"So he blames the late and unlamented Bjartmar personally for all his problems."

"Pretty much," Ívar Laxdal said. "And quite possibly with very good reason. What concerns me more than anything about this case is that it may well be impossible to find a jury that would convict him. My feeling is that the best we can hope for is a plea of insanity and a verdict that reflects that."

"This is already a high-profile case. It was all over the news yesterday and again this morning," Gunna observed. "It's going to dominate everything for a few weeks, I'd expect."

"Quite possibly, and it's certainly going to divert attention away from Svana Geirs for a day or two."

"More than likely," Gunna agreed.

"Gives you some peace and quiet, in that case," Ívar Laxdal said with a shadow of a smile. "But you might be interested to know that one of the Rigel Investment properties that Jón Jóhannsson worked on was the block on Lindargata where Svana Geirs lived. He's a plumber, and he fitted her bathroom and kitchen, along with a great many others, of course. Thought you might want to know."

"Tell me, Jón," Helgi said softly. "What was it about Bjartmar?"

"Everything," the big man replied quietly. A calm had come over him since the policewoman had led him from the bank with one hand on his elbow and the other holding his mutilated shotgun. Now he was relieved that he hadn't harmed that stupid boy who worked there.

"You had a dispute with him?"

"Did I ever!"

"Did you speak to him?"

"Only on the phone a couple of times. Never face to face. But I saw him about often enough."

"When was that?"

"At the block on Lindargata when I was fitting all those bathrooms and kitchens for Ingi Lár. We used to see him wandering about in his suit and wearing a helmet, looking like a twat. Then, after that, I used to notice him around his house. It's only a street or two above my place." He coughed. "What used to be our place until the bank had it off us," he corrected himself. "Look, I've already been through this with your mate, the fat bloke. Why do I have to tell you as well? Not that I have other plans."

"That's because I'm working on another investigation that concerns Bjartmar. So was this the only time that you spoke to him face to face?"

"You mean when I told him just what a bastard he was and then shot him?"

"That's it."

"Yup. That was it. Never spoke to the man in person before."

"So how did you know it was Bjartmar who was responsible for your financial problems?"

"Ingi Lár told me all about it," Jón said with heat. "I know Ingi and he wouldn't lie to me. He's come out of it badly as well, poor old feller. His company went bust because Bjartmar's company declared bankruptcy. Because Ingi didn't get his bills paid, he couldn't pay me, although he helped us out with what he could."

He smacked the table with a palm. "Ingi's broke as well now. He's sixty and doesn't have two pennies to rub together, so he's doing odd jobs for people who used to work for him. Good, eh?"

He sat back and scowled.

"Who's Elín Harpa?" Helgi asked.

Jón shrugged. "Some woman I did a job for. I think I left my phone there, but I figured I wasn't going to need it in prison, so I didn't bother going back for it."

"Where does she live?"

"Off Hringbraut somewhere," Jón said uncertainly.

"Where off Hringbraut?"

"Can't remember."

"How was she involved in your plans?"

"She wasn't," Jón said animatedly. "Look. I got a call asking if I could replace a kitchen tap. I did the job, took five thousand for it and that's all. I might have left my phone there. Or I might have dropped it somewhere."

"Where does she live, Jón?"

"Like I said, one of those streets off Hringbraut. I can't remember which."

"All right. If you won't tell us, we'll find her."

THE RAMBLING HOUSE on Álfhólsvegur was closer to the road than its neighbours were, and Gunna could see people inside as she pulled up and switched off the engine. Not that many years ago, this had been a quiet residential street, but it had since become a thoroughfare from one end of Kópavogur to the other, with cars taking it as fast as the vicious speed bumps allowed.

"I'm looking for Högni Sigurgeirsson," Gunna said to the wrinkled woman who answered the door. "Is he here?"

The woman didn't answer, but stepped back and to one side to allow Gunna in, letting out a yell of surprising volume from someone so diminutive.

"Högni! Someone for you, boy!"

Gunna closed the door behind her and followed the woman into the kitchen, where an elderly man sat at a table and leafed through Morgunbladid while drawing on what Gunna could smell was a filterless Camel even before she saw the overflowing ashtray at his elbow.

He nodded and returned to his newspaper as the woman went through another door, calling out without getting a reply other than a blast of cold air. A door from the house's living room leading to the garden swung open and showed where Högni had disappeared.

"I can't understand it. He was here just now," she grumbled. "Láki! Where did Högni go?" she called to the man at the kitchen table.

"Dunno," he wheezed.

"Who are you anyway?" the woman asked finally, looking up at Gunna. "I'd have thought Högni's girlfriends would be a bit younger."

"I'm from the police," Gunna said stiffly. "This is the address he gave us, so I was wondering who you are?"

"I'm sorry, dear. I'm his mother's aunt. It's terrible about poor Svanhildur. The lad's awfully upset, you know. Would you like a cup of coffee?" She took unsteady steps into the kitchen and fetched a cup without waiting for a reply. "Sit down, dear."

"And have you found out who did it yet?" the man rumbled. "She was a lovely girl, Svana was. A crying shame what happens these days. And what do the police do about it? Nothing," he went on, oblivious to Gunna's presence as he continued to leaf through the newspaper.

The old woman poured coffee as black as tar into the cup. Gunna sipped doubtfully, but found that it was excellent.

"How has Högni been?" she asked.

"Æi. He's taken it badly, the poor dear."

"Is he here much?"

"No, we don't see a lot of him, but we're up early and in bed early, not like you youngsters."

"Is he working, do you know?"

"He can't work much, not since his accident, so he only does a few hours. He broke his leg a year ago."

"Two years ago," the old man corrected.

"Two years ago. Lord, but time flies. Yes, he's a martyr to his bad leg, the boy is."

Not so much a martyr that he can't shift quickly out of the back door as soon as the police show up, Gunna thought, draining her cup.

"Do you know where I might find him?"

"Couldn't tell you, dear. His car's not there, so he might have gone to work."

"And where's that?"

• • •

GUNNA STOPPED AT the traffic lights and fretted as the driver of a battered Mazda that had once been canary yellow revved its engine in front of her. She could see that there were four youngsters in the car and the driver was riding the clutch, waiting to be away the second the lights changed.

She pulled away gently as the Mazda raced ahead with a squeal of rubber, and eased to a halt behind it at the next set of lights, this time noticing the missing licence plate. The boys in the Mazda again pulled away with a roar from its cracked exhaust. Gunna let them go, and then swung the latest hired Audi into the outside lane but kept under the speed limit.

At the third set of lights, she was still moving as they flashed to green and she cruised easily past the Mazda, indicating to pull into the inside lane ahead of it. This time she saw that the car's front licence plate was also missing, and her jaw set in irritation.

She was ready to slow right down and force it to a halt when her communicator buzzed.

"Ninety-five-fifty, zero-five-sixty-one."

She clicked the button on her earpiece and replied, keeping an eye on the Mazda in the mirror.

"Zero-five-sixty-one, ninety-five-fifty."

"We've a sighting of the grey Opel you're looking for. It's outside a pizza takeaway in the Bakki district shopping centre. Pizza-K, the place is called."

The Mazda roared past and the driver looked at Gunna, tapping his forehead with one finger and mouthing an obscenity.

"Thanks for that. I'm just turning into Stekkjarbakki, so I'll check out the shops. Are you there now?"

"Yeah. We're heading back on to Reykjanesbraut. You don't need backup, do you?"

"No. I'll be all right. But there's a dirty yellow Mazda just overtaken me well over the speed limit, four young men in it. You might want to see what they're up to."

"Will do. Did you see the vehicle's registration?"

"No licence plate, front or back."

"Even better. Thanks. Out."

Gunna took the turning off the main road and cruised slowly around the row of shops and takeaways that served the suburb. It was a long time since she had been in this part of town, and it looked shabbier and more tired than when she had been here last. She drove into the car park and looked around for Pizza-K, finally locating it under its garish red and white signboard on the far side. She parked where she had a good view of the place, but Högni's grey Opel was nowhere to be seen.

"The bugger's gone," she cursed, clicking her communicator. "Zero-five-sixty-one, ninety-five-fifty. 'Where did you say you saw that grey Opel?'" she asked.

"It was right outside Pizza-K ten minutes ago."

"OK. He's gone. Can you keep an eye out again, please?"

"Yeah. Will do. My mate's just booking four idiots in a clapped-out Mazda that looks like they bought it from a scrapyard, thanks."

"Pleased to hear it," Gunna replied. "Out."

She checked her phone for messages and looked up to see a grey Opel pull up outside Pizza-K and the familiar bulk of Högni Sigurgeirsson haul himself out. She got out of the Audi and walked towards the shop, looking the Opel over carefully on the way.

"Yeah?" a young man with pocked cheeks and a white hat behind the counter greeted her.

"Grey Opel outside. Whose is it?"

"'Scuse me. Don't speak good Iceland," the man said with a pout. "Grey car," Gunna said clearly, pointing. "Who?"

"Is Högni car."

"And where's Högni?"

"He here," the man said without interest, turning away to deal with something on the counter in front of him. He looked up to see Gunna's police badge held out in front of him, just as Högni, a red-and-white baseball cap on the back of his head, appeared from the kitchen with a pizza box in his hands.

"Högni. This look for you," the man behind the counter announced as Högni's face fell.

"The man I've been looking for," Gunna said cheerfully.

"Look, yeah. Er, I'm working right now, see. I can't talk to you."

"You work here?"

"Yeah. I deliver pizzas sometimes," he said sulkily.

"Well you'd better get someone else to deliver that one, because you and I need to have words."

Högni made for the open door at a trot and Gunna stepped in front of him. His bulk would have been enough to bowl her over, but he stopped short.

"Now."

Högni looked bewildered.

"Hey, Ahmed," he called to the man behind the counter. "Can you get someone else to take this one?"

"Yeah. Z'OK. Andrzej back soon. You go. Take with you police," he said shortly, almost spitting out the last word.

Högni followed Gunna outside and she opened the door of the Audi for him to sit in the passenger seat. Infuriatingly, the craving for a cigarette came over her as she got into the driver's side, but she ruthlessly banished it and took a square of gum from the pack in the door pocket.

She chewed slowly and looked at Högni as he sat rigidly.

"Why did you do it, Högni?" she asked softly, and watched as he crumpled in the seat. Tears started to roll down his red cheeks and he wiped his nose with the Pizza-K baseball cap.

Gunna handed him a tissue. The overbearing bluster that had been the main feature of any conversation so far with Högni had disappeared. He sniffed and his face relaxed with what she guessed was a release of tension now that he was no longer guarding a secret.

"I'd like you to tell me exactly what happened, Högni, OK? No pressure, and this is between us. We'll have to do it formally later, but tell me the story first. Did you find Svana?"

Högni hiccoughed and nodded. "She said I could come round and see her around half one, two. We were going to go to the gym and work on some fitness regimes for me."

"So you were training together?"

"Yeah. She said I needed to lose ten kilos at least. She was going to try and get me fixed up as a personal trainer. But she said I couldn't be an unfit personal trainer."

Gunna appraised the young man's baggy form and compared it to his late sister's toned figure. She could only agree with Svana's diagnosis that losing the double chin and some of the belly would probably make him a happier individual.

"So you went to her flat? You have a key?"

"Yeah," he said, sniffing hard and pulling a ring of keys from his pocket. He picked one out and held the bunch by it. "And I knew the alarm code."

"So you let yourself in. What then?"

"I never hurt her," he said plaintively. "I would never have done that."

"I can see that, Högni. But you have to tell me everything you can. Even a tiny detail could take us to the person who really did it."

"I knocked, opened the door and went in. The alarm wasn't on." He gulped. "So I called out and went into the kitchen and saw her there on the floor."

"Did you move her at all?"

Högni shook his head.

"So when we arrived at the scene she was lying just as she fell? Is that right?"

Högni nodded vigorously and his chin quivered. "I touched her cheek. And her hand."

"But you knew she was dead?"

"Her eyes were open but she couldn't see anything."

"And you answered the phone, didn't you?" Gunna asked.

"How do you know? Yeah. The phone was there on the side. It started to ring and so I picked it up."

"Do you know who was calling?"

"Dunno. Didn't look at the screen. It was some guy and he wanted to know where Svana was so I just said she was busy right now and couldn't talk to him," Högni blurted out before drawing a breath. "He got a bit angry. Asked who the hell I was and why I was answering Svana's phone, so I told him I was her brother and he just laughed. Then he said he needed to talk to her and I should give her the phone. I said no, I couldn't and he wanted to know why."

"You told him?"

"It's all fuzzy now. I think so. I think I said she won't wake up, or something like that."

Högni was starting to collect himself. The gasps for breath had calmed and the hiccoughs had disappeared.

"What was his reaction to that?"

"I don't know. He must have hung up."

"All right. So what did you do then?"

"I don't really know."

"You mean you panicked?"

"Ummm."

Högni nodded a second time and Gunna sat in thought. She had suspected that Högni could have been responsible for his sister's death in a furious outburst, but the man's obvious distress now was going a long way towards convincing her otherwise.

But knowing that Svana was already dead by the time the last conversation on her phone took place was enough to open up other possibilities.

Högni saw the look of determination on Gunna's face and immediately quailed.

"What's going to happen now?" he asked.

Gunna looked up and shook herself back to the here and now. She started the engine.

"You have a lot of questions to answer. Put your seat belt on, please. We've going to Hverfisgata to finish this. It's going to take a while, I'm afraid."

"But I'm supposed to be at work. I'll lose my job," Högni protested. "And what about my car?"

"Sorry, work's going to have to wait," she said sternly, and clicked her communicator. "Zero-five-sixty-one, ninety-five-fifty. Busy?"

"Not right now. What can we do for you?"

"Can you meet me by the Arnarbakki shops, outside Pizza-K?"

"Will do."

"Give me your car keys, please, Högni," Gunna instructed, and he meekly handed them over. "We're going to Hverfisgata and I'll have to ask you to make a statement and account for every single thing you remember from the second you walked in the door of Svana's flat. Understand?"

Högni nodded as a squad car appeared at the far side of the car park and nosed through the traffic towards them to pull up next to the Audi. Gunna wound down the window to greet the two officers sitting in it.

"All right?" the one nearest to her said with a dazzling smile.

Gunna leaned out of her window and passed Högni's keys across.

"Grey Opel over there, guys. I need one of you to bring it down to the station for me. But first, will one of you go into

Pizza-K and tell the snotty bastard behind the counter that this young man's not been arrested, but he'll be helping us with an enquiry for the rest of the day and it's not his fault?"

Högni slumped in the chair. The release of tension in the young man had already exhausted him. Although Gunna would have preferred to treat him gently, a gut feeling told her that this also needed some quick and determined handling.

Eiríkur handed her a photocopy of Högni's newspaper interview and sat back to listen, while Gunna pushed it across the table towards him.

"This is what made me think," she told him, tapping it with one finger. "It was the worst feeling of my life seeing my big sister, who we all loved and admired so much, lying dead in front of me," she read out, and waited for a reaction.

"You know, Högni, Svana is still in the mortuary at the National Hospital. I know your father identified her, because I was with him. He'd already told me that you and your mother couldn't face it, which was one of the reasons I made sure I was there as well. It's not an easy thing to do, and it's a lot harder on your own," she said, quickly stifling the expected but unwelcome pangs of loss that fought their way to the surface of her mind.

Högni's eyes were blank pools, staring at his hands in front of him. "Are you aware, Högni, how she earned a living and could afford to live in a place like that?"

"Yeah," he muttered, looking down, his voice barely audible. "Mum and Dad don't know."

"I think we'll try and keep it that way," Gunna said. "Did you know any of the men, or ever see any of them?"

"Svana knew tons of people and she was always hanging about with someone different. I never knew who most of them were."

"You left the flat. You didn't think to call the police or an ambulance?"

"No. I was just really confused. I knew she was dead and an ambulance wouldn't be able to help her. I was scared it looked like I might have done it. . ." His voice tailed off into silence.

"Why's that?" Gunna asked softly.

"Because we'd had an argument a few days before. It was when she told me how she really made her money with those guys. She said she'd tried being married and didn't like it, so this was like being married to four rich men at the same time but without having to cook or wash smelly underwear." He sighed. "We had a real screaming argument in the street outside Fit Club. I yelled at her that she was a slag and she screamed back that I was an idiot who should go back to the fish factory where I belonged."

"When was this?"

"I'm not sure exactly. A few days before."

"So you made up?"

"Sort of," Högni said. "She called me and asked if I'd come round in the afternoon. She said she had some good news and wanted to tell me, said she was going to be back on TV and she could pack in the rich men. She said she'd see if she could find herself some toyboy who would cook and wash her underwear for her."

"So what did you do with her phone?"

"Dropped it, maybe. I don't remember."

"You closed the door of the flat?"

"Don't know. Don't think so."

"Did you see anyone on your way out of the building?"

"Nah. Don't think so. Or there could have been the cleaner on the bottom floor. I'm not sure."

"Did you go anywhere else in the flat, or notice anything out of place? Anything unusual?"

"I don't think so," Högni said. "But the rose wasn't there, neither was the bat," he added darkly.

"Bat?"

"Yeah. She kept an old baseball bat behind the front door, just in case, she said."

"What was that about a rose?"

"She had a little porcelain rose on a plate, about so big," he explained, making a ring of his thumb and finger. "When she didn't want to be disturbed, the rose was hung on the door."

"You mean when one of the syndicate was there?"

Högni nodded. "Yeah. I suppose the only ones who knew about that were me and the . . . men," he said with hesitation. "But I didn't know why until the day before we had our argument. I went to see her and rang the bell, but didn't get an answer. I didn't have much to do, so I thought I'd wait, and sat outside. Then she came out, hanging on this guy's arm, an old bastard, way too old for Svana."

"What do you call old?"

"Shit. As old as my dad, I guess, and he's past sixty. This guy was a stocky feller, bald and old."

Jónas Valur, Gunna thought, recognizing instantly the description of the man's domed forehead.

"Did you know any of Svana's rich men? Did you ever see any of them?"

"Nah, only that old bastard," Högni said, and for the first time Gunna heard a note of uncertainty in his voice. "I just knew there were four of them, because she said so, and she said she was going to stop seeing them soon."

"Do you know if the men themselves were aware that she was planning to bring this arrangement to an end?"

"Dunno. Don't think so."

"Do you think she'd tell you or them first?" Gunna probed. "Dunno," Högni repeated. "But I'd have thought she'd have told me first after we'd had that argument."

"Right. Thank you, Högni. That will do for the moment. You're free to go now, but I'll certainly need to speak to you again tomorrow. Will you go home?"

"Yeah." Högni looked down at his hands.

"Go and get some rest. I'll call you in the morning."

"Will I go to jail?" he asked in a small voice.

"WHAT'S THE RUSH this time?" Helgi demanded, stifling his irritation at being bundled out of the building and into a car.

"Nothing like striking while the iron's hot," Gunna replied with determination in her voice. "Listen up. According to that greasy pudding, Svana Geirs was about to bring the syndicate to an end and give all her sugar daddies notice to quit."

"Right?" Helgi said, an eyebrow shooting up. "Win the lottery or something, did she?"

"Nope, not that good," Gunna told him, slipping the car into the stream of traffic. "It seems she was getting a second chance at TV, so I reckon that between Fit Club and telly, she reckoned she could afford to give up shagging for cash."

"All right, so where are we going now?"

"You're going to see Bjarki Steinsson. Push him hard on when he last saw Svana. Ask for all the details you can get, confiscate his laptop if you have to and get in touch with his internet provider if you think that might produce an alibi. Don't forget that we know now that Högni answered Svana's phone at thirteen fifty-three and she was already dead then. I'd been working on the premise that she answered her own phone. Miss Cruz said between twelve and three, but now we know it was between twelve and thirteen fifty-three, which shoots down Hallur's alibi in flames."

"If I'm going to grill the accountant, where are you off to?"

"I'm going to go and pay Jónas Valur a visit and ask him just the same. Call me when you're finished with Bjarki Steinsson and we'll both go and see Hallur Hallbjörnsson. All right?" Gunna asked, pulling up outside the office block where Bjarki Steinsson's fourth-floor offices overlooked the building sites of Reykjavík's Shadow District.

A few minutes later Gunna parked outside the modest old building that disguised Jónas Valur's office.

The grim-face secretary looked her over with undisguised hostility, but gave way and rang through to Jónas Valur.

"He'll see you now," she informed Gunna primly.

Sitting in the half-dark behind his antique desk, Jónas Valur exuded gravitas. A desk lamp illuminated the papers in front of him and the light from the screen of a small but sleek laptop in front of him shone on the dome of his forehead.

"Good afternoon, Inspector," he said smoothly as Gunna's footfalls echoed on the wooden floor towards him.

"Sergeant, actually," she said, taking a seat.

"For the moment," Jónas Valur said with a smile, quickly extinguished. "How's my old friend Chief Inspector Örlygur Sveinsson?" he asked, stressing the Chief Inspector.

"If you know him well, then I suppose you'd know he's still on sick leave. I've no idea how serious his condition is, but we're hoping he'll be back soon. How come you know Örlygur? I wouldn't have thought someone like you would move in the same circles as a lowly copper," Gunna said, looking down at the desk in front of her and noticing for the first time the red and gold Masonic ring and the man's surprisingly long and delicate fingers.

A musician's hands, or a craftsman's, Gunna thought, suddenly recalling her father's shovel-like hands that could nonetheless repair the most delicate machinery with a skill and patience that she would have loved to be able to master herself.

"When was your last contact with Svana Geirs?" she asked bluntly.

"I thought we'd already been through this?"

"Maybe we need to go through it again."

Jónas Valur reached for a diary on the desk in front of him. "The sixth. That was the last time I saw her."

"Five days before she died?"

"Precisely."

"How long did you spend together? Did you go anywhere you might have been seen or where someone else could confirm this?"

"Officer, our last meeting consisted of a disappointing DVD of some slushy film that Svana wanted to see, a reasonable takeaway from Ning's and some rather energetic sex—not necessarily in that order. We spent the night at her apartment and I left in the morning," Jónas Valur said with the return of his narrow smile.

"So you last saw her on the morning of the seventh? I asked what your last contact with her was. Emails, phone calls, maybe?" Jónas Valur shook his head with a show of regret. "I'm sorry, but I can't help you with anything subsequent."

"I see," Gunna said. "I was wondering who could be the JVH she called on the ninth and had an eight-minute conversation with?"

A sudden spasm of anger flashed in his eyes and was instantly suppressed.

"I have no idea, officer. There are surely plenty of people in Iceland with those same initials."

"Actually, you'd be surprised just how few there are, according to the National Registry. It seems a coincidence too striking to ignore that Svana Geirs would know two people with the same initials. It also seems odd that she wouldn't have your name and number in her phone memory when the rest of the syndicate are all there."

With one hand in her pocket, she pressed the green button on her phone that her thumb had been hovering over, while looking Jónas Valur in the eyes.

"It may well seem odd. . ." he began, shutting his mouth suddenly as a faint buzz could be heard from his jacket hanging on an old-fashioned hatstand in the corner. His eyes narrowed and Gunna immediately sensed the man's fury.

"I take it that's your phone ringing over there?" she asked sweetly, lifting her own phone from her pocket. "If you answer it, you'll find yourself talking to me."

"Probably nothing important," Jónas Valur said dismissively. "I receive dozens of calls every day."

"But you don't," Gunna corrected him. "I happen to know that your personal mobile number is carefully given out to only a few selected friends and your business calls come here to be screened by the witch next door."

Jónas Valur stood up and leaned forward with his knuckles on the surface of the desk. "I think I've told you everything I have to say without a lawyer present. So if you don't mind, I'm a busy man."

His eyes indicated the door.

"What did Svana talk to you about?" Gunna asked, remaining seated as he loomed over her.

"I have said everything I'm prepared to say."

"Did she call you to let you know that the syndicate was being closed down?"

"What the hell are you talking about, you stupid woman? Don't you know what's good for you?" Jónas Valur hissed, lifting his knuckles from the desk and impotently balling his fists.

"If I'm expected to take that as a threat, then it might be as well to continue this conversation at Hverfisgata," Gunna said in a voice that she did her best to keep even.

"On what grounds?" he sneered. "Sleeping with a murder victim? That doesn't mean that I had any hand in her death."

"Or Steindór Hjálmarsson's?"

Jónas Valur sank back into his chair and his face hardened. "What did you say?"

"You heard me."

"I had nothing whatsoever to do with that."

"That's not what I've heard."

"That was all Bjartmar's doing."

"And he's conveniently no longer with us."

Jónas Valur's eyes bulged with fury that he concealed with a humorless smile. "Nonetheless, it was Bjartmar's affair entirely. He was a good friend, but the man had a temper that he sometimes found difficult to rein in. I knew nothing of this until long after the event, and then only through unreliable hearsay. Needless to say, I never asked Bjartmar about these rumours."

This time Gunna stood up and towered over him.

"In that case you won't have any objection to making a formal statement to that effect. Nine tomorrow morning at Hverfisgata? Ask for me at the main desk," she said crisply, turning to leave Jónas Valur glaring at her as she closed his office door behind her.

Gunna hunted around for the car, cursing the department's finances that left them short of vehicles and forced them to hire cars to fill the gap. She clicked the fob, saw lights flash and strode across the car park to where today's Audi waited for her.

Her phone trilled as she started the engine, and she fumbled for it as the car began to bump forward through the puddles.

"Gunnhildur," she barked without bothering to check the caller ID.

"Hæ, it's me. Busy?"

"As always. What can I do for you, Skúli?"

"Ah. It's more a case of what I can do for you."

"Go on," Gunna instructed, intrigued, letting the car come to a halt. She heard Skúli take a deep breath.

"It's about Gulli Ólafs. I've been talking to a friend of a friend and thought you might be interested to know there's a rumour around the news desk that he and Helena Rós are more than usually good friends. You know, Hallur Hallbjörnsson's wife?"

"That's very diplomatically put, Skúli. I don't suppose you could name a source, could you?"

"I could, but I'd best not."

Gunna put the car into gear and it jerked forward, splashing its way through a deeper than usual pool of rainwater.

"That certainly throws a new light on things. Thanks for letting me know, Skúli. It's appreciated."

"That's not all, though. Listen . . ."

Gunna braked and the car ground to a halt a second time.

"There was a journal meeting this morning and a load of the usual old stuff came up, but there was also a mention by one of the senior editors that he has someone sitting on a story about Svana Geirs and her little club. There was a bit of an argument about whether or not we should actually use it when it shows up, as it's definitely going to upset her family."

"And what was the verdict?"

"That we use it. If we don't, someone else will, so we might as well have it," Skúli said quickly. "It'll have to be under an in-house byline, as the guy who's done the legwork on it would probably be sacked if his employers find out he's freelancing as well. So are you thinking what I'm thinking?"

"Gulli Ólafs?"

"I reckon you'd be right, especially taking the rumours about Helena Rós into account."

"Thanks, Skúli. I'll keep that to myself for the moment. But I'd really appreciate it if you let me know when this is going to hit any headlines. OK?"

"Will do. Got to go. There's someone coming."

The phone went dead in her hand and Gunna sat with a puzzled frown on her face as the raindrops started to rattle on the car's roof.

"MESSAGE FROM THE Laxdal," Helgi said as he jumped into the car outside Bjarki Steinsson's office building.

"Which is?" Gunna asked, letting out the clutch and roaring into the traffic.

"First, turn on your communicator. Second, he formally requested the Portuguese police pick up Sindri Valsson, but by the time they got round to knocking on his door, he'd done a bunk. He's in Iceland, apparently, according to his neighbours."

"Like hell," Gunna grunted. "I'll bet he's sunning himself in Tortoiseland or whatever the bloody place is called."

"Tortola, chief. It's a tax haven in the British Virgin Islands."

"I was just about to say that. But I suppose it's out of our hands and he'll surface eventually. What d'you reckon on Bjarki Steinsson?"

"Bloody hell, chief. The man's distraught. He couldn't have been more upset if had been his wife who had been murdered."

"Still?"

"Yeah. Even more so because it seems Svana had gently given him the push, along with all the others."

"Ah! Högni was telling the truth on that bit, at least."

Helgi looked doubtful. 'Who knows? I reckon he probably did it. They had a shouting match and he bashed his sister over the head in the heat of the moment. That's what Sævaldur thinks, and I'm inclined to go along with him on this one."

"Don't bring Sævaldur Bogason into it. I don't care if the man's a chief inspector; he has neither imagination nor common sense."

"Fair enough. Hallur next, then?"

"Yup, the oily bastard himself."

"How was Jónas Valur?"

Gunna swerved to overtake a heavily loaded truck and cursed as the car behind flashed its lights.

"Yeah, piss off, or I'll have you for dangerous driving," Gunna yelled as the jeep sped past. "Let's say that I'm more than likely not on Jónas Valur's Christmas card list, nor likely to ever be on it, and my description is probably being circulated right now among the funny-handshake brigade with instructions to blight this bloody awkward old cow's career at all costs."

"A productive day's work, then?"

"We'll see a bit later on what happens. We'll have an Interpol alert out for Sindri Valsson. I've told Eiríkur already that I want Jónas Valur tailed to see where he goes, and hopefully we'll be able to track his mobile as well."

"Serious stuff. Where are we seeing Hallur?"

"We'll try his office to start with."

Gunna parked close to the City Hall, flashing her warrant card at a parking attendant who saw them walk away from the car without buying a ticket. Inside the old building they found only a secretary, who seemed pleased to have company.

"He was here this morning and said he'd be back soon, but I haven't seen him since," she said plaintively. "His diary's blank for the afternoon."

"No idea where he is?"

The girl shook her head. "Haven't a clue. Maybe you could try his mobile?"

Gunna and Helgi sat outside in the car.

"What d'you reckon, chief?"

"No idea. He's not in Parliament, he's not in his cubbyhole, he has no official business, otherwise the secretary would have been aware of it. He's not shagging Svana and I somehow doubt that he's at Fit Club. So where's the least likely place a man like Hallur would be?"

"At home, I reckon."

"We'd best try there and then give it up as a bad job," Gunna said, starting the car once more.

It was a ten minute drive to the leafy suburb where Hallur Hallbjörnsson lived in the Vogar district, but it could have been a different world. There was birdsong instead of the incessant grumble of traffic, and Gunna wound down a window to let in a little fresh air as she took the car gently along the deserted street, looking out for twitching curtains in kitchen windows.

"Someone's going to call the police in a minute, I expect," she said grimly. "That's his place, there."

She pointed and drove slowly past.

"Car's there," Helgi said, peering through the sparse hedge as they passed the house, and Gunna reversed into a driveway to turn around and go back. Helgi screwed up his eyes to see better, staring at the antique Mercedes tucked as far along the driveway as it would go.

"Is he in the car?" Gunna asked. "Can you see him, Helgi?"

She stopped where they could see along the length of the driveway to the car half hidden behind some bushes.

"He's been sitting there a while now."

Gunna switched off the engine and tapped the wheel with her fingertips as they waited for Hallur to either finish his call and get out of the car, or else drive away. After what seemed an age, her patience snapped.

"The bloody man must know we're here by now, surely?"

"You'd have thought so," Helgi said thoughtfully.

"Hell and damnation," Gunna grated and got out of the car. Helgi rolled down his window and watched, expecting to see Hallur put his foot down and reverse out into the road, but nothing happened as Gunna approached. He watched her suddenly pick up her pace and run to the car door, where she pulled her scarf from inside her coat and turned towards him.

"Helgi! Quick! Ambulance!"

"Control, zero-two-sixty. Request ambulance urgent to Hrìmvogur 44," he said as calmly as he could into his communicator, watching Gunna wrap her scarf around her face as she opened the car's door and dragged an unconscious Hallur

Hallbjörnsson by his shoulders out of the driving seat to sprawl full-length on the gravel drive.

"Zero-two-sixty, control. On the way. Can you advise?"

"Carbon monoxide poisoning, I'd guess," Helgi replied, speaking as he jogged across the road.

Gunna had already dragged the unconscious man away from the car and was kneeling over him, one hand gripping his head by the chin and the other under his neck. She swooped down and locked her mouth over Hallur's, and Helgi could see the effort she was making to force air into the man's lungs. She lifted her head, looked to one side to see the fall of his chest, then turned to breathe again. Helgi reached for the man's wrist and felt vainly for a pulse.

"Any heartbeat?" Gunna asked quickly between breaths.

"Not yet. Stop a moment," he said, feeling for a pulse in Hallur's neck. "Yeah, faint, but it's there."

Gunna resumed, while Helgi felt again for a pulse in the wrist of the limp hand.

"We've got company," he said, as two small boys on bicycles stopped and stared at the end of the driveway.

"Hey!" Helgi called out.

"Me?" one of them shouted back. "What are you doing?"

"He's injured. There's an ambulance coming. Can you go to the corner and wait for it? Make sure they come to the right place?"

The two boys hurtled away just as the faint wail of a siren could be heard in the distance.

"Let me know when you want to switch," Helgi said quietly.

"Doing all right. Turn the engine off, will you?" Gunna said between breaths as the siren whooped and fell silent, its howl replaced by the rumble of tyres as it stopped in the street and two paramedics jumped out and trotted to the scene. One of them clipped a mask around Hallur's head and placed a clear plastic bladder in Helgi's hand.

"Here you go, squeeze that, will you, mate? Now, what happened?"

"Turned up to interview this chap and found him spark out in his car."

"D'you know if he's been drinking?"

"No idea. And the house is locked up."

Gunna sat on the tarmac and took deep breaths while the second paramedic linked up an oxygen cylinder to the mask.

"Is he going to be all right?" she asked.

"Couldn't say. D'you know how long he'd been in the car, or if he's taken anything?"

"No idea. We just turned up and watched him I suppose for a minute or two before I went and had a look to see what was up."

"Hard to say, then. We'll get him off to Casualty. Might be a bit touch and go, though."

"You reckon?" Gunna said.

"Yeah," he said without looking up from Hallur's face. "If it was a new Volkswagen with a catalytic converter, he'd probably be as right as rain in ten minutes, apart from a bastard of a headache. But an old heap like that Merc's bound to be bloody deadly. Gunnhildur, isn't it?"

"Yeah."

"Thought so. If you ring up in an hour or so, they'll tell you if he's still with us. Who is he, by the way?"

"Hæ, Mum. Bad day?" Laufey asked brightly.

Gunna hung her coat on the back of a chair and then dropped into it.

"Why? Does it show?"

"Duh. Yeah."

"Sorry, sweetheart. Since you asked, it has been a pretty crappy day. Where's Steini?"

"Don't know. Haven't seen him. Isn't he at work or some-thing?" Laufey asked with a trace of irritation in her voice.

Gunna realized as she pulled off her shoes just how tired she was and how draining trying to breathe life into Hallur Hallb-jörnsson had been.

"What were you doing, Mum? You look shattered."

Gunna yawned and started to undo her blouse.

"I shouldn't tell you things like this, but I've had to inform a lady that her husband tried to commit suicide this afternoon and that it's still too early to tell whether or not he'll be per-manently brain-damaged afterwards," Gunna said grimly.

Laufey sat wide-eyed. "Wow. Heavy."

"And when she heard that it was me and Helgi who stopped the idiot from killing himself, she told us we should have let the bastard finish the job and then burst into tears. So right now she's sedated in the same hospital as he is."

"Definitely a bad day."

"That's what it's like when you get to rub shoulders with the rich and famous. Anyway, it's been a bloody long day and I need a shower, badly," Gunna announced, her blouse balled in one hand and wrinkling her nose. "Is that my smelly feet or yours?"

"Yours, Mum, definitely." Laufey laughed. "What's for dinner?"

"Dinner? You mean you haven't cooked something ready for your old mum?"

"I thought Steini would be making dinner tonight."

"Apparently not," Gunna said through a second jaw-breaking yawn. "A takeaway, then. Decide what you want and we'll go and get it when I'm out of the shower."

"Woo-hoo! Junk food!"

Gunna stopped in the bathroom doorway.

"Not pizza, though," she decided. "Well, you can have pizza if you want. Some of that deep-fried fish would be good if they have it. See you in a minute," she said as Laufey pounced on the local shop's takeaway menu. "And ice cream," she added through the closed door as the hot water started to run.

"Ice cream? Aren't you on a diet?"

"To hell with the diet. I want ice cream," Gunna yelled back. "Because I'm worth it."

Thursday 25th

"WHAT DO YOU have for me, Gunnhildur?" Ívar Laxdal said with no preamble, overtaking at a smart trot as she made her way up the stairs deep in thought.

"What? Oh, sorry, I was miles away. What did you say?"

"Come with me. A quiet word before we both get busy."

Ívar Laxdal took Eiríkur's chair, while Gunna sat scanning her own desk and the junk piled on it.

"Three primary suspects. Jónas Valur Hjaltason, Bjarki Steinsson, Hallur Hallbjörnsson," she said. "I think one of these three either murdered Svana Geirs or possibly made sure that she was murdered. All three of them had left fingerprints in her flat in the week before she died."

A questioning black eyebrow crept up Ívar Laxdal's forehead.

"It could be any one of them. Jónas Valur is a vindictive old bastard and he's supposed to be here at nine to give a statement. You're not a Mason, are you?" Gunna asked suddenly.

"Why?"

"Just because. Jónas Valur is, and it seems he's a mate of Örlygur Sveinsson's."

Ívar Laxdal grinned and shook his head.

"Bjarki Steinsson is a bag of nerves and completely distraught," Gunna continued. "Most likely because Svana had called time on the syndicate, so there's the theory that he was so upset, he lost it and clobbered her. As for Hallur, who knows what his motives could be? Certainly he stood to lose his political career if the story came out."

"Sure? Plenty of people have stayed on in politics after being caught with their trousers round their ankles."

"Yeah, admittedly. But this wasn't your run-of-the-mill fuck on the side. He'd been paying her upkeep for the best part of two years. Somehow I don't think his career could have survived that."

"And the brother?"

"Possible, but I don't believe so."

"Sævaldur thinks Ómar Magnússon is the killer. He's killed before."

"Or not. We certainly have enough to look very hard at Sindri Valsson as the man genuinely responsible for that killing."

"And he's gone to ground somewhere, which a cynical man would see as an admission of a guilty conscience."

"Someone cynical like me," Gunna agreed.

"What next?"

"Clear some of the paper." Gunna looked with distaste at the contents of her desk. "Listen to what Jónas Valur comes up with, pay a visit to Hallur's poisonous wife and then start putting pressure on Bjarki Steinsson. There's something about this syndicate that none of them have been telling us, and I reckon he's the most likely one to crack."

"I'll leave you to it. Let me know how you get on," he commanded, and made for the door. "Don't screw up on this, Gunnhildur. We have to get this one right. If we don't . . ." He merely shook his head sadly.

GUNNA WAS DEEP in paperwork when her desk phone rang. She snapped out of updating her case notes and heard Sigvaldi on the front desk announce gloomily that she had a visitor.

"Eiríkur," she called out, rapidly signing forms without bothering to read them a second time. "There's a good friend of the police downstairs. How would you like to go down to reception and bring him up here to an interview room?"

"All right," Eiríkur replied, rising from his seat. "Who's that?"

"Jónas Valur Hjaltason. Delightful man, a philanthropist and a gentleman," she said drily. "Tell him I won't keep him waiting."

But Gunna did keep Jónas Valur waiting, delayed by an encounter with Sævaldur on the way, and their disagreement over charging Ómar Magnússon left her devoid of the good humor she had acquired by having signed off long-overdue paperwork.

"Apologies," she said irritably, bustling into the interview room where Jónas Valur lounged in one of the chairs while a dark-suited man with a greying combover who nevertheless put Gunna in mind of a wolf sat upright next to him.

"Good morning, officer. I've been waiting for some time now and I'd like to remind you that my time is valuable," Jónas Valur drawled.

"And so is mine," Gunna snapped more sharply than she had intended.

"My lawyer, Ólafur Ja–"

"Ólafur Jacobsen. Yes, we've crossed swords before."

"A regrettable miscarriage of justice," the lawyer sniffed.

"A miscarriage of justice in which your client had a bag of coke in his pocket and two more in the car he was driving."

"There was nothing whatsoever to link my client to the narcotics. A mistake, easily explained."

"The judge didn't think so."

"Evidence can be misleading."

"If you're implying that there was anything irregular with

that particular case, which is long closed, then I'm sure you're aware of the proper channels."

The lawyer frowned and pouted, and Gunna wanted to laugh but restrained herself.

"Just so my client is aware of circumstances."

"I'm sure you've told him everything he needs to know on the way here," Gunna said smoothly, turning to Jónas Valur. "You're prepared to give a statement?"

"My client has prepared a statement," the lawyer said, interrupting Jónas Valur before he could speak and sliding a single sheet of heavy paper across the desk between them. Gunna picked it up and sat back, taking her time to read it, while Jónas Valur gradually began to twitch and the lawyer fidgeted.

"So according to this, you were at your office from nine in the morning until after three on the day that Svana Geirs was murdered? You are aware that this contradicts your answer when I asked about your whereabouts before?"

"A mistake with his diary, my client assures me. He was in his office the whole day."

"And who will corroborate this?"

"Anna Fjóla Sigurbjörnsdóttir."

"The secretary?"

"Yes."

Gunna looked long and hard at Jónas Valur, who gazed clear-eyed back at her.

"When I spoke to you a few days ago, you recalled clearly that you had been working at home that morning and had lunch at the City Café before going to your office, where your secretary confirmed that you arrived at twelve thirty. Now you're claiming that you didn't leave your office all day long? Isn't that unusual?"

Jónas Valur opened his mouth to speak, but the lawyer beat him to it once again.

"My client has told you that he made a mistake when checking his diary. It's a simple enough error, and he has apologized for the oversight."

"He hasn't told me anything—only you have. It strikes me as highly unusual for your client not to leave his office at all for a whole day. Odd for a man who likes to take a walk around lunchtime?"

"Possibly," the lawyer rasped, tight-lipped.

"I think we've established beyond any reasonable doubt that you had a phone conversation with Svana Geirs shortly before she died. What was that about?" Gunna asked, looking directly at Jónas Valur, who glared stonily back at her.

"My client has no comment to make."

"This is the number of your personal mobile phone?"

Gunna showed him the seven digits she had noted down. Jónas Valur nodded imperceptibly, while the lawyer shook his head.

"No comment."

"You don't deny that you and a group of men had a simultaneous relationship with Svana Geirs, and that between you you all contributed to her livelihood?"

"My client prefers not to comment."

"In that case we appear to be at a deadlock," Gunna said, her patience wearing thin. "So that's it for now," she added. Jónas Valur immediately shoved his chair back and rose to his feet.

"Can I have an assurance that my client will not be harassed?" the lawyer asked in a flat voice but with a sneer on his face.

"As long as I can have an assurance that your client won't obstruct a murder investigation," Gunna snapped back. "I'm sure we'll have reason to talk again soon," she said as Jónas Valur and the lawyer left the room without another word or a backward glance.

In silence, Gunna escorted the two men down to the front

desk and watched them leave the building, Jónas Valur holding his tie in one hand to prevent a vicious wind from whipping it up, while Ólafur Jacobsen placed a hand on the top of his head to prevent his carefully arranged coiffure from collapsing.

Eiríkur appeared silently at her side as she glumly watched the two men get into a smart Mercedes that stopped for them outside.

"Right, my lad. I'd like you on your bike this minute. Get down to City Café to start with and see if Jónas Valur was in there the day Svana died. If not, try the other eateries and whatnot round there. Go out there and ask. See if we can demolish the stupid statement that evil-minded oaf wrote for him. All right?"

PICTURES IN ORNATE frames decorated every wall of the living room that stretched away into the distance. Some were garish abstracts; others were sepia-toned portraits of groups of children at various stages of adolescence, unconvincingly contrived to look as if they had been taken a century ago.

Gunna looked with unconcealed dislike at the display of bad taste on the walls while she and Helgi waited, standing uncomfortably next to a dining table that shone like a mirror, as Bjarki Steinsson carried on a muted argument with his wife just out of their earshot.

"I'm sorry. We can talk in my office," he said apologetically, leaving his wife mouthing impotently in the middle of a bitter whispered tirade. Gunna was struck by how drawn the man appeared, with black bags under his eyes and a look of not having slept for many nights.

He ushered them into a small room and stood behind the door as Helgi sat on the small sofa against one wall and Gunna took the deep leather chair by the desk.

"I'm sorry," Bjarki apologized, gesturing at the door. "Kristrún will listen . . ."

"We can take this to the station if that's a problem."

"No, no," Bjarki protested with fright in his eyes.

"On the eleventh, the day that Svana Geirs was murdered, you stated that you were with her all morning."

"Until soon after eleven. I don't remember exactly when I left," he said guardedly, then jumped as Helgi's phone rang.

"Yup?" Helgi answered and listened. "OK, mate. That's great. Yeah, you'd best tell her yourself."

He handed the phone to Gunna. "Eiríkur for you, chief."

"Any luck?" Gunna asked sharply.

"Oh yeah, chief. Jónas Valur had lunch at City Café. I got the manager to go through a stack of receipts and there it was. He has a tab there, pays once a month, lunch for two on the eleventh, clear as day. He definitely left the office that morning and the manager confirmed having seen him there."

"Good. Doesn't tell us much other than that he's lying," Gunna said. "Yeah, but that's not all, chief," Eiríkur went on.

Gunna listened, before handing the phone back to Helgi. She looked up at Bjarki as he hovered by the door.

"So what did the Svana Syndicate have to discuss on the evening before Svana died?"

"What do you mean?"

"You all had dinner together at City Café, you, Jónas Valur and Hallur, the night before her death. The only one missing, it seems, was Bjartmar Arnarson, leaving the three of you to talk something over, as you were there until close to midnight."

"He was in America," Bjarki said, a look of misery on his pale face as he leaned back on the door.

Suddenly he lurched forward as the door opened and his wife appeared.

"D'you want coffee?" she demanded.

"No, Kristrún, of course not. We won't be long, dear," he added, flustered.

"Actually, I'd like a cup if you're making some," Gunna said with a sly smile. "You too, eh, Helgi?"

"Yeah, definitely, chief."

With a look of fury, the woman departed to make the coffee that she had been certain nobody would want.

"Right. You have two minutes while your wife's not listening at the door. Talk," Gunna instructed.

"Svana had called us all. She said that she didn't want to continue with the syndicate any longer as she was going to be back on TV. I was . . . upset, to say the least. The others didn't seem too concerned, except Hallur. He was furious."

"Why?"

"Svana told me that someone had been pestering her, someone who clearly knew about the . . . the arrangement." He gulped. "I told Hallur and he went wild."

Gunna looked at Bjarki expectantly.

"We were all terrified of publicity. Well, Hallur and I, at any rate. I can't deny that . . . my wife . . ." He left the sentence unfinished. "Jónas Valur was almost amused, I think. He seemed to think that Svana was spinning us a yarn."

"In what way?"

"He's very shrewd and can be extremely suspicious. He seemed to think that Svana was looking for a payout."

"Blackmailing you all?"

Bjarki blanched. "That's an ugly word."

"So is murder," Gunna reminded him. "And Bjartmar?"

"I didn't speak to him myself, but Jónas Valur had called him earlier in the day. He said that Bjartmar's marriage was a wreck anyway, so he wasn't concerned on that score, but if we wanted to split the price of her silence four ways, such as the flat she was living in, that was fine with him. That was the message, anyway."

"So the ones with something to lose were you and Hallur?"

Bjarki nodded miserably.

"Coffee!" called an angry voice beyond the door.

"Yes, dear," Bjarki replied.

"Make it quick, before she comes to get you," Gunna growled.

"If the story came out, it would wreck my marriage," Bjarki said with wide eyes. "My wife . . . her social position, you understand . . ."

"Yes. Go on. And Hallur?"

"God, it would destroy his career. He's always had ambitions, but he was fishing for something higher up the ladder and would probably have got it fairly soon."

"Until he wound up in intensive care."

"What . . . ?" Bjarki Steinsson's eyes reminded Gunna of saucers. "On the news they said he'd been in an accident, and I couldn't get through to Helena Rós last night. You mean . . . ? Will he be all right?"

"Who knows? What happened? What did you decide between yourselves?"

"We tried to talk it through with Jónas Valur, but he'd had a few drinks by then. Hallur was beside himself, asked what the hell they could do to keep Svana quiet, and he pressed Jónas Valur harder than I would have done, asking whether she would keep quiet even if she'd been paid off, whether the whole thing would start up again next time she ran out of money."

"And?"

"Jónas Valur said we could . . ." He hesitated and looked up. "We could all start screwing her again if she hadn't got too slack by then," he quoted in a clear voice. "Hallur was beside himself, said that it was all right for the rest of us, but it was different for him with a career ahead of him to think about. So Jónas Valur just said, 'Well you'd better sort it out then.' That was it. He left. I saw him sign the chit at the bar and that was it, the last I saw of him."

"So who killed Svana Geirs?" Gunna asked, staring straight at him.

"I don't know," he whispered almost soundlessly as a tear threatened to overflow the corner of one eye.

To Bjarki Steinsson's dismay, the dining table's deep shine had been covered by a cloth, on which were arranged plates of cakes and biscuits, cups and little jugs of cream and milk.

"Please, now you'll have to stay for a while," he whispered to Gunna, staring at the table. She saw Helgi's eyes light up and her heart softened.

"Certainly. Actually, there's another matter I wanted to speak to you about," she said, settling herself in one of the matching high-backed chairs as Bjarki Steinsson's wife poured coffee into dainty cups and Helgi filled a delicate-looking plate with slices of cake.

"What's that?" Bjarki asked, still blank-eyed after the conversation in his office.

"Kleifaberg. You did the accounts for Kleifaberg?"

"You mean Kleifar, Jónas Valur's company?"

"No," Gunna corrected, sipping the aromatic coffee and nodding her thanks to Bjarki's wife, off whom anger still coming in waves. "The company that Jónas Valur, Bjartmar Arnarson and Sindri Valsson ran between them until a few years ago."

"Oh, Kleifaberg," Bjarki said, as if a ghost had come back to haunt him. "Yes. We prepared their accounts for several years."

"Good. What really went on there? They bought property, developed it and it sold. Nothing unusual about that. But as far as I can make out, the real profits came from buying some plum sites at extremely low prices."

"Yes . . .?" he said uncertainly. "I really think you'd have to speak to them about that."

"Bjartmar is dead, Sindri Valsson has disappeared

somewhere in southern Europe and Jónas Valur is far from inclined to be co-operative right now. Off the record, I'd like you to tell me what went on. It would be, let's say, helpful on your part."

"Strictly off the record?"

Gunna nodded and sipped while Helgi popped another delicate biscuit into his mouth and smiled his appreciation.

"Well," Bjarki sighed. "It was one of those things that wasn't strictly speaking illegal, but . . ." He tailed off sadly.

"Less than ethical?" Gunna finished for him, and watched him nod in glum agreement.

"Hallur was on a lot of committees and he made sure some sales of land went through quietly to Kleifaberg without being discussed or advertised. Like I said, it wasn't illegal, but it wasn't exactly acceptable either. Kleifaberg developed some sites themselves with housing complexes, and other parcels of land they just sold on after a while."

"You did the accounting for this scam?"

"I don't know if I'd call it a scam," Bjarki said with the first sign of any kind of authority that Gunna had seen.

"What do you call it, then? What would the newspapers have called it if they had found out? What about Steindór Hjálmarsson?" she asked suddenly, and Helgi looked up quickly.

"Who?"

"Come on. A young man who was a bookkeeper at Kleifaberg. He died in 2000 after smelling a rat."

"Oh, him. Very sad. Didn't he get beaten up or something? It was a long time ago now."

"It was sad. But he's no less dead for it having been ten years ago."

"I, er, I don't know. It's not something I could safely comment on."

"I assume Kleifaberg made a considerable amount of money out of this," Gunna said flatly, and Bjarki nodded.

"It was a highly profitable venture," he said finally.

"Where did all the cash go?"

"That's not for me to say."

"We're off the record, don't forget. I know you did the tax returns for Jónas Valur and Bjartmar's companies. So where did it go?"

Bjarki shrugged helplessly. "Abroad, mostly. Bjartmar was already running Landex, and a lot of his cash went into setting up Sandex in Spain. Sindri bought two hotels and a golf course in Portugal. It's a delightful place. We've been there a couple of times," he said wistfully, and then regretted his words.

"I hope you had a lovely time," Gunna said acidly. "What I want to know is how Sindri Valsson was made aware that Steindór Hjálmarsson found out about this scam—because I have no doubt as to who battered him to death."

"No? Surely not?"

"There's enough evidence to make a case," Gunna lied as Helgi coughed discreetly. "Maybe you weren't aware of quite how ruthless these people are? Come on, Helgi, I think we'd better be on our way."

Helgi dusted crumbs from the front of his jacket and rose unwillingly to his feet, taking a longing glance at a banana and chocolate cake on the table that he had already done some serious damage to.

"This was off the record, Bjarki," Gunna warned him. "That goes for both of us, and there's no need for you to pass any of this conversation on to Jónas Valur or anyone else, otherwise what you've told me might suddenly be on the record. Understood?"

"Understood," the accountant said, looking miserably after them as they made for the door and he clicked it shut behind them.

"There's a man who's in the shit up to his neck," Helgi said knowingly, as they heard the muffled sound through the heavy door of Bjarki Steinsson's wife asking him questions of her own. "Where now, chief?"

THE DOCTOR ON duty was a woman with greying roots and serious eyes behind unfashionable glasses in heavy frames.

"How's the patient?" Gunna asked as she matched her pace to keep up with the striding doctor and Helgi scurried behind.

"As good as can be expected," the doctor said, an answer that they both knew meant nothing. "But there's something I really think you need to see."

Hallur Hallbjörnsson lay in a pristine hospital bed. An oxygen feed was connected to a tube leading into one nostril, and his face appeared peaceful.

"Is he . . . ?" Gunna asked, but lapsed into silence as the doctor put a finger to her lips.

"He's heavily sedated but may be able to hear us," she murmured, beckoning Gunna closer and gently rolling Hallur's head to one side to part the brown hair.

"See?"

A livid bruise was visible beneath the thick waves.

"This is recent? You mean he was smacked on the head?"

"Hit or fell," the doctor said. "Could be either."

Gunna stared at the discoloured bruise.

"That puts a whole new complexion on things," she said. "You're certain this happened prior to the incident in the car?"

The doctor folded Hallur's hair back and stepped away, beckoning Gunna to follow.

"The question is, did it happen while he was being manhandled out of the car?" she said severely. "Because it certainly didn't happen after he was brought in here."

Gunna thought back frantically to the events outside Hallur's house.

"I grabbed his jacket and pulled him out of the seat. When he was leaning half out of the car, I gripped him under the arms and hauled him out," she said, half to herself and half to the doctor, putting out her arms to demonstrate. "I dragged him backwards away from the car and laid him down. No, he certainly didn't receive a blow to the head then, I'm certain of that."

The doctor nodded slowly. "In that case, I think you might have some investigation ahead of you, because with a blow to the head like that, it's doubtful that he'd have been able to tie his own shoelaces, let alone rig up a car with a hosepipe and get in it."

"Attempted murder, not suicide, then?"

"You're the detective," the doctor replied. "But it looks that way to me."

GULLI ÓLAFS WAS alone in the Verslun office, picking at a laptop with one hand and holding a sandwich in the other.

"Busy?" Gunna enquired.

"Hell! You took me by surprise," he said, his head jerking back as the sandwich dropped from his hand.

"Sorry. The door was open. Where's the rest of the staff?"

"There's some kind of team-building exercise going on for an hour or two. Rubbish, really, but I said I'd look after things to get out of going."

"Sensible man," Gunna said. "I won't keep you. Which newspaper were you working on when Steindór came to you with the story you told me about the other day?"

"Dagurinn," Gulli Ólafs answered. "My first proper job. It was very new then, back when it was a real newspaper and not a freebie propaganda sheet."

"So who did you tell about the story?"

"The editor was Arnar Tómasson. He died a couple of years ago. He was getting on a bit and smoked like a chimney, so it wasn't a surprise. I think he'd had three or four heart attacks already by then."

"And who else knew about it?"

Gulli Ólafs looked down at his laptop as it pinged quietly and he rattled the keyboard in a flurry of fingers. "Only Arnar. He was quite interested, but a couple of days later he told me to back off."

"What conclusions did you draw from that?"

There was no hint of laughter in his grim smile. "The obvious ones. That Arnar had asked a few questions and found out that one of his cronies had a stake in it, so he wanted it glossed over."

"And what research had you done? Did you approach anyone about it?"

"Oh, yes. The mayor's office. No reply, as far as I remember. I tried the committee that was responsible for what was then called spatial resources as well, but didn't get far."

"Do you remember who you spoke to?"

Gulli Ólafs laughed and gestured at a copy of that morning's paper on his desk.

"Him."

Gunna looked down at a black-and-white portrait of Hallur Hallbjörnsson smiling from a lower corner of the front page.

"That's the guy. It says here he had an 'accident at his home,' but the word is he tried to do himself in yesterday."

"What was his reaction when you approached him?"

"Very positive, actually. He seemed keen to meet so he could refute any wrongdoing. But then . . ."

"Then what?"

"Arnar quietly warned me off," he said, squinting as he peered down at the newspaper. "Then I had that rope round my neck in the car and figured I'd best leave well alone. Putting your job on the line's one thing, but your life's something else."

"You didn't think to go to the police at the time?"

"God, no."

"You'd recognize the voice if you heard it again?"

"Absolutely," Gulli Ólafs said firmly. "It was a long time ago, but I assure you it's burned into my memory. A death threat's not something that happens every day."

"WHAT D'YOU RECKON, chief?" Helgi asked. "Hallur's place next?"

"Yup," Gunna instructed, stabbing at her phone. "Somebody let Sindri or Jónas Valur know that Gulli Ólafs was sniffing around, and presumably they put two and two together to figure out where the leak had come from. Gulli gets a warning, and Steindór gets a punishment that went too far. That's my take on it."

"Sounds about right to me," Helgi said morosely, changing lanes too fast and earning an angry blast on the horn from the car behind. Slowing right down, he negotiated the quiet street, where Hallur's Mercedes now occupied a place in the road instead of the drive.

"Hæ, Eiríkur," Gunna bellowed into her phone. "Where are you?" Oh, right. No, listen. A little task for you, and it needs to be done today. But first I'd like you to tell Technical that I'm at Hallur Hallbjörnsson's place and we need them to cast beady eyes over something, OK? As quick as you like."

As Helgi waited patiently, he looked up the drive towards Hallur's house, where a small face peered from the corner of the kitchen window at them. He smiled back and the face disappeared.

"Clutching at straws here, Helgi, but it's worth a go," Gunna said grimly, appearing at his side and marching towards the house. She noticed that the carved wooden sign proclaiming that Hallur, Helena Rós, Margrét Anna and Krist'n Dröfn live here was now protruding from the dustbin by the gate.

Helgi reflected that it seemed to be a day for angry women. Helena Rós sat with ill-controlled fury in her pristine front room, while two small girls sat quietly in the next room, engrossed in the television.

"How long has this been going on?" she demanded.

"Has what in particular been going on?" Gunna asked.

"How long had my husband," she snarled the word, "been seeing that woman?"

"Ah, you mean the affair with the late Svana Geirs," Gunna said. "Some considerable time, several years. Unfortunately, we're not in a position to ask the lady herself."

Helena Rós picked irritably at a plait that snaked lazily over one shoulder of her sweater, a traditional knitted one but with a modern cut that did without arms and which Gunna thought looked ridiculous.

"Several years? Jesus," she muttered to herself. "Years?"

"How is your husband now?" Gunna asked, trying to speak gently.

"You mean how is my soon-to-be ex-husband?" Helena Rós snapped back. "I don't know and I don't care. Last night he was awake but sedated. I haven't been to the hospital today, and I don't think I'll bother. I guess his parents and his brothers are there to soothe the poor boy."

"Obviously we will need to ask him rather a lot of questions once he's fit to answer them. Have you spoken to the doctors today? Do you know how he is or what the prospects are?"

"No idea. He may well be brain-damaged," she said in a voice that fizzed with emotion. "Why the hell did you have to come and drag him out of the car? Why couldn't you just have left him there for a few more minutes?"

"I'm afraid . . ." Gunna began, taken aback by the virulence of the woman's fury. "I don't need to tell you that would amount to murder. I have to ask you about your husband's movements, in particular what he was doing on the eleventh. Are you aware of where he might have been that day, or what he might have been doing?"

"No idea. He leaves the house. I have no idea what he does or where he is until he comes back."

"You didn't suspect that he was having a liaison outside his marriage?" Helena Rós stood up and paced back and forth in front of the window with short, sharp steps.

"Of course I suspected. He's that kind of man. I thought I had that side of him under control, though, at least since the girls were born. But what the hell do I know? The bastard, how could he do this . . .?" she said, as much to herself as to Gunna and Helgi.

"We need access to some of your husband's bank details. There are transactions that need to be traced and his business interests need to be accounted for."

"Feel free. You know where his office is," Helena Rós snarled. "You were down there with him long enough the other day."

"When were you aware that your husband was being blackmailed?" Gunna asked, letting the jibe sail past without acknowledgement.

"He was what?" Helena Rós screeched, knotting her elegantly manicured hands into fists. "How dare you?" she demanded, her face turning a deep red.

"It's possible that your husband's mistress was blackmailing him, probably for a considerable amount of money."

"Good God." Helena Rós suddenly gulped, letting herself fall back into a chair. "I don't believe this. The bloody man, the bloody, bastard, bloody man. I knew there was something, just knew it."

"Do you have a joint or separate bank accounts?" Gunna asked.

"Both. We have one for the family finances and we each have our own accounts for anything else. God knows how many accounts Hallur had. I think he'd lost count himself," she said, and Gunna noticed that she was already referring to her husband in the past tense. "Why on earth couldn't you have come five minutes later or five minutes earlier? That way he'd have been either dead, or at least alive and healthy enough to be made to suffer," Helena Rós wailed. "Do I need a brain-damaged husband? Me?"

At last a flood of tears broke and she ran for the bathroom, hand to her face to stifle the nosebleed that Gunna saw with satisfaction had left a trail of bright drops on the rich cream of the carpet.

"Not easy to feel sorry for her, is it?" Helgi observed.

"Not really," Gunna agreed. "She feels so sorry for her bloody self that any pity from us would be overkill."

"Next, chief? Think we'll get anything out of her?"

"Nope, but I'm going to leave you here, if you don't mind, Helgi."

"What? With that witch?"

"Yup. I want you to go down to Hallur's office in the basement. She'll show you where it is. Start going through it and see what you can find." Gunna stood. "I need to get back to Hverfisgata and see if Eiríkur has finished the little job I asked him to do."

ANNA FJÓLA SIGURBJÖRNSDÓTTIR's lips pursed into a thin, bloodless line as Gunna appeared in the doorway.

"Good afternoon, Anna Fjóla," Gunna offered, willing herself to be civil. "Is the lord and master in?"

"I think so," the secretary said quietly. "I'll see."

She gingerly opened the door behind her and said a few muttered words before swinging the door open and unwillingly ushering Gunna in.

Jónas Valur sat behind his antique desk, and Gunna could sense immediately that her appearance was less than welcome.

"What now, officer?"

The light from his desk lamp cast sharp shadows over the hands that held a sheaf of papers, neatly clipped together.

"Why did you state that you'd been here all day without a break on the eleventh?" Gunna demanded without waiting.

"What do you mean?"

"I have witnesses and evidence that put you outside this office around midday on that day. You were out and about for at least an hour."

"Jesus, are you never going to let this go?" Jónas Valur groaned. "All right. I may have gone round the corner for a bite to eat. I don't remember."

"Anna Fjóla would, and pressuring her to commit perjury on your behalf is hardly a reward for all those years of loyal service, is it?"

Jónas Valur glowered back and said nothing.

"How much was Svana Geirs after?"

"What do you mean?"

"Svana had called time on the syndicate, and she wanted a goodbye present. How much?"

"I don't know what you're talking about."

"Then what was the emergency meeting of the syndicate the night before she died all about?"

"Again, I don't know what you're talking about, officer," Jónas Valur said coldly.

"Bullshit," Gunna said brusquely. "Jónas Valur, where is your son?"

"How dare you speak to me like that? Watch your step, Sergeant, I have plenty of influential friends."

"I'm supposed to take that as a threat, am I?"

"As far as I am aware, my son is travelling on business. As I expect you know, he no longer lives in this country."

"If anyone knows where he is, I'm sure you do."

"I have no comment to make," Jónas Valur said, his face visibly pale even in the warm cast of the desk lamp.

"You'd best give your friendly lawyer a call, in that case,

because I'll be back," Gunna said, sweeping from the room without waiting for a reply and closing the door behind her.

"I assume you heard most of that?" she said to secretary, who was sitting behind a pile of binders and pretending to be busy. "Just so you're aware, perjury is something the courts take a dim view of, and the women's prison isn't a particularly cozy place."

IT WAS GETTING dark, and a brisk spring wind was sweeping in off the sea to batter the windows with raindrops as Gulli Ólafs sat in the interview room.

"Thanks for coming in," Gunna said, yawning. "I'm sorry. It's been a long day."

"What am I here for? To make a statement or something?"

"I think you might want to," Gunna told him, opening the door. "My colleague will be right with us and there's something I want to show you. That's all."

Eiríkur bustled in with an open laptop in his hands and put it on the table.

"That was quick, young man. How did you get it all done so fast?"

Eiríkur fingers flickered over the keyboard. "Simple, chief. I got one of the warders to do it for me and then email me the sound file. Your mate Bjössi over at Keflavík did the other one. Said you owe him a huge favour now."

Gunna glowered. "I'll bet the foul-mouthed old goat said something a bit more graphic than that. Am I right?"

"Um. You're not wrong," Eiríkur admitted, plugging a pair of small speakers into the laptop. "Ready?" he asked, looking up at Gulli Olafs.

"Ready for what? What do you want to show me?"

"I'd like you to turn your chair around and face away from the desk for a moment, if you don't mind," Gunna said, moving towards the door. A perplexed Gulli Olafs did as he was asked.

Gunna nodded, and Eiríkur clicked the laptop's mouse as she dimmed the lights.

"Back off. Leave it. You know what," a harsh voice rasped.

"Familiar?" Gunna asked. "Want to hear it again?"

"Shit . . . you could have warned me," said Gulli Olafs plaintively.

"Sorry. But does it ring any bells?"

"No. That's not the same voice."

Gunna nodded again at Eiríkur, and this time Gulli Olafs jumped to his feet, his teeth chattering, as a deeper voice, thicker and slower, intoned the same threat.

"F-f-fucking hell . . . that's him. That's the voice," he gibbered. "The bastard. You know who it is? You must do, surely?"

"You're absolutely sure?"

"Completely. Two hundred per cent certain."

"All the same, I'd like you to listen to them both again, just to be sure."

Gulli Olafs sank back into the chair and listened in stunned silence as both voices read out the same threat several times.

"No doubt. The second one. Absolutely no doubt," he said.

"Thank you," Gunna told him, flicking on the lights and opening the door. "In that case, you're free to go and my colleague will show you out. If this goes further, I'll call on you for a statement in the next couple of days."

GUNNA WAS FRETTING over what she might have overlooked when she was hauling a half-dead Hallur Hallbjörnsson from behind the wheel of his antique Mercedes, wondering what she had not seen that she should have. It could take less than ten minutes to die of carbon monoxide poisoning in a closed car. Whatever had happened at Hallur's house had taken place only moments before she and Helgi had turned up. Now Helgi was back at the house, this time with a technical team to sift through whatever evidence could be gleaned after the trail had gone cold.

Pacing furiously, she opened her mobile and called Helgi's number, listening to it ring as she strode twenty paces one way and twenty back. "Helgi? Yeah. What news?"

Helgi's voice crackled through a poor connection and she could hear both traffic in the background and the puttering of a generator.

"Blood spots on the headrest, chief. They're taking samples, but I'd bet any money you like that Hallur was in that car with a sore head when the engine was started."

"Sure, Helgi? Sure he didn't fall or something and then try to drive himself to hospital afterwards?"

"What? With a hosepipe gaffer-taped around the exhaust and put through the back window? I think not, somehow."

"Of course," Gunna replied. "What are you up to next?"

"I'm having the car impounded and then I'll start knocking on doors."

"All right. Get some uniform chaps as well if there are any spare."

"There are never spare uniformed coppers these days, chief. But I'll get hold of some for an hour or so all the same."

"Good man. Look, got to go. Let me know what happens," she told him, and prepared to end the call.

"Hang on, chief."

"What?"

"In Hallur's office. Nothing useful in any of his files that I could see, but I had a look in the bin as well, just to be sure, and there it was."

"Make sense, will you, Helgi? What was there?"

"At the bottom of the bin, screwed into a ball. A letter demanding twenty-five thousand euros in cash. You were right."

"Bloody hell . . . Anything on there that could lead us anywhere?"

"Nah. It's on the way to Forensics to be checked out, but I don't expect there to be anything useful somehow."

ANNA FJÓLA SIGURBJÖRNSDÓTTIR sat with pinched cheeks by the reception desk.

"You wanted to speak to me?" Gunna asked, surprised.

"I do. But not here."

"There's an interview room upstairs we can use."

Anna Fjóla looked sour. "I'm not a criminal."

Not yet, anyway, Gunna thought, realizing that there had to be a very good reason for this prim woman to come to the police station in person.

"I take it what you want to discuss is sensitive?"

"And confidential."

"Come with me, then."

At Café Roma, Anna Fjóla sat at the furthest table from the window as Gunna returned from the counter with coffee in a mug and tea in a cup.

"Now, what did you want to tell me about?"

"My employer, Jónas Valur Hjaltason."

"What about him?"

"He's not a bad man, you understand." Anna Fjóla hesitated. "He's a fine businessman, but he's . . . weak in other ways."

"Such as?"

"Women in particular."

"Such as Svana Geirs?"

"Yes," Anna Fjóla whispered.

"How long have you worked for him?"

"Nineteen years."

"So you remember Steindór Hjálmarsson?"

"Of course. A pleasant young man. Such a shame about him." Anna Fjóla finally took a sip of tea.

"He worked there for about six months, as I remember," she continued haltingly. "But the company was bigger then. There were the exports to Spain and Portugal that we still have today, but there were also the property and entertainment businesses that were Sindri's interests. There were three bookkeepers then, myself and some salespeople."

"And Sindri Valsson?"

Anna Fjóla glanced up sharply and immediately looked down at her cup.

"How did Sindri and Steindór get on?"

"Not well, but not badly. We could all see they didn't like each other. Steindór thought Sindri was a spoiled brat and he didn't do a very good job of hiding what he thought. Sindri thought that Steindór stuck his nose into things that didn't concern him."

She took another sip of tea and wiped her lips delicately on a handkerchief from her handbag.

"I daresay they were each partly right about the other," she said with a thin smile.

"So why are you here today, Anna Fjóla?" Gunna asked gently.

"It's been nagging at me for days, what you said," Anna Fjóla said quietly. "The day that woman was murdered, Jónas Valur was out of the office for part of the morning."

"What time was that?"

"He came in a little later than usual, around nine thirty, and left at eleven. He was back soon after twelve, as far as I remember."

Gunna had no doubt that Anna Fjóla remembered correctly. She frowned to herself and thought out the possibilities. The timing put Jónas Valur as able to have been at Svana's flat at the edge of the time frame that Miss Cruz had given them.

"You're certain?"

"Yes," Anna Fjóla said in an icy voice, as if the possibility of her being mistaken was a ludicrous idea.

"You realize the implications?" Gunna asked grimly. "That's why I want to be sure you're certain of the timing."

"I'm certain."

Gunna sat back and finished her coffee while Anna Fjóla sipped delicately.

"I'm just wondering why you're telling me this, after all the years with Jónas Valur."

Anna Fjóla's thin shoulders rose and fell with a barely perceptible shrug. "To set the record straight, I suppose. I have worked hard and honestly for all these years for a salary that's reasonable, but no more than that. But next month I'll be joining the unemployed and I suppose I'm, well, upset about that."

"How come?" Gunna asked.

"Kleifar is being sold. Jónas Valur is selling his shares and I happen to know that Sindri has already sold his. Between them they owned eighty per cent of the company."

"Who's it being sold to?"

Anna Fjóla smiled. "That's just it. On paper it's a fairly simple transaction. A few thousand euros change hands and Kleifar has new owners. But so that Jónas Valur can retire somewhere warm near his son, the new owners will quietly make over to him a couple of large villas in Portugal. That's the real price of the company. The new owners get an established saltfish trading company in Iceland at a good price, and Jónas Valur gets the value of it without having to worry about currency restrictions."

"And how do you know all this?"

"Please. After almost twenty years, I know Jónas Valur as well as I know my own husband—better, if anything. Jónas Valur has never been able to remember a password or a username, and if I didn't have all that information at my fingertips, the company would come to a halt tomorrow. I check his emails, bank statements, everything, even the ones he thinks are secret."

"And when is all this due to happen?"

"It's been going on over the last few months. Jónas Valur thinks I don't know what's been happening under my nose. His friends Bjarki and Hallur are part of it as well, not to mention that Ólafur Jacobsen."

"The legal expert."

"Yes, a vile man. Bjarki Steinsson has been falsifying figures for the last year to make the company look less profitable so that the low purchase price doesn't appear suspicious, and Hallur Hallbjörnsson arranged for the port authority to buy the office building. The port doesn't need it and actually can't afford it either, but you should never underestimate what Jónas Valur can get his friends to do for him."

"And what happens to you? Don't you get to work for the new owners?"

"I don't think so," Anna Fjóla said with a thin smile. "They don't want an old woman telling them how to run their business. Kleifar will officially cease to exist and may well even be insolvent if Bjarki Steinsson has done his work well. Its activities will be absorbed by a holding company, so there's no need to worry about redundancy for an old woman."

"Another quick visit to Jónas Valur might be in order," Gunna mused, half to herself.

Anna Fjóla drank the rest of her tea, put the cup down firmly in front of her and stood up. "In that case, I'd suggest you don't wait too long. All the contracts have been signed and I don't believe he has much left to wait around Reykjavík for."

She marched out of the café with her mouth pursed and her nose in the air, leaving Gunna wondering what was in the thick envelope that she had discreetly left on the table where her handbag had rested.

Friday 26th

GUNNA DROVE THE few kilometres to the Keflavík police station, where Bjössi lounged in his habitual smoking spot by the back door, chatting to Helgi. As she parked, he crushed out his cigarette and shook the last drops of coffee from a mug and let it hang on his little finger.

"Good morning, gentlemen. And how are you on this lovely day, Bjössi?" Gunna greeted him.

"Tired, got cold feet, my hair's still falling out, I hate my job and it's going to rain. Apart from that, fine," Bjössi grumbled back at her as she marched into the station. A muffled angry mutter of distant shouts could be heard from deep inside the building.

"What's the racket, Bjössi? Got the choir practising in there?"

"Bugger the choir. You know what that is," Bjössi told her grimly.

"Ah. Our friend, is it?"

"I don't know about our friend. Not the cleverest in the class, but he's all yours."

The volume of sound grew as they approached the cells, and the hammering on the steel door echoed throughout the building.

"Æi, shut the fuck up, will you?" Bjössi yelled, banging on the door and lifting the flap to give Gunna a view inside. "You really want to go in there? He's bouncing off the fucking walls."

"Yeah. We'll be all right."

Björssi shook his head in resignation as he slid back the bolt and the hammering inside faded away.

"About fucking time . . ." Skari rasped, falling silent as Gunna stalked into the cell with Helgi trying to look tough behind her and Björssi standing by the door. The bruises on his face had subsided, but there were still livid patches across his cheekbones where the stitches had been taken out.

"What the hell are you doing here?" he challenged. "I told you before—"

"Sit down, Skari," Gunna told him coldly.

"I don't have anything to say to you. I told you that before, didn't I?"

"For fuck's sake, sit down and shut up for a few seconds, will you, you selfish twat?" Gunna spat at him.

Taken by surprise, Skari dropped onto the bunk and glowered back at her, muttering under his breath.

"What did you say?" he demanded, scowling. "Fucking . . . brutality, that's what it is. Bastards . . ."

"Skari, give over, will you. Now listen. Two thousand, remember that year? I have you positively and reliably identified as issuing threats. There's no ifs or buts here. Understand?"

"Is that what that bloke wanted yesterday?" He nodded towards Björssi. "Asked me to read something out for him?"

"Precisely. Bang to rights, Skari."

His brow darkened as he struggled to take it in. "That was fucking years back."

"But it's still an offence and the victim would be only too happy to press charges, even at this late stage. You could be looking at a year or two for this, even now."

Skari's hands curled into fists and the anger turning his face red was plain enough. Björssi stepped forward and Helgi took his hands out of his coat pockets.

"You've three minutes to come up with the whole story. Otherwise there'll be a formal charge and not much chance of bail."

Cornered, Skari's eyes flitted from Bjössi to Helgi and back to Gunna. "Mum said you were a hard bitch."

"Your mum wouldn't say anything of the kind. Who wanted you to frighten this guy?"

"Come on. This was years ago."

"Who?"

"Sindri."

"Sindri Valsson?"

Skari nodded and hung his head.

"What, precisely, did Sindri want you to do?"

"I don't remember. It was a long time ago, for Christ's sake."

"Then start remembering," Gunna said with quiet menace. "You have another minute."

"Sindri said there was this bloke who worked in an office on Skipholt. Didn't tell me his name or anything, just gave me the number of his car. He said the bloke'd come out around seven, and I should scare the shit out of him and tell him to keep his nose out of what's not his business. So I did."

"This was just Sindri?"

"Sindri and his old man, both of them."

"Where did this conversation take place?"

"At the club."

"Blacklights?"

"Yeah."

"When?"

Skari shook his head as if he were talking to an idiot. "It was years ago. How the fuck should I know?"

"How soon was this after you beat Steindór Hjálmarsson to death?"

In a second, Skari was on his feet. "I didn't! That was

Sindri! It wasn't me and you can't prove anything!" he yelled, eyes bulging.

"Sit down, Skari. I know it was Sindri."

"So why d'you say that?"

"Because I wanted to be sure," Gunna said sharply. "Now I can be. What do you know about it? Did you see it happen?"

"Might have."

"Tell me what you saw."

Skari heaved a deep breath. "Bjartmar was there. He pointed this bloke out to me and told me to kick him out, said he was a troublemaker."

"Bjartmar did, not Sindri?"

"Yeah. I collared the bloke and walked him out, easy as you like, and slung him out the back door into the car park." He paused. "Sindri just laid into the guy. I don't know why, I'd never seen him before. Sindri fucking hammered him, knocked him flying and kicked him a few times, then went back inside like nothing had happened."

"And he said nothing to you?"

Skari shook his head. "Bjartmar just said, 'You saw nothing, right?' And that was all."

"You know who Gunnlaugur Ólafsson is?"

"Who?" Skari asked, mystified.

"Bjarki Steinsson?"

"Look, I don't know who you're on about," Skari replied angrily. "Who the hell are these people?"

"Högni Sigurgeirsson?"

"I said, I don't know who these bloody people are. All right?"

"Who was it who beat you up and put you in hospital?"

"Told you," he said, dropping his eyes to the floor. "Polish bloke."

"No, Skari," Gunna corrected him. "I'm sick of listening to this particular broken record. Most of the Poles have already gone home and there isn't a single Pole, Latvian, Lithuanian or even Mongolian who answers your description. So how about you come clean and admit it was Ommi?"

"What?" he asked, eyes wide. "Because . . ."

"Because what? I know you and Ommi go way back, but that's not going to make a bit of difference."

Skari hung his head and at last his fists unclenched.

"It was Ommi," he muttered angrily. "Ommi and some little pipsqueak mate of his. I'd have had Ommi on his own, but his mate batted me round the head with a plank and I couldn't think straight after that."

Gunna turned to Bjössi in the doorway. "Got that?"

Bjössi nodded back at her and she looked down at Skari, sitting on the bed clenching and unclenching his big fists.

"And you're going to give my colleague a statement to that effect, aren't you?"

"Can I go home after that?" he asked hopefully.

"Make a statement and you can go home to Erla and the kids."

"Everything?"

"Everything," Gunna said firmly. "All right, Bjössi, we'll leave this chap to your tender care. Can you sort him out a lift home when he's made a suitable statement?"

"Statement, yes. Don't know about a lift, though. We're a bit short-handed today and a car down as well."

"Then put him in a taxi and tell the driver to take him to Hvalvík without going past the booze shop," Gunna instructed. "And Skari?"

"Yeah?"

"Give your mum my regards when you get home, would you?"

HELGI DROVE, KEEPING steadily to the speed limit as cars and trucks whistled past them in the outside lane of

Reykjanesbraut. As they passed the spot where she and Laufey had come across the accident a few days before, Gunna could see nothing to indicate that anything had ever happened there.

"Hæ, Eiríkur. Can you hear me?" She called into her mobile. Suddenly the car emerged from the black spot and she could hear him perfectly.

"Anything on that note?"

"Nothing much. No dabs. It's printed on an ordinary laser printer of some kind, but there are thousands of those in use, so that's no help. Nothing special about the paper, either. There are a few prints on the envelope, but nothing that we've been able to identify so far. We're working on it, but I reckon they're more than likely Hallur's own."

"But we fingerprinted him to eliminate him from Svana's flat, didn't we? So we'll have those prints on file. Check the dabs, would you, and let me know as soon as you have anything?"

She ended the call and sat brooding in the front seat, hands in her coat pockets, watching the lampposts flash past.

"Was Svana being blackmailed, or was she doing the blackmailing? If so, is that why someone broke her head open, possibly with her own baseball bat?"

"Where to, chief?" Helgi asked as they approached the Hafnarfjördur outskirts.

"Skari had nothing to do with anything recent. All this stuff going on around Svana Geirs and her syndicate, it's nothing to do with him. The same goes for Ommi. So who stands to gain on all this? Who's doing the blackmailing? Is it someone who knows which of these bastards killed Svana, or is the person who killed Svana trying to cash in on the others? Someone within the syndicate? Högni, maybe?"

"You know, I don't bloody know. It gets more complex by the minute," Helgi grumbled. "A few straightforward break-ins would be nice for a change."

"If that's the case," Gunna went on, as if Helgi had said

nothing, "why so little? Twenty-five thousand euros is a stack of money for you or me, but for any of these high-flyers like Jónas Valur or Hallur, it's small change."

"Unless it's not about the money."

"It's always about the money."

"I mean, if it's a smokescreen of some kind."

"Could be, I suppose," Gunna conceded, unconvinced. "I'd like you to dig into Hallur's basement again today."

"Where to, chief?" Helgi asked again. "Back to the station first?"

"Ach. Let's take a little ride around Kópavogur on the way, shall we? There's nothing like staying away from the shop for five minutes to stimulate the grey matter. There's a bakery at Hamraborg, so we can stop for an early lunch break."

LATER THAT AFTERNOON, Gunna bustled past Sigvaldi at the desk with her phone at her ear, but was rewarded with only Eiríkur's voicemail. On the way up the stairs, she met Sævaldur on the way down for the second time that day.

"We're going to have to stop meeting like this, Gunnhildur," he warned her.

"Nothing to worry about, Sævaldur," she shot back. "Nobody would ever believe it."

Sævaldur stopped a few steps past her. "The guy who topped Bjartmar. He's the one who sent all those blackmail demands. Thought of that?"

"Come on."

"All right. So there's an accomplice."

Gunna stopped and looked back at him. "Like who?"

"Like his wife. It's obvious enough."

"You are joking, surely?"

"No, of course not."

"Good grief," Gunna muttered to herself, making her way back up and leaving Sævaldur on the stairs.

Back at her desk, she remembered that Eiríkur was busy. She drummed the desk with her fingers and dialled Helgi.

"Any joy?" she demanded as soon as he replied.

"Sod all. The man has reams of paperwork and at least half a dozen bank accounts. His wife was delighted to find a couple with a good bit of cash in them that she didn't know about. No big withdrawals, though."

"Fair enough. Going to be long?"

"No, don't think so."

"All right. Eiríkur's running an errand for me elsewhere, and I think it's time I had another chat with Jónas Valur. I've been handed copies of half a dozen letters he's received."

"I'm sure he'll be delighted when you show up. You don't want to wait for me and we'll go mob-handed?"

"No, just give me a call when you're finished and on the way back here. It feels like it's been a bloody long day. I'll see if I can find Jónas Valur and then go home from there."

THERE WAS NO sign of life at Kleifar's offices. Gunna rattled the door and got no response. She stepped back and looked at the building's corrugated-iron plates that had once been red but were now closer to pink after decades of alternate sun and rain. She crossed the street for a better view and noticed a faint light behind one of the windows, as if an internal door had been left open. Curious, she walked to the corner of the building in the hope of being able to see through one of the end windows, but there was nothing but darkness.

Back in front of the building, she was about to give up when the faint light winked off. She rattled the door a second time. Again there was no response, and this time she walked quickly to the far end of the building and round the corner, where she could see Jónas Valur's black Mercedes tucked away in a corner of the car park, enclosed on three sides by the backs of buildings. Suddenly the car's internal light came on and Gunna hurried towards it.

Jónas Valur had emerged from the back door of the building, hauling behind him a suitcase on wheels that bumped down the steps. "Good evening, Jónas Valur. Going away somewhere?" Gunna asked as the car park's security light clicked on and flooded them with its harsh glow.

Taken unawares, Jónas Valur didn't even bother to hide his scowl of displeasure.

"This is bordering on harassment, Sergeant," he groaned.

"Quite the contrary. I've been very gentle and understanding."

"Look, I've had you or your colleagues prowling around for days, dogging my tracks and asking all kinds of questions about my movements. Don't you think enough is enough?"

"When you've answered all my questions truthfully, then enough will be enough," Gunna said, unfolding a sheet of paper from her pocket and handing it to him.

"What's this?"

"Have a look. I'm wondering if it's something familiar."

He held it out at arm's length and shook his head.

"Rubbish," he said unconvincingly.

"And how many of these notes have you received?"

"I don't know what you're talking about," he rasped, handing the note back to her.

"It's a copy. Keep it and compare it to the rest of your collection," Gunna told him. "Now, you wouldn't be Shorty by any chance, would you?"

"Who the hell are you?" Jónas Valur grated, and Gunna saw the man's eyes widening with surprise as he glared past her. She was halfway through turning to look over her shoulder when her head felt as if something had exploded next to her and she sensed the taste of iron on her tongue as the world went black.

• • •

GUNNA SHIVERED AND wondered why she was unable to move. She knew she was lying on her back, and lifted her right hand to put it to her throbbing head. She kept her eyes firmly closed, sensing that opening them was going to hurt.

In the event, it wasn't so bad, lying in half-darkness. She closed them again and tried a second time to move her legs and left arm. It was then she realized that something heavy was holding her down. She made an effort to open one eye again, and decided that the acrid smell of aftershave had to be coming from somewhere very close by.

With both eyes open and her free hand behind the back of her head to support it, she realized that the heavy weight on top of her was Jónas Valur, and that he was completely inert. Gently lowering her own head back to the cold ground, she fumbled for the man's head, running her fingers from the top of the gleaming scalp down the face to try and locate a pulse among the folds of his neck.

There was no pulse to be found, and no breath from Jónas Valur's open mouth. Raising herself as far as she could, she could see that the side of the head that was lying on her chest had been battered, and blood had seeped on to her shirt. For a moment she was thankful that the blood on her fingers wasn't her own, and wanted to go back to sleep, safe in the knowledge that she was still alive.

Gunna made an effort that set her head ringing and dragged herself from under Jónas Valur's bulk, letting his body roll on to its side as she sat up and held her head in both hands, resting her elbows on her knees as she felt her limbs drained of strength. She fumbled in her coat pocket for her phone, but came up with her communicator instead and thankfully pressed the emergency button.

She made another effort to get Jónas Valur's attention, but soon grasped that he was beyond any help, and sat back as a siren howled close by until the flashing blue lights filled the yard and reflected painfully from the dark windows of Kleifar's offices.

SHE HAD BEEN expecting Steini, but instead Ívar Laxdal and Miss Cruz sat waiting for her.

"Feeling better?" he asked, standing to greet her.

"Yes thanks," Gunna replied, settling gingerly into a chair. "My head feels like it's been under a bulldozer, but otherwise fine."

"You took quite a knock," he told her seriously, switching to English for the benefit of Miss Cruz.

"Yes, a blow to the right side of your head," Miss Cruz said, looking over her glasses. "I had a look at you last night when you were brought in here."

"Did you?" Gunna asked. "It's a bit hazy."

"It looks as if you turned so the blow glanced off the side of your head instead of hitting you squarely, while the victim took a single blow to the centre of his forehead with something round."

"A baseball bat, something like that?"

"Something narrower, maybe a length of pipe," Miss Cruz said. "Difficult to say at this stage."

"Did you see the attacker?" Ívar Laxdal asked.

"No. I was talking to Jónas Valur in the car park and he wasn't very pleased to see me. I remember he saw something over my shoulder, so I started to turn to look, and, bang. Out like a light."

"Not someone you'd be able to identify?"

"No chance. I take it the same attacker belted Jónas Valur a bit harder than he did me?"

"It looks that way. It must have been quick, because the man landed right on top of you. Any idea how long you were lying there?"

"Haven't a clue," Gunna said. "Jónas Valur had a suitcase, a small one on wheels. The kind you see pilots walking along with at airports. Any sign of that?"

"Nothing. His car was taken as well and left at the bus station."

"What? At Hlemmur?"

"No. BSÍ."

"So who the hell took it?"

"It's being fingerprinted right now, so we should know soon enough. But I think we'd best leave you to get some rest," Ívar Laxdal said, pointing to where Steini and Laufey could be seen waving from the reception desk.

"Fair enough," Gunna said, struggling to her feet. "Helgi and Eiríkur are getting on all right, aren't they?"

"Gunnhildur, they're doing fine, and they're not taking the slightest notice of Sævaldur Bogason's frequent useful suggestions. I thought I'd tell you that to put your mind at rest."

"Good. I'll be back tomorrow and pick up where we left off."

"You'll be back in a week, if I have my way," Ívar Laxdal said sternly. "Let's be off," he said to Miss Cruz in English. "Gunnhildur has some more important visitors."

GUNNA WATCHED TV with the sound turned low, determined not to think about work but unable not to. Her head ached dully and she said a quiet prayer of thanks for extra-strength painkillers. Steini lounged across an armchair, a book open in front of him.

"You're not going to work tomorrow, are you, Mum?" Laufey asked.

Gunna yawned. "Tomorrow afternoon. I have to go to the hospital for a check-up at twelve, and I'll go to the station for an hour or two after that."

Laufey frowned, less than half satisfied, and went towards the kitchen. "Laufey, what are you wearing?" Gunna asked, her frown almost as deep as her daughter's.

"New trousers. Got them in Reykjavík when I went there with Finnur last weekend."

"They're a bit, well, tight, aren't they? Shouldn't you wear a skirt or something with those?"

"They're OK. Everyone wears these now, Mum."

Steini shook his head as if to say that this was a discussion he would never be qualified to take part in.

"I know, sweetheart. But it's just that they're so, what shall I say? Revealing. You might as well walk around in nothing as wear those."

"Mum!"

"It's true. Is there even room for underwear under them?"

"Yes, of course there is. What's the matter? Can't I wear the same as everyone else?"

"I suppose so," Gunna said, regretting that her question had elicited such a waspish reply. "It's just that every man you encounter will be sizing you up. Right, Steini?"

"Don't bring me into this," Steini grunted, lifting his book higher.

"Oh, Mum, don't be so old-fashioned," Laufey scolded, nose in the air as she marched to her room and shut the door firmly behind her.

"Æi, why did I say anything?" Gunna groaned. "I should know better by now."

"She's getting to be a big girl now, quite a grown-up young lady."

"I know, that's what worries me," Gunna said, stretching to reach her mobile as it trilled. "Gunnhildur."

"Hæ, chief. Högni's dabs are all over Jónas Valur's car. How's your head?" Eiríkur asked.

Sunday 28th

GUNNA STUBBORNLY REFUSED to use the lift and tackled the stairs in two stages, taking a breather halfway up to ease the pounding in her temples. Sigvaldi on the desk had asked tenderly, albeit gruffly, after her health.

At her own desk she waited while Eiríkur and Helgi marshalled chairs. Several other people looked curiously at her as they passed, and even Sævaldur Bogason offered a few mumbled kind words.

"All right, boys. Tell me the worst," Gunna instructed, looking up to see Ívar Laxdal appear in the doorway, his eyebrows knitted in disapproval.

"Come in, please. Just a quick chat and then I'm going back home," she assured him.

"As long as that's all," Ívar Laxdal growled.

Gunna turned to Helgi. "Any sign of Högni Sigurgeirsson?"

"Nothing, chief. No sign of his car anywhere yet, but Jónas Valur's Merc was abandoned at the BSÍ bus station," Helgi said, flipping through a sheet of notes. "You'll be interested to know that during the house-to-house questions around Hallur Hallbjörnsson's place, there was a mention of a grey Opel, same model as Högni's, in the next street, and the timing fits."

"Interesting. If it was Högni, he must have gone pretty much straight from being questioned here to Hallur," Gunna agreed. "No doubt on the vehicle identification?"

"None at all. The woman in question has the same model of car, so she was certain. No registration number, though."

"Shame," Gunna said.

"If this man is a suspect for the killing of Jónas Valur, you think he may have attempted to murder Hallur Hallbjörnsson as well?" Ívar Laxdal asked.

"Certainly," Helgi replied.

"So what next?" Gunna asked, wondering if the investigation was out of her hands and in Helgi's charge.

"We're looking for the weapon used to assault you and Jónas Valur. The door-to-door stuff is still going on and there's a search in progress through all the bins and nooks and crannies for anything that might fit the bill. It could be a long process," Helgi replied sadly.

"ALL RIGHT, ARE you?" Sigrún asked with concern.

"Ah, not so bad," Gunna admitted. "And you? Heard anything from . . . ?"

Sigrún's face brightened. "A little bird whispered to me that Jörundur's all alone now."

"Really?" Gunna said. "What happened?"

Sigrún sat down and opened a bag of home-made biscuits straight from the deep freeze. She dipped one in her coffee and skilfully lifted it out and into her mouth a moment before it was ready to disintegrate.

"Left over from Christmas," she said, munching. "I baked too many and froze what was left over."

"Never happens at my place. I swear my Gísli can sniff out cakes and biscuits a mile away. Come on, what's happened with Jörundur? He's not on the way home, is he?"

"No, it's his lady friend, this Gígja who went out there with him. They'd been carrying on a good while. I can see it now, all the signs were there, but I refused to acknowledge it,"

Sigrún said with a shake of her head. "I should have known better. Well, I was talking to Mæja Dís the other day."

"The girl who works in the office at Hvalvíkingur?"

"That's her, the personnel manager I think she is. Well, Mæja Dís knows this Gígja a bit, because Gígja's ex used to be a cook on one of the boats; Einar, his name is. So Mæja Dís ran into Einar at the petrol station in Keflavík and he said that she was back."

"Already? That was quick!"

"Apparently Einar said that Gígja had given up her job and let her flat to go to Norway with Jörundur, but once he'd been on the drink once or twice, she packed her stuff and got a flight back. Now she's living with her daughter, because she can't have her flat back until the end of the year."

"Amazing, isn't it, how some people fall out of lust the moment they see the other half's true colours?"

"That's not all," Sigrún added gleefully. "I don't want to crow, but she had sold or given away almost all her furniture and everything. So when she does get her flat back, she'll have to start by buying a new fridge and a washing machine. I don't want to crow," she repeated, "but it's karma. She's gone from having a nice flat and a reasonable job to stealing someone else's deadbeat husband, and now she's got no job, no flat and no bloke either. Great, isn't it?"

Sigrún smiled radiantly while Gunna shifted uncomfortably in her seat.

"All right, are you?"

"Ach. Stiff after my little adventure, that's all."

"D'you think you should still be doing this sort of stuff?" Sigrún asked seriously.

"Absolutely. Can you see me managing for long with a desk job?"

"You did it here for long enough."

"Yeah, but that was different. There was only me and old Haddi at the station here, so we both had to do a bit of everything, and Haddi was quite happy to sit in peace and quiet and look after the paperwork."

Gunna hauled herself to her feet. "Well, Laufey's disappointed you're not going."

"Why's that?"

"Krummi. She was really looking forward to having a rabbit living in our bathroom."

"WHERE ARE WE going now?" Helgi asked. "You know, we hard-working public servants have enough to be getting on with. Especially when some of those public servants ought to be at home nursing a sore head."

"Yeah, yeah. I know."

"Why so secretive?" Helgi asked, looking sideways at the determined side of Gunna that he had heard of but never seen close at hand.

Gunna sighed and brought the car almost to a halt so she could check the café's interior.

"Here?"

"Yup."

"Why?" Helgi asked, baffled.

Gunna screwed up her eyes against the bright midday sun that she felt was trying to drill holes in her head and strolled across the road. She pushed open the door, nodded to someone Helgi could hardly see in a corner and poured coffee for both Helgi and herself at the counter, offering a note to the dark-eyed girl behind the till. She handed Helgi his mug and nodded towards another table in the far corner, where Helena Rós' gaze followed Gulli Olafs' as he looked in horror at Gunna and Helgi bearing down on them.

Gunna smiled broadly, taking a seat at the end of the table. "How sweet. The wronged wife and the investigative journalist meeting for lattes in a bookshop café."

Both looked embarrassed as Gunna sat back and surveyed them, while Helgi pulled up a chair next to her.

"We're . . . er . . ." Gulli Olafs floundered.

"Gunnlaugur is writing an article about this whole affair," Helena Rós said sharply. "He wanted to interview me about Hallur's part in it. Haven't I helped you enough with all this already?" she asked, her voice petulant.

"Certainly," Gunna said. "My officers have spent a lot of time trawling through your husband's effects. How is he, by the way?"

"As close to being brain-dead as before," Helena Rós snapped back.

"Now I'm wondering if we were looking in the right places."

"What do you mean?"

"What I mean is that I'd like you to accompany my colleague here. He's going to go to your house once again for another look around, while Gulli has a chat with me."

Helena Rós' face was set as firm as rock. "Am I under arrest for something?"

"Not so far," Gunna said coolly, opening her briefcase to pull out a file. "But that's an option if you decline to cooperate."

Helgi looked puzzled. Gunna opened the file and extracted some sheets of paper that she placed on the table. "Of course, these are just copies, as the originals are still at the lab."

Gunna watched the blood drain from Gulli Ólafs' face as he saw what had been put in front of them.

"Can we, er . . . can we take this somewhere else?" he said in a strained voice.

"We're just about to do that, don't you worry," Gunna told him, and turned to Helgi. "See if you can rustle up a patrol car to take this lady home, would you? When you get there, you'll need to impound all the computers and printers in the house."

"How dare you!" Helena Rós spluttered, her cheeks acquiring pink spots of fury beneath the make-up.

"And you," Gunna continued, transferring her attention to Gulli Ólafs, "I'm asking you to come with me to your office and we'll go through the same procedure there."

The tension that had been gnawing at her all morning had disappeared, replaced by a serene calmness that she knew would be followed later by a draining exhaustion.

"I want to make a statement," Gulli Ólafs said abruptly while Helgi muttered into his communicator.

"And so do I," Helena Rós spat.

"All in good time," Gunna assured her, as a patrol car appeared outside and two officers emerged from it.

"Magic, chief. Eiríkur should be here in a few minutes as well," Helgi assured her. "Shall we go?" he asked Helena Rós in a voice that left her in no doubt that she had no option.

"What about my car?"

"One of these gentlemen will bring it, if you'll give him the keys, and we'll go in the patrol car."

Helena Rós numbly handed over a bunch of keys hung with a fluffy effigy of a white dog, and Helgi took her elbow in his hand as they made their way over the road, leaving Gunna facing Gulli Ólafs.

Her face hardened and she glowered as Gulli Ólafs began to shrink into his chair. "Do you want to make a statement at the station, or do you want to tell me the story?"

"Jesus. . . I, er . . . I don't think I should . . . I mean . . ."

"Make sense, will you?" Gunna's finger stabbed at the transparent folder on the table. "You wrote these, right? I don't doubt that we'll be able to trace these documents to a computer you have access to, and we'll match the inks to your office printer without too much trouble."

"God. . . Yes, I wrote a couple of notes and posted them to

that evil old bastard Jónas Valur. But I didn't do anything more than that."

"Where's the money?"

"Money?"

"Don't play games."

"It's at home. It was all Helena Rós' idea. She knew her husband had been seeing Svana, and she knew he was terrified of the publicity after he got into Parliament. She wanted to give him a hard time."

"And the cash you got out of Hallur Hallbjörnsson and I suppose Bjarki Steinsson? At your home as well?"

Gulli Ólafs nodded miserably as Gunna looked out of the window to see a second patrol car draw up across the road, this time with Eiríkur in the passenger seat.

"Come on. We're going to have a little trip to Hverfisgata," Gunna said, getting to her feet. She took his arm and steered him discreetly out of the door.

Outside, Gulli Ólafs blinked owlishly in the bright sunshine. Gunna felt him tense, and took a firmer grip on his elbow just as he ripped his arm free and sprinted across the road. A bus coming towards him screeched to an undignified halt. Gulli Ólafs dodged around it and splashed frantically through the puddles until Eiríkur, the length of his spindly legs giving him a clear advantage, caught up with him in a tackle that laid both of them full length in the street.

Trying to free her mind of the image of Eiríkur as a galloping giraffe, Gunna walked towards where Gulli Ólafs had been brought down in a patch of gravel with his face in a puddle. Eiríkur was panting and holding the man's right wrist in a lock behind his back. Gunna kneeled down and snapped handcuffs around his wrists.

"Thanks, Gulli. That makes things so much easier," she said with satisfaction.

• • •

"Talk," Gunna instructed. "Everything, please. We have all day ahead of us and as much of tomorrow as we need."

"Where shall I start?" Gulli Ólafs asked plaintively, as if to himself. He was hunched in the chair, while Gunna sat back with her hands on the desk in front of her.

"You and Helena Rós. How long's this been going on?"

"Almost a year."

"Before or after she found out about her husband seeing Svana Geirs?"

"After. She was going to divorce him and come and live with me."

"Who had the idea of these threats and demands?"

"What?"

"Come on. The demands that Jónas Valur, Bjarki Steinsson and Hallur have been getting. The inks on some of these letters match the printer in your office."

"There are hundreds of printers like that about," he said dismissively.

"Actually, no." Gunna smiled. "It seems it's a fairly unusual type, and there aren't more than a handful in various offices. My colleague spoke to the dealer and found out that these were introduced right after the crash when nobody had any money, so they only sold half a dozen."

"So? How does that implicate me?"

"Because other ones were printed on a cheap inkjet printer that matches the one in Helena Rós' study. So who had the bright idea?"

"Well I did, sort of. I said something about it one day as a kind of joke." He twisted his fingers in his hands.

"A joke?"

"Yeah. I said something about it to Helena Rós, just in passing. Then she came back with it a few days afterwards and she was serious."

"So how did she find out about Hallur's relationship with Svana Geirs?"

"I told her," Gulli Ólafs whispered miserably. "I truly wish I'd kept quiet."

"And how did you know about the Svana Syndicate?"

"Newsroom gossip. This kind of thing leaks out and it's impossible to keep anything completely secret, but these rumours stay that way, just rumours. There are dozens of things going on all the time that we could never, ever use."

"Like a story about property fraud involving some prominent people?" Gunna asked.

"Exactly. This stuff gets talked about but that's as far as it can go. Nobody dares to go out on a limb with it and nobody will be quoted. So I followed Svana discreetly, watched her flat, saw who came and went." He shrugged. "Easy enough. I was interested because of the connection with Jónas Valur and Bjartmar Arnarson. They screwed me over before and I've been looking for an opportunity to return the favour ever since." His voice oozed bitterness as he spat out the names of the two men.

"And now they're both dead."

"Nothing to do with me! You have to believe that, surely!"

"You heard about this group who were sharing Svana Geirs between them, and knowing that Hallur was one of them, you told his wife, right? Why?"

"I, well . . . I've known her for years. Good friends, but never . . . you know . . ."

"You thought it might bag you a good story, return the favour to the people who screwed you over before and help you into her knickers, all at the same time?"

"That's . . ." he began, and sank down and nodded.

"And it worked?"

He nodded again. "I was going to leak it to a gossip magazine or a website. That would get it out into the open so I could follow it up. That was the idea, expose Hallur as a man who was cheating on his wife. That would have made it a lot easier for Helena Rós to end the marriage. She's a prominent figure in her own right and doesn't need any mud thrown at her."

"So you were going to engineer a scandal with Hallur as the bad guy?"

"I'm not proud of it. Not now."

"I'm not here to pass any judgement on you. That's for the jury."

"Jury?"

"Undoubtedly. This will go to court."

"Jesus . . . Look, it was Helena Rós who wanted to put pressure on her husband, not me."

"Right, let's backtrack. You say she wanted to apply pressure to her husband. When was this?"

"About three weeks before Svana Geirs died. Hallur was a bag of nerves after he got the first demand. Helena Rós is vicious. She wanted to pressure him and screw as much money out of him as she could. It wasn't because she needed it; just to make him squirm. She knew he had money hidden away that she didn't have access to, but didn't know how much."

"So she wrote the letters?"

"I did that, some of them anyway. Then Helena wrote more."

"You sent them to his office or his home?"

"Both."

Gunna felt her head throbbing but forced herself to concentrate. "You also sent letters to Bjarki Steinsson, Bjartmar Arnarson and Jónas Valur Hjaltason?"

"A few text messages as well," he sighed. "They all responded, except Bjartmar. Maybe he just didn't care. I don't know."

"Why?"

"I wanted to make them suffer too. I'm damn sure that bloke

who threatened to strangle me was sent by Bjartmar or Jónas Valur, or that bastard of a son of his."

"And you needed the cash, I suppose?"

"Shit, yes, all right. I bought a flat two years ago, not long before the crash. The payments on it have gone through the roof and I thought I'd be out on the street otherwise. The place has been for sale for the best part of a year and it's only even been viewed twice."

"So your flat is safe now?"

"For the moment."

"Good. Interview suspended, fourteen twenty-five," Gunna intoned, stopping the recording. "Maybe you'll be able to rent it out while you're in prison. We'll take a break now."

At the mention of prison, Gulli Ólafs' eyes glazed over.

"I HEAR HÖGNI's been picked up," Eiríkur said, sitting down at his desk and running his hands through his hair to dislodge some more of the gravel collected during his tussle with Gulli Ólafs.

"Do we have room for him?" Gunna asked, shaking painkillers from a jar and washing them down with lukewarm coffee.

"Yup. There's a cell upstairs reserved for him. Helgi's back," he added. "Has Helena Rós been arrested?"

"Not yet. But she has plenty of questions to answer."

The door swung silently open and Ívar Laxdal stepped inside. "Progress, Gunnhildur?" The trace of a smile on his normally deadpan face told them both that he was already aware of what had happened.

"Oh yes. Högni Sigurgeirsson is on his way and Helena Rós is sitting in an interview room waiting for us."

"Hallur Hallbjörnsson's wife?"

"That's her."

"Her father's a well-known figure, you know."

"And he's a lawyer."

"What progress with the hack?"

"Singing like a bird. Can we get some extra bodies to search his flat and his car? I could do with someone to go to his office as well and bring his computer back here for Albert to have a look through."

"I can get that done," Ívar Laxdal said.

"What we have at the moment is Helena Rós and Gulli Ólafs helping us with enquiries. It's crystal clear that between them they were blackmailing three of the four members of Svana's Syndicate, but I have no idea yet how they're linked to the deaths of Svana or Jónas Valur, or the attacks on me or Hallur," Gunna said, pausing for breath as Ívar Laxdal's eyes widened. "On the other hand, we have Högni Sigurgeirsson, who is a seriously fucked-up young man and has plenty of questions to answer about Hallur's injuries. It seems that Gulli and Helena Rós had already started their little campaign some time before Svana's murder, and it was aimed mainly at wrecking Hallur's marriage, as well as digging Gulli Ólafs out of his financial difficulties, after which he was going to play house with the man's wife. It's something I should have twigged earlier and followed up."

"Don't blame yourself, Gunnhildur. You've been busy."

"Albert's work has been outstanding," she continued. "There was a dog hair in one envelope at Hallur's parliamentary office that matches Helena Rós' poodle. Now Gulli Ólafs and Helena Rós Pálsdóttir are in separate interview rooms desperately blaming each other. But Gulli Ólafs wasn't the one who smacked Hallur and tried to poison him, or the one who bashed Jónas Valur's head in, although he was probably the person Jónas Valur was expecting to see. Both Gulli Ólafs and Helena Rós were elsewhere at the time, and that's already been confirmed. The house-to-house enquiries and CCTV have turned up sightings of a grey Opel that fits, so I have our pizza delivery boy pegged for that one. But we'll see."

"If you think Högni may be responsible for the attack on

you and Jónas Valur, then that interrogation ought to be handled by someone else," Ívar Laxdal decided.

"Not Sævaldur, surely? Not after all the work we've done."

"Sævaldur's busy elsewhere. Helgi can do it."

GUNNA SAT QUIETLY next to Eiríkur in the interview room.

"Interview with Helena Rós Pálsdóttir, officers Eiríkur Thór Jónsson and Gunnhildur Gísladóttir present," Eiríkur recited for the benefit of the recording. "Helena Rós, can you tell us where you were on the day your husband was attacked at your home?"

"At a fundraising event."

"Fundraising for what?"

"For the National Theatre, at Hotel Borg."

"And there were people there who will confirm your attendance?"

"Of course."

"Have you any idea who might be responsible for the attack on your husband?"

Helena Rós folded her arms and glared, head back. "You've already asked me all these questions."

"How long have you been in a relationship with Gunnlaugur Ólafsson?"

"Who says we're in a relationship?"

"I'm asking," Eiríkur said. "Are you saying there isn't a relationship between you?"

"All right. About a year."

"How long have you known Gunnlaugur?"

"Since we were at college. Twenty years, something like that."

"And how did you become aware of your husband's arrangement with Svana Geirs?"

"Do I really have to answer these questions? This is very personal."

"But it's also a murder inquiry."

"Surely you don't suspect me of murdering that woman?"

"Would you please answer the question?"

Helena Rós fidgeted with the ends of her scarf. "I knew there was something going on. Hallur has always been easily led astray, especially by pretty women, but since the children were born he's kept his dick in his trousers, or so I thought. This was different. To answer your question, it was simple. I checked the SMS messages on his phone while he was in the bath. He must have realized, because after a while he started taking his phone with him to the bathroom."

"Was this before or after your relationship with Gunnlaugur began?"

"Before. Gulli confirmed it and told me what the arrangement was."

"Which was what?"

"You know perfectly well," Helena Rós said in a voice that dripped scorn.

"I'd prefer to hear it from you."

"Hallur and three other dirty old men were paying to take turns on that plastic Barbie doll. Is that what you wanted to hear?"

"That will do nicely, thank you," Eiríkur said politely. "You know Jónas Valur Hjaltason?"

"Of course. He sits on a couple of committees with my husband."

"He's dead."

"A heart attack, I suppose?"

"You don't seem surprised," Eiríkur said with a frown.

"He was overweight and unhealthy."

"He was murdered. It's not public knowledge yet. Where were you on Friday evening?"

"At home, I think. Yes, I'm sure of it, I was at home."

"Anyone who could corroborate that?"

Her cheeks flushed pink. "Gulli. He stayed the night and left early in the morning."

"What time did he arrive?"

"Eight-ish. Something like that."

Eiríkur shot a glance at Gunna. "The threats and demands posted to your husband. Who had this bright idea?"

"I have no idea what you're talking about."

Gunna opened the file on the desk and passed two sheets of paper across. Helena Rós ignored them.

"There are more," Eiríkur said. "Some of these were retrieved from the bin in your husband's office at your home. A couple more are from his parliamentary office."

"So who was blackmailing my husband?"

"That's what we'd all like to know, and I have to consider your involvement in it."

"This is absolutely ridiculous! How dare you!" Helena Rós lifted herself to her feet and towered over Eiríkur.

"Sit down, will you?" Gunna growled, speaking for the first time.

"Idiots," Helena Rós hissed, ripping the two letters into shreds and dropping the pieces with a flourish on the desk as she dropped back into the chair.

Ívar Laxdal rubbed his chin irritably, the first indication Gunna had seen that he might be tired.

"What's the situation with Hallur now?" he asked.

"He's not doing well. It seems he has a level of brain damage due to oxygen starvation. It could be weeks or even months before we can understand quite how much damage has been done, and all the indications are that he may never be fit to stand trial. One doctor says he's going to be a twelve-year old for the rest of his life. Another says he should make at least a partial recovery, so we'll have to wait and see."

"But there is some good news for you," Ívar Laxdal said.

"Högni Sigurgeirsson is being flown back to Reykjavík right now from Tórshavn."

"What? Out there in the east? What was he doing there?"

"No, Tórshavn in the Faroes. It seems he arrived there the day before yesterday. Showed up on a flight from Reykjavík with a bag full of money, still with Jónas Valur Hjaltason's name tags on it, and brandishing Jónas Valur's passport."

"Sounds weird, doesn't it?" Eiríkur asked. "Why the Faroes?"

"He had a ticket for the next morning to Copenhagen, but Faroese customs only picked him up as he was waiting for his flight from there to Kåstrup, not when he landed from Reykjavík," Ívar Laxdal explained patiently.

"If you want to fly to Denmark, there are direct flights all the time. Why go through the Faroes? It doesn't make sense."

"It does if you want to avoid the airport at Keflavík, where he would have been picked up like a shot," Helgi pointed out. "But the only flights leaving the country from Reykjavík airport go to the Faroes, and I suppose he was travelling on Jónas Valur's ticket. How much money did he have on him?"

A phone rang shrilly on a desk and Eiríkur swept it up, speaking in an undertone as Ívar Laxdal continued.

"A hundred and ten thousand euros in cash and he's saying nothing. Faroese customs took one look at him and decided he wasn't Jónas Valur, then had a look in his baggage and found the cash. He refused to tell them who he really is and we got the identification from pictures of him that the Faroese police sent as soon as he couldn't pretend to be anything other than Icelandic. Once we was realized who it was, we asked them to send him right back."

"So he knocked you on the head, banged Jónas Valur a bit harder, grabbed the man's car keys, suitcase, tickets and passport, and ran for it. Is that what you reckon, Gunna?" Helgi asked.

Gunna cradled her chin in her fingers. "It sounds plausible, doesn't it? It also sounds like I was just in time to see what

Jónas Valur was up to, if he had flight tickets and some pocket money on him. I don't think he was coming back, y'know. Maybe I held him up long enough for Högni to intercept him on his way out of the country for good. I assume they were one-way tickets that he had?"

"Sounds about right to me," Eiríkur interrupted, with the phone to his chest and the palm of one hand over the mouthpiece. "But you want some more news? Bjarki Steinsson has disappeared. His wife's reported him missing, hasn't seen him since last night. His car's missing as well. Do we put out an alert for him?"

THE FAINT AROMA of something spicy hit her nostrils even before Gunna had left the car. It was late, and she felt exhausted by the tension of the long day. At the door she kicked off her shoes and left wet prints across the kitchen floor.

"Hæ, people," she offered as Steini looked up from the book in front of him and Laufey acknowledged with the briefest of nods that her mother was home before turning her attention back to a TV sitcom.

"Good day?" Steini asked. "We thought you were only going to be an hour or two."

"A bloody long one, and I've lost count of the number of people I've pissed off."

"A successful day, then?" Steini grinned. "We kept some food for you. Chicken and stuff with it."

"Spicy?"

"Oh yes."

"Will I need a litre of milk to wash it down?"

"Not that hot."

"That's all right, then."

Gunna heard the ten o'clock news start on the TV through the bathroom door just as the hot water had started to wash away the day's aches. She emerged swathed in towels to find a steaming plate waiting for her and Laufey sitting at the kitchen table. Steini's eyes were closed and the book had slipped down to his lap. Work seemed blessedly far away from Hvalvík, where only an occasional car could be heard in the distance to break the soft quiet.

"How was school?" Gunna asked.

"Not bad, same as usual. Mum, I had lunch at Sigrún's today and she's still so angry at Jörundur."

"Well that's understandable. It's something that really knocks you sideways when that kind of trust is betrayed."

Laufey nodded slowly. "Has that happened to you, Mum?" she asked quietly. "With Gísli's dad?"

A shiver went down Gunna's spine at the question she had expected for years, and she instinctively looked around to see if Steini were awake.

"Sort of. Gísli's dad is a strange man and I haven't seen him for years. Not since Gísli was about ten, I suppose. We never lived together, just were together for a little while, and didn't get on all that well. So there was no real betrayal like Sigrún's going through. It was a million times worse when we lost your father, sweetheart."

"I think Gísli's seen his dad recently."

"You're sure?" Gunna asked in sudden alarm, but warned herself to think rationally. "There's no reason why he shouldn't, and I suppose it's something he ought to do. He's a big lad now and doesn't need to ask me for permission to do anything."

Laufey yawned.

"You should be asleep soon, young lady," Gunna observed. "Homework done, is it?"

"Yeah. Steini helped me with the maths. It's easy when you know how, all those cosines and things," she said, getting up and trying to stop herself yawning again.

"Put that in the dishwasher, would you?" Gunna said, handing her the plate and fork. "I need my bed as well."

Laufey disappeared to her room and Gunna turned off the kitchen lights. In the living room, she looked down at Steini and leaned forward to place one fingertip gently on the end of his nose. His eyes opened and he looked up.

"I'm shattered, so I reckon it's bedtime."

"I don't need telling twice," he said, and smiled back.

In the darkness, Gunna stretched out, feeling her toes tingle as the fatigue drained out of them and Steini settled beside her with a sigh. Exploring fingers gently stroked her thigh and she stretched a hand to cover and encourage them when the phone on the floor beside the bed began to buzz and chirp.

"Hell!" she swore, fumbling for it in the darkness. "What?" she barked into it.

"Tucked up with Steini already, are you, you randy old cow?"

"Björssi, always a pleasure to hear from you. Yes, I'm in bed and I've been on my feet since six."

"Well you'd better get out of bed, darling. We've got someone out at the airport you might want a word with."

"So what made you want to leave so suddenly right now, with so much money?" Gunna asked.

"Just trouble," Bjarki Steinsson replied in a voice laden with despair that echoed in the bare interview room at Keflavík international airport. "Always more trouble. The phone calls and the texts."

"What calls and texts?"

"Demanding money, more and more money. Threatening to tell Kristrún."

"Who was this?"

"I don't know." He waved a hand towards the jacket hanging on the back of a chair. "Look in the pocket. You'll see."

Gunna gestured for Björssi to look as Bjarki continued, speaking faster, his voice rising from a whisper to a more normal tone.

"Yesterday there was a text as well. So I thought, why bother? I'd just go. I have enough to live on. I was just going to walk away and leave whoever it is to tell Kristrún whatever he wants. I don't care any more. The house and the business are all in her and the children's names. She can keep the lot, all those stupid crystal knick-knacks and pictures that give you a head-ache. I've had enough."

Behind her, Björki carefully unfolded a sheet of paper, typed with a dozen lines. Gunna saw with relief that he had put on gloves to read it. "Have you any idea where these demands were coming from?"

"Some man. I have no idea who. Just a phone number, nothing else."

"And the note? How did that get to you? Post?"

"It was pushed under the windshield wiper of my car yes-terday morning. I heard about Hallur and then Jónas Valur, and I decided that was all the warning I needed after I went to see Hallur in hospital yesterday."

"What do you know about what happened to him?"

"Only that he would never have taken his own life, never," he said with conviction. "Hallur always comes out smiling. He's one of nature's survivors."

Gunna turned to Björki. "What is it?"

"Demand for cash. Twenty thousand euros. 'Have it ready. You will be told when and where to hand it over,' it says here."

"A classy sort of blackmailer, then, wanting foreign currency."

"Understandable, I'd have thought, considering how valu-able Icelandic cash is these days."

"All right. We'd best get that to Technical as soon as we can and see what they make of it," Gunna said, and turned back to Bjarki. "I'm sorry. I can't allow you to leave the country."

"Am I under arrest?"

"Not yet. But you tried to leave the country with a large amount of foreign currency, which I'm sure a man in your position is aware is illegal. Plus you're a key witness in a serious case. If you attempt to leave the country, I'll make sure you're stopped and I'll get an injunction to prevent you from travelling."

"I can't go back to Kristrún," he said with certainty.

"In that case we'll get you a hotel room for the night. I'll be along to see you again in the morning, and then you can make other arrangements."

Tuesday 30th

GUNNA BANGED WITH a fist on the door of Bjarki Steinsson's room, with Eiríkur behind her.

"Don't tell me the bloody man's not here. Eiríkur, run down
to reception again, will you, and find out if anyone's seen him.
Failing that, get somebody up here with a pass key," she
instructed. Eiríkur left at a jog along the corridor, his footfalls
soundless in the deep beige carpet.

Beige and boring, Gunna thought. Just like Bjarki bloody
Steinsson.

"Bjarki! Open the bloody door, will you! It's the police!"
She yelled, hammering on the door again.

She paced the corridor back and forth, banging the wall
with her fist and feeling her knuckles sting. Eventually Eiríkur
appeared at the far end of the corridor with the portly figure of
the hotel's manager puffing at his side.

"Open that, will you?" she instructed the manager.

"It's extremely irregular," the manager grumbled. "I can't
open a guest's room just like that."

"Yes you damn well can, and quickly. We've had enough
bodies as it is," Gunna told him grimly.

At the mention of bodies, the manager's eyes bulged in
immediate alarm and he swiped a card through a slot. The door
swung open and he stood back to let Gunna and Eiríkur enter
the room first. The clatter of running water was the first thing

Gunna noticed, followed by the steam coming past the slightly ajar bathroom door, and the reek of sulphur.

"Bjarki!" Gunna called out. "Are you there?"

The bedroom was empty, the duvet on the bed thrown back. Gunna took a deep breath and pushed open the bathroom door. A cloud of steam billowed past her. She peered into the gloom, the room's light hardly piercing the steam and reduced to a white orb in the middle of the ceiling. She could see the water running at full power in the shower cubicle, and a dark shape against the cubicle wall showed her where Bjarki Steinsson was.

Here we go again, she thought, turning to Eiríkur. "We're going to need an ambulance, I reckon. Get one called, will you?" she told him and gingerly opened the cubicle door.

Gunna looked down at the body curled against the wall and breathed a sigh of relief as Bjarki Steinsson gazed up at her with water cascading through his thin hair and down his face. There was misery in his eyes—but at least he was alive.

She gestured to Eiríkur to take a step back before she squatted down on her haunches and looked into Bjarki Steinsson's blank brown eyes rimmed with red.

"Bjarki?" she said gently. "What happened?"

"It's just too much," he said hollowly.

"Look, come on out of the shower, will you? You've been in there for a long time."

"It doesn't matter," he said finally, after a long moment's thought. "None of it matters now."

Gunna stood up. She leaned over him to turn off the flow of scalding water and there was a sudden silence. She pulled a thick towel from the rail, opened it and held it out to him.

"It's going to be all right," she said softly. "Come on, we'll get you dried off and sorted out. All right?"

He nodded dumbly and dragged himself unsteadily to his feet, every movement seeming to cost him pain. Gunna was surprised at just how thin his limbs were as he stepped, shivering already, from the shower cubicle. He immediately sat on the closed toilet seat and his shoulders hunched forward, emphasizing the pale paunch that contrasted with the thinness of the rest of his body. She wrapped the towel around his shoulders and pulled another from the rack.

"Get the manager out of here, and make sure he keeps quiet," she said to Eiríkur in a matter-of-fact voice so as not to alarm the forlorn man sitting in front of her. "And look out for that ambulance, will you?"

Eiríkur disappeared, taking the manager with him.

"All right, Bjarki. They've all gone. Stand up again, please."

He obeyed as if in a trance, and she reached around him to wrap the second towel about his waist before taking his hand to lead him to the bedroom. She sat him down on the end of the bed and crouched down in front of him.

"Bjarki, tell me what happened. Have you taken any pills or anything like that?"

The question seemed to spark him into consciousness.

"God, no."

"What then?"

"I was just going to go away. Away from everything. I've wanted to do it for years, just walk away."

"Where to?"

"To the house in Spain."

"You have a house there?"

Bjarki nodded. "Nobody knows about it, not even the witch," he whispered. "Bjartmar fixed it up for me at a good price. I was going to go there and not bother coming back."

"So what went wrong?"

"You did," he said with a first flash of animation. "Stopped me at the airport yesterday."

"Customs stopped you leaving the country with an illegal amount of foreign currency," Gunna reminded him.

"Illegal, crap. All the top dogs can do it. If you know the right people, you can do what you want."

"But why yesterday? What brought this on if you've been planning it for so long?"

Bjarki shook his head. "We went there a couple of times, Svana and I. Nobody knew us. It was perfect. Then she died."

Gunna felt a presence behind her and look round to see Eiríkur and a green-suited paramedic. She looked back at Bjarki Steinsson, who seemed to have slipped into a trance.

"He's all yours," she told the paramedic. "Look after him. He's had a bit of a tough time."

The man nodded. He kneeled down where Gunna had squatted and patted Bjarki's knee.

"All right, are you? My name's Siggi and I'm here to help you," he said cheerfully.

Gunna squatted again and looked at Bjarki's blank face.

"It's going to be all right, Bjarki," she said softly. "These gentlemen are going to take you over to the hospital for a few checks and some rest. I'll look in on you later if that's all right."

GUNNA FELT HER head spin as she sought out Ívar Laxdal. As the last few days had become increasingly complex, she had found the man's presence in the background a reassurance that she was on the right track, even when she seemed to be getting nowhere.

"Gunnhildur," Ívar Laxdal's rich baritone intoned behind her. "Coffee? I'm just going to the canteen."

"Good idea."

"What's happened? Did you locate Bjarki Steinsson?"

"Yup. Last night at Keflavík, trying to skip the country like all the rest of Iceland's brightest and best criminals. Put him in a hotel and took his passport away. He seems to have suffered a breakdown during the night. He's at the National Hospital now, under sedation and observation."

"Has his wife been informed?"

"Not yet." Gunna smiled. "I thought we'd spare the poor man that for the time being at least."

"You want to question him further?"

"Absolutely, the sooner the better. Yesterday he visited Hallur Hallbjörnsson in hospital, and that's a conversation I'd like to have listened to."

"What do you propose to do next?"

Gunna thought for a moment, taking the opportunity while Ívar Laxdal punched buttons on the hulking machine that had replaced the canteen's percolator.

"There are buttons for all sorts of weird and wonderful drinks here, but no mention of ordinary, old-fashioned Icelandic coffee," he grumbled.

"You'll find number 56 comes closest," Gunna said.

The machine hissed, threatened and administered a plastic beaker of brown liquid that he passed over to Gunna.

"At the moment I have Högni Sigurgeirsson and Gulli Ólafs in cells, Helena Rós Pálsdóttir spitting venom in my direction, and Bjarki Steinsson and Hallur Hallbjörnsson in hospital, not to mention Svana Geirs, Jónas Valur and Bjartmar Arnarson on the slab, plus Jón Jóhannsson on suicide watch. Doing well, don't you think?"

"It looks to me like you have all the ingredients there. All you have to do is fit them together," Ívar Laxdal said with a rare smile.

"I hope you're right. Helgi's starting on Högni soon, and then I think I'll have a run over to the hospital."

"Jónas Valur and Bjartmar are both dead, and I have every reason to believe that you were responsible for both of those deaths," Helgi suggested.

"I wasn't!" Högni yelped. "I never touched Bjartmar!"

"You did harm Jónas Valur, then?"

"I never said that," Högni said, retreating and throwing an uneasy glance at Gunna, sitting behind Helgi.

"My colleague was speaking to Jónas Valur when you attacked both of them." Helgi nodded his head slightly sideways towards Gunna. "What happened? You attempted to murder a police officer, and then assaulted Jónas Valur with fatal consequences?"

"It wasn't like that . . ."

"So how was it? I've all day to listen to you tell us."

"Jónas said I was an idiot and if I thought he was going to hand over any money then I'd better think again. I told him I didn't know what he was on about. He laughed when your mate hit the ground," Högni said, looking at Gunna.

"Was Jónas Valur expecting someone else?" Helgi asked.

"How should I know?"

"I'm asking you. Could he have been expecting to see you?"

"No," Högni said truculently. "Why?"

Helgi looked sideways at Gunna and raised an eyebrow, at which she nodded back.

"Jónas Valur was being blackmailed for a considerable amount of money, and you're the most likely candidate. I believe that he refused to hand over the money in his suitcase when he saw it was you, so you attacked and killed him."

"I didn't!"

Högni pounded the table with the flat of his hand while the silent lawyer sitting next to him flinched and the uniformed officer by the door took half a step forward until a quick shake of the head from Gunna stopped him.

"So how was it, Högni?" Helgi asked quietly.

"He laughed at me, said I was a fool. He said the city wasn't a place for people like me and I should go home to the country." Högni's eyes bulged with recalled anger as he carried on. "That bastard said Svana had got what was coming to her and he wasn't going to hand over a penny. Then I got angry."

His fists bunched into thick balls and trembled on the table. The officer at the door looked doubtful.

"So you and Svana were blackmailing Jónas Valur and your sister's other men? And when Jónas Valur refused to pay up, you cracked his skull?"

"No! Nothing like that!" Högni howled. "What's this blackmail shit about?"

"And Svana?"

"No! Svana'd never do anything like that."

"She had every reason to, so she could cash in on these guys."

Högni shook his head wildly. "No, it wasn't like that. She was packing them in, going back on TV again with the fitness show. She wanted to get rid of them."

"Why? Surely it was a profitable arrangement for her?"

"I don't know. But she said that somebody had found out about it and had been stalking her, sending her texts. She said she just deleted them and never replied, but she wasn't happy. She was edgy, bad-tempered."

"So what happened when you had that argument with Jónas Valur?"

"I hit him and he fell down. So I ran for it."

"But you took his car and luggage with you?"

He hung his head. "Yeah."

"So you knew he had a flight booked and you decided to go instead when you saw all the money in the case?"

"Yeah."

"What did you hit my colleague and Jónas Valur with?"

"A bit of wood. It was a chair leg once."

"And where is it now?"

Högni lifted and dropped his shoulders. "Dunno. By the road somewhere."

"Where?"

"Near the airport, I suppose." He sighed. "What's going to happen to me?" he asked, suddenly deflating and in a small voice.

"I'm sorry, that's not for me to say. But this weapon you used, was it the same one you used to assault Hallur Hallbjörnsson when you tried to choke him?"

"Yeah."

"And you fixed up the car so it would look like he had committed suicide?"

Högni nodded. "He's dead, isn't he?"

Helgi ignored the question and carried on. "And the same weapon you used on your sister in her flat?"

"No!"

This time Högni's hands smacked hard on the table and he half rose from his seat.

"I never hurt Svana!" he yelled, his face going an even deeper shade of red, and the officer by the door took a step closer, ready to intervene.

"We have witnesses who have stated they saw the two of you having a serious argument outside Fit Club a few days before her death."

"That was different!"

"Sit down," Helgi instructed in a calm voice, but Högni continued to rap at the table with his fists and seemed ready to jump from his chair, unable to stay still.

"Sit down, please, Högni," Gunna said quietly, speaking for the first time and looking squarely into his eyes. Högni gradually became less agitated and sank back into the chair as the officer at the door and the lawyer both visibly relaxed.

"I didn't know it was you," Högni mumbled.

"What do you mean?" Gunna asked.

"I didn't know it was you there talking to that bastard Jónas Valur," he repeated. "Otherwise I'd never have . . ." His voice tailed off as the lower half of his face disappeared into his chest and fat tears rolled down his cheeks. "I never hurt Svana. I just found her there and she wouldn't wake up."

• • •

HELGI AND GUNNA walked to the canteen and sat in silence in the deserted room over mugs that steamed in front of them.

"That was an ordeal, wasn't it?" Helgi said eventually, breaking the silence.

"Right enough."

"D'you think he did his sister in?"

Gunna shook her head. "No."

"So who was it? Gulli Ólafs, maybe? I have to admit I can't understand where these people get the energy for all that sex. That Svana must have been like a machine," Helgi said appreciatively.

"Not Gulli Ólafs. He didn't have enough of a motive. Svana would really have been more use to him alive. I'll bet you any money he was the one on her tail. We'll see what the search at his home and office turn up. If there's a phone with a number that ties up with the SMS messages that Svana, Bjarki and anyone else had been receiving, then we have him bang to rights," Gunna said with a yawn.

"So who was it? It could have been any of the Svana Syndicate apart from Bjartmar."

"We'll see," Gunna said and pulled herself upright. "Will you carry on with Högni? I have to go over to the hospital."

THE SAME DOCTOR who had attended to Gunna's bruises a few days earlier was on duty.

"Basically the man's had a nervous breakdown," he said laconically, stretching his legs out in front of him during what was clearly a long-awaited opportunity to sit down. "It's a combination of stress, acute anxiety and depression. He needs some long-term recuperation and that's not going to happen here, I'm afraid."

"No?"

"We don't have the resources these days. Endless cutbacks being pushed through right now. You're a public servant. Surely you're seeing all this as well?"

"Hell, yes. There's a block on recruitment unless it's absolutely essential, and even then you have to fight tooth and nail. As for equipment, it's a nightmare. Anyway, Bjarki Steinsson. What's his condition?"

"Physically he's as fine as a non-smoking middle-aged man who takes minimal exercise is likely to be. Mentally it's hard to say, and I'm not a specialist."

"I really need to speak to him."

The doctor looked pensive and wrinkled his nose doubtfully. "I'd prefer it if he could be left in peace to recuperate for a few days."

"This isn't something trivial, I'm afraid. This is a murder case. Two people dead and another victim in here as well."

"Good grief, who's that?" the doctor asked with a sharp intake of breath.

"Hallur Hallbjörnsson."

"What? The MP who tried to commit suicide?"

"That's him, only it seems it wasn't suicide and I need Bjarki Steinsson to shed some light on it."

The doctor tapped the top of the cluttered coffee table. "All right, but I think it would be best if I could sit in. I'll have to call a halt if he gets overstressed."

The corridors were quiet, and music played softly somewhere distant as they walked towards Bjarki's room.

"His wife's been with him," the doctor said. "She's been there practically since he was brought in."

"And I don't suppose she's helping much towards his recovery."

"Really? Why's that?"

"She's not the most pleasant of people," Gunna said as the doctor knocked and eased the door open.

"Bjarki, a visitor for you," he said, a kindly bedside manner clicking into place automatically.

"Who is it?" Gunna heard Kristrún's frosty voice ask. "The police again," she said in a flat tone, answering her own question as she caught sight of Gunna.

"Hello, Bjarki," Gunna said gently. "Feeling any better? I need a quiet chat if you don't mind."

"I really think—" Kristrún began.

"If you'd like to leave us for a quarter of an hour, I'd appreciate it," Gunna said firmly.

"I don't think—"

"Fifteen minutes will be enough."

Kristrún stalked from the room and Bjarki looked gratefully up at Gunna from the deep chair where he sat swathed in a blanket.

"I really need you to tell me the rest of the story, Bjarki," Gunna said, keeping her voice soft and taking a seat next to him. She saw with alarm how wretched he looked and watched as he twisted his fingers constantly. "What really happened at that meeting the three of you had the night before Svana died?"

"We had an argument," Bjarki said eventually. "It wasn't very pleasant."

He fell silent and looked down at his fingers, pale against the dark wool blanket. "Svana wanted to end it. Jónas Valur and Bjartmar didn't care."

"The meeting?" Gunna prodded.

"We had all been getting these threats and demands. I don't know how whoever it was knew who we were. But it was worst for me and for Hallur. We both had so much to lose, especially Hallur with his career in Parliament just starting."

His hands trembled and his eyes stared out at her. "I'm sure you couldn't understand how distressing it all was. Jónas Valur is a hard man. He said he didn't care about publicity, but if we were concerned, then we should do something about it. He called Bjartmar in the States and told him what he'd told us, that it was our problem, mine and Hallur's. Jónas Valur is divorced. Bjartmar was estranged from his wife anyway. Such a shame, a lovely young woman." His dry voice fell silent as he reached for a glass of water that shook and threatened to spill as he lifted it to his lips and sipped.

"So Jónas Valur said that it was your problem—yours and Hallur's?"

"Yes. That was it."

"What did you decide to do?"

A look of discomfort passed over Bjarki's face, and Gunna wondered if he was going to cry again.

"Hallur said he would talk to Svana."

"To reach a settlement?"

"Yes," he whispered. "Hallur thought the demands were coming from Svana and some journalist he said had been sniffing around her. I told him I didn't believe it."

"When was this?"

"I saw him."

"You saw Hallur when?"

Bjarki gulped and his eyes misted over.

"The day she died," he said with an effort. "It was the day she died. I was there in the morning to . . ."

He paused and swallowed, reaching for the water glass again. "I was there in the morning. I never stayed overnight with Svana. We met mostly during the day. Often we'd meet at her flat in the mornings for a few hours, when it was easiest for me to get away from the office. We'd have breakfast and then . . ."

"And the day she died?"

"I left her flat around eleven. She was still in bed and said she was going to sleep for another hour before going back to the gym. I went to the bakery on the corner to get some pastries to take back to the office, and I saw Hallur go into the building."

His eyes focused on something far distant, outside the little room. "Did Hallur tell you what happened?"

Bjarki Steinsson snapped back to reality and he looked up at Gunna with desperation in his eyes. "He told me that they'd argued. Svana denied anything to do with trying to blackmail anyone. He said they had a furious argument . . . That's all he'd say."

His voice tailed off and he twisted the fingers of one hand frantically in the other as the doctor looked at Gunna and pursed his lips in concern.

"And what happened?"

"I don't know. I mean, I can't be sure. But Hallur can have a terrible temper sometimes." He paused. "I think it was Hallur. I know it was. He lost his temper and I think he hit her without knowing what he was doing." He lapsed into silence. After a few moments his shoulders began to shake until he finally drew breath and leaned back to stare at the ceiling.

"I think that's going to have to be enough," the doctor decided, pressing a button on the wall to summon a nurse.

"GUNNHILDUR. I CAME to see you a couple of times before. Do you remember?"

They were outside in the hospital's grounds, enjoying some unexpected sunshine that had finally bullied its way through the last of the inkblot clouds. Hallur stared down at his hands, which were fiddling with a tattered magazine. Gunna could see a deep frown furrowing his brow. His face cleared and he shook his head as if trying to dislodge something stuck in his mind.

"I'm not sure, but I think so . . ."

"I want to ask you about a friend of yours. Her name's Svana. What can you tell me about her?"

This time Hallur's face lit up, then rapidly darkened. "Svana . . ."

"When did you last see Svana?"

"I don't remember," he said finally. "Before I came here."

"Do you recall going to her flat?"

Hallur nodded slowly with a thoughtful look on his face.

"I used to visit her sometimes," he said, and grinned to himself.

"But you don't remember having an argument with her?"

He looked blankly back at Gunna. "With Svana? No. I don't think so."

"What did you do when you went to visit Svana?"

"We had a lot of fun."

"What sort of fun?"

"You know," he replied with a sly smile. "Bedroom fun."

Gunna took a few paces forward and Hallur followed. "I want you to think back very carefully. Do you remember anything of the day you were injured?"

"I was at home and then I was here."

"Do you remember what you were doing that day?"

"Stuff at home, I think. Nothing special."

"Did someone come to the door?"

Hallur sighed in exasperation. "I want to remember but I can't. It's not there in my head."

Gunna turned quickly to face him and found herself looking into confused eyes that suddenly stared innocently back at her. She was certain that she had seen a rapidly concealed spark of cunning.

"All right. That'll do. I don't think I need to ask any more questions, at least not right now," she said, cupping his elbow in her hand to lead him back to the building. "I think Helena Rós is here to take care of you," she said, looking across at him, and was pleased to see a spark of irritation appear in those captivating brown eyes. "Who knows? Maybe you'll soon be well enough to go home with her?"

Hallur's arm tightened suddenly in her hand and immediately relaxed again.

GUNNA'S HEAD WAS throbbing again, and she gulped down two painkillers with a mouthful of water.

"Still rough, chief?" Eiríkur asked.

"Yup. And I've had enough for today."

Helgi opened the door and dropped into his chair. Gunna looked at him expectantly, but he had his face in his hands, kneading his eyes with the heels of each hand.

"Have an interesting time at the hospital, did you?" he asked. "Shit. What a day. Oh, the Laxdal will be here in a moment. Saw him coming up the stairs just now."

He had just lifted his face from his hands, his eyes red, as Ívar Laxdal appeared silently and swung a chair under himself, sitting down in one smooth movement.

"Just so you know, there's an international arrest warrant out for Sindri Valsson," he announced. "That's the good news."

"And the bad news?"

"The Portuguese police want to get hold of him as well, so we might not have first crack at him."

"But we will eventually?"

"Eventually," Ívar Laxdal said grimly. "I hear congratulations are in order," he added with the nearest thing to a smile any of them could recall.

"Really?" Gunna asked, stifling a yawn. "Has our lottery ticket come up?"

"No, chief," Helgi said. "Högni's weapon was apparently a chair leg that he picked up from a pile of firewood behind his great aunt's house. Eiríkur's already been out there and been through the pile, and we have the other three legs. So at least we know what we're looking for. It would be handy to have the murder weapon, but I reckon we're watertight enough without it."

"Excellent. How about Gulli Ólafs?"

"Hard to say," Eiríkur said. "His lawyer's whispering all sorts in his ear, so he's refusing to speak in case he incriminates himself. But we're going through his work and personal computers to see what Albert can dig out, and there's a handful of phones from his flat and his office that Albert's playing with now,"

"We have the number that was used to send SMS demands to Bjarki and Hallur, and Albert's retrieving what he can from Svana's phone as well," Gunna said, eyes half closed as she waited for the painkillers to chisel at the throbbing in her head. "Högni wasn't after cash—just revenge, plain and simple. But it seems that Jónas Valur and the rest of the syndicate believed that they were being blackmailed by Svana and Högni, when in fact it was Gulli Ólafs and Hallur's wife who were sending treats and demands to the syndicate and to Svana."

"So we can pin Jónas Valur's murder and the assault on Hallur on this man?" Ívar Laxdal demanded.

"That's it," Eiríkur answered.

"No connection with the man who murdered Bjartmar Arnarson?"

"None whatsoever."

"Högni murdered Jónas Valur," Ívar Laxdal said. "So which of this syndicate murdered Svana Geirs?"

"We're still working on that," Eiríkur said.

"It was Hallur," Gunna broke in. Helgi and Eiríkur swung round to look at her.

"You're sure?" Ívar Laxdal asked, eyebrows lifted.

"As sure as I can be. Unfortunately he's not the man he was since Högni's assault on him. It seems his memory is cut to ribbons and there isn't a lot of the past few weeks that he remembers. So, conveniently, this whole episode has been erased from his mind. Sorry, guys, I should have told you. I've just now come back from the hospital. Bjarki Steinsson says that Hallur was convinced they were being blackmailed by someone with Svana's complicity. We know now that it was nothing to do with Svana, but it seems that Hallur went to confront her. The result was an argument, with Hallur losing his temper and cracking her over the head, all in time to be back at work after lunch."

"Evidence?"

"Sorry. That's as close as I reckon we're going to get unless something new turns up."

Ívar Laxdal stood up and swung the chair back under the desk it belonged to as Gunna rose to her feet, looking at her watch.

"I'm going to leave you two gentlemen to clear things up, if that's all right with you. I assume Högni's been charged?"

Helgi nodded.

"As Litla-Hraun is full to overflowing, I suppose that Gulli Ólafs may be granted bail on the blackmail charge, but we ought to ask for a travel restriction," she instructed. "Don't want him skipping the country like Jónas Valur was about to."

"Will do," Eiríkur agreed.

"See you all tomorrow, then," Gunna said, pulling on her coat as Ívar Laxdal held the door for her.

Halfway down the stairs, he caught up with her. "Gunnhildur. A question."

"Go ahead."

"What do you make of Hallur?"

"He's in no state mentally to face a trial. The doctors don't even want us asking him questions. I had to bully them to get five minutes."

Ívar Laxdal nodded pensively. "But you're sure he's the perpetrator?"

"As sure as I can be."

At the door, Gunna paused and zipped up her anorak in spite of the spring sunshine.

"The guy bugs me," she admitted.

"Why's that?"

"The doctor said he would expect to see a significant level of recovery in time, although not as much or as rapidly as he would with a younger casualty. I can't help feeling Hallur's not as impaired as he lets on."

"You think he's faking?"

"The man's a politician, so lying's second nature to him, but he's going to be under supervision and the moment he slips up I'll be on him like a ton of bricks. If it's an act, he's going to spend the rest of his life playing that part, so I suppose we can look on the bright side."

"Which is what?"

"The man has a choice, assuming it is an act. Either he can snap out of it and face the music, or else he can pretend to be mentally impaired. Not much of a life."

"Better than prison, though," Ívar Laxdal said.

"I'm not so sure. I suppose he'll be released eventually into Helena Rós' care, and considering how fond she is of her husband, I think prison would be the more pleasant option."

"Not as good as prison, but close, you mean?"

"As good as a life sentence," she said, letting the door close behind her. "See you tomorrow."

OTHER TITLES IN THE SOHO CRIME SERIES